The last twenty years have been vigor... Australian literature, and this marvellous collection of... one stories is a celebration of women's very particular contribution. The voices of Thea Astey, Beverley Farmer, Helen Garner, Barbara Hanrahan, Elizabeth Jolley, Olga Masters, Judith Wright, and Fay Zwicky are well known; others are less familiar, but all show a wonderful talent for story-telling. Here the bizarre rubs shoulders with the mundane; men, women and children love, laugh, argue – and misunderstand each other; immigrants and expatriates regret or rejoice in lost inheritances, and the landscape, beautiful and brutal by turns, etches itself on to consciousness and memory. These are stories as diverse as they are compelling: the Babe has always been wise, but here she gets listened to.

LYN HARWOOD was a dance and drama consultant for many years and is now a partner in Pascoe Publishing. She has a son and lives at Cape Otway, Victoria.

BRUCE PASCOE is editor and publisher of *Australian Short Stories*. He is also the author of *Night Animals*, a collection of stories, and *Fox*, a novel. He has two children and lives at Cape Otway, Victoria.

PAULA WHITE is a publisher and bookseller, and has written a book of traditional Australian recipes. She lives in Melbourne with her husband and child.

The BABE is WISE

Contemporary stories by Australian women

edited by
Lyn Harwood
Bruce Pascoe
& Paula White

VIRAGO

Published by VIRAGO PRESS Limited 1989
20–23 Mandela Street, Camden Town, London NW1 0HQ

First published in Australia
by Pascoe Publishing Pty Ltd 1987

A CIP record for this title is available from the British Library

Printed in Great Britain by Cox & Wyman Ltd, Reading, Berkshire

Introduction

The Babe is Wise is the title taken from Lina Bryan's painting on the cover of this book. This collection is a celebration of a particularly influential period of Australian fiction. The emergence of so many good new writers in the last two decades requires a collection such as this. We've included some stories written earlier than 1970 but they are stories which have lived on.

We invited a select group of writers to submit new or little published stories for *The Babe*. It is a beautiful book and we will not conceal our pride in presenting this collection for your enjoyment.

The Babe may also serve as a tribute to the spirit of Olga Masters and the contemporary women writers of Australia.

June 1987
Lyn Harwood
Bruce Pascoe
Paula White

Acknowledgements

The following short stories were first published in the sources mentioned; 'My Hard Heart', The Festival Edition of *The Adelaide Review* 1986; 'A Lover of Nature and Music and Art', *Australian Short Stories* no. 14; 'Whatever it Takes', *Australian Short Stories* no. 15; 'The Game', *Billy Blue Magazine*; 'Maralinga', *Australian Short Stories* no. 12; 'My Sister's Funeral', *Meanjin* vol. 44 no. 2 June 1985; 'Hitler's Driver', *Flesh* April/May 1987; 'The Midnight Shift', *Australian Short Stories* no. 13 and *Hecate*; 'Judith. 510 Pieces', *Australian Short Stories* no. 15; 'Buttercup and Wendy', *Australian Short Stories* no. 16; 'As Time Goes By', *Australian Short Stories* no. 11; 'The Plain Clothes Man', *Australian Short Stories* no. 13; 'The Mincer', *Australian Short Stories* no. 3; 'My Father's Moon', *Australian Short Stories* no. 17.

We express our gratitude to publishers and authors for permission to reprint. 'A Lover of Nature and Music and Art', by Barbara Hanrahan appeared in *Dream People* published by Grafton Books, London 1987. Permission to reproduce the story has been granted by Barbara Hanrahan care of Curtis, Brown (Aust.) Pty Ltd; Permission to reprint 'The Dugong' was granted by Judith Wright who retains copyright. 'Irene' is from *The Estuary* by Georgia Savage published by University of Queensland Press 1987; 'The Test is if They Drown' is from *Bearded Ladies* by Kate Grenville published by University of Queensland Press 1984; 'Travelling' was first published in *Sister Ships*, by Fremantle Arts Centre Press 1986; 'Brown and Green Giraffes' is from *The Rose Fancier* by Olga Masters published by University of Queensland Press 1987; 'As Time Goes By' appeared as 'Home Time' in *Home Time* published by Penguin 1986; 'Write me, Son, Write me' is from *Hunting The Wild Pineapple*, published by Nelson 1979; 'My Father's Moon' is copyright by Elizabeth Jolley 1987.

Thank you to the photographers for the following photographs. Judith Wright by Attila Kiraly; Fay Zwicky by Jaqui Mitelman; Meredith Michie by Deirdre Tolmer; Mary Anne Baartz by Bruce Devine; Carmel Bird by Ruth Maddison; Joan London by Victor France; Helen Garner by A. T. Bolton; Barbara Hanrahan by Michal Kluvanek; Elizabeth Jolley by Tania Young; Judy Duffy by Bryan Gilkes; Sue Hancock by Brendan Hennessey; Carolyn van Langenberg by Angus McIntyre.

Contents

Helen Garner

Helen Garner was born in Geelong in 1942. She was a teacher but now writes full-time in Melbourne. Her published works are: *Monkey Grip* (1977), *Honour and Other People's Children* (1980), *The Children's Bach* (1984) and *Postcards from Surfers* (1985).

My Hard Heart

Do you call that Soul, that thing that chirps in you so timorously?

Rainer Maria Rilke

I met my husband at the airport, and there he told me some things that wiped the smile off my face. He put his suitcase down outside the Intercontinental Bar and leant his face and arms on the fire hose: he wept, I did not. We drove home. He lay on the bed and sobbed. I went downstairs and sat beside my daughter on the couch. She was watching a Fred Astaire movie and did not notice how I gazed at the side of her smiling face, as if in that glossy skin I might find meaning.

I lay beside him in the hard bed and listened to him talking, explaining, crying. I said nothing. My limbs and torso swelled. Slowly I ballooned. I became tremendous. I was colossal, a thing that weighed a ton, a bulky immovable slab of clay set cold, baked hard and heartless. Somewhere in the centre of this inert mass was a tiny spark, hardly a spark at all, only barely alight.

In a day he was gone. The smell of the house changed immediately. I got up in the morning and stepped out of my bedroom. The door of his old room, the front one with the balcony, stood open, and across its empty air fell a slice of sunlight.

The front of the house was festooned with great twining loops of wisteria. People walked slowly past, gazing up. A delicate, warm scent puffed out of the dangling flowers, and when I sat on a cushion on the doorstep and played my ukulele I saw that the flower clumps were full of bees.

I knew it was a passing euphoria, but all my senses were working. Crowds parted as I approached, old men and boys and babies smiled at me in the street, waitresses spoke to me with a tender address. When I tried to play, notes placed themselves under my fingers. Milky clouds covered the sky, a warm dry wind blew all day, shocks of perfume came from behind fences. I remembered being a student, the delicious agony of exams in spring.

'You wait,' said Suzie in the wine bar. 'In six weeks you'll be walking on rocks. You'll have a brick wall six inches in front of your face.'

I bought a Petpak at Ansett and took our cat to Vanessa's place in the country. I set him free at the door and he bolted away into what would one day be a garden. Vanessa was wearing sagging purple socks. I sat with her at the kitchen table. She showed me a book by C. G. Jung which contained a series of mandalas painted by one of his patients. The first pictures were grim prisons of rocks and stones, but as the series progressed, oceans appeared and the air inside the circular frames flushed, thinned and became breathable.

'What is a mandala?'

'I don't know. Is it a picture of the soul, at a given moment?'

I pulled a chair over to the big window and sat watching the movements of the long grasses in the wind.

'Will I be walking on rocks?'

Vanessa shrugged. She lives alone in a house which from the outside looks small and square but which encloses, with a light touch, one enormous room, a space of unusual flexibility. The kitchen is right in the centre: everything else radiates from there.

The cat returned at five in the morning and began to complain and cry. At home I would have thrown him into the kitchen and shut the door, but here, because of the huge room in which Vanessa also slept, I had to feed him and bring him on to my bed. When at last he settled down with my hand on his side, I remembered the nights with a newborn baby: the alarm, the broken sleep, the silently turned doorknob, the plodding from task to task; the despair of fatigue, but the weary patience and the acceptance of the fact that it is absolutely required of one to do these things: the bearing of duty.

I approached our house in the evening. It was 'lit up from door to top'. I knew there was no-one inside it now but my daughter: I felt her tough little spirit burning away inside its many rooms. I cooked a meal and we tried to eat it elegantly, facing each other across the white tablecloth. She put on an old Aretha Franklin record: my daughter is not like the girl in the song, the one who 'don't remember the Queen of Soul'. At those feathery cries we rolled our eyes and gave each other shy smiles.

We washed the dishes together. I put my forehead on the window sill and cried with my hands still in the hot water, and she said, 'I know this is much worse for you than it is for me.'

In the cafe Elizabeth told me her husband was dying of a tumour.

'I used to think there was justice,' she said, 'and fairness. That there was a contract, that things meant something. Now I know your foot can go straight through the floor.'

'And what's on the other side?'

'Nothing.'

'Nothing?'

'*Nothing*.'

Tears, black with mascara, poured off her face. She cried in silence, without sobs.

'I think what I'm trying to do,' she said, 'is to die. Because I can't *bear* him to have to go out there on his own.'

I was ashamed of my story when she asked for it, a simple tale of marriage betrayed, but she listened with respect.

'We were bright girls, weren't we,' she said. 'What bright girls we were.'

We kissed goodbye, and sat quietly. I put my hand on her stockinged leg. 'Aren't those boots beautiful,' I said.

We looked at the boots without speaking. In perfect unison we heaved two great sighs; and then we began to laugh.

I saw my husband sitting in the cafe with a woman we both knew. I went without thinking to the same table; the three of us said good morning and they went on reading the papers. When my husband got up to go to work he nodded to me and said to the other woman, 'I'll pay yours.'

At home I answered the phone. A young woman asked for my husband.

'He's not here,' I said, 'at the moment. This is his wife speaking.'

'Oh yes!' said the young woman. 'He told me he was involved with you.'

'*Involved*!' I said. 'He's married to me.'

'Oh well,' she said with a careless laugh. 'Married . . . involved . . .'

I filled the bucket and got the mop out of the yard and began to wash the kitchen floor. The tiles were filthy and I had to scrub: their edges chipped and crumbled in the foam. My daughter came into the room behind me and opened the fridge. She uttered a dramatic cry of pain. I was used to this.

'What happened?' I said, without turning round.

'I hit myself in the *eye*. With the corner of the freezer *door*.'

'How'd you manage to do *that*?' I said, and continued to mop.

She said nothing, and did not move. When I looked around, she was still standing at the closed fridge door with her palms over her eyes. I stripped off the rubber gloves and went to put my arms round her. She was as stiff as a rail.

'Are you all right?'

'Obviously not,' she snapped from behind her hands.

I flinched. 'Oh — don't talk to me like that.'

'You never know!' she burst out. 'You never know how to comfort somebody who's hurt themselves! And now I'm the same — I can't either. I've picked it up from *you*.'

I met Steve in the bank. He had come from Sydney in a panel van so heavy with carpentry equipment that he parked it under a tree outside my house and went everywhere by tram. He had a very small black bible which he carried in his shirt pocket. I knew his brother, but I didn't know him. He put his budgie's cage on the highest kitchen cupboard and we watched the cat licking its lips. The budgie perched on my daughter's shoulder while she played the piano, and accompanied her with thrilling inventions.

'Have you ever been married?' I said.

'No,' said Steve. 'But I'm familiar with the pain.'

We watched an American gospel show on TV: the pastor stood waist-deep in a brown river and dunked them one by one: up they came, spouting and fighting and babbling in strange tongues. Their faces were distorted, their eyes were closed, their bodies bloated or emaciated. Somebody somewhere was picking at a banjo: that tricky, tough, humble music.

Between the gospel show and 'Six Centuries of Verse', we took the dog out and walked a figure-of-eight round the enormous park. The night was starry, the air was cool, the big avenues of elms looked low and humped beyond the ovals.

'Did you get baptised in a river?' I said. It was a kind of flirtation, but he never bit. He looked at me with his face open, ready to laugh.

'No,' he said. 'At a beach. In the ocean.'

'What happened, exactly?'

'Oh — I don't know if all that detail would be useful to you.'

'Are you trying to be "useful" to me?' I said sharply.

He turned and looked at me. 'You asked me,' he said, 'and I'm trying to answer.'

We walked. The dog heard possums in the trees and sprang helplessly into the air at the base of the thick, ridged trunks. Half a mile away, along the western boundary of the huge park, silent headlights moved in a formal line, as if in convoy to a funeral, or a wedding.

'I haven't slept with anyone for a really long time,' he said. 'For years.'

'You must be absolutely radiant with it,' I said.

He laughed. 'It's not orgone, you know. I'm celibate, but I'm not asexual. It's not so bad. It's not bad at all. I was like you. I had a heart of stone. I was all black. I was grieving over everything. I'd feel an impending relationship, and I'd know I had nothing to give. So I stopped. In Ezekiel, I think it is, he says "I will take away your heart of stone, and I will give you a heart of flesh".'

14

That night the poet on 'Six Centuries of Verse' was Milton. Across the screen stumbled different Adams and Eves: in various postures denoting shame, humiliation and grief, they staggered into exile.

When it was finished he stood up and leaned over me, and kissed me on the cheek.

'Goodnight!' we said. 'Sleep well!'

In my room I pulled the curtain open and lay down in a current of night air. I heard a tram go chattering through the intersection. The little flame stirred in its cage of clay: I felt it shiver, and begin to move.

Judy Duffy

Judy Duffy is at present experiencing the best of three worlds: living in the country — St Andrews — with her children; writing in Carlton in a 'room of my own' and writing full-time, thanks to the assistance of a Literature Board Grant.

Scars

Angela shudders with the shame of it, her mother flaunting herself, flirting, lifting her skirts before the open fire, warming her arse, laughing, loudly, toothless, swilling pot after pot of beer bought for her by Jim, Old Jim the Driller, who was using her. Everyone knew for what!

Now he was slapping her exposed buttocks, saying what a superb meal she had cooked, calling her Mother because everyone called her Mother, when she had a perfectly good name, Tillie, and Tillie was laughing so much that her breasts were shaking, unashamedly, under her floral dress.

The dress was the only familiar thing about her. Everything else had changed, swung full circle back to the 'wild youth' Tillie talked about sometimes, the 'wild youth' that had ruined her life, drained her soul dry.

'Be warned by what happened to me Angela!' Tillie would say. 'Be a lady!'

For years, before *he* came, Tillie had been a lady; a quiet woman, minding herself, doing her job and going on home, just the two of them, going on home together.

Angela curls herself tighter into 'her' corner, on the window box, under the frosted 'Bar' sign, where she has waited almost every night for the past sixteen years for her mother to finish cooking in the kitchen.

'If looks could kill!' Tillie whispers, tipsy, nodding towards Angela.

'I'd be a well-scarred corpse!'

They laugh again. The two of them. And he has said *it*. The word 'scar'. And so it will begin. The ritual. First he will search his body for a scar. He can produce one for every tale he tells. Scars add authenticity, he claims, to his tales, tales already extravagant with images of ex-wives, eyes glinting behind flashing meat cleavers, cuckholds red faced and raging chasing him with sawn-off shot guns,

17

bewitched maidens pleading sylph like and innocent for his body, his love, then offering him delicacies disguising arsenic, offering him death. The tales prove, he insists, that although his big-boned body is sagging *now* about the middle, and slightly stooped, its survival has been a miracle! Well! When you consider how it has been abused, so thoroughly abused . . .

'By Love!' he concludes dramatically, laughing.

'And who'd be dead?' he beams, anticipating the applause that always succeeds his stories.

Only Angela doesn't laugh. She sinks her head even further into her shoulders and stares out the window into the night. Normally Tillie cares when Angela is miserable. Now Tillie won't even look at her.

'It's like having a mother again myself,' Tillie tells Old Jim.

'Way she sits there watching me, judging.'

'She's a grown woman now. And I've told her all I know. Keep yourself whole, I've told her, until the time's right.'

'Otherwise,' Tillie explains, 'she could find herself with a kid weighing her down, forcing her to go on, day after day, forcing her to provide, to survive.'

'And that's a far stretch from living.'

Tillie empties her glass.

'You've done a good job, bringing her up on your own.' Old Jim seems genuinely impressed.

'But she's still a little girl Mother. Remember that!'

Tillie doesn't want to remember that.

If she looks too long at Angela she might see a little girl and she might give in and go home and sit by the fire Angela will make for her, sit in that dim familiar quietness drinking endless cups of tea and reading, for something to do, the glossy magazines Angela loves so much, with women in them who want for nothing.

'I went back to her once before.' Tillie fights a memory. 'That's how it all began . . .'

'Steady on Mother! I'll get another beer. We can't have you getting maudlin.'

Tillie hadn't intended coming back that time, long ago. She had rugged the child up warm, given her a bottle of juice and some biscuits, locked her in the truck and parked it on the side of a busy highway. It was three days before she crawled back out of the bush. She'd taken all the pills but they weren't enough and she'd come back dazed and retching, foul in her own excrement, with the single obsession, she remembered it clearly, that if no-one had found the girl, she too would be covered in her own waste. It had motivated her to stumble back to the truck. To find her still there. The world hadn't cared. The Bastards would have left her there. To rot!

She had dragged the child wimpering and clinging to the creek and washed her, and then herself. The water, brown and cold had loosened their filth, carried it away with their clothes downstream. In time the icy water numbed her pain. Only Angela was warm. Only Angela.

And now Old Jim was hugging her. Kissing her cheek.

'Come on now Mother! Cheer up! Life's too short to waste on the bad memories.'

Old Jim was right. Tillie was tired of missing out on life. It was time, she decided, for change. For too long now she'd thought herself past loving. Too old, she'd thought. Too ugly. But now Old Jim thought different and certain things didn't matter so much. Like always pleasing Angela. Like going home every night. Like being a good mother.

'Like that did you Mother?' Old Jim asked, the first time they made love and their laughter escaped the thin walls of the hotel bedroom and was heard in the bar where Angela said, 'I hate you Tillie!' Screamed over and over, 'I hate you Tillie! I hate you Tillie!'

It was Ernie Duggun who tried to calm her.

'Give her a go girl! Let her have a bit of fun. It won't be for long. Old Jim don't stay in the one place long. He'll be gone soon and things'll get back like they was. You'll see. Give the girl a brandy. Here! Bill! Mother won't be worrying. Now quieten yourself girl. Trouble's the last thing Mother'll want. First sign of trouble and Old Jim'll be gone.'

'We gave her brandy Mother,' he told Tillie later. 'Had to give her a lot to quieten her down. Young Bill here will drive her home. Won't you Bill?'

19

'You can trust me Mother.'

'He'll take care of her.'

'You've been ogling her for years Bill Thomas,' Tillie hissed.

'Only admiring Tillie.' But he was blushing, scarlet.

Years now Tillie had worried about Angela waiting all that time in the bar with the men talking about her as if she wasn't in the room, saying how her body was filling out beautiful and how it was crying out to be filled. Tillie told them if they looked twice at her girl she'd have their guts. Slow poisoning she promised and they didn't doubt her.

Tillie drives home in a black night, talking all the time to the old Bedford truck whose glowing eyes stretched the gravel before them, cold and orange. Angela is slumped against the door, shivering and dazed, her head bashing against the window at every bump. Tillie tells the truck to go carefully. Is it trying to punish her? At home she puts the girl to bed.

'I won't be staying Angela,' she says. 'I won't be giving him up too easy.'

All her life Angela has slept with Tillie in the same bed. Since her father left and Angela was only two then. So don't trust men Angela, Tillie says often. Keep a part of yourself still and safe so you can survive without them. And sometimes she'd say, 'You're my beautiful daughter Angela. My beautiful girl. Tillie's child. Cuddle up warm with me. There's plenty of time to grow up. Plenty of time.'

'It won't be forever,' Tillie says now. 'And I'll be back Angela and we'll go on sharing things like we've always done.'

Sharing everything, even the grubby underclothes scattered about the room. They'd never bothered with who owned what. But Angela wouldn't be sharing anything, not any more. She would be going, to the city, and never would she be coming back.

'It's your life Angela,' Tillie tells her daughter. 'You live it the way you want. But you take care. You hear?' And Angela sobbing fit to shatter and Tillie holding her, together, comforting.

'You can stay girl. You don't have to grow up just yet.

You don't *have* to go. Just don't cause me any trouble.'

Angela didn't go. She sat every night in her corner watching Tillie and Old Jim, watching them teasing, laughing, drinking. Tillie acting like a young girl in love, spoiling Old Jim, stealing delicacies from the kitchen for him, calling him 'My Man'. And Old Jim still calling Tillie, 'Mother' and saying,

'No love more loyal than a Mother's love!' And beaming proudly.

Tillie stayed with Jim at the hotel and every Sunday they went to Tillie's house in Berwick. Not to stay. Old Jim said Angela wasn't ready for that, not yet anyway. Tillie cleaned the house, saw Angela had clean clothes for the week ahead. Jim cut the wood, collected rubbish. Angela stared at them accusingly, like a creature abandoned for a whim.

Sometimes, at night, in the bar, Old Jim could coax a smile from the girl and sometimes it seemed that smile might extend into laughter. But the moment Tillie arrived Angela would return to her corner and sulk and sip the brandy she had taken to drinking.

Every three months Tillie went to the city to give blood. Giving blood cleans your head out, Tillie always said. Your blood builds up, she believed it, gets thick, slows you down so you can't see clearly the way you're going.

'And I'll be going without you this time Angela,' Tillie said. 'I need to get out from under your eyes. It's getting so I can't feel anything but your shame of me. It's spilling out your eyes and tarnishing me.'

When Tillie came back she had teeth, a mouth full of teeth, a Luna Park's Laughing Mouth, Angela thought, watching everyone laughing and kissing her, a laughing stock, laughing with Old Jim.

They'd been married, they said.

'So I'll be coming home with you now Angela,' Tillie tells the girl. 'We'll both be coming home with you now.'

She stands before her daughter, proud but pleading.

'You got no need now to be feeling shame. Your mother is married and Old Jim will be staying for a long time. He's promised.'

'Can't you smile girl? Can't you smile?'

21

There is champagne, scavenged from the basement, dusty old bottles produced with pleasure and corks bounce crazily to the ceiling and echo there like gun shots.

Someone finds grapes, enormous green grapes and drops them into the glasses and they float there in the sparkling liquid, a delicate green, almost transparent.

Old Jim is explaining the suddenness of their decision.

'Mother here saved a life, with her blood. A young woman who haemorrhaged after her kid was born.'

He pauses, grinning, enjoying the attention.

'Now I ask you,' he says, 'could a man like me let an act like that go unrewarded?'

He joins the laughter, his arm casually about Tillie's floral body. Champagne swirls in her glass, slops carelessly on to the floor and it seems to Angela that Tillie will never stop laughing, never stop laughing with him.

'You're a dirty old cow Tillie,' Angela screams. 'I wouldn't want you back. Not now, not any more. You're a dirty old cow on heat Tillie!'

'Angela! Girl!' Tillie is crying but her face is still.

'Mother!' Angela hisses the word, a curse. In a stunned silence Tillie tells them, 'She ought never have said that, never.' Old Jim puts an arm about her shoulders.

'Words! Just words Mother! Come now girl tell your mother.'

'Words like that leave wounds that don't heal over,' Tillie tells her child.

'She don't mean them Mother.' Old Jim is worried.

'Tell your mother girl!'

At his approach Angela moves suddenly and slams a glass hard into his face and blood surfaces there, rimming a circle, a full red circle on his forehead before it spreads quickly down his face. He grabs the girl, holds her arms back behind her.

'Keep out of this Mother!' He shouts to Tillie who emerges from the ensuing confusion her face tight with anguish.

'You'll be doing yourself no good girl!' Old Jim speaks quietly to the girl while she struggles, a frantic bird, against his hold, her black hair flicking into his face spreading blood across his cheeks, his neck. He holds her until she calms then he pulls her back into his body, her head against his shoulder.

'We'll look after you girl. Your mother and me. You got nothing to fear.'

Angela is quiet. She turns her face towards Old Jim and smiles. Then she lunges her teeth into his cheek. With a wail of pain he sends her crashing into the far wall.

'You stupid little bitch!' he screams. 'You need your flaming arse belted.'

Young Bill rushes to Angela but Tillie pushes him aside.

'You'll not touch her.'

Her eyes are squinted, steely. She helps Angela to her feet, checks she is unharmed before she folds her into her large soft body and stands rocking her, swaying, comforting. Angela cries quietly, clinging.

The silence is heavy and the men look away, embarrassed. Only Old Jim keeps the women in his eyes. Tillie can see that his concern is genuine. But he watches, Tillie realizes, suddenly frightened, with a curious indifference. He will fall in with fate, without argument, without struggle.

Angela begins to wimper.

'Take me home now Tillie. Come back with me . . .'

Tillie holds the girl away from her, forces her head up. She can feel the young man, Bill, watching, waiting . . .

Tillie holds Angela in her eyes.

'It can never be again, like it was Angela. Just the two of us. I'll not come back to that Angela. No matter what.'

Angela breaks free of Tillie's hold and is gone, the glass panelled door slamming hard behind her and Tillie sees young Bill, his face alive with purpose, rush out after her. But Tillie's face is set.

Old Jim is worried.

'Go to her Mother! Try to calm her!'

Tillie shakes her head.

'She's waiting for you Mother, out in the truck.' Ernie Duggan is anxious.

Old Jim brings a stiff brandy.

'You can't abandon her mother! She's still your daughter!'

Old Jim can't understand.

Tillie drinks the brandy. Her hands are shaking.
Outside the truck lights flash on and off, on and off, sending yellow warning streaks through the dimly lit bar.

'Young Bill is with her Mother. He says he's only trying to calm her.'
The truck engine roars, frenzied, demanding.
It's urgency chills Tillie's spine. But she will not move.

'Bill says he'll take her home Mother. Bill says for you not to worry.'
The truck thunders into the night.

Old Jim holds Tillie, wipes her face. They sit a long time together, silent, staring into the fire. Sparks are errupting there, like disasters, like tomorrows, Tillie thinks. Then she sees that the blood on Jim's face is drying and she begins to clean his wounds, wash them gently.
After a time he begins to tease her.

'They will make fine scars Mother. They will remind me always of the dangers of coming between a mother and her daughter.'
It is meant to cheer her.
But Tillie doesn't smile. She can see him, telling the tale, in a different bar, in a tomorrow without her.
She tries to explain.

'Nothing *can* come between the girl and me Jim. She's all I've got, really. Don't you see?'

Lyn Hughes

Lyn Hughes was born in 1952 in South Wales, UK and lived in South Africa for 18 years. She has published both poetry and short stories and is currently co-writing radio monologues for ABC Radio with Sydney writer Dorothy Porter. Lyn is also working on a collection of short stories set in South Africa and now lives in Mount Victoria in the Blue Mountains.

The Plain Clothes Man

Jonas Msinga worked for the Church of our Father in Dreifontein. Five days a week he walked the pavements of the white suburbs, collecting clothes and money for the church. This was not entirely a charitable exercise on his part, although if challenged he would have vehemently denied any self-motivation. Citing hostile dogs, the heat, the arduous nature of his work, not to mention the white rebuffs and hostility which was his daily lot. Ai, no man would willingly subject himself to this, day in, day out, without the love of his brother being uppermost in his heart. So his mother praised him to neighbours, friends and anyone else who would listen. 'God has placed his finger upon Jonas' heart,' she would say with barely restrained pride. Once Mrs Msinga had had other hopes for Jonas. Moses Thembela had done well for himself in the mines. Amos Tzimvimbulu had risen to undreamed of heights, only recently being appointed a Storeman with a big city firm. But Mrs Msinga was well content. Few, she knew, were chosen and Jonas was one of the few. Sometimes she did wonder why her only son had been singled out amongst his peers but, she would remind herself, 'God works in mysterious ways.'

Jonas looked up at the hot blue sky, shielding his dark eyes from the glare, and gripped his plastic carrier bag more firmly. Enoch Dlutu, his next-door neighbour, was leaning against the wire fence that fronted the dusty road, his arms dangling loosely before him, his fat stomach straining at the buttons of his shirt. 'Ai, Jonas,' he smiled broadly, 'you still collecting for that church, man?' Jonas shrugged his shoulders deprecatingly and smiled in return. 'A man tries to help his brothers, Enoch,' he said mildly. Enoch's smile broadened. 'Ai, talking of help, Jonas, you got another of those nice shirts for me?' Jonas

26

glanced quickly back towards his house but his mother had already turned and the front door was shut. 'Enoch, I know you're hard-up, man,' he hissed, 'and I tried to help you out of Christian kindness. And now you want to tell the whole street!' Enoch looked puzzled but quickly recovered his smile, 'Sure, Jonas,' he said in subdued voice, 'just between you and me, but my brother Joseph is getting married next week and he needs a new shirt. He gets paid on Friday, he can give you the money then.' Jonas frowned, 'I'll see what I can do for your brother, Enoch, but I can't promise mind. Some weeks pass without my seeing the cuff of a shirt. Some weeks I'm lucky to run fast enough from the dogs!'

'Aiee, it's a hard life,' Enoch agreed without any trace of sympathy in his voice. Jonas gave a dismissive wave of his hand and walked on and Enoch remained leaning against the fence, looking after him. He smiled to himself. Ai, that Jonas! Everyone in the township knew of his wheelings and dealings. Why, only last week his wife had seen Mrs Empela wearing a new checked coat that only a white woman could have had the money for. And he was paid two Rands a day by Father Terblanche. It was enough to make any man take to God, he reflected. He yawned widely and stretched his arms above his head. Ai, he felt pretty sure Jonas would manage a shirt for Joseph. Perhaps he should have asked him about trousers, too. Still, not to milk any cow dry.

Jonas stood on the train and thought of Enoch with distaste. A man tried to help his brother and what did he get in return. Now he must help his brother's brother, and then there'd be no end to it. He tried to do what he could, a shirt here, a coat there. But always giving a full bag to Father Terblanche each day. There was no end to their greed. Well, Joseph could go to his wedding in an old shirt and that was the end of it. Why only yesterday old Themba had asked him for a pair of shoes! The train was full, Jonas had never known it any other way, but this morning he found himself gradually being pressed by the packed bodies into the back of a woman. He tried to distance himself, drawing his long arms in towards his body, but the

27

pressure continued until he fitted quite snugly into the contours of her body. Jonas felt alarmed. He looked down at the head slightly below his and his teeth clenched. The dark cropped head was young, rounded and elongated into a neck that was unusually white, and soft. He didn't know how he knew the softness of that neck but he could almost feel its pale silk under his fingers. He gritted his teeth, holding himself as rigidly as he could. Ai, would they never stop! Greed and soft skin mingled uneasily to bring the sweat onto his forehead. He was imprisoned. He couldn't even reach for his handkerchief to wipe away the sweat that had begun to dribble into his eyes. Jonas, in his alarm, searched for some thought to banish this Eve, this apparition of sin on the morning train. 'Blessed are the meek for,' the downy hairs on her neck were darker than the surrounding skin, 'Though I walk in the shadow,' her shoulders were narrow, delicate as, 'Lead me not into the ways of,' he could almost feel every bone in her thin body . . . There was a sudden screeching of brakes and the train stopped abruptly, throwing people violently against one another. Jonas felt a sharp blow to his ribs from the woman in front and then he was pushed bodily towards the door. He stood unsteadily on the platform, weakly resisting the engulfing black wave. The woman had disappeared and he stood for a while watching the receding crowd. No doubt a cheap woman, who bleached that fine skin with Karroo Cream and smoked and drank like a white woman! Ai, these loose women, surely the day of retribution would net them from their sea of sin. Slowly his pulse returned to normal and he took a folded handkerchief from his suit pocket and wiped his face thoroughly, and then his wet hands.

He took a bus from the station to Swartfontein. Father Terblanche had warned him not to collect from the wealthy Johannesburg suburbs, Houghton and their like. 'It's hard to explain, Jonas,' he'd said wearily, 'why the rich find it harder to give than the poor.' Jonas hadn't questioned his words, he knew well enough the trained dogs, the high glass-topped walls that barricaded the rich even from their white brothers. He was quite content to ply the middle-class suburbs, changing each week from one to another. Not that it would have mattered if he'd approached the same house week after week, his black skin gave him anonymity in white eyes. His damp shirt stuck to his back and he sat morosely ignoring the overtures of the man seated beside him in the bus. Everyone wanted something from him, he thought irritably. Enoch, who thought he could produce shirts from thin air. Themba, who begged shoes. Did Themba think of *his* feet, blistered and aching from walking, day in, day out. A man could bear much for Christ, but sometimes a brother's burdens weighed heavily. And a woman could test the will of the strongest man, flaunting soft skin for a stranger to . . . He shifted in his seat, taking out the crumpled handkerchief again and wiping his face roughly. Ai, this heat! It softened a man's brain. He must be strong in Christ, he knew these lewd thoughts were the devils own sent to test him.

By midday Jonas' carrier bag was half full and he made his way to a familiar street corner and sat down on the wide grass verge. On the opposite corner a group of nannies sat in their neat uniforms and doeks, some accompanied by their white charges. Jonas waved his hand, recognising a few, but ignored their calls for him to join them. Let them think what they liked, he was in no mood for their idle chatter. He ate his sandwiches without appetite, idly watching the play of light on the shimmering tarmac. The women had become noisier now and two men, one of whom he recognised as Mlamleli, the gardener at No. 54, had joined them. Relenting, Jonas stood up with a sigh and wiped the grass from his suit. He crossed the street and sat down beside the two men, a little apart from the women. Mlamleli introduced him to the young man sitting beside him. Jonas hadn't seen him before, he was sure. He was one you wouldn't soon forget. He was sharply dressed, his thin legs moulded into faded jeans, his hairless chest exposed in the vee of a bright red shirt. A gold medallion hung from his sinewy neck. A city man by his look, Jonas thought disapprovingly. A ladies man he could tell, from the banter he was exchanging with a pretty young woman who was laughing immoderately. Jonas had relented knowing how much he depended upon groups such as this, that gathered on street corners all over the white suburbs. He valued and often used their information. 'Don't bother with No. 32, the missus works all day.' 'No. 34, she's okay, she'll give a little something.' 'No. 36, now she's a mean bitch, with a look that could sour milk.' So much they observed unknown to their white Madams, who thought them inanimate as the furniture they polished and cleaned. The groups bound them together in an environment that was alien and barely tolerated them. Dora, an enormous woman with a pock-marked face called to him. 'Hey, Jonas, there's a new Madam at No. 40. You should try there, last week she gave money to my daughter's school.' Jonas thanked her politely. And then, in amazement, he watched as Dora took a white baby who had been grizzling in its pram and drew the child into the folds of her vast stomach. Brazenly unbuttoning her uniform she offered the child her own breast. The baby sucked greedily and was quiet. Dora drew a blanket around them both, hiding her from Jonas' disapproving stare and any passers by. 'Now don't you start, Jonas Msinga,' Dora said defensively. 'My Madam won't give her the breast. Shame on her! Every day she's out shopping or visiting and she leaves me with the baby. "Feed the baby, Dora. Warm the bottle, Dora. Not too hot, not too cold." "Yes Madam . . . yes, Madam . . . Aiee, Madam!" And then the baby cries. I can't bear the baby crying, such a thin baby too, all bones. And all I have for her is a bottle. So one day I give her the breast. My Madam would kill me if she knew! And now the Madam says, "Dora, you're a real treasure. The baby is so contented with you." So the Madam's happy and the baby's happy. Now, what's wrong with that Jonas, you tell me! I've had six babies of my own and I never knew one that could tell the difference between white milk or black!' she finished with a sour laugh. The other women laughed with her and Jonas exclaimed hotly, 'What's wrong, you ask, Dora! Going behind your Madam's back is what's wrong. Why do you hide the baby behind your blanket, if it's right?' he added sternly. Dora shifted uncomfortably. 'Aiee, Jonas, but the white Madams are so cold,' she said sulkily. The city man who had been listening to their conversation suddenly joined in with a hoot of laughter. 'Aikona, Dora,' he said loudly, 'not all the white Madams are so cold! Some are hot as hell-fire, believe me!' The pretty young woman gave a shriek of laughter and covered her face with one hand, looking coyly through her fingers at him. 'Ai, listen, it's true man,' he said seriously, taking Jonas' blank look as one of disbelief. But Jonas turned away in disgust. This man confirmed his worst fears. Johannesburg had become the breeding ground of sin, spawning men such as this who openly bragged of fornicating with a white woman. And Jonas was shocked at the niggling worm of envy that had stirred in him at the man's shameless words. Such was a day a man had to live through, he thought with sudden realisation. Surely the devil himself had come to tempt him. The women began to disperse and Dora placed the baby back in its pram. 'Jonas, remember No. 40,' she called after him. Jonas, walking slowly up the street, acknowledged her with a wave, but didn't turn. His feet felt leaden and unready for the afternoon that stretched endless as the hot tarmac before him.

For most of the afternoon he avoided No. 40. Not deliberately, but he approached other houses, houses in parallel streets, in streets that intersected the one that contained No. 40, for something held him back. One who had given money last week would be unwilling to do so this week, he reasoned. The pickings in that particular street were often lean. He would stick to his regular houses, his regular Madams. Surely it was better not to deviate from routine on a day such as this. But by late afternoon his bag was barely full, and he had no shirt for Joseph. Dora had often proved reliable in the past, he conceded, as he finally made his way up the neat brick path. The house was set back from the road on a wide swathe of lawn and there was no brick wall, no 'Beware of the Dog', 'Hawkers Prohibited', signs to justify his uneasiness. He leaned against the stuccoed white wall and held his hand on the doorbell, hoping that the Madam was out. That he could turn his back and leave the solid door closed under its canopy of bright bougainvillea.

She opened it almost at once, a thin young woman dressed in brief shorts and a loose shirt. Jonas was unnerved by her proximity. There was no security door separating them, no spy-hole to secretly observe an unwanted supplicant. She had opened door, sight unseen, to a stranger and stood smiling, the corners of her blue eyes creased, one brown hand fiddling with some strands of dark hair that had unravelled from a loose knot. Jonas looked over his shoulder, but he was alone. The smile was for him. He met her eyes uneasily and then looked down, stubbing the doormat nervously with a black shoe. He didn't want her to think him brazen or impolite. Strangely it seemed important what she thought. Her smile was joined by a puzzled lift of one eyebrow and Jonas fumbled in his pocket for his donation book. She took it and pointed to the official rubber stamp. 'You're collecting for the Church?' she asked. Her voice was strange, sweet and musical, he thought suddenly. The poetic turn of thought threw him into confusion. 'Ai, Madam,' he said looking past her. 'If you could give a little something? Old clothes. Perhaps a little money.' He couldn't meet her eyes, unnerved by the fluttering lightness in his belly. She handed the book to him and he took it gingerly, avoiding the long brown fingers, the blunt white nails. She smiled again, reassuringly, as though she guessed his discomposure. 'I think I've got some old clothes for you. David has some old shirts, they're missing a few buttons though, I'm afraid.' She tucked the loose strands of hair into place. 'I could look now, if you don't mind waiting?' she said. 'No, no,' Jonas said eagerly, 'the Madam's very kind.' She turned, leaving the front door open. Jonas stood on the doorstep, annoyed at his ingratiating tone. He had anticipated a challenge, a wary scrutiny, a pointed locking of the security door. How could any Madam be this reckless, turning her back on a stranger? Someone like the city man would walk softly through that gaping hole and steal. Money, a radio. Or worse. Someone like the city man would take a welcoming smile as an invitation he thought in confusion. 'Some Madams are as hot as hell-fire, believe me!' Jonas turned but he was alone. There was only the bougainvillea, rustling in the afternoon breeze.

She came to the door carrying an armful of clothes. 'I've been waiting for a chance to get rid of these,' she laughed. 'David can't bring himself to throw anything out.' She spoke to him casually, as she might speak to a neighbour, he thought wonderingly. Perhaps this white Madam came from some other place. He had heard there were lands where whites and blacks lived together. He had heard, but hardly believed. He took the clothes from her and stuffed them into the plastic bag, mumbling his thanks. And he turned to go, unwillingly. There was no reason to remain and yet he looked for some opening, a wedge to drive into the closing door. 'Ai, Madam, it's been so hot today. Perhaps the Madam has a glass of water for me?' It was inspiration, breaking every rule Father Terblanche had instilled. Not to bother the whites, not to endanger their continuing charity. 'Don't ever make a nuisance of yourself.' Jonas could hardly believe the words were his own. But she didn't falter. 'Of course,' she said pleasantly, and was gone. Almost immediately her voice called from inside, coming nearer. 'Perhaps you'd prefer a cup of tea? I was going to make one for myself.' And then she was standing in the open doorway, beckoning with a thin brown hand. 'You could sit down and rest for a while. While I make the tea. It must be hell walking around all day in this heat.'

Disbelievingly Jonas walked through the open door. Obediently he sat where she motioned, placing his clumsy shoes lightly on the plush carpet. He sat on the very edge of the soft armchair while she went to make the tea. Dimly he heard the clatter of cups, the shrill whistle of a kettle, her voice humming softly. He sat deep in thought, his body rigidly calm, his mind racing through the events of the day. Weaving the loose threads into a whole. The woman on the train, Dora's open deceit, the city man's shameless words, and now this white woman who offered him her home, herself?, as though she had been waiting for his knock on the door. A day of shadows and forebodings. This was no chain of events without a link. He was no fool! As a man of God he prided himself on being well-versed in the ways of evil. Ai, but he had been blind, not to see the devil's work in her welcoming smile, her beckoning hand!

A conviction formed in Jonas as solid as the leaden weight in his belly. As palpable as the sweat that trickled down his collar and into the small of his back.

The woman returned carrying a tray, neatly laid out. The cups were of a delicately patterned china with matching saucers. There was even a plate of biscuits. Jonas wondered at her cunning. Ai, but she had overplayed her hand, he thought with satisfaction. The delicate china was a false note. There were no chips on the cup she handed him, the handle was intact, the delicate saucer dwarfed by his sweating hands. And then she took a cup of the same fine stuff from the tray and sipped slowly at the hot tea. This extravagance of equality was transparent to Jonas. He eyed the door but it was closed. He would have to match her cunning. She was talking now, a thoughtful frown playing between her blue eyes. 'Perhaps you find this strange,' she said hesitantly, 'coming from a white woman, but I don't agree with this rotten system.' Jonas nodded his head in agreement. He said nothing. To say nothing, he knew, was best. He gulped a mouthful of hot tea and watched her warily. She looked puzzled and then quite suddenly, as though resolved, stood up. Taken by surprise, Jonas watched her advance across the stretch of carpet towards him. Soundlessly, he thought, as one scarcely human. She smiled, 'I'm sorry, I haven't even introduced myself,' she said and stretched her thin hand towards him. His own hand, as though possessed of a will of its own, reached out to meet hers. They were almost touching when Jonas came to his senses. A strangled wail came from his mouth as though he had tasted hell-fire itself. He jumped from the armchair, flinging the cup and saucer towards her. The woman gasped in pain as the hot tea splattered on her clothes, but Jonas didn't hear. He ran towards the door, grabbing the plastic carrier bag with one hand, wrenching at the doorhandle with the other. It flew open, the hinges cracking with the force of his escape.

Dora, who was pushing the pram past No. 62, watched in amazement as Jonas ran, jacket flying behind him, down the road. She laughed. 'Ai, Jonas,' she called, 'you got the devil at your heels, man?'

34

Barbara Hanrahan

Barbara Hanrahan was born in Adelaide in 1939. She has published nine novels and a collection of stories, *Dream People* (1987). She has recently completed a new novel, *A Chelsea Girl* to be published in 1988. A printmaker, as well as a writer, she has had 25 one-woman exhibitions, and her work is represented in the Australian National Gallery, State and regional galleries. After many years in London, she now lives in Adelaide.

A Lover of Nature and Music and Art

F red studied Jesus Christ in Sunday School and wanted to be just like Him, he thought Jesus was Number One. Vic Ryan, Fred's gymnastics teacher at the Unley Boys' Club, was his other hero. Once Vic had been a little skinny lad like Fred, but then he trained that hard with gymnastics he became a beautiful build — what they called the tapering build with great big shoulders. Vic had terrific muscle and was the only man in the Club who could hold on to the Roman rings and do the crucifix. When he taught you he put everything he had into it, he'd always encourage you; if you were doing something on the parallels he'd say, 'That was good, laddie, you're doing real well.' He'd go to the Magestic Theatre and see a new tumbling sequence in a vaudeville act and train his boys up to do it — three of Vic's boys went to work at Wirth's Circus as acrobats. Fred never did a full-length giant swing, he had a fall trying to do that, but he could do all the other things, even the dead drop.

One doctor reckoned Fred was born with nerves. It was an affliction with him; he'd get big moths in his stomach instead of butterflies. Fred's mum had a bit of it, too, and when she got nerved up she'd hit the bottle — she hid sherry bottles in her wardrobe. Fred often wondered if his mum had had one of her bouts when she was pregnant with him, because his sister, Alvina, was smart with a good memory but Fred had a shocking memory. And he'd had brain fever when he was twelve, through eating green quinces — he'd had hallucinations and seen the water coming up and wanted to get on top of the cupboard. When Fred was thirteen his dad took him along to the Boys' Club on account of his shyness (there was a scoutmaster who gave the boys badges for carrying on with him in the lavatory, so Fred's dad wouldn't let him join the scouts). Fred's nickname at school was Snail, because he was so slow at picking things up (but he was slow through shyness), and it hurt his feelings a bit.

Once Fred and Alvina used to walk down the street together and they both had fair ringlets and people called them the two little girls. But Alvina grew up to be a real fiend; she was a wild little devil, a hot pants type, with a terrible attraction for the boys. There was a Seventh Day Adventist down the street called Moonlight Moggy who pinched the clothes off people's lines at night. He made a hut of boughs in a paddock and Fred often saw Alvina and her girlfriend go in with him; it was a wonder Moonlight Moggy didn't put them in the family way. Alvina got very nasty when Fred said he'd tell Mum about it (Fred had forty different birds' eggs, all labelled and laid out on cottonwool in a specimen case in his bedroom; Alvina chucked them out the window and broke the lot).

Auntie Em had drunk herself to death. Wine could be a curse and Fred's mum would pass out at least once a month, though Fred pleaded with her to leave the bottle alone. She'd been brought up a real society lady in every way; she had a gold filagree brooch but didn't look after herself as far as appearances went. She hated the Labor Party and the Aborigines and would've shot the lot of them if she could've. She wished she'd married her first boyfriend who'd been kind and thoughtful, but only had one arm, though he did penwork with an Italic nib on ornamental scrolls.

The shark was an irritable creature because it had a very large liver; Fred's dad smoked a pipe and cigarettes and the doctor said his liver was twice the size of an ordinary man's. He was vain and kept trimming his moustache into different shapes. He was the manager of the Manchester in one of the big Rundle Street shops and could touch a piece of material and know what it was without looking at it.

As well as Jesus and Vic Ryan, Fred loved Nature and Music and Art. He was always out bird-nesting and if he found a rare egg he'd give it to Mr Pennyfold who lived nearby and worked at the Museum. He was mad on the fife and played *Rule Britannia* on it in the Unley School band. He drew flowers and birds and won every prize for freehand and they carted him round the school with his drawings.

Mr Tuck was the headmaster and he had a lady's bike so he wouldn't have to cock his leg over. Mr Gerlach, who'd been to India and took malaria turns, had a hollow blackboard stick that the chalk just fitted into and he'd shoot chalk at anybody who played up, like the pigmies shot their poisoned arrows — and he was accurate, too. Miss Fanny Luke was a tyrant with two dents in her forehead from one boy throwing a pencil-case at her and another, an ink-well. She kept swigging at a bottle of Clements' Tonic to calm herself but one day she bashed Fred for contradicting her when she said Jesus was perfect.

A chap round the corner in Fisher Street had cut the throats of his kids and his wife and himself because he'd been out of work in the 1914 Depression, and now the house where they'd lived was haunted. There was a liquorice-root paddock on Unley Road behind Mr Saint's house and an old man skinned the roots and sold them in bundles outside the Star picture theatre for people to chew. Sammy Sellick's tailor shop was just up from the Star and he was a Sturt footballer, one of the best, who could kick the ball over his head and get a goal. There were open-air pictures on the Unley Oval, it was a wild place where girls and fellows carried on under blankets, and Fred liked Tom Mix, William S. Hart and Elmo Lincoln who was Tarzan. Fred got up on the chimney to see Captain Harry Butler, the great aviator, fly in to land on the Oval in his plane, the Red Devil — he'd looped the loop and been injured that many times his face had been remodelled.

Fred's dad came into some money and sent him to Scotch College where the art teacher was Miss Priest, a manly type who didn't show her emotions. She'd put a boot up on the table and Fred would draw it, and he left Scotch College with the drawing prize and a gold medal for gymnastics.

The thirty-first chapter of the Book of Numbers said that God commanded His soldiers to kill all the male children and take all the women that hadn't lain with a man for themselves and kill the women that had — Fred read his Bible right through but couldn't understand it all; some parts upset him, there were too many contradictions. He wanted to be a missionary but didn't have enough brains for it. Instead, he was apprenticed as a precision toolmaker to Mr Len Sen who made water meters and clocks. Fred had a watchmaker's lathe and made every gear and all the plates and tiny pinnions with little teeth.

Fred was still skinny but he'd grown so tall his nickname at work was Long'un. He was good at high-jumping but once he couldn't rise off the ground because he'd had such a big feed of his mum's bread and butter pudding for lunch. He reckoned he broke the South Australian record practising for the high-jump at the YMCA sports, but when it came to the competition he packed up with nerves. Such fine work on the lathe was bad for Fred's nerves, so to calm himself down he took up the flute. His teacher was a manufacturing jeweller who cast rings in the back of cuttlefish; he was a funny old gawky bloke with a stoop and kept peacocks and parrots from all over the world till the neighbours complained and he had to get rid of them; he'd had three wives and when the last one died having triplets he got a message from the King.

Fred wasn't too popular at home with his practising. His dad wanted to cut his flute up, though it wasn't the noise that worried him. He said Fred should make a man out of himself — playing the flute was for sissies, and he was a religious maniac because he went to church, and he ought to smoke.

But Fred's teacher only taught amateurs and Fred's flute was a little old one; Fred was ambitious, so he saved up and bought a better flute from the flautist in the Wondergraph orchestra and determined to learn from Mr John Gilbert. Mr Gilbert was an expert who played at West's pictures and Tottie del Monte, the famous Italian opera singer, had offered him big money to tour the world with her. Fred kept going to West's and pestering Mr Gilbert at interval; Mr Gilbert thought him a damned nuisance, but Fred worried him so much he took him on. But the flute Fred bought wasn't responsive because the Wondergraph flautist had been half drunk when he'd played it, and the alcohol coming out of his skin had worn right through the covers of the keys, so he'd had sixpences soldered over the tip of them. Mr Gilbert had to send away to England for some special gold alloy springs with more kick in them to make Fred's flute respond. *Hark, Hark the Lark* was a very hard piece that had cadenzas running right up to glory; Fred learnt to play it, though he wasn't a champion player and when it came to a solo he wasn't much good. When he played at the Unley Boys' Club break-up concert, his lips shook with nerves all the way through, and his mum was there watching.

It was any excuse for a party with Fred's sister, Alvina, and on Saturday nights in the sitting-room there were often people playing Postman's Knock and Cupid and the other kissing games Fred hated because he was shy. Though he loved girls, and always had his eye on a few in the choir at church, they'd gone to the Methodist Ladies' College and were too flash for him, so he decided the best way to meet some who were his type was to learn to dance.

Mr and Mrs Pullman had a garden in Arthur Street, and supplied florists with wedding bouquets and funeral wreaths, and next door to their house was a hall where they taught dancing. All Unley learnt the Alberts and the Schottische, the Circular Waltz and the London Foxtrot at Pulley's. Fred started there on Thursday nights when he was eighteen; you didn't have to tog up, but you had to look smart, and Fred wore a collar and tie and his Sunday serge suit and changed into his dancing pumps in the cloakroom. Before he was allowed on the floor, Mr Pullman inspected his soles to see if they'd been in the gravel — if you had any gravel marks, he wouldn't let you dance. One section of the floor was very fast, like glass; the other, for learners, was fairly slow and painted with circles and numbers to show them where to put their feet. Mr and Mrs Pullman demonstrated, and their daughters, Iris and Elma, took turns to play the piano. No one ever carried on with the Pullman girls while the old man was there — you dared not fool round or you'd be out on your neck quick. Fred wore his white gloves and always bowed in front of a girl and said, 'May I have this dance?' He had to have his arm out when he was dancing and when the girl had her hand on his shoulder, her elbow had to be so it didn't drag (there was no hugging tight or faces together).

Fred met Enid at Pully's. She was extra good looking and had a dress with a handkerchief hem. He took her to the pictures and she was the first girl he kissed. Enid was a nice girl but she wasn't made for a man, she was too moody for Fred — sometimes she wouldn't talk on the way home from the pictures, and she'd go to her room for no reason at all. Enid's mother gave Fred cream cakes and cocoa for supper and betted him to keep on with Enid, but he couldn't be bothered and chucked her up.

The *News* Symphony Orchestra played *Madam Butterfly* style of music, so Fred joined it and started going out with Hazel, the leader of the second violins. She was a music teacher, a golden-haired girl, and her hair was all over the place like a mad musician's till Fred said why didn't she do something about it. She had it treated to stop the untidiness and Fred thought she looked beautiful; he might have married her, but her stepmother ruined things. She had a fellow picked out for Hazel — one of her pupils, about twelve years younger, who had plenty of money. Then the conductor ran off from his wife and five children with the first violinist, and the *News* didn't keep the orchestra going.

Madge was an artist who painted scenery, not portraits — Fred met her when he studied object drawing at the School of Arts. She was lonely and would rush out and have a yarn with him before classes. He took her to the Teachers' College dance, but some of the student teachers carried on and Madge was disgusted. Fred was reasonably narrow, but Madge was narrower still, and he wasn't sufficiently attracted to her so they never really went together.

Dorothy was a pale-faced dainty little thing, rather frail, who was nuts on Fred. She would have been perfect for him but his mate, Tom, a plumber, had met her first so Fred kept away from her. Tom was arrogant, bossy, a big loud-mouthed coot, and morally not much good. Once he stopped the lift of one of the stores in Rundle Street half-way between floors and tried to assault the lift-girl and she screamed and screamed. Fred's other mate, Bert, was a lens grinder for an optician; he had an operation for appendicitis and was just about right when Tom came along and told him he's seen his girl out with another bloke and then Bert just dropped his bundle and died.

When Fred went to work at Holdens he was tense all the time, because they found out he was used to fine work and pushed it on to him. Then the Depression came and things got bad. But there was always a demand for sugar overseas and even ministers of religion were jumping the rattler, getting on the train and going up to Queensland to be cane-cutters. People died through suicide and Fred would buy a couple of pasties and ride about the parklands on his bike, looking for some poor beggar who was up against it. He got fed up teaching Sunday School at a church where most of the congregation were hypocrites, talking about their new dresses or the people next door, so he went down to the slums of Brompton and started a boys' club — there were shocking conditions and some houses had dirt floors and bags for doors. Fred took his boys camping in the Adelaide Hills and taught them tumbling and matwork; they gave him a terrible time but he felt they loved him. Then Fred was out of work himself and walked the streets every day for six months, looking for a job. He got so desperate he offered a foreman at Kelvinators ten bob to give him one, but in the end he was taken on again at Holdens.

When Fred turned thirty he thought it was the end of the world; he'd had a few disappointments with girls and was scared he'd be left on the shelf. One night his mum persuaded him to go to a dance at the Palladium. He always waited till everybody was up and then if he saw a wallflower he'd ask her to dance, he didn't care if she was big and fat (Fred was sensitive and hated to see a girl sitting out all night, he reckoned it was awful for a girl to have to go home and tell her mother she'd never got a dance). He danced with a girl called Muriel who'd been sitting on her own for a long time; she wasn't much to look at, she stopped and wobbled when she walked, but she had big brown eyes and if she'd done herself up she might have been very nice. She was a dressmaker and only eighteen and she kept smiling so he took her home. He didn't intend to get serious with her, she was too young, but she really worked on him.

Anyone that chases you, you think they must love you. Muriel was interested in Jesus and her father was a pig (he pigged to you, he grunted, he couldn't talk to you properly). Fred had never met such a horrible man, and her mother was a hateful woman. Fred felt sorry for Muriel and got his first music teacher, the manufacturing jeweller, to make up a diamond ring and then Fred and Muriel were engaged.

They had a big wedding, done properly, with bridesmaids and a flowergirl. Muriel wasn't keen on a honeymoon; she said, 'This honeymoon business is over-rated,' so they didn't get round to one. The house they'd rented was in such an awful state that Fred and Muriel spent their honeymoon cleaning it out. Fred had got a friend to make a special bed and Muriel's father had bought the kitchen furniture, but Muriel had no interest in furniture and carpets so Fred had bought some more stuff secondhand. Muriel had the lounge suit covered, but she chose a shocking pattern — she had no idea, and it was a lovely lounge too.

She changed almost overnight. She didn't take a pride in her clothes. He said he'd write out a cheque and she could pop into town and buy some new dresses, but she said if he didn't like her as she was he could lump it. She wore things she'd worn at school, all faded. She'd made out when he'd met her she loved everything he loved, but after they were married she changed right round. She was a hypocrite. She'd made out to be religious but she wouldn't read her Bible, and he was a great one for prayer, but she wouldn't even pray with him. She turned out to be a morbid type, like her mother and father. She used to go out in the shed and cry.

Fred thought Muriel was one of those women who were brought up for two purposes — to produce children and do the cooking, that was about their lights. She was a reasonable cook and Fred wanted to have children straight

43

away and she did, too. Fred got into trouble with her father who expected them to wait a few years, but the doctor said, 'She's a good healthy woman. Don't you wait at all.'

Muriel said Fred was a no-hoper and anybody could have him; she said he just went to his boys' club to show off, and Fred was dedicated to youth and it hurt. When there was a row she'd fall over as if she'd fainted. She was determined to beat him and keep him down, but Fred wasn't the sort to be crushed by anybody. She was going to chuck herself in the river a couple of times — he got frightened the first time, but she came back knocking at the door to get in. One day when she was going to have the baby she slapped him across the face with a big bunch of dead roses — Fred didn't know what made her do it. He picked up her photo, once, and smashed it.

The baby was dark with Muriel's brown eyes and they named her Effie, after Fred's mum. Muriel made a bad mistake with Effie when she dipped her in water that was almost boiling and scalded her. Muriel always looked miserable, so Fred had to teach Effie to smile.

When Fred went to work at the munition works during the War, it was a time when Russia was the ally and people cracked up old Joe Stalin (they didn't realise he was a bit of a butcher), even the military sang away about Stalin our King. Fred was dead anti-Communist, he hated the sight and sound of them because he was so religious. He put up a big argument, but one bloke at the munition works kept at him and gave him a book to read on atheism. Fred kept it in his top drawer for ages, he couldn't dare go near that book, it was like poison. But one day he got up a bit of cheek and started reading it. It was about prayer and asked how was it that if God was such a loving God and knew all your worries, you had to get down and beg Him to give you something. And how was it that there were all those poor people in Poland who'd never sinned in their lives, and they'd prayed and prayed but were blown to bits with their babies — where was God to help them then? The book made Fred think and he thought about Jesus Christ's miracles. How was it that when Jesus Christ was walking through the streets, the people who were strong enough to go and touch his robe were cured but the poor beggars who couldn't get near weren't? It didn't seem right and Fred lost all respect for prayer. He did a lot of thinking and started to think there might be something in the Communists. Fred had always believed in Jesus Christ, he'd thought the salvation of the world would be through Him, but Communists didn't believe in religion. Old Marx said religion was the opiate of the people, it kept them humble, and Fred thought when you boiled it down there was a lot in it. And how could the King of England and the Pope live in those palaces with gold embedded in the roof when people were dying of poverty? And when you went to Court you had to swear on the Bible — the Old Testament was full of filth.

Fred stopped praying and reading his Bible and going to church when he lost his faith. He tried to talk to Muriel about it, but she rushed outside screaming, 'You dirty bloody Communist,' so everyone in the street could hear.

Things got worse and worse. Half the fridge was for Fred's stuff and half the fridge was for Muriel's stuff and they lived separate lives. Muriel bred hatred into Effie and kept having hysterics and jumping out the window when Fred wasn't even near her. Once Fred chased Muriel round the side of the house and, being a nervy type, he might have gone beserk and killed her.

Though Fred had his own engineering business in the back yard now, he knew he had to get away. He told Muriel he wanted a bit more tool-room experience and left everything he'd worked all his life for — the house and his machinery, his books and art and music and insects — and went to work up north at Whyalla. Muriel always put on a shocking act when he came home at weekends.

She was the biggest hypocrite in the world and never let anyone know what she was really like. When Fred's Socialist friends visited she'd agree with them, but when they left she'd change right round. And she wouldn't tell Effie the facts of life. It wasn't a man's place to do it, but Effie was getting on and Fred didn't want her to make a mistake. Effie's eyes popped out when he told her.

Effie got hayfever so she had a plastic wedding bouquet,

and the day she was married Muriel put on one of her acts. She didn't want Fred to give Effie away and said he'd just come down for the wedding to take all the glory.

Fred saw a job advertised at the sugar mills in North Queensland and when he got it he told Muriel he was still hoping things would come right with them, and he'd send her a cheque every month. She would have performed something terrible if she'd known he was leaving her for good; he had to clear out in a sneaky sort of way.

Some fellows up North Queensland had never seen an overcoat, they wore a pair of shorts and a singlet through the year. There was a colony of Aborigines out on Palm Island and Palm Island goats were famous, but on the mainland where Fred lived there were mainly wild pigs and they were savage devils too. There were rain forests with elk ferns and cedar trees and black oaks, so tall they shut out the sun. You couldn't grow stone fruit like peaches and plums up North Queensland; you grew tropical fruit like pawpaws.

Fred bought a block of land and when a cobber built him a house he had a lovely little set up. The place was thick with bandicoots, wallabies and swamp pheasants and one day Fred saw a great big swamp snake on his patio. He thought it might be poisonous so he got his 410 shotgun and finished up shooting ten holes through the asbestos, and then he did in eleven louvres.

A solicitor talked Fred into a divorce, not a separation, though Fred didn't believe in divorces. Muriel was a bitter woman and said she'd get every penny out of him.

Fred felt he'd like to live with someone and advertised for a lady in the Brisbane *Courier* and the Townsville paper. He got a lot of replies and some sent photographs, but out of about forty there were only two or three really nice women. Fred had mentioned in the advertisements he had a little bit of property, but when they saw it they turned lukewarm — they were mostly opportunists after a gold-mine. Some of them were supposed to be Fred's age, but when he met them they were a damn sight older. One was blind in one eye and her other eye was nearly gone; another one was all crippled up. One was a homosexual who said he'd like to meet Fred in Brisbane — Fred had said a lady and the thought of a man upset him. One woman said he was a surprise to her; she thought North Queensland people had big stomachs, on account of being heavy drinkers. One of them, Fred could have married; she was a dear, but she changed her mind. Life was a funny business.

When Fred retired from the sugar mills, he had a skating rink on top of his head and wore a copper bracelet for arthritis, but he still fitted into the navy-blue suit he'd had since he was thirty. He sold up and bought a bungalow at Sunbeam, on the South Australian coast, and took to gardening. Fred's tomatoes were South Australian Mighty Reds and Tom Thumbs that grew like glory. His strawberries were red as the devil, but always mis-shapen. His figs were too big for a sugar fig and they weren't a Turkey, but they were delicious.

Sunbeam was full of widows and Fred upset a few of them because he wouldn't have a regular dancing partner. But every Wednesday night he went to the Sunbeam Social Club 60/40 dance in the Sunbeam Hall. They were a happy crowd, just like a big family; everything was done in the old country style of the ancient days. They didn't play Beatles' songs, they stuck to good music and danced the Maxina, the Marcella, the Gipsy Tap, and Pride of Erin and the Queen's Waltz that were graceful and nice. They had a supper of fruit squares and lamingtons, and all the other things you shouldn't eat, and then went round and found out the birthdays and announced them and everyone clapped. The old-style dance attracted a decent class.

Fred wasn't keen on the Pensioner's Society (they made out they were religious and sang hymns) so he joined the Senior Citizens, who had eighty at their Christmas break-up in the R.S.L. Hall and sang *The Song of Australia*. But a lot of gossiping went on and one loud-mouthed woman was always running someone down. She reckoned her husband was the rottenest alcoholic mongrel in the world, but people who knew him said he was a nice chap. And another woman went round telling people not to vote for the Labor Party, because when they got in they were going to put a needle into the old people and kill them off.

The Labor Club met in the Church of England Hall once a month. It was a happy little gathering and they had the fun of their lives and a basket supper afterwards. Fred didn't approve of all their ideas but there was nothing filthy in the Labor newspaper, it was pure truth and happiness in every way in Fred's opinion.

Fred hated smutty things and anything pertaining to filth. There were some shocking things in the newspapers and on the radio, and there was a show on TV he couldn't watch (they had a girl running round with nothing on up top). He didn't watch rubbish but there was nothing wrong with a good clean Western and as far as the shooting went, that was just fantasy. And Fred liked anything to do with circuses and gymnastics and ice-skating and ballet — anything that had terrific skill.

But you could be driving along and you didn't know if the fellow in the next car had been on drugs or something — there were drug addicts all round the place. And there were homosexuals, you couldn't pick them half the time, but some seemed born like it and Fred couldn't understand.

Fred had a clean mind. He treated women with respect, no matter who they were. Even a prostitute, Fred would still treat her with respect, she was a human being. Fred knew a girl once — an innocent girl from Wallaroo who couldn't get a job in the Depression, and she finished up on the streets. He saw her once, dolled up, and he could see she was a bit degraded.

The Field Naturalists' Society went on a bus each month to different places and Fred's favourite spot was prehistoric, with tree roots tens of thousands of years old. The bus driver would boil the billy while they wandered through the scrub, looking at birds and plants, and then they'd come back to have their dinner. The Organ Club met in members' homes to have recitals. Everyone had a piece to play and then they'd have supper and a yarn.

Fred bought a baby organ — a portable Yamaha, electric and battery, that you could carry round like a suitcase and the shop girl gave him a special price. It had a nice tone on it and Fred was learning *The Rose of Tralee* and *Beautiful*

Dreamer, but he wasn't too good on *Gipsy Love Song*. Fred was still a mass of nerves — he did all right till someone was around and then he packed up.

You had to keep busy doing something when you were living on your own. Fred was always referring to *What Bird is That?* and he could whistle just like a blackbird and even taught one a tune (blackbirds were great imitators). And Fred walked on the beach and picked up moonlight shells and stones with unusual colouring, and he got all the equipment and taught himself gem polishing. Any nice stone he kept for someone special. And he had an onyx from Tasmania, a tiger iron from Western Australia, a Mexican crazy-lace agate, an Australian jade with bits of crystal in the middle, and snowflake obsidians. He sold gem stones for the Labor Club barbecue and onyx and crazy-lace were the best sellers.

Lallie Lennon

Lallie Lennon was born 56 years ago near Granite
Downs Station, and has lived all her life in, and
north of, Port Augusta. Her Antikirinya name is
Kantjuringa. Since going to the Davenport Aboriginal Adult Training Centre in 1975 to learn to
read and write, Lallie has worked with the South
Australian Health Commission. Previously Lallie
did domestic work on stations. Lallie has presented
information about her Maralinga experiences to
various enquiries and appeared in the documen-
tary, *Backs to the Blast*. This picture was taken not
long after the bombs.

Maralinga

The oral history of LALLIE LENNON
as recorded by Chris Warren and
Adele Graham at Port Augusta in November 1984.

I was married at the time with three children, and my husband, Stan was doing fencing at Mabel Creek Station. We came down and it was a new Ghan running then — first time — used to be old steam engine — I came down on the steam engine — we was that pleased to get in this flash new Ghan — hiding our billy cans and all that — anyway kids were crying and we were trying to stop people looking — we was embarrassed I think — I was anyway — the billy can dropped out and we'd try to hide it. Banjo Walkington and his wife were on the train with us — she was carrying too I think.

We were going back to Mabel Creek. We got off at Kingoonya and got a ride with Mr Dingle, mail driver, he had all this petrol — right up high it was — forty-four gallon drums — some underneath and some on top — and I was big — just about to go in. Anyway had to climb all the way up there — got off the train and had to get on these drums — I don't think they cared about Aboriginal woman sitting on drums — he was only a boy, Mr Dingle — and I had to hold on to the kids — Stan wouldn't do it — they all sitting in the front there — and I'm holding on there — can't you hold this — asking Stan. Oh — shut up — he answers — anyway — I just had to put up with it and kids behinds was burnt with petrol — the petrol was leaking — mine was burnt with petrol — one place and I can't move with big stomach and trying to hold on to the kids — ropes — you know ropes was tied had to hold on to the drums — it was very cruel. Anyway we got to no. 7 and they said come in for a cup of tea Dingle — anyway — they went in — and one woman came out but I couldn't get down I was stiff and everything — burnt — skin was burnt — petrol — and

I was so wild with Stan — anyway they got down and got their scones and that and cup of tea — I had my cup of tea up top there with the kids.

Anyway we got started back to Mabel Creek — got off 12 o'clock in the night I suppose — gee I was pleased to get off — so burnt with this petrol. Put vaseline on ourselves and all — so wild with Stan — anyway we stayed there for a while. We lived down the Creek — I was ready to go in — I said can't I go back to Port Augusta — baby's ready — I shouldn't have went to Mabel Creek. Anyway lived in the creek there — I thought oh well if I have the baby — if anything happens it doesn't matter — no help see — anyway baby starts giving me pain — that was '53 — anyway I went up the creek and had the baby myself — cut the cord and that — kept it wrapped up like that. Stan never gave a cup of water or anything — I just had to stay there — I thought Aboriginal women have them like this — I might as well be like them — stayed there for a while and Mavis brought some water and that — I had Jasol with me but I didn't have water see.

That was when trucks was going through with these big things — didn't know what that was — I was ready to go home then with the baby — and all these big trucks going through — and all these people you know — dressed up — uniforms — they were everywhere — I didn't know what was going on and they had a big thing on top of a rise there and I was in camp then — dust was getting on us from the trucks going through — Stan goes up on the station but never comes back and tell me what it was — when I try to ask he says — Oh I dunno, just trucks that's all. I just live along like that — anyway next minute this big war tank went past — one — first time we saw it — guns sticking out you know — was frightening — I thought — I wonder if they're going to kill us, I kept thinking to myself — because I couldn't get anything anywhere. Oh they're going that way doing tests on bombs — Mavis said — what Stan told her — anyway stayed down the creek for a little while — Stan was walking around with them — that was a long way from us — anyway they went on.

They said they're bombs. After that when they went up

— a few days after — they said bombs going to go off directly — Mavis said Stan told her they going to let a test go and I said oh gee its going to blow us up — I was scared — I said well what's going to happen? Oh it's just going to go off — we'd better watch it you know. I was frightened — getting up there and worrying about the kids — what's going to happen — they'd be screaming — thinking you know. I supposed they'd be screaming and thinking and running to me — I don't know. That was just going through my mind. Everybody else wasn't worried but I didn't know much see. Tried to ask Stan and it was nothing — so I just live along like that. I thought well if it goes off it goes off.

Anyway we were watching out for this — it was in the afternoon — must have been about 3 or 4 — we all watching you know and I was thinking I wonder if it's going to blow us up. It went off and a big rumble came on through — all right around — big noise — rumble — ground's shaking and everything. Anyway — saw this big mushroom thing go off and it just laid there you know in the sky — it was just like a white sky — like a cloud — you see a wide cloud just laying there — was just like that — next day when we got up that was gone.

Anyway after that I'm not sure if it was three that time. Two weeks after — that kind of thing — I'm mixed up with that one and the third one — I don't know whether we went back the third one or the second one — back to Mintabie. Anyway this bomb — they was talking about they was going to let another one off — I wasn't worried then because I knew it was going to go up like the other one. Anyway we went back to Mintabie for a holiday looking around for opals. June was only little. She might have been just starting to walk — I don't know so far back. Went back there and was looking around for opals.

We had our breakfast — got up early because we was anxious to look for opals. Had our breakfast. Bombs going up again this morning. Oh yeah. I was thinking long way from the bomb now. You know I wasn't so frightened. Oh yes it's going to go off this morning. We listen to the little wireless we carried around. We had our breakfast and washed up our things — put 'em all away and it's nearly time to go off now — we was watching out for it — made that same kind of noise only it was bit closer this time. It sounded a bit close but we couldn't see it — we was in a hollow — could only see the top of it. Little while after — didn't take long — suppose it'd be about 7 I suppose — you can see the smoke coming through the trees and the sky going — you know blowing — blowing through. It was sort of slow down the bottom coming but up the top it was sort of going fast. But oh gee, any way we could smell the gunpowder and Alec Woody was there with us and none of us were too sure. He said quick put the rag over your nose and he had a hanky over his nose — he was scared of it — was laughing.

Anyway at the same time I was looking around for this tree — it had sugar in it you know and I was going to suck it — like honey always runs down — I was going to give it to the kids and Alec said don't touch that — it could be poison. Lucky he did. That's when I noticed the dust was on the trees. Sort of a grey/black, you know — not much — but you can see it on the trees — how it settled. That could be poison he reckoned — don't touch em. Anyway I wouldn't touch it — got frightened of it. It was only through him — I was a bit scared — it was making me scared — that could be poison you know — white fellas letting these things off. I never thought like that. And Stan said Ah! — he was laughing — he went up on top of the hill trying to look for some opals. But oh gee, anyway — it was that time — don't know what time the kids starting getting sick — you know vomiting and rash and I thought they're getting flu — forgot about the bomb — they must be getting flu again and I sort of felt sickish you know and then kids were vomiting — all that. They had little bit of rash — sort of a red — and I'd bath them in the water — we wasn't allowed to use too much water — only one drum of water we had — and if the truck breaks down we mightn't get water for weeks, so I just washed them in a dish and put their same dirty clothes back on — it wasn't worth it — red dirt. Anyway — I said these kids are getting sick and June was only little and she was sort of taking a fit or something — jumping — I think she was overheated or something — too hot — anyway we packed our things and came back to Mabel Creek — Welbourne Hill. We came back and I was telling Joan how these kids was sick. Anyway she said why don't you give them something — I gave them castor oil before I came away because I only had a little bit in the bottle — thought this'll clean their stomach out anyway — I thought — gave them that and told Mrs Giles that they was sick and that and told her must be flu — bit of a dry cough you know — I didn't feel too good neither.

Anyway she said, keep on taking the castor oil. She gave me another bottle and she gave us — its a brown stuff — you put two drops in the sugar — I know the name of it — I can't say it. Its for cold or anything like that. Or if you have a big cut you put that on — that brown stuff. It's not iodine — it's that other one like iodine — pretty smell I reckon it's pretty smell. Friar's Balsam! Yeah — that's what we were having all the time. Anyway we were travelling on to Mabel Creek — I had dysentry — kids had dysentry — all sick — it was terrible. Anyway we got there late so we camped in the creek and I was so sick with this you know. I told Stan to get something from the station and they gave me these white tablets to stop the dysentry — gave us some of that — take it four times a day or something you know — couldn't understand anyhow — take them anyhow. It helped. Jennifer wasn't too good at all — she was so sick. She just sort of didn't know us — she was looking at herself — looking at her hand — looking at everyone's hand — she was sort of funny. I was worried. And June was taking fits. I had handful.

We wanted to go in Coober Pedy. Stan started growling — I don't know what you're running around for. I said there's no doctors there's no nothin' — I wanted help because station people — they don't help that much — didn't even come down and see us. That Mary Rankin she never come down and see what was wrong with us. Anyway I wasn't satisfied — I wanted to go in Coober Pedy. Stan took me in there — wasn't happy — but I was worried about the kids. We went in there and Mrs Brewster gave us cough mixture and said if they still take them turns bath them in mustard water — so I was doing that — mustard water — tablespoon full in this water. See I didn't know them people you see. Only she was a shopkeeper — Mrs Brewster. I don't know what she was she just told me to put them in the mustard bath and that's what I done and they were really sick.

I didn't know what to do — I thought oh well — just carry on look after them like that and then she gave us eucalyptus. If that brown stuff not making them any better give them eucalyptus in sugar — together — mix it up together and rub them all over with olive oil and eucalyptus — or don't give them eucalyptus — give them olive oil — plenty olive oil with this sugar — they just eat it — you know — they loved it. They couldn't eat much — just giving them milk and that you know — every time they have milk — bring it up you know. Jennifer was taking fits. June was taking fits. It was so hard for me. It must have been only a few days — no, a week after those tests.

We came right through in a Blitz. That's a big truck — an army truck — Stan had that — that was Stan's father's. Truck — old Blitz they called it and we had a little house on it — sort of like a tent on it and we had the tank under the campsheet too, tied around the drum — just get on the drum and up into the tent. We was living in that. Must have been a week they was sick. Think we only had one night from Mintabie, Welbourne Hill — then we had — I can't remember — I think we camped from Mintabie somewhere along the road there — next day we got to Welbourne Hill and from there we got to Mabel Creek and then Coober Pedy — and they were sick then all the time.

They were sort of weakish — I was sick myself — old woman was looking after two kids — old Toddy — she used to live in the dugout — so she helped me out with the kids — she took one — she's old lady, she was, and I didn't know her — a stranger but she helped me — she said I'll look after the baby while you look after the other ones — that was good help — and she used to rub them up and put them to bed. I was worried because she was in the dugout you know — inside — thought they might suffocate but they were okay. I used to go in and have a look — they used to go down the stairs and then go in like that. She helped me out. Barney was there with his mob but they were okay — it was only us who were sick.

I remember this bloke MacDougall he was trying to take the people away from Maralinga — shift them away — because he knew the tests — he didn't like it — he didn't like it at all — but they just done it. He was working hard; never used to preach or nothing. He went up there and he tried to tell them people and he couldn't understand their language and that kind of thing but he had a — he reckoned he had an old man there — he was talking to him — Maralinga — all around there — he was so tired trying to tell them people to keep away — big fire was coming he was trying to tell them — and they reckon the people — soon as he came away went back that way somewhere — telling the people to get going and them people went back and they never seen them people again — that's what I heard — Mr MacDougall was talking about it and Mr Bartlett was there. He was so tired poor thing — on his own. Had red — no had blond hair. Had fair skin and freckles — poor thing. He tried his best. He came back when everything was finished — he got all these people and took them to Woomera — we had to go and get our chests done and that. I think it was for TB that test. X-ray kind of thing. They never told us what is was for. I got this rash thing but they wouldn't tell me about it. I've still got that rash — go on until I die. On our heads too. I went down talking to them about it and they don't want to tell me. Tell me my father had it and my father *didn't* have it. We can't use soap — skin comes off. Bruce is bad, worse than I am. Bruce was outside with me — we both got the rash. Jennifer was playing with the baby inside the tent when that was happening — I had Bruce on my arm — watching.

There were other people around but we didn't mix with them. That Giles from Welbourne Hill, he died from cancer on his liver. Mrs Giles'd have a story to tell. The smoke went over them too. She was worrying about her orange trees. — Orange trees don't look too good. — Wonder if that smoke's doing that. After that again we went back.

We're always going back that way because we were lonely. We didn't know it was dangerous — just thought it was bombs going off. Mr MacDougall use to help get injections for the kids — and Mr Bartlett — they were so good to the Aboriginal people — they were the only ones.

Meredith Michie

Meredith Michie was born in Mount Gambier and grew up in country towns, inland and coastal, in South Australia, New South Wales and Victoria. For many years, though, Melbourne has been home and she lives with her daughter and son a few blocks from the beach in South Melbourne. For a crust, there's been a lot of thising and thating; at present she works part-time as a publisher's editor. Not for a crust, she was on the Editorial Board of *Tabloid Story* for several years in the '70s. Her work has been published in *Australian Short Stories*, *Island* and *Westerly*.

Whatever It Takes

As usual, morning eventually comes. Squinting, I confirm last night's suspicion. Yes, that'd be right — mushrooming on my wrist, a ringworm. Rose's felines? Or, Rose?

Morning again. Again, shaping in the dim light is the fungusey stain of possum, under the weight of which the soggy cardboard ceiling sags. I'll get around to them again one day, these furry occupiers of my eaves — after I've had a go, that is, at evicting the furry occupiers of my mind.

Already the poultice heat sucks. Throat's a dried-up river bed of parched pebbles, clacking away. And behind the eyes, hot grit.

Without looking, without reaching out to feel, I see and feel Rose's dimpled bott hogging our bed's sagging centre.

Dull bones ache from rainlessness and muscles, craving rain, knot.

I give it a squeeze, Rose's bott, and as usual it shrugs irritably but doesn't budge.

Time was when it did though. It doesn't take much and I am transported by memory of her dazzling flesh thirty years ago in another place, when I was not so old and she was young. I was taking up her hem. It was yellow, the dress, and so becoming on her in the shop I'd handed over the five pounds proudly. But after, she nagged that it was dowdy and there was a tantrum. She dug her heels in. So on a Sunday morning with the good roast spitting and the ABC burbling cosily she passed me the pins and hopped up onto the kitchen table.

I was not good at this sort of thing and embarrassed by inadequacy. I wanted to escape outside and clip the edges and move the hose around a bit, maybe even get the mower out. But warm Sunday morning sunlight swathed her and her golden leg hairs gleamed. She'd got me. In that warm suburban kitchen.

The dress was yellow. It was also cut on what I think is

called the bias, full and swirly. I was all thumbs.

Restlessly she shifted her weight and I clutched at the cloth, trying to bunch it into some semblance.

Impatiently she shifted again, and again the impossible hemline dipped.

I kneaded the fabric.

She fidgeted.

I pinpricked her calf.

She jiggled.

I jabbed.

She jumped, and stooped and yanked my hair.

I would have gone for the scissors then, but giggling, she suddenly pirouetted. Her laughter swirled about her, the cloth blossomed out around her yellowly and, oh lord, I could have eaten her. My chest was full of feeling.

Another place, another time.

In my chest now, a heavy stone, slowly heat-splitting.

Climbing out over Rose's bulk produces further bum-shrug and sleepgrunt. I am always up hours before her and her dogged occupancy of the outside of the bed is a silly, but not to be changed convention. She feels, she says, hemmed in against the wall, and says she must have elbow room. Conventions and convictions, Rose has them. She has pretentions, too.

Like the way she dug her heels in all that time ago when things got bad and we came bush. Coming bush was acceptable — Rose had notions about living in the country. Rather, her obstinacy was over where and how. She was for a trim white farmhouse in verdant setting. Of course there'd be an orchard, and from every window pretty hilly vistas dotted about with grazing palominos. Palominos! Yes, Rose had notions.

I let her dream on, having learned you can't move a mule by flogging, that carrot is the only way. So while she concocted I scavenged and came up with these bush acres leased cheap and long term.

It's second-hand sort of bush, tired, but we're on a creek and that was one carrot. We'll bathe in ferny water holes and glittering fish will spring into our arms, I whispered. (Never mind that the block's so steep you'd need witch's cloak and broomstick to make it down to mosquito and blackberry infested sludge.) We'll terrace, I murmured seductively. Garden steps and secret winding pathways. Little rustic bridges, I cajoled. I crooned, we'll plant. Ferns and orchids and growths luxuriant. We'll make a paradise, I warbled, and birds of paradise will come. Already there are bellbirds — harken to their chimes, I carolled.

And so it went, inch by inch.

It was harder going with the house, or shack you'd have to call it. If the bush was played out, you'd have to say the shack was knackered.

So things were only middling here for a while until Rose fell in with potters. For the upturn I was thankful, but for the influence on Rose of those arty layabouts I despaired. I pointed out to her their rough-thrown bowls, their lop-sided jugs, their patchily and pukily glazed plates. I mistrusted their slow ways and fast philosophies, their thin and waffly notions. But Rose mixed muesli and took to soaking lentils. Everywhere, beans! There grew in her a hankering for hand-made, greasy wool garments.

Fanning, I shuffle to my smelly heap of clothes. They're on the nose all right. Tee-shirt and overalls, loose, for any flukey draught that's going. Bellbirds is right! The monotony of their ceaseless tinny clappers is broken only by the outraged rasps of some thirst-crazed parrot.

The sudden yelp is my own as I pad across the main room for the boots. Stung? Bitten? On the sole. I peer. That Rose. Oh sloppy Rose. I've stumbled straight into her little pile of nail parings from last night and, like a thorn embedded, one creamy horny sliver has pierced even my cast-iron pad. Impaled on Rose's toenail — that'd be right. I hop to the kitchen mantlepiece for the pointy-nosed pliers and wrestle myself into a parody of Buddha for the extraction.

I'm too long in the tooth for all this. I should just let go. But am losing Rose again, and must go along with whatever it takes to hold her. Whatever it takes, because I love the slummock. Even from the kitchen I hear her sleeping — her darling little whiffles and whistlings, the tiny hoots. Like a pup. I love her.

She hurts though. Take last night, which had been building up for weeks. She was in a mood all right — her weapon, disdain. I was nervous and placatory and over our bean and rabbit stew I asked her how the pottery was going. Not that she ever fires anything — it's all just clay play. But I called it pottery and enquired.

Eye-to-heaven-rolling silence.

I offered to take her swimming, to the Living and Learning Centre pool, no less, because of Heenan's Hole having all but dried to a puddle. The water galumphings of bulky over-eager Rose are an embarrassment and people turn to watch then turn away, but I'd have done it.

Silence.

The deafening furry whirrings of moths churned in the silence.

So I feigned indifference. But it sets the blood churning, indifference, when it is feigned, and is the hardest thing of all for me to sustain.

It didn't work. She left me sitting there in mid-mouthful and I soon heard the snap, snap of the nail clippers, each snap a deadly little insult. Moths pinged on the light globe, in the stifling air.

I went for a wander outside and mozzies descended. Slapping, I scuffed along the firebreak I'd cleared around the shack this summer, kicking at the dry clods which instantly disintegrated. And I was swamped with longing for spongy suburban cooch, edges to clip and a hose to shift around — a hose with a sprinkler that I could turn on Rose to set her squealing and cavorting to accompaniment of drops on hydrangea leaves — coolest of sounds. Here there was no sound.

Light from inside where Rose was prettifying came down over the verandah and lay across the ten foot wide scar I'd created, in the middle of which the shack now sat exposed like a grubby peeling scab. Not pretty, and I hadn't relished taking out the woody fuschias and straggly agapanthus which had hugged the sides — remnants of my brave long past attempts at camouflage. Not pretty, and I'd got buggery from Rose, but safer because smoke was often in the air this summer.

I mooched over to the vehicle parked in its own fire-break facing up the track leading to the main road for a quick getaway if necessary and if God and vapour-lock didn't prevent. There was water stashed under the front seat and, in case it came to it, blankets. I switched on the ignition and let the engine run awhile. It sounded rough but willing to my attuned ear. The headlights arrested a munching ring-tail which went stock still. The silence intensified when I switched off. God. I sat there with Rose in my chest like a stone.

When I went back in she was humming self-absorbedly, surrounded by her beautification paraphernalia which our pension cheques can't cover, still clipping. She did not look up.

'Would you like me to paint your nails, alluring Rosamunda?' I pleaded with desperate jocularity, swiping instead of patting her head as I'd intended.

She ducked and hummed louder. Snap, went the clippers.

I was gruff and clumsy. I was ridiculous. But I was full of need.

'Come on Rose, give us a go at your toes, like I used to.' Snap. Snap.

I circled her, wheedling. 'Want a back rub, Rosie?' Snap.

I'll show you snap, haughty miss, I thought, and brought in the firearms from the kitchen for a clean. Ever since I'd had to shoot the moth-eaten gelding, Rose has hated my weapons, though the lord knows they've been the means often enough of keeping the wolf from the door. It worked. As I inserted the brush up the first bore she ignited.

'Trigger-happy!' she hissed.

Got her.

'Titivator,' I taunted.

Her deliberate fart. Because of the beans, a beauty.

'Better out than in,' I sang, brightly controlled.

Two more tight expulsions.

'Sourpuss!' I yelled, uncontrolled.

'Old mean-mouth crazo!' she shouted. 'Stringy-bean!'

'Fatso!' I bawled.

'You make our life *thin*!' she screamed. '*Thin-thin-thin-thin*!'

Drumming.

She'd got me. I sat there.

'Nothing *happens*!' she howled, and sent flying her little bottles and gadgets as she crashed off to bed.

I heard her flinging things. I heard the familiar bed springs.

The silence then was absolute. Then in the room no moths flopped and the night was frogless, cicadaless. The whole world, Roseless. I sat on, enveloped in the sweet familiarity of her haunting Rexona talc, and cleaned and reassembled and replaced in the rack all the weapons.

Later, lying alongside her, I listened to a hot hissing wind get up. All the night was filled with wind and a far-off single fox's barking, on and on persistently. And I thought of the hidden birds out there balancing in the seething trees and the possums holding on with all their claws.

It is dead still again today though, and any sympathy I might have felt for the tenacity of possums wilts with the cough, nearer to hand, of one of the beggars dragging its slow body across my ceiling.

I get the boots on, go for the hat, and untie the flywire which on its one loose hinge falls back crookedly. *I* fall back crookedly. Because catching me on the hop comes the cats, Rose's gang of snarlers, swarming in. What a turn-up. Usually they melt when I appear — at worst they keep a baleful distance. But now, everywhere, disregarding the greasy lumps of stew still floating in last night's plates. All around, humming, in the same state of furious ecstacy that possesses them when Rose remembers to feed them and deliberately strings it out, sending them crazy and over the edge.

Hydatids? Heat? Impending bushfire?

My moths go gutty — I mean, mothy. My guts flutter as I spot up there on the mantlepiece the ring leader, the *ringworm*-leader, sick. Orange and bigger than a fox, it crouches, its tail whipping. The growl bubbles in its throat and its one eye is milky with unreason.

Old instinct stirs and the body responds. I don't have to crunch through cat-strewn debris. Only my arm moves, flowing out to the familiar firearms rack. Unlike a dog's which would look away, the unhinged eye is snagged on my gaze. Down with the Brno, transfer it to the left arm smoothly. Then from the ammo ledge, the silencer, for Rose's sake. I screw it on, not rushing. Now the cartridge packet. I slip a .22 standard up the breech and with the click of the bolt the eye flicks. Tuck butt into right shoulder and take, as Rose would say, deadly aim — the lovely action, the old hard harmony.

The sick mad eye sits in the steel vee. My juices flow in harmony with the rhythm of my breathing — deep, slow, steady.

My heart like deep, still water.

Breathing suspended.

Take up pressure.

Now.

It's clean. Clean, quiet and quick. I take it in mid-air in mid-spring and even as the spit of the Brno registers, cat is thrashing meat on the floor.

It is the only way with sick things. Sick or threatening things.

The shocked pack scatters and I examine the still jumpy carcass, noting with the inevitable little pull of pride the clean, fatal entry and exit of my shot. The animal's been scouring and the green ooze around its ring is sour, but surprisingly, apart from the one moth-eaten patch on its head, the pelt is free from mange. I'll peg it out and get Shirl Hempel, who owes me, to make a trim of it for the collar of Rose's parka. Rose'll like that — I'll tell her I got a fox and she'll never know the difference.

But how I am busting.

I get the hat and stepping out onto the verandah sense, before I see, the presence. There, in the battered old lopsided lounge at the other end. An apparition? In grey shroud? I prop.

'The sword!'

What's this then?

'Whoso . . . *Whom*soever uses, uh, *weilds* the sword will die by it,' it sniggers, muffled by sheet.

Oh lordy me.

'I am chosen to warn you, be warned!'

'Oh. Yes . . . well . . .' I cough.

Sunstroke? No, too early.

'A lemonjuice, perhaps?' I try. 'To drink?'

'You cannot oil around me for you have been sprung, uh, *witnessed*. The sword will smite you, you who live by it,' it leers.

'It was a twenty-two,' I blurt. 'A Brno.'

'All God's lambs must be venerated!' it smirks.

'It was a chook,' I protest. 'I mean, a sick. I mean *cat*. It was a cat — a sick cat.'

Oh boy.

'Look,' I rattle on, 'this is all very nice but I'll be back in a minute.'

And, still clutching the Brno, scuttle down the steep steps, perilous with rot. Lord, if there's not already enough on my plate without this visitation by deranged, bean-eating potter!

The morning, so still, yet debris everywhere from last night's strange wind. I slither, all ungainly, down over the dry slippery leaves to the seclusion of the patch of bush in which this summer I am rotating. For Rose's sake we got around to a septic, an inside one, but it's hardly used — it never occurs to me except if it's raining pick-handles, or hailing. And at night, if she has to, lazy Rose squats over a pot she keeps under our bed — the big blue china potty she had as a kid. It is me, of course, who eventually has to do the emptying.

Leaning the rifle against a rusty drum, I face downhill and plant my feet. Down I go, all bone-ache and muscle-knot.

She's an oddie, Rose, and I often mull over how she is not fully furnished. One day she was — the next, not. I thought I'd have to shoot her, but it hasn't come to that. The sickness got her soon after we came to this place those years ago when she, probably moping for the horse I was trying to talk her out of and pining for the potters I was discouraging, was in the wrong place at the wrong time and was bitten by the wrong mozzie. Well, that's my theory. But anyway, the mozz was on her. She got a fever on the brain and that was it — the old encef.

I haunted the hospital while they battled for her. *I* battled for her. Oh my darling, let it be me instead — let me be the sick one. God. Let it be me, take me instead. My heart, my darling heart.

She didn't know me.

Bone-ache and muscle-knot. After the first hot spurt I control the flow and let it trickle over my wrist — an old remedy and nature's way. *Piss on your ringworm/Watch it squirm . . .*

I broke a bone in my hand one night in the hospital grounds punching and punching the gleaming trunk of a silver birch. It went into plaster. And once, some nurses found me wrapped around the same tree, trying to squeeze the life out of it they said later, and prized me off and put me into one of the wards with a shot. They thought I was having a fit, they said, but found I was choking on the earth I'd crammed into my mouth — though I don't remember.

You'd have to say I'd gone to pieces.

Here, the very air is brittle. All around are small crackings of dead wood endlessly falling on the crisped ground litter, and all around the tinny plinks of soulless bellbirds. Long pale leaves drop silently and silently a lizard, a little bloke and almost underfoot, is panting uselessly.

Then one morning she knew me and asked for a back rub. And never was there such a rubbing of back, one-handed because of the plaster, and never, as my tears fell on her, such a salty lubrication. That triumphant morning there was an outbreak of hospital geese which arrived in a triumphant rush on the lawn overlooked by Rose's room. My chest was full of feeling as we celebrated those indignant speeding geese and the antics of pursuing not so speedy gardeners.

Even now, geese sometimes flurry through my head.

They said we were in luck, her coming out of the coma as well as she did, but that I'd have to adjust to certain changes. Just so. Her moods oscillated from near-normality to long bleak vacancies to frenzied activity and shitty rages. She was capable of cunning. She got greedy and fattened. I guarded, anticipated, responded, gauged. I became her watcher. Several times I had to save her when her head was especially heated. I went into hock to get the gelding for her, and supplies of clay. Waking and sleeping Rose occupies me.

Sometimes I nearly lose heart and wish for a soybean simply to go down the wrong way. There'd be a brief carry-on, but then it would be over. That'd be that. Natural. Rose is partial to beans.

The crack, like a shot, of a dead wattle falling somewhere further down snaps me out of reverie.

Trudging unwillingly back up I ponder the identity of the shrouded occupier of my verandah. The voice, nasal. The tone, smug yet hectoring. The utterances, frogshit. Definitely a potter. But how long on my verandah I don't know, the fine tuning of my hearing faculties being on the blink again.

But it doesn't take any fine tuning to hear the blood-curdling whinny of Rose's laughter — the sound of her when she's out to impress. The load in my chest slips sideways and is wedged. From the bush at the edge of the clearing I squint up at the verandah. She's plonked on the bedroom window sill, one cheek bulging over, still in the voluminous yellow nightie with the butterfly sleeves. Her back is to me but I know she is flirty and overheated. Their heads, his now uncovered, are close.

I see it is the Baxter boy, aspiring potter, and know that he's just playing with us, that there's a bet involved.

Playing with us — that'd be right.

I raise the rifle and step into the clearing to be seen.

He sees.

Elaborately I aim.

He stiffens.

With the rifle I motion him off.

His eyes pop.

I gesture again.

He is off the verandah and down the steps before slow Rose connects.

His foot goes through the rotten bottom step which launches him into a thudding belly-whacker in the dust at my feet.

'Only a joke,' he rasps as he gets his wind back.

I am unmoved. 'Up!' And he edges past me to the track.

His cringing gait, slack mouth and flicking eyes is a measure, I know, of my boiling heart, as is my spray on his cheek.

'Get!'

Robbed Rose has heaved herself out through the window and is hanging over the verandah rail babbling, imploring the lentil-head to stay. The stone in my chest moves. Sideways, his fear-sickened eyes still on me, he begins to manoeuvre up the track.

But now, as he crabs along at the end of the verandah, she lurches into an unbalanced pirouette. Her wild giggles swirl about her, the yellow nightie blossoms grotesquely around her. And then, oh lord, she blunders up onto the old couch. Bouncing up and down on the couch. How nice of you to call, do visit again soon, you must see my clay works next time, she bellows with desperate gaiety. Up and down — bounce, bounce.

That gets him, and in an instant she's hoisting up the long nightie, tugging, wriggling, wobbling, balancing and stepping out of her pants. Her pants are pale blue. With them, as with hanky or flag, she waves him off, braying and cackling, exhorting him to come again.

Semaphoring with her pants.

Her blue pants.

Legume's eyes rush to mine. Then he clamps his hands over his ears and runs. He ducks his head and tears up that track like there was no tomorrow.

Slowly I lower the unloaded rifle. The stone, my burden, cracks. Standing here, I feel it split and am aware of a lightening. I am aware, too, that Rose has subsided and, flopped on the lopsided lounge, has fallen to moping again.

Tink! go those dreary, dreary bellbirds. Tink!

It might as well be now. I confirm the ammo in my pocket. It is no good a body going on with mad heart, mad mind. Now'd be the time and I know a spot. Bone-ache and muscle-knot dissolve. My mind starts to clear — its furry occupiers departing. I feel easier — my heart stilling like deep water.

I turn and start down. I do not look back.

But, the cat. Even as I remember the cat, Rose's roar stops me. In waves, roar upon roar rolls down. She's found the cat and the carry-on has a worse than usual edge. Intention falters. Whirry furrings — I mean, furry whirrings return. *I* return. There seems nothing else for it.

Rose carried on last night. Mean-mouth, she said. Well, that's the way things go sometimes, especially after sixty-six years of life's eventualities being only middling. She screamed that nothing happens. 'Every day, nothing!' Nothing happens is right. Then, it seems, everything happens — just take this morning. But 'everything', around here, doesn't signify . . . I suppose. There seemed to be so many possibilities once — all around, choices. But now, it seems, as I return, none.

I come up the steps slowly, rubbing on my overalls my itchy wrist. What now? Whatever it takes, I suppose. Though what?

She quietens, then backs off as I enter the kitchen and bring out the cat. For the first time in months I feel upon me her full, intense attention. On *me*. New intention stirs and there comes a flutter of feeling, that old mix of hope and anxiety — rebirth of the stone, I suppose.

If only I can get it right. For once, when Rose is around, my actions are deliberate and uncompromising. My head clears again. I prop the Brno, unsheath the knife and drop the furry body, unresisting thing, on the verandah table. Without looking, I know that Rose is rooted to the spot. Intention forms.

I spit on the stone and start sharpening, absorbed in the act and by the feel of steel on stone, the lovely response of one to the other. The arc of steady strokes — steady stroking, heel to tip, side for side on the blade. Steady pressure.

Like an anxious animal, Rose, despite herself, draws closer. I test the blade. My mind feels as sharp, bone and muscle alive. The tension in Rose is palpable. Intention firms. And is affirmed by the growl of sudden thunder. Thunder! With all these goings on I'd forgotten the elements. What a turn-up. Had nature been going to create this day, I'd have sworn she'd have given us fire.

71

I stretch the cat out on its back and spread wide the hind legs. The front legs flop uselessly, at variance with the taut belly.

The verandah darkens under thunder as I push the blade under the skin at the hock.

'No!' gasps Rose. 'Don't cut cat!'

'What a turn-up,' I murmur with calculated vagueness, cutting up along the first leg, across under the balls, and down the other to its hock — a precise and clean-cut crescent. Not bad for one who fumbled at a girl's hem thirty years ago.

'Ire!' she yowls. 'Ire!'

'Mmm?' And taking care not to pierce the stomach cavity, my knife unzippers the animal from crutch to chin. As I part the flesh along either front leg and across the chest — the second crescent — I know I've nearly got her.

'Stopput, Ire! It's going dark! Ire-*us*, stopput, I'm dying!'

'Is that so.' I pull the skin off one knee, push the leg bone forward and peel it down to the foot. 'What a turn-up,' I say as I break the bone and cut the foot off. 'What a turn-up.'

'Turnip! Turnip! Waddaya talkun turnip!' Spittle forms. 'Old turnip-head Iris!'

It won't be long now. There are bubbles of snot and a sequence of tiny farts. I love her. It is, as she says, going dark — indeed, so overcast has the day become shapes are beginning to blur. I drop the cat on the floor and, with my foot on each hind leg in turn, work the skin free up to the buttocks.

'Iris! Bum-bum-bum! Turnip-bum!'

But she's mewing now and the fingers are cramming into the mouth. She is collapsing. Stay intact, intention. Whatever it takes, remember?

So I smile, and cut the skin where it joins the sour crusty ring, work it free around the tail butt, then pull up hard. The fur peels off the tail bone right to the tip.

Her whimper almost undoes me.

Come on, Rose, come on, I pray. Still standing on the hind legs I sit the carcass up and, like undressing a sleeping child, start rolling the skin up to the forelegs.

'Maa-aa-aa!' Her eyes like blue china potties.

'Rosie?' I acknowledge. *Proud, bright-eyed geese come rushing through my head.*

'Maa-umm!' she bleats.

Got her. *Behind my eyes, the whooshing of triumphant flapping geese.*

I let the carcass drop and at last turn to her.

'Mummy?'

My darling. *In my head now, beautiful geese serenely preening.*

And, crooning, I gather her to me again and we stand here in the gloom, us two old women, clamily locked together, rocking, as the first spits of rain hit the iron. It doesn't matter that my hands smear her nightie. There is, I see, a ringworm on her neck and joyfully I vow to fix first thing our fungi.

Olga Masters

Olga Masters was born in Pambula, New South Wales. Her first job, at seventeen, was with a local country newspaper, where the editor encouraged her writing. She married at twenty-one, and with a family of seven children and part-time work in journalism, she had little opportunity to develop her interest in writing fiction until she was in her fifties. In the 1970s she wrote a successful radio play and a stage play, and between 1977 and 1981 won nine prizes for her short stories. *The Home Girls*, her first book, won a National Book Council Award in 1983 and her first novel, *Loving Daughters*, was highly commended for the same award. *Loving Daughters* is now being made into a major film. Her third book, *A Long Time Dying*, a collection of linked stories, also received critical praise. Olga Masters died in 1986 after a brief illness. She was at work on her fifth book, a collection of stories, which will be published late in 1987.

Brown and Green Giraffes

George Carr mourned for a suitable time following the death of his wife then began to think a lot about a successor. George had an only child, a daughter who was high up in education, as he expressed it to anyone asking. She was married to a Canadian, also high up in education and together they wrote books on teaching methods. Barbara came home for her mother's funeral, distressed that she couldn't stay longer than a week because she was giving a paper at a conference in Calgary. As it was she had to change times with another speaker. She had worked right up to the time her plane left making neat little asterisks on a pile of programs ready to go in delegates' places drawing attention to the change, explaining on the bottom margin the reason for it.

'I insist,' she said. 'I feel less like letting everyone down.'

After the funeral she offered George puzzling compensation for letting him down by leaving so soon.

'I'll take the fruit girl,' she said sweeping a figurine from the mantlepiece, a girl with a basket of fruit on her hip. She said she would have it touched up by the experts at home in the more culturally advanced country and George saw with a deepening depression the shabbiness of the porcelain ornament when moved to a new light. When Barbara carried it off to pack it among her fashionable clothes he felt he should move the other things on the mantlepiece to close the gap but didn't think he could manage this and was miserable at the thought of looking at the space for the rest of his life.

But the space was filled when he came home after taking Barbara to the airport. Mrs Oates from next door had let herself in to leave a macaroni cheese on the kitchen table and pick through the flowers from the funeral, making new arrangements of those still fresh. She put some cream roses in a brass jug and made the mantlepiece look quite different after forty years with the fruit girl there.

George found the macaroni still warm and although it was only eleven o'clock in the morning, hardly lunch time, he sat with the dish on his knees and ate, staring at the roses.

'A woman's touch,' he said aloud. 'There's nothing like a woman's touch.' He dropped the empty dish in the sink with such a klunk he snatched it up again and ran his hands around it looking for a crack.

In the bedroom he took off his jacket and as was his habit all his married life, flung it on the bed, wondering at the difference there. Usually the quilt was on smooth as a billiard table as Jess made it, then Barbara while she was home.

'Blimey,' he said and went to look in the second bedroom where Barbara had slept. He pulled the quilt back and saw the pillow naked of its slip, the blankets turned back on the mattress.

George looked stupidly for sheets, even looked over the bed end at the floor.

He remembered then seeing Barbara early that morning on her way to the laundry with a great bundle of something coloured green. He went there and looked about him. A big white washing machine, above it a dryer, the door of which he opened and felt surprise nothing was inside. Nothing in the washing machine either, he saw when he lifted the lid. He removed the lid of a wicker basket. There were the sheets looking as if a plum pudding was inside them.

'Blimey,' he said looking at the neat arrangement of packets and bottles on a shelf and below it a line of hooks from which hung brooms, mops, dusters, dustpan and brush. He saw there were curtains at the small window with a design of giraffes on them, long necked brown giraffes, some very silly looking with half their legs off or a rump missing where the material was cut and hemmed. The curtains were familiar to him although he never went into the laundry. Although he thought the giraffes were green. Then he thought, ah I've got it, and trotted to the kitchen where, yes, similar curtains hung above the sink except the giraffes were green. There's nothing slow about you George, he told himself and went to the living room to sit in his chair and stare at the dark grey face of the television and think about the curtains. He imagined Jess shopping for them. She couldn't decide between brown and green, he supposed. He always thought of her as a silly indecisive woman and here was proof of his intelligent judgement. Then he remembered she was dead and he should be charitable. He decided to think of her as clever, taking a colour for each room when she was unable to choose between them.

She knew how to spend money, no doubt of that, George thought, then had to pull himself up again and in guilt and some confusion he switched on the television and stared for a while at a demonstration on raising African violets, then switched off and wandered to the window to look out on Jess's garden.

This had been her main hobby. He would sometimes come from golf or a business luncheon (although retired from the taxi company where he was secretary for thirty years, he was still a shareholder) and find her, a stoutish woman in a grey skirt and green jumper, pressed between the shrubs working furiously with a digging fork.

She could sprout something herself, George often thought, mildly irritated that she might have neglected dinner preparations. Of course she hadn't. In the kitchen he would see her little shiny tightly lidded saucepans of vegetables ready on the burners, and since he watched his weight and favoured grills, the steaks would have thawed on the enamel plate, lapped gently by their own bloodied juice. In a little while she would be in, her gardening gloves gone, a big flowered apron over her jumper and skirt, her large arms shaking their flesh as she lit the gas and turned the saucepan handles inwards as she had done since Barbara was a year old.

He could never understand how she could have everything ready at once, even the baked custard warm the way he liked it. He went to the kitchen now and stared at Mrs Oates's dish with a yellowish crust formed on the inside.

He should fill it with water, he supposed. Or wash and dry it and take it to her. She might then ask him to eat dinner there. He stood in the middle of the kitchen with his hands in his pockets. He was incapable of removing them to wash the dish, incapable of drying it. He searched the room for tea towels but could see none, the steel rack above the stove empty. They must usually hang there for George had never seen the bars exposed before. He tugged at the green giraffes and yes they were outside spinning on the clothesline. He should bring them in he told himself, but he had never done such a thing in his life. He looked nervously about him as if there was danger of his thoughts exposed to an onlooker.

He sauntered through the house to the front in time to see the afternoon paper spin through the air and land on the stone floor of the porch. He picked it up shaking it free of leaves, thinking they were not usually there, and started to think why they were allowed to be and switched the blame quite quickly from Jess to Barbara. She had always been a selfish girl, her mother doing everything for her while she was at school and University, then allowing her to go off overseas when she had been teaching for only a year, and all that money spent in bringing her home for her marriage to that fellow Edward. He didn't come out for the funeral which he should have done and they could have stayed and Barbara look after him as it was proper for a daughter to do. Back inside he looked into the double bedroom which he supposed they would occupy, himself in the other room. He picked his jacket up and laid it down again and felt renewed irritation with Barbara blaming her for the tangle of blankets and sheets as if she and Edward had passed the night there and she had failed in her duty to make it. It would not be a good idea though to have Edward here. He wouldn't fit in, not liking golf, football and fishing, and never having heard of the Melbourne Cup. Perhaps Barbara would come back alone. She could well be deciding that on the plane at this very moment and would be back before he had dirtied all the crockery in Jess's cupboards and used all the sheets in Jess's linen press. He made his way to the living room slapping his thigh with the paper.

A few weeks later he was there again in his chair, a board on his knee backing a pale blue sheet of paper he was filling out. He was up to the question *How would you describe yourself? Careful / generous.* George looked at the vase of dead roses on the mantlepiece in place of the figurine. 'Generous!' he said aloud. 'Very generous!' But he didn't write it down. George knew women. There would be some who would not stop at brown and green giraffes. Just think of all the other colours giraffes could come in.

Judith Woodfall

〜

Judith Woodfall has had short stories published in many Australian literary magazines and newspapers including the *Bulletin*, *Westerly*, *Island Magazine* and the *Canberra Times*.

The Game

The winter of 1984 had been cold and snowflakes had fallen onto Lottie and Percy's property that July night when they played their game. Their house is tucked away in the valley up Monkey Creek Road only a few miles from Yea, where the ironstone hills are like the Big Dipper at Luna Park, and the granite outcrops covered in velvet-green moss make bumpy slides for their grandchildren.

That July night was bitterly cold and puffs of cardboard cut-out like smoke from the lounge room fire gathered around the eaves and didn't budge from the chimney pot.

Percy stuck his head out the back door to look at the night, whispered to the dogs King and Bluey, 'As soon as she's toddled off you two can come in out of the cold,' and then walked slowly back into the lounge room, rubbing his knotted hands that always played up with arthritis this kind of weather.

'Your pea soup's got nothing on this, Lottie. It's really crook outside.'

'Don't you like my pea soup?' Lottie asked, putting down the pot holder she was crocheting for the Yea Presbyterian Church Fete.

'Look, I didn't say that. Trust you to take it the wrong way.'

'I'd've thought after fifty years' marriage to me you'dv'e learnt a bit of tact, Percy.'

'Oh shut up Lottie.'

That did it.

It was on again for young and old.

Lottie flung the pot holder onto the floor, put her head, covered in white fluffy curls a bit like cotton wool, into the air and stalked sedately off to the bedroom.

'Come on boys, in you come,' Percy called to the dogs. 'We're in for a bad bout of no-speakies again from the boss.'

The dogs, sometimes enemies, sometimes friends, yapped and whimpered and knocked into each other and sent the sugar bag they had been sleeping on off the verandah and down onto the concrete courtyard.

'King and Bluey,' said Percy, 'shut your traps or the three of us will pay.'

Lottie and Percy lay in the double bed as far away from each other as possible. Percy hung his legs over the edge of his side and Lottie huddled her body, 'shaped like a knitting needle' Percy reckoned because she was always crocheting and knitting, into a tight ball. They both had trouble breathing and they both wanted to have a bit of a cough. But if they coughed it would be breaking their mutual coventry.

Lottie hadn't the time to go to the outside lavatory before she'd stormed off to bed, and even though she kept a jerry under the bed for these night-time emergencies, she wasn't going to let on to Percy that she wanted desperately to go. Not that she'd go in the jerry when they were not speaking, it somehow kind of made it seem vulgar and her more vulnerable. Anyway, he always said, 'Niagara Falls got nothing on you, Lottie, once you start.'

The only way for Lottie to retain her dignity was to hold on for as long as she could and then make a speedy dash for it when it sounded as if Percy had gone to sleep. Sometimes she tricked him and went in the bath, leaning her skinny flanks over the edge, and then quietly turning on the tap to get rid of it all. But last time he'd tricked her, and slunk in, almost like Jack the Ripper, she thought, and just as she was nearly finishing and moving her bottom from side to side to get rid of the last drop, he'd flicked on the light and she was caught red-handed.

'Well, well, Lottie,' he'd said. 'I must say the Vicar would be impressed with that, I don't think. Although they do say it's the best disinfectant of all,' and he'd laughed and slunk back to their bed.

That particular night she was so furious that she'd made up the bed on the couch and covered herself with the thin eiderdown and had got herself a luke-warm hot-water bottle. She'd listened to Percy snoring away like a thrashing machine.

She wasn't about to repeat that particular humiliation of being caught with her pants down in the bathroom, so she waited till she heard his stop-and-start snoring, and hopped out of the bed and headed for the outside lavatory.

Percy was very very untidy and Lottie was very very neat. Lottie had spent years trying to train him to put the farm equipment away in the shed into alphabetical order. 'It's easier to find, Percy, and you won't be rooting around like a rattlesnake looking for things.'

'Yes dear,' said Percy scratching his head.

But Percy always won in the end because he maintained he forgot his alphabet. 'Does S come before P or what, boys?' he asked King and Bluey.

That night, Lottie tripped over the sugar bag on her way to the lavatory and as she was straightening herself up, she missed seeing the spade leaning against the south wall of the lavatory.

Percy had meant to put away his spade, but he'd heard his longtime friend and neighbour, Isla Billings, come puffing up the back track, so he carefully propped it against the wall. Ah ha, he thought, no point in starting a fight with the old girl. We'll just leave the spade hidden here away from Lottie's searchlight eyes. Time for a cuppa now. We'll finish digging up her vegetable patch after Isla's gone home.

Well, that's how Lottie tripped and fell over the spade.

Because of Percy's continual carelessness and her urgent call of nature.

The spade was hidden amongst the black-eyed susans and jasmine vines and only the wooden top peeked out. She was so intent on reaching her destination and had her hands covering her head from the snowflakes that she just didn't see it.

She ran smack bang straight into it and fell and hit her head on the concrete edging of the pavement near where her freesias were growing in healthy clumps.

Oh no, she thought, I reckon I've done in my ankle. Trust him, trust him, not to put away his tools. Tricked again by his constant blathering and yapping to Isla. If I'd known all of this before I married him, I doubt if I'd've gone through with it.

I could cut his darn throat he's so careless. I won't make a squeak and that'll make him suffer when he finds me here in the morning frozen to death and looking like a large green iceblock.

She'd reckoned without Percy's animal cunning.

He'd been aware of when she'd left the bed and after about twenty minutes he became worried.

I'll just put the light on in the kitchen, he thought, and flick it on and off like the Pt Lonsdale lighthouse light. Then she'll twig to the fact I'm up and about and she's not forgotten.

If he went searching for her it meant another big fight and him being accused of being a sticky beak.

He lit up the stove again with the remains of the kindling, stacked more wood onto the lounge room fire, muttered to the dogs,

'We'll have to thaw her out, boys, when I've worked out a plan for her rescue,' rubbed his weatherbeaten hands together, and went back to his bedroom to put on his bottle green parka so as he wouldn't get wet and just have a bit of a mosey around the place and see where she was hiding.

The parka was missing.

'Look, this time, she's going to wait. Pinching my damn clothes all the darn time,' he said as he pulled on his gum boots and old burgundy dressing gown.

He whistled the dogs. 'Well boys,' he said, 'We've got to come up with a darn good plan this time to get her back into the house or we'll have her snuffling and snorting the rest of the winter. Now, remember, she's playing her "come and get me" game, and we have to find a way for both of us to win and neither lose face.'

The dogs nuzzled against his dressing gown.

'If I go looking for her, she'll lie low, and tomorrow will accuse me of being as weak as cat's piss.'

Percy walked into the kitchen and poured himself a medicinal sip of Chatelle Napoleon brandy, kept for emergencies. He got out his pen and paper and started to write down his plan. Percy, he muttered to himself, let this be a rescue operation that Rommel the Desert Fox would be proud of. Percy, think of this farm as if it's the African Desert. He wrote down on the top of the paper Rommel's words prepared as an introduction to his account of the war in Africa. 'It is my experience that bold decisions give the best promise of success. One must differentiate between operational and tactical boldness and a military gamble.'

Percy worked with speed and cunning and after fifty years' experience at the same game, came up with a possible solution.

He put his decision into practice.

Isla Billings lived about two miles away as the crow flies, and if she drove over the back tracks she could be at the farmhouse pretty quickly.

Percy rang her.

'Look Isla,' he said. 'Lottie's up to tricks again — yes, it's no speaky time. I reckon she's hiding out from me down by the blasted dunny — she didn't go before she stormed off to bed, and she's probably got her foot caught in that damn wire I was supposed to put round her damn vegetable garden.'

Percy took another sip of brandy.

'Yeah, it drives me batty, Isla. Yeah. You'll help? Get over here quick as a flash. Trust me. Pretend I'm Rommel the Desert Fox. Isla, the plan is this . . .'

Lottie tried to crawl towards the house, but her ankle was throbbing as if it had been bitten by a giant gnat, and her other foot was trapped in the fencing wire left hidden amongst the clover by Percy.

Lottie's nose was parallel with the freesias and she started to sneeze. She knew the only way out of her dilemma was to pray to God. 'Dear God,' she said, 'don't let me freeze to death, he's just not worth it. My legs are hurting and I'm starting to sneeze from the close contact with those freesias he was supposed to pull out last summer. Oh hurry up God and help Percy find a solution!'

Lottie started to cry with cold and rage and pain.

A light drizzle had started to fall and she lay on her side and watched the leaves moving in the old river red gums above her head. At least I've got on my slippers and his warm parka, that'll save me, she thought.

Perhaps if I pretend I'm a trapped dingo, she thought, that'll give him an excuse to speed up his operations.

She gave out a few plaintive cries which sent King and Bluey into a frenzy and she could hear Percy yelling at them in the kitchen telling them to heel.

Ah ha, she thought, at least he's still awake and on the job.

Percy ignored her.

Isla drove her ute to within a few hundred yards of the homestead and then stealthily crept down the back track. She was clad in her gum boots and dark grey plastic rain-coat and her drop amethyst earrings swung against her jonathon apple pink cheeks. She'd listened carefully to Percy. 'Yes,' she'd said. 'I agree that surprise is the essence of the future victory, dear.'

She crept past the farmhouse, and tapped lightly on the kitchen window.

'Stop!' Percy commanded in a clear ringing tone, from just inside the back wire door. 'Who goes there? I'll shoot to kill.'

'It's me, it's me!' yelled Lottie, who of course, hadn't heard Isla's spy-like footsteps.

'It's only Isla, Percy. I've brought over some geranium cuttings for Lottie. Yes, dear, I know it's early, but I'm on my way to Buller to do a bit of ski-ing. You been on the grog, Perc? How's Lottie?'

'She's as fit as a trout, still asleep in bed, lucky her. I couldn't sleep,' said Percy very loudly.

Lottie knew then that he was a wake-up to her and wasn't going to rescue her. Just going to let her die.

H'm, she thought. He and that Isla Billings have prob-ably been planning this for some time. She's been eyeing him off since Sunday School at Bonnie Doon. H'm, I bet

86

the Vicar is a wake-up to her. Oh well, she deserves him. They're one of a kind, their property will be like a pigsty, just like the one on the Flowerdale Road . . .

Lottie ignored Percy.

'Help, help,' she whimpered to Isla.

'Did I hear a baby crying, Percy?' said Isla, her plump hand cupping her ear, her head on her side. 'I'll just pop over near the lavatory and see what's there.'

'All right, Isla,' said Percy. The plan's working to perfection, he thought.

'Percy,' screamed Isla from near the lavatory wall. 'Quickly, Percy. Lottie is lying here with her feet doubled up under her and is smelling the freesias.' Isla bent down and touched Lottie's cold cheek. 'Lovely perfume, haven't they, dear? I don't think I'd be bothered getting that close to them though on such a very cold night. You're soaking, dear. Have a bit of an accident?'

Percy piggy-backed Lottie into the house and straight into their bedroom. He tucked her up into bed and placed two hot-water bottles near her feet. He gave her two disprin in a hot lemon drink with three teaspoons of sugar, dried off her wet hair with a towel and rang the Yea doctor.

He then stoked up the fire, placed thick slices of white bread onto the toasting fork and held them over the open fire. He spread blackberry jam in big clumps onto the toast and placed them on a tray painted with a picture of Sydney Harbour Bridge and the Opera House. He placed the tray on Lottie's side of the bed, then pushed back the blue lace curtains and let the blinds up with a bang.

The moon had almost gone, the snowflakes had stopped, and the first pink and lavender light of dawn was edging over the ironstone hills.

'Doctor'll be here soon, Lottie,' he said. He sat on his side of the bed, his feet beating time to Harry Secombe singing *In a Monastery Garden* on the radio.

Lottie started to eat her toast and her eyes shifted to her husband's face.

He was waiting for her to break the silence.

She nodded her head to say thanks for the toast, Percy.

She was not going to be rushed though.

'That Isla gone home, Percy?' she asked.

'Yes, Lottie.'

King and Bluey stirred by the fire playing their sometimes-friends role because of the cold weather.

Lottie and Percy lay together on the bed, their old fingers entwined. They listened as Isla started up the ute on the back track and drove home.

'Oh Percy,' said Lottie. 'You're a silly drongo. Don't you reckon it's time we grew up and stopped playing silly games?'

'We'd've died years ago, Lottie. You'd've lost interest in me.'

'Yes, Rommel.'

Judith Wright

(Mrs J. P. McKinney)

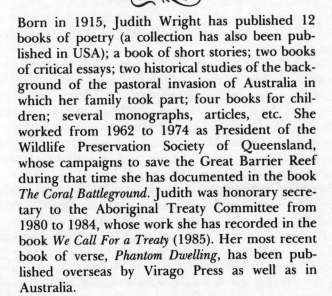

Born in 1915, Judith Wright has published 12 books of poetry (a collection has also been published in USA); a book of short stories; two books of critical essays; two historical studies of the background of the pastoral invasion of Australia in which her family took part; four books for children; several monographs, articles, etc. She worked from 1962 to 1974 as President of the Wildlife Preservation Society of Queensland, whose campaigns to save the Great Barrier Reef during that time she has documented in the book *The Coral Battleground*. Judith was honorary secretary to the Aboriginal Treaty Committee from 1980 to 1984, whose work she has recorded in the book *We Call For a Treaty* (1985). Her most recent book of verse, *Phantom Dwelling*, has been published overseas by Virago Press as well as in Australia.

The Dugong

When Ida gets married,' old Jim had often said, 'I'm leaving. A man's a fool to stick with his children too long; he's just a nuisance to them when he gets the pension and sits about the house. When Ida's married she won't see any more of me, 'less she comes and brings Eric for a holiday.'

'Where'd you go to, Dad? You'd be that lonely you'd soon be back, I bet.' Ida and Shirley and Margie didn't believe him.

But when Ida came back after the honeymoon there was the note on the table. 'Gone to the Island. Look after Eric good and remember man's stomach is key to man's Heart. Love from Dad.'

Jim had always been a bit odd, and in his later days he had grown odder yet, the neighbours thought, collecting things — sea-shells, ropes and compasses from old broken-up ships, stones and queer-shaped bits of wood. He took them all with him. Ida cleaned his room, mourning but a bit relieved all the same. The house was theirs now, hers and Eric's.

On the Island, Jim was both happy and frightened. He had chosen for his own a patch of bush far off the only road that crossed the almost deserted island; what belonged to the Crown belonged to nobody, he said. He cut down some of the thin box-trees and banksias that grew in the dark sand, and with them made a framework for a two-roomed floorless cabin; he covered it with iron from dumps, and odd scraps of timber left behind by the Army when they had camped there during the war, and made himself rustic furniture with pieces of banksia and branches that had been too crooked to use for the cabin.

He was deep in the bush, just as it had been when he was a young man and took fencing contracts far out, those times he had talked about ever since. At first, lying at night in the moving forest where stars and possums travelled through the branches, where wallabies thumped suddenly in the dark, causing his heart to shrink as though it were clutched in too tight a grip, he felt more fear than pleasure at his boldness and at the loneliness he had so long looked forward to. But soon he had identified the noises of the forest, separated the sounds of the night sea as the tide rose and fell across the stairway of rocks at the point half a mile off, and begun to interpret the movements of the stars and planets, half-remembered from his few sea-voyages in youth. He began to accept this new life and to move in accordance with its rhythms, fitting his meals and sleep in with the tides and the weather.

He had his bit of garden in the blackish sandy soil — cabbages and onions and geraniums and ferns, in beds edged with whitewashed stones and beach driftwood. He grew staghorns and small string-like unobtrusive orchids prised from rocks and trees; he fished in the surf on the narrow beach, standing for hours braced against the rush of waves, and on Saturdays he dressed in trousers instead of shorts, took his battered fibre suitcase and a sugarbag, and walked the three miles of sandy track in to the little island settlement, to meet the Saturday launch and collect his groceries and bread, and the pension Ida drew for him in town.

As he walked this track, he often found himself talking aloud, in a kind of apprehension, practising as it were for this unusual contact with his fellow-creatures. Ida would say he was getting to be more of a crank than ever, if she knew; and he stopped himself sternly.

Ida and Eric had come over now and then at week-ends, but it was a long trip on the launch and back on Sunday nights, and after the baby came he seldom saw them. Margie was nursing in Sydney and never wrote, and Shirley had three children now and her husband was playing the horses. Sometimes she sent a postcard, but they had never been very friendly, and Jim was beginning to forget her.

He knew Ida didn't like the island, didn't like the shanty so buried in the bush that few people knew it was there at all; and the knowledge put a defensive self-justifying note into his monologues, when he thought of it. But more often he did not think of it. What went on in his mind, nowadays, was the noise of the sea and the leaves, the knowledge of tide-times and the best spots for fishing, and an obscure feeling that was a mingling of the desire for company and the need to be alone. This feeling was behind the care he took over the making of a house-name for the shanty, a sign made of crooked banksia-boughs, each letter a triumph of ingenuity. He searched the bush for months looking for boughs of the right thickness and shape, and when the sign was finished and framed in driftwood, he took it out to the road and nailed it to a tree. 'LAST-HARBOUR', it said, with a banksia-bough arrow pointing down the secretive track off the road.

It brought him a few visitors, now and then — curious bushwalkers, holidayers from the single guest-house at the settlement, expecting a cafe with tables and tea and disappointed to find only the shanty and the tall loquacious old man in neatly-mended shorts. But if they were willing to listen and humour him for a while, he would take them round his curios and his garden, lead them out to the point and explain the geology of its rocks, and tell them where the fishing was best and at what times of day, give them tea in cracked white cups on the kitchen table now growing greasy and dark with wood-smoke. Sometimes they sent him bundles of papers and old copies of American magazines, before they forgot him. He had quite a library of magazines in the corner, with the old Nautical Almanac and the seedsman's catalogue for 1936 and the book on geology and the old Postal Guide.

One of them, coming back to the island for a second holiday after a year's absence, brought him a dog. Ida had told him once, on one of those weekends that now seemed long ago, that he needed a dog for company; but he preferred the old grey cat that for years now had killed mice in the kitchen, cleaned up the fish-heads that otherwise Jim would have had to bury, and kept his feet warm on winter nights, sharing his narrow bunk. Jim thanked his visitor, but he was doubtful about the dog, which had begun by putting Tiddy up a tree from which she had to be brought down again.

He tied it up with a rope to a sapling till nightfall, while he went fishing, and when he came home it had scratched up a bed of cabbage seedlings near the tree, and had half-strangled itself with the rope by dragging at it, so that its eyes started out of its head and it wheezed miserably. Jim untied it and looked at it without pleasure; it had an ugly stupid head and a thin whip-like tail. It would want to come with him to the beach when he went fishing; like as not it would steal things from the kitchen; he would have to carry meat twice a week instead of once from the settlement, and that would make a difference to the pension.

'Tiddy's got more sense than you,' he said to the dog. 'I don't want you round.' Yet it was something — alive, forlorn, uncared-for. He let it stay, half-liking, half-disliking its dependence on him, its anxiety when he tied it up and went away to the beach, its gratefulness for scraps.

It was a tie; it asked too much, demanding attention, demanding food; and the devotion it was ready to give in return was something he did not want and shook off. He felt the bond as somehow unclean, not like the relationships of the wild things to each other — the wallabies that mated, brought up their young and then forgot them, the birds and lizards that sought their own food and defended their own lives. He and his dead wife had had their children; they were grown and were forgetting him, and that was as it should be. He did not answer the dog when it fawned and asked for petting; and he was not particularly sorry when, later, it picked up a scrub-tick and died of it.

His favourite days were the working-days from Monday to Friday, when he had the whole length of beach, bare, empty even of footprints, all his own. On Saturdays and Sundays he never knew when fishermen or holiday-makers might come strolling along, looking with curious eyes at his patched shorts, the grey hairs on his chest that was now burned almost black with sunlight, his straggling hair that he cut himself, with scissors, now and then. On these days he stayed home, wore his shirt, half-expected visitors and was relieved and disappointed when they did not come. But on Mondays he would set out early and with secret joy for his empty beach, as though he had won a victory and driven the intruders away. The fish he caught and cooked that night were always especially good to his taste, after the week-end butchers' meat. He threw Tiddy the bones and fish-heads and rubbed her ear as she crouched beside him.

'We'll do, Tiddy. We don't need much but our wits and a good line and hook. We don't depend on them, eh?'

It even pleased him when the week-ends were spoiled for holiday-makers by rain — not from any special malice, but rather from a feeling that visitors to the beach were trespassing on something they did not understand or care for as he did. What did they know of the tides, the banks and rocks under them, the sounds of the sea at nights, the places where fresh water soaked through the sand and the wallabies and possums drank? His feeling for this stretch of coast-line was not one of ownership, but of unity, as though he had grown there as the creatures did, and understood each day and night and season only in their impact on one piece of bush and beach.

Accordingly, he was not displeased when a cyclone blew up one week-end and kept the Saturday and Sunday launches from running. By Monday evening it had blown out to sea, and the sky was clear. He could hear the crash of waves on the rock-stair at the point, and the long following blur of sound as the water raced back to the sea. There would be a big swell for days. Next morning he would go down — low tide was soon after daybreak — and see what the waves had brought up to the beach.

He still collected shells — there was nothing he liked better than to wander with concentrated gaze along the curves of high-tide litter on the beach, after heavy weather. He wanted a pearly nautilus, a complete shell — the one he had was broken and imperfect.

Day came with the hazeless clarity of after-cyclone weather. The sun was ready to rise as he set off to the beach, bare-footed and carrying an empty flour-bag, to look for treasure. The growl of waves grew louder as he came to the point and stepped from the tangle of trees that crouched below the crest of the hill, bent away from the sea-weather.

There was a strange black bulk on the beach near the

rocks; so large that he would have thought it only another rock, if he had not known there was no rock there. The suck of receding waves had left it lying in a little pool, where the sand had been dragged away from its sides by the run of water; and the pool was a strange pink.

He had to shade his eyes to look at it, for the sun had come over the horizon and the water glared white beyond the line of breakers. But it seemed to have no proper shape at all.

He started cautiously down the great smoothed stairway of rock to look at it, for it was not far from low-tide mark, and the waves still washed up over the rocks. They crunched underfoot with tiny purplish barnacles, and were slippery with weed. The thing seemed to move as he drew near; but it was only the drag of a wave on one black flipper that hung inert in the pink pool.

'Dugong,' thought Jim, as he stood on the rock above it and stared down. He had never seen one before, in spite of the sea-voyages, but he had heard of them. 'A siren,' he added to himself, to emphasize his knowledge.

The creature raised its head sluggishly; there was blood on one side, under the tight rounded skull. Its split lips moved, as though it were eating or whispering. 'Or praying,' Jim said.

He stood undecided. The creature let its head fall again on the sand; its flipper moved helplessly, defencelessly, as the sea played with it.

Jim could not think what to do. He sat down on the rock, his hands round his knees, and watched the animal. He was moved, but he had not yet decided whether his feeling was of pity or merely astonishment.

'They're rare here. Very rare nowadays,' he said to himself, testing out his feeling cautiously. 'Nearly all killed out. A half-grown one, by the look of it.' He wondered if it was male or female, but he could not be sure.

At last he slipped down the rock, holding a loose stone in one hand as a precaution, and approached the dugong. It moved a little, but vaguely, as though stunned; and at last he stood beside it. It smelled of the sea, a cold salt breath.

He touched it — hairy, harsh, and thick, yet strangely

warm. Of course: the thing was not a fish, he remembered; it was warm-blooded like himself. It was a siren, and an ugly one. But 'If it was good enough for Ulysses,' he said to himself, airing another piece of knowledge, 'it's good enough for me'; and he drew his hand meditatively over its flank and bent to see how deep its wounds might be.

There was a long cut on one side of its curious face, and blood ran down sluggishly and dripped into the pool. One flipper was bent beneath it and twisted. Jim looked at it carefully. He would have to lift the dugong to straighten that flipper out.

Up at high-tide mark he saw a long board or spar lying where the waves had left it. He brought it down and slipped it under the dugong's bristly pig-like side. It was then he saw, with a strange feeling, that the creature had opened its eyes and was watching him.

He moved back with a start, holding its glance with his; but it seemed to him that there was nothing to fear in that look. It came from something lost in pain and resignation, something past struggling. Yet the creature tried to move, tried to release the bent flipper that looked so uncomfortable, so that Jim drew in his breath quickly in sympathy, feeling his own arm bent and hurting as that must. He raised the dugong with his board, carefully, talking to it as he levered the big weight upwards. 'Now, try to move it, boy. See if you can get it out.'

But the flipper did not move, even when the dugong was levered clear of the sand. Clearly something was broken. Inch by inch Jim worked his hands down the levering-board, and carefully touched the flipper, watching all the time in case that blunt stupid head swung round at him. He manoeuvred it gently, so that it lay naturally on the sand, then reached for a few loose stones and slipped them in to support the dugong's body. He slipped the lever out. The creature sank back, and as it sank it made a small cry, a grunt half of pain and half of relief.

At that Jim's heart moved a little. He had helped it, evidently; the sound might have been addressed to him. It was the kind of noise a sick child might make, half-confiding and half-protesting, as its mother moved it on the pillow.

96

The sound made a bond between them, a kind of gesture towards language.

But the waves running up and back were moving the flipper from side to side. It must be splinted. Jim went back to the hut, eagerly, swinging up over the rocks as he had not felt the need to do for years. He found a stick or two for splints, and an old elastic bandage he had had once for a sprained ankle and kept by him. Tiddy was bewildered and indignant that he did not wait for breakfast; she even followed him halfway back to the point, mewing like an injured wife.

Down on the beach again, he set to work on the flipper, and the dugong, still dazed perhaps, struggled once or twice but then lay quiet. He moved the flipper carefully, found what seemed to be a break near the body, and tied it as well as he could against the splints. Then he stood up and thought what he should do next.

The creature must not go back to the sea until he could take off the bandage, perhaps in a week, perhaps in a fortnight. Already the tide was turning; soon it would be high enough to float the big body. He must wait here until the waves were strong enough to lift and carry it, then guide it up the beach to the deep cleft in the rocks where water stayed in a pool after the high tide. That was near enough to high-water mark; the waves would not wash the dugong out.

It ate sea-weed, he thought; he might be able to gather enough on the rocks to keep it alive. Or it might eat bread and cabbage-leaves, if he brought them. At any rate, he was determined now that it should survive. He gathered what weed he could on the rocks between tide-marks, hoping it was of the right kind; then he sat down to wait for the tide to rise. He had quite forgotten his breakfast.

Hour by hour he dragged and pushed it as the bigger waves came in, sat and waited, dragged again. The creature did nothing either to help or hinder; it only looked at him sometimes with that patient inhuman eye accustomed to the fields of seaweed and the undersea reefs, and sometimes made that small protest. He answered it, patting the round stupid head, encouraging it with words.

At last he had it safe, in the narrow pool through which the high-tide waves swished shallowly, and had propped it there with small stones and laid out the flipper easily. Now he rolled up a couple of rocks to bar it in, and made a shade over them with criss-crossed driftwood and branches of trees. He set down the bundle of weed near its head, and suddenly felt tired and hungry. The hot sun of afternoon blazed down as he made his way back to the hut, threw Tiddy a half-can of beef and ate the rest on thick chunks of bread.

Next day he chose a few green things from his garden-beds, took some stale bread and went to the beach, after breakfast, with his fishing line. The dugong lay still in the pool. It had not moved, but it was able to lift its head and chest a little from the water and look at him. It twitched its lips at the bread and the beet-leaves and cabbage, but ate nothing.

Jim was not discouraged. 'Feverish,' he said to it reassuringly. 'Bound to be, after a bashing. You'll feel better in a day or two. Just take a bit when you feel that way.'

He fished off the rocks that day; it somehow gave him pleasure to know that the creature was there. High-tide waves spilled into the pool and refilled it, cooling the water; Jim had become anxious about the heat.

Next day it seemed stronger; it moved quite sharply when he came near, and made a menacing noise, but did not object when he bent down with the day's leaves and bread. Some of yesterday's food had gone, he saw; crabs maybe, but perhaps it had eaten a little. Later in the morning, when he came back from fishing to look at it, it had a beet-leaf in its mouth. He was so pleased that he laughed out loud. 'You'll do, cocky, you'll do.'

And next day it had actually moved, dragged itself round in the shallow pool so that it faced the sea. He looked at the splint anxiously, but it still held.

'Wanted to look out for your friends, eh? I ought to have known you wanted a sight of the sea. Now you just stay still a few days more and we'll have you right.'

But suppose it dragged itself down to the sea on the next high-tide, before the splint was off? It would be helpless, not able to swim yet; it would be beaten on the rocks again, most likely. He dragged up more and more boulders, made a barrier to keep it there, cutting off its view of the sea remorsefully.

'It's all for your own good, boy. Can't have you checking out before the doc's given you your pass. Now keep quiet. Here's your breakfast.'

Next day was Saturday. He must go to meet the launch and get his bread and meat and groceries. He spent the Friday afternoon camouflaging the dugong's shelter, for the week-end was dangerous to it. Boats sometimes crossed the bay on Friday nights and early Saturdays with picnic parties and campers and amateur fishermen; children and their parents came to the guesthouse; idle and aimless youngsters wandered along the beaches. He must go, but he would be back as soon as he could.

He told the dugong so, explaining it all. 'You better lie low, see? They'd take you to a zoo or something as soon as look at you, and then what's your life worth? You stay still till I get back, and then I can keep an eye on you, see?'

But the dugong was getting stronger. Its head-wound was healing; it moved about occasionally in the pool, and was eating a little more. Jim was dubious about leaving it. But there was no bread left and nothing to eat for the week-end, and the fishing had not been good. Tiddy was complaining.

He left early, but the walk was long and it was noon when he came back. He dropped the suitcase and the sugarbag on the table, and went straight down to the point, for he felt disquieted. Something might be wrong.

The driftwood and branches had been dragged down — he saw that as soon as he reached the crest of the hill. Then he saw the young men, two of them. They stood on the rocks above the pool with big stones in their hands, taking aim deliberately. Jim ran down the rocks; he had his stick in his hand. One young man had already thrown his stone, but the other turned and looked.

'You let that damn sea-cow alone,' Jim screamed. 'You hear me? I'll have the hide off the both of you.'

'Aw, you will, eh? It's yours, eh?' But the second young man had dropped his stone.

'It ain't mine, nor it ain't yours either. I can have the law on you. You ever heard of the Protection Laws? I'm the ranger on this island.' Jim was lying, but the young men would not know it. 'Now, I want your names and addresses. Both of youse.'

The young men were bluffed; they ducked over the stone stair and started to run. Jim screamed after them, 'No use running. I got your descriptions; I can find out who youse are. Damned lousy couple of cowardly lairs.' But the young men were gone.

Jim went down into the shelter. The dugong lay still; it had stopped bleeding. Stones were scattered thickly over it. They must have been at it half the morning.

He dragged it to the water's edge again, with painful difficulty. It was half-tide; out beyond the end of the stone stair was the steep rock-edge where the deep water began suddenly, and where the dugong must have had its first injuries in the grip of wind and water. He dragged it further in, further yet, bracing himself as the big waves dragged at the great inert bulk of the creature and forced it landwards. Deeper, deeper still. He caught the moment between two waves, thrust it out with all his strength, and saw it sink slowly down.

The next wave caught him off balance. He fell and floundered for a moment, then struggled out, panting with a deep-drawn groan like that of a winded man who tries to get his breath again. He sat for a while on the rock above the water, with his head in his hands, panting and groaning.

At last he pulled himself to his feet and walked back to the hut, his back bent and his lips pulled tight and masklike across his face. Tiddy had pulled the newspaper from the meat with her claws, and was feasting on the kitchen table. She looked up snarling, ready to run.

But Jim did not notice her; he lay on the bunk so quietly that soon she began to eat again, cautiously and with many glances towards him. The extra loaves of bread spilled from the mouth of the bulging sugarbag.

Molly Guy

❧

Molly Guy is a Tasmanian writer currently working on a collection of short stories. She has had a number of stories published in *Australian Short Stories*.

Incubus

S he's just this woman I know. She's this scrawny woman with grey stains on her teeth, and she's getting to feel like a poltergeist. She's spectral, she won't leave me alone.

She hangs round the flat. Her fists hammer my door. She peers in windows. Her face is crushed against glass — her lips move, they writhe, slither, they leave a sticky trail. She's a grotesque hag and she's driving me nuts.

She rats on her husband. The patter's always the same. A poisonous litany. He's sadistic, a psychopath. Her hubby's a cheapskate fascist. Dickhead! Her voice is a monotone, 'He beats me if his food isn't cooked in fat. He says he likes his food lubricated, he likes his chips, chops, his fried eggs greasy. He likes meals that slip, glide down his gullet. His throat's a long drop, spiralling shute, a funfair ride — he smiles when his greased snags, T bones PLUNGE, TOBOGGAN down his oesophagus.

He's surly. I ask him for housekeeping money and he blacks my eyes. I remind him we've run out of breakfast cereal, bread — we've squeezed the last worm of Colgate from the tube — He tells me I'm extravagant; he advises me to buy low cost brittle toilet paper. And fruit's cheaper if it's overripe. Meat's half-price when it's green. He says don't waste money on vegetables. He explains low-cholesterol veggies are unpalatable, expensive — they make him fart...

The bastard's monosyllabic! I plead with him, I say primeval muttering, gutteral grunts are decipherable, but WORDS are bonds. Words exercise the intellect — He tells me my blah blah all day long, my mindless yakety-yak makes his earholes thrum!'

I bolt doors, I lock windows, I shut blinds. Her slippered feet crunch gravel. I will the hag to go away, to go home. To leave me alone. I watch her from curtain chinks. She's agitated. She whispers, she knows I'm in the flat, she can sense my warm breath, my rhythmic respiration, tepid exhalation of carbon dioxide and nicotine. She says she's come round for a cuppa and a chat. She knows I'm lonely living on my own. And she understands my emptiness — she KNOWS about solitude, about desolation, about pining to hear another voice, a human voice in the void called Life. The gaping abyss Existence. She cajoles, open the door my pet and I'll chatter in your ear, your pink and curving sensory organ. Goosepimples erupt on my spine. My teeth chatter. Her dulcets are coaxing. She tells me *he*'s gone out to the pub and she's a captive of silence, she's solitary, she's one when she wants to be more. One when she wants to be the nucleus of a swarm — core of social interaction, of confidences exchanged. We could pledge friendship, she and I. Friendship for ever and ever. Comrades until apocalypse. She says HE's gone out, the selfish wanker. Snail excrement! He's slunk off to the pub, *he*'s quaffing XXXX, he's munching Samboys, salted peanuts, he's mouthing off to his mates, he's laughing, his Adam's apple's bobbing like a cork, he's having a great time; *he*'s chatting up his pal, he's slavering over his buddy Hal. And she's on her lonesome — she's on her own. She's all alone — alone with her manic depression, her feelings of inferiority.

She says, 'Did I tell you hubby's hot for his good buddy — hot for his Pal Hal? I didn't? Hal's his companion. Harold's his bestest mate. Hal's his sexual obsession — I've seen them; I've watched them sitting in the kitchen sopping tinnies, eating pizza, arm wrestling. I've pressed the gleamer to the keyhole. Their fingers interlock, arteries on their forearms bulge. Their shirt sleeves rub together. They strain against each other, they subside — I've seen the two of them. Perverts! And they're into MEANINGFUL conversation. Can you imagine it. Doesn't it make you want to throw up your Ryvitas and Camembert. He *talks* to his mate, buddy. Prick! I'm his spouse and I get the rough edge of his tongue. Hal gets poetry, politics, moral dilemmas. Harold gets the heavy stuff. The sharing stuff. I get the, spread your knees and keep your mouth shut dialogue. Well I used to. Not so much anymore. Still plenty of the keep the mouth closed.'

If I respond to her door pounding I'm brushed aside, I'm trodden underfoot as the crone heads for the kitchen, ransacks my cupboards, puts the kettle on to boil. She clacks her ruined teeth in disapproval. The raisin bread's bearded with green. Teabags aren't so great recycled. She says I'm a slob and squalor is a symptom of failing self-esteem. She tells me I need to smarten up, get out more, I need friends. I need people dropping in, people gorging my stale food, gulping my spurious tea. I need disruption, distraction. I'm getting to be egocentric, introverted. If I don't rethink my lifestyle I'll start picking my scabs in public. I'll forget to shave, use a deodorant. I'll stink. I'll be a menace, an embarrassment, an incontinent non-conformer, foul-mouthed fringe dweller, degenerate punk. She says have you got any Montecarlos? Any Jam Fancies? A cold chop? A bit of cheese? How about magazines? Playboy? Wheels? Zoom? National Geographic? No? Well up yours then. She tells me her hubby's a bore. He repeats himself. He boasts about his family —

'He brags his sister's great looking, a honey. His mother's the sweetest woman alive. His Dad's got a heart of gold. I make snide remarks. I laugh behind my hand. I remind him his sister's a bikies' whore. I say your kid sister's fucked every Hell's Angel. She's had crabs twice. Your sister bangs like a dunny door in a storm. And she doesn't look that good anymore. She's getting to be a bag. Her points are fouled up. She could do with an overhaul. I say your mother isn't sweet natured. Your mother isn't compliant. Your mother's a vegetable. I tell him you need a brain to make waves, to stand up for yourself. I say your father's heart is tinfoil.

He gets abusive. He tells me I suffocate him. I pry. I nag. He's tired of me badmouthing his family, his cronies. He says I'm envious. He says I'm hardly a woman anymore. I'm something else. Something less. A cross to bear.

He says, you think you're so superior. You think you've got these great powers of observation. You imagine you're omnipotent! You file people away in alphabetical order, A-arse-hole. You're only ever critical. You only know how to be destructive.

He wants to know why I can't be like other women in the suburbs. Bovine, passive — a soapies addict. He tells me I should see a headshrinker. A psychologist would mainline me Valium. A psychologist would exorcise my discontent. He tells me giving in to barbiturates is painless. He says brain death won't hurt a bit. He says relinquishing the will to live is free of side effects.'

She slurps my tea, she guzzles, slobbers. She tells me when she was young she was this gorgeous chick. She had allure, she had wow-appeal. Guys tried to crack on to her; they were attentive, deferential. Now she's a bag-of-bones, it's like she doesn't even exist. Everybody looks right through her. She says if I could turn the biological clock back 20 years you'd buy me Montecarlos. You'd share your Penthouse. If I could hone a quarter of a century off my life, if the ivories sparkled again and the peepers were stars, if the ankles were still shapely, my bum a peach — I mean *really* peachy, curved provocatively, a wiggle in the walk. If my bum hadn't deflated like a tired balloon and my arms weren't sharpened sticks, you'd be hospitable. If I still had my eye-popping good looks you'd anticipate each of my visits, squirm with impatience — you'd buy me cream horns, danish pastries. You'd offer me seconds of everything. Seconds of sly gropes, you'd blow in my ear. You'd prostrate yourself and you wouldn't care if I had strength of character, or no character. I could be psychotic, vindictive. I could crap you to tears and you'd beg me to read your bloody Bulletins, watch your tele, use your bog, listen to your Heavy Metal collection. And probably I'd turn you down because I'm hooked on agony. I adore seeing little faces screwed up with pain, with self-disgust. I'd scoff your Danish, then I'd disappoint you.

Sometimes I hint she exaggerates. I suggest maybe hubby and Harold are just good friends. I say it's usual for best mates to share a few beers, a pizza — I tell her guys arm wrestle all the time. I say maybe she should lay off hubby's family for a bit. So her in-laws are moronic, philistine, she should still try to be courteous. She says why don't I mind my own business, keep my imbecilic advice to myself. I don't know what I'm talking about. I'm a meddling thickhead. Her life's fraught with trauma. Her life's tedious. Her in-laws are pricks getting under her skin. Her husband's a deviant. Her husband's insensitive to her needs.

She says, 'I dream of escape. Of a clean break. A new life. I want to be where they pass out second chances.

I want to be somewhere beautiful. No more sprawling ugly suburbia. No more suburban housewife syndrome. I want to be somewhere where Boredom is Prohibited. Where Misery is a Capital Offence.

I want to be on the side of the fence where the grass is greenest. I want to be footloose and free of what's-his-name — Fuckwit . . . Free of HIM!'

She's nosey — She pokes her oar in where it's not wanted. She asks personal questions. She speculates. She wants to know why I'm living alone, why a spunk, a hunk, someone well-hung, a guy my age, isn't shacked up with a tart with great legs, libido. She says, okay so maybe I got carried away, so you're not hung, you are young — what's wrong with you? Have you got Herpes — Do you reckon you're God's Gift and no-one's good enough for you? Are you narcissistic, do you do it with mirrors. Do it on reflective surfaces. She says have you ever done it at all. That's it, isn't it! You're a virgin. You're craven — you're dying to, but you don't know how. You're afraid of rejection. You're clumsy. You leave bruises and teeth marks. You blunder, you don't score. You've shut yourself up in your flat and you're sulking.

She says, why didn't you confide in me earlier — I can tell you about women. I know what women like. What floosies fancy. What sluts crave. I can tell you what they *don't* like. They don't like wimp masturbators who reuse teabags!

She says, who's the weedy ponce I saw at the flat yesterday? You know, the wacka with the acne, the nervous twitch, planters warts. An old friend is he? A relative? Something more than a friend, a relative? Something less? On the dole too, is he? She hammers at my door. She pounds at my consciousness. She's a voyeur. I feel her hanging off me like a leech. She's engorged, she's disgusting. Her voice is ugly, 'HE'S going to be a loathsome OLD man. He'll be a ghoul. I'll be expected to fetch, to carry. My back will be humped. I'll be bent double. A posture of supplication.

HE tells me my self pity is an art form. HE says martyrdom is my whole life.'

She's mercenary. She sucks. She sucks after advantage. She's a threadbare vulture. Wheeling. Hovering.

Like I said before, she's this woman I know. She's thin. Her teeth are stained . . .

Robin Sheiner

Robin Sheiner lives in Western Australia with her husband and three teenage children. She has many Aboriginal relatives in the north of the state who are an inspiration to her. Her short stories have won prizes in competitions and have been published in various magazines and anthologies. A novel was published in 1983, another one has been put away in a bottom drawer and she is currently working on a third.

My Sister's Funeral

The grapes arrived on the day of the funeral. We loaded them onto the back of the truck with the beer then everyone climbed on afterwards. My Japanese friend had to be helped up, Billy on one side of him, and Rosa on the other. He is a very old man now but still he doesn't speak English. He was pleased about the grapes, though. I could tell by the way he smiled. Since he had his teeth pulled out he doesn't smile very much because he can't enjoy a good feed of meat. He always liked a feed of meat but now he has only five teeth at the top and three at the bottom. I think he'll like the grapes.

He came here in 1920 to dive for pearls. They all came then, the Japanese, because they wanted the pearls, and knew how to get them. No-one else did. They liked the coloured girls and were nicer to them than white men were. They made the girls dive but didn't beat them or make them lie down with them afterwards.

I didn't know my old Japanese friend then, even though I lived in this town. Well, not really in the town. My husband and I lived in one of the old boat sheds, with all our kids, out across the mangrove swamp. At night we could hear the swamp gurgling beneath us and sometimes the big mangrove crabs climbed in and walked across us sideways. Our kids had a lot of fun chasing them around the shed. It was allright until the hot came and then the mozzies, ouch, you should have seen them, as big as dragonflies. At least we had shelter, not even the mozzies could drive us out to join other coloured people who slept along the gutters.

There are black and white and yellow people in the town, there are others half and half, and there are others all mixed up so they came out cream. My father was a very important white man. He owned a big station and had three black wives and one Malayan wife. My mother was one of his black wives. He loved her and he loved us, his

109

kids. When they came in a car and took all of us kids away to the mission he wasn't there because he had gone down to the big city to visit his relations who are the people who grow grapes. They have lots of land in the city with grapes like you've never seen — red and glittering like rubies, black like opals, white and shiny like pearls with no seeds. I know this because some of my cousins' kids went down there once. They went all the way. Don't ask me how they got there but they did, and they went to work on the vineyard picking grapes but they weren't treated so good. I told them they should have told the owners they were their relations. Nobody makes their relations live in kerosene tins that let in the sun so bad, and the flies. Some people say black people like the flies. I tell you now, while my sister Rosa writes, we don't like the flies. They get in our eyes and make us go blind. Even now I don't see so good and I am telling this story to my sister Rosa to write down.

Rosa is married to a Malayan, his name is Kim Bin, and she has electric fans in the ceiling of her house to keep her cool. There are only two of us sisters left now because of the funeral. It was three days ago. The beer flowed for two days and Rosa and I were the only ones who didn't drink. Now we are home again and tired and I am asking my sister Rosa to write down how our sister Marcellus is gone. The nuns gave Marcellus her name but our father gave us ours — Clara and Rosa — pretty names to show he cared for us. I have found out from Billy's uncle, who knows everything, that our father died on the other side of the country, a lonely old white man. Where he lived they used to call him the captain and he would walk along the beach with pockets full of lollies for the kids who followed him everywhere. I think he was wondering all the time about us, his own kids who were took away young to be brought up at the mission.

Our sister Marcellus who died never left the mission, she stayed on as a helper in the kitchen to the nuns for forty years. For her funeral everyone, all of us, except the white relations from the city, came. We all went up from here and you should have seen us on the back of the truck. I wouldn't let anyone sit on top of the grapes. It was funny

110

that we didn't ever ask who'd sent them or how they'd known that Marcellus was gone. We were so sure they'd been sent for Marcellus' funeral that we didn't bother to ask. We have learned not to ask questions, especially my old Japanese friend. He could learn English easily if he wanted to but he doesn't try. They tried to make him talk when he was sent away from here to be kept wired-in during the war. They tried to get him to say that he knew who was bombing us. Still he didn't talk. They thought he might be dumb. Big bombs came. We were lucky in the boat shed over the mangrove swamp because they didn't hit us. My husband was sick during the war. Too many mozzies. I couldn't do anything except wring out his singlet in the cool swamp water and lie beside him. There were no Japanese around then, they were wired in, so the pearl luggers were sitting empty not far from our shed. There were lots of sea planes on the water, too, funny looking things like giant birds, and when the bombs tried to hit them they hit some of the luggers instead. I don't think, if it was the Japanese dropping the bombs on us, they would have bombed their own Japanese boats that only wanted to look for pearls.

I was pleased my Japanese friend came for Marcellus' funeral. She would have been pleased, too, because she loved everyone like the nuns had taught her, even Japanese, because Jesus would have done, she said spitting on her hands and rolling out the pastry for the nun's steak and kidney. I didn't care much for Jesus when I was at the mission even though the nuns crammed him down my throat. Our mother would come to the mission gate every day and cry for us to come back to her and cry and cry when the nuns wouldn't let her take us out. So much for Jesus. I could see her crying behind the fence that kept us in and I know what my Japanese friend must have felt like, all wired-in but no-one cried for him to get out. People were glad. So, when he had his teeth out I sat with him and made him warm cloths to put across his cheek because I can guess what it feels like, when all your teeth are gone.

He looked comfortable in the truck, squatting on his heels near the beer crates. We hid the beer when we got to the mission. Some had been drinking on the way and fell over at the mission and couldn't walk straight. It didn't worry us. We were used to it but the nuns didn't like it, especially at a funeral. They let Rosa and me look at Marcellus when she was lying in the coffin, open, and they had done her up nice and put a flower in her hand and dressed her in her best white dress that she wore for Holy Mass. Rosa started to cry so I stood up very straight and was glad for her sake, and for Marcellus', that I had worn my hat and white gloves. Some people in our town say what does a coloured woman want with hats and white gloves but it doesn't worry me if I am dressed up. Let them worry. My father who owned a station would have been proud of us: Rosa who married a Malayan and Marcellus who worked her life to the bone for the nuns, and I who wear a hat and gloves because they don't think I'd dare. I looked down at Marcellus and she was still the blackest of us three sisters.

Some of the others outside the room with the coffin in it were starting to make a lot of noise, especially the drunk ones who had started wailing and the nuns couldn't quieten them, even when the priest said the holy dedication. The nuns are not happy because the mission is going to close now that there are no more half black children they can bring. No-one these days will let kids be snatched. They used to bring all the ones who had white fathers and black mothers. There weren't any who had black fathers and white mothers because the black men didn't go near the white women. They didn't like them smelling of soap and stiff with corsets, and they would have been hanged if they did. My father's brother, my uncle, hanged lots of people. He was the magistrate in our town and lived in a big house and had black people fan him with banana leaves. Lots of them would run fast past his house because they thought he was the devil, and the nuns had scared them of the devil.

My Japanese friend is not scared of anything, even when he dived for pearls and saw crocodiles as big as boats and great big sea snakes with yellow stripes like lightning. He was not wailing like the others when Marcellus' coffin was wrapped up in the ground but he was sitting down on a little stool I had brought for him and he was smiling because in his hand he had a bunch of grapes and it didn't matter with grapes that he had no teeth. Soon someone brought out the whole box of grapes because they were too scared, even the drunk ones, to bring out the beer in front of the nuns who could be very fierce if they wanted, especially now their mission was closing. Next thing, all the grapes were gone, the juice of them dribbling from our mouths as we stood there and the sun opening up the sky to let in all the light across Marcellus' grave. My Japanese friend lay a bunch of grapes next to the flowers my sister Rosa had brought, across the sun on the grave. The flowers were withered because we had come such a long way in the truck and it was a hot day but the grapes were firm and shiny. My Japanese friend said the gods would like them and they would be kind to Marcellus but I didn't think Marcellus would be happy about it, so when he wasn't looking I picked them up from the grave and gave them to the twins, my grandchildren who are growing tall and fat.

The priest gave a talk about how nice it was that all of us who had been half-caste children at the mission, and looked after so well, had come back to see one of our own buried with the grace of God. Then he said, much louder, that drink was the temptation of the devil, and we should cast it from us. But I knew from what Marcellus had told me that the priest drank the altar wine when he could and that she had seen him without his cassock and with his fly undone, and had been so frightened she had said ten holy Mary's, then burnt the cup cakes that she was going to cut up to make angels' wings. When she went to confession and told what she had seen, the priest said she was very wicked and must scrub the big black pots every night until she washed away her sins. Marcellus was obedient, not like Rosa and me. We were proud and did not let anyone put us down or call us half-caste good for nothings. Rosa learned to swear at them in Malayan if they did, and I would walk on past, knowing how much it annoyed them to see me in my hat and gloves.

113

'Why do you think our father let them take us?' Rosa asked when we were trying to get everyone back into the truck. I couldn't answer her because I knew he could have got us back if he wanted to, an important man like that who had relations who almost owned the city, so my cousins' kids, who went to work for them down there, said. 'It broke our mother's heart,' Rosa told me as we hugged each other.

The sun was going down and everyone was tired. It was good the grapes were gone because it made more room in the truck. As we went along we saw something very funny. There were a lot of emus trying to get through a wire fence, getting very mad and tangling themselves up. We all giggled so much we rolled about the truck and one fell off and we had to stop but he wasn't hurt, so we lifted him back on. It was my cousin's son and his name is Billy. He has seen the city, picked grapes for our relations and come back, drinking worse and worse, sometimes beating his wife who is the daughter of my second cousin Mary.

My Japanese friend squatted on his heels in the middle of us all like that, so quiet with his eyes squinting. He is a good man and never minds being with us half and halfers, neither one thing nor the other but in the strip between. His wife was a mixture, cream-coloured. He had married her in a Japanese ceremony, that was when there were lots of Japanese here because there were so many pearls. They had their own temple, even their own graveyard. It's still there with Japanese writing on the headstones. His wife had been a beauty, like all the cream coloureds, and she had run off with a white man, down to the city in a ute. They didn't have no kids. Just as well. He lives with me now in the house the government sold cheap when they were trying to do something about us, tidy us up. In the drawer of the cupboard he made for me he has two big pearls and sometimes he takes them out to look at them. I think he's keeping them for if his wife comes back.

He has given me some pearl shells and I wanted to send one to our white relations when I thought they were kind enough to send us grapes for Marcellus' funeral. I only found out about the grapes when I went down to the big

114

store to buy some powder so my nose wouldn't be red if I cried. 'You,' the shop man said. 'Them there are for you.'

'How do you know?' I asked.

'Ask no questions and you get told no lies,' he said. He is a white man who has been hit on the head with a black man's bottle and he sometimes acts up stupid. But there it was blurred across the side. Even with my eyes blinded from flies I could see it, Clara, my name. I held myself proud. 'From my relations in the city for my sister's funeral,' I told him. 'I'll call my cousin's son to carry them. Hoy there Billy, come over and carry this box of grapes for your aunty.' He came across from the hotel where he had been playing snooker with some white friends, just to carry it for me, back home so it could be loaded on to the truck. He's the one who fell off the truck and I'm glad he wasn't hurt through laughing so much at the emus. We have a lot of fun. It's the black side of us. I don't miss out on much. My father laughed a lot but he wasn't like other white men, having all us black kids made him different, and anyway I don't think he could have laughed too much after we were gone. Blacks can laugh at anything, birds dropping shit from the sky, bungarras racing up white ladies' skirts looking for the trees.

It was a long trip home from the funeral and very dusty so we stopped at lot even after Billy fell off and soon all the beer was gone and half the men were snoring on the back of the truck. I was glad my cousin Paddy was driving because he can drive straight even when he is drunk. When it got dark we stopped and all curled up warm together there on the back and my Japanese friend rested his head on my knees. It was nice there looking up at the stars and all together, though I felt sad about Marcellus who had never got away from the mission and was so small, smaller than Rosa and me, when she was taken that she couldn't remember where she had come from.

In the morning we washed ourselves in a pool left by the dried-out river. My cousin Paddy always follows the river road, when it's not flooding in the rainy season, because his truck overheats all the time and needs water for the radiator. There aren't any garages on the way to the mission and if there were there are lots of whites who wouldn't even give water away to blacks. It was nice to be clean. My Japanese friend washed his feet and slicked down his hair.

I put my hat and gloves back on so I would be ready when we arrived back at the town to see anyone and look them in the eye. That's my white side. It doesn't bother me if a white man puts his evil eye on me because I give it to him straight back again. Except I wasn't ready for the policeman who met us at the door of the house the government sold to me, and I wish they hadn't, it's damper than the boat shed in the rainy season.

'Which one here stole the box of grapes?' he asked, and we were all struck dumb.

I climbed down from the truck first. 'They were my grapes,' I said 'sent to me from my relations who grow grapes in the city.'

'Garn. Tell us another,' the policeman said. 'They were addressed to Mrs Clare, the station owner's wife and she gets them sent up regular. Seen you before, haven't I? Hanging about with whites in the hotel?' He moved across to Billy. We knew what that meant. Billy melted into us and we closed up tight around him. Everyone had climbed down from the truck, even those with hangovers so bad they couldn't make any sense of day or night; the children glad to be home had run off whooping.

'You pay for the grapes, or else,' the policeman addressed us all.

It wasn't pension day but that didn't worry me. It was that my relations hadn't known about Marcellus' funeral after all. They hadn't cared that she'd died there like that in the mission, that she'd never got out not for forty years and now she was there forever, buried in the ground. So the grapes hadn't been for her, they had been for the white lady who ordered them regular. A mistake had been made. I took off my hat and crumpled my gloves up small inside it.

My Japanese friend knows what it's like to be wired-in, and I know for certain he didn't scream when the dentist pulled out his teeth. He stood forward, separating himself from us half and halfers, and he spoke his first words in

English. If I hadn't heard it with my own ears I wouldn't have believed it. 'Fuck your grapes,' he said.

Kate Grenville

Kate Grenville was runner-up in 1983 for the Vogel Australia Award with *Dreamhouse* and in 1984 she won the award for *Lillian's Story*. She has published in magazines and anthologies in Europe, USA and Australia and her own collection *Bearded Ladies* has been highly praised. She has just completed a novel commissioned by the Bi-centennial Authority entitled *Joan's History of Australia — a Romance*.

The Test Is, If They Drown

Miss Spear in number forty-two is a witch. From the street we can see her sometimes on her verandah, spreading her hair over a towel on her shoulders to dry in the sun. We gather at a safe distance and whisper across the sunny air — Witch! The hiss fades before it reaches her. She never looks around at us.

Behind her house, up on The Rock, my gang and Mick's gang meet. From high above we can look down into her garden, where the cat stalks among great clumps of vine-smothered rose bushes, and sometimes Miss Spear herself comes out and drags ineffectually at the consuming creepers.

Miss Spear is what happens to you if the orange peel doesn't make a letter when you drop it on the ground. It nearly always makes an S. That means you'll marry Steven or Sam or Stan. Sometimes it makes a C and you take a second look at Carl and Conrad. Miss Spear's what happens to you if you don't step on all the cracks in the footpath between the school gate and Spencer's shop. Miss Spear's what happens to you if the numbers on the bottom of the bus ticket don't add up to an even number. She's what happens when you lose a game of Old Maid.

When she leaves the house to shop, she wears a skirt that reaches her ankles, and sandshoes. She's never been seen without the unravelling straw hat with the feathers stuck in the band. The cat comes to the gate with her and sits with its front paws tidily together and its eyes narrowed waiting for her to come home.

Mum calls her *Poor Miss Spear*, and says there's a sad story there somewhere. Dad says that Miss Spear wasn't ever anything to write home about. Mum shakes her head and mashes the spuds with a great rattle, punishing them, her lips gone thin. She thumps the saucepan down on the table and says that it's a good thing Miss Spear's got her house and a bit of independence at least. Dad laughs as he pulls the potatoes towards him and says he reckons she's got a bob or two stashed away in there.

At the shops she buys fish and milk and according to Mr Spencer the grocer, more eggs than you'd believe. The butcher skilfully rolls the corned beef and ties it with string, living proof that no-one needs more than two fingers on each hand. He tells Mum that Miss Spear comes in once a month for a piece of best fillet. He doesn't see hide nor hair, he says, then regular as clockwork there she is wanting a bit of best fillet. The butcher says he supposes Old Spear's harmless, and Mum agrees with a sigh as she puts the corned beef in the basket.

Of course Miss Spear isn't really just an old maid whose dad left her the house when he died, like they say. She can't really be just an old stick whose cat gets fish every day while she makes do with eggs except for a treat once a month. An old lady wearing funny clothes living in a big house with a cat must be a witch. No way she can be any-thing else. A witch a murderer a gobbler of children a creature from another planet. An alien.

Up on The Rock we watch her cat stalking a butterfly through the long grass, sliding on its belly, ears flattened to its skull. My gang has just beaten Mick's gang at spitting. All us girls got it further than the boys. And in spite of her ladylike pucker, Sonia got it furthest of all.

Mick shifts round restlessly, looking for a way to impress us.

'Betchas don't know what she did, the Witch,' he says. 'Betchas can't guess.'

I lean back and pick a scab on my knee. I'm not worried, I can beat him at anything except Indian wrestling and even then I can usually trick him into losing. I'm better at nearly everything than the boys. Pam and Sonia are hope-less the way they're always worried about getting dirty or being home late for tea. But they're my gang and I'm the only girl that's got one.

Mick hasn't done too well with the suspense so he hur-ries to the punch line.

'She murdered her mum. Got this carving knife see and chopped her in little bits.'

Stewart and Ross are impressed. Ross wipes a fleck of saliva from the corner of his mouth and says avidly:

'Geez what she done with the bits eh Mick?'

Mick hasn't thought that far.

'That's, um, a secret.'

He purses his lips and pretends to be very interested in the way a bird is flying past above us.

'Aw come on Mick tell us, tell us.'

Pam and Sonia won't let him off the hook.

'Betcha don't know, come on tell us or that means you don't know.'

An impressive pause from Mick. Stewart and Ross lean forward agog.

'She buried the bits in the garden. Right down there.'

He points dramatically down into the tangles below.

'S'that all?'

Pam and Sonia are openly contemptuous and even Ross and Stewart are disappointed. Mick's eyes dart around as he tries to come up with an embellishment. This is my moment.

' 'Fraid you've got it all wrong,' I say casually.

They all look at me expectantly. Girl or no girl they know I always deliver the goods.

'It was her dad. She killed her dad.'

Mick is beginning a shrug. Mum or dad, so what?

'With cyanide. One drop in his tea every day for six months. She mixed it with the sugar so when he put sugar in his tea he got the cyanide.'

The awed silence seems to demand some more details.

'And then when he was dead . . . she stuffed him. Like Phar Lap. He's in a glass case in her bedroom. To keep the dust off.'

Stewart's mouth is hanging open and he's breathing loudly through his nose as he always does when concentrating.

'Geez what a weirdo eh.'

Mick jabs him with a sharp elbow and shouts:

'Oh yeah, sez who. You gunna believe a girl, fellas?'

Stewart snaps his mouth shut like a carp and nods. But his eyes are still glassy with the idea of such a sweet and unsuspecting death.

Ross glances at Mick and mutters to me furtively:

'What did she stuff him with? She pulls his brains out his nose like them Egyptians did? What she done with the guts?'

I've got all the answers. But Mick's tired of having his thunder stolen.

'Shaddup stoopid, she doesn't know nuffin. What ja believe her for?'

He hawks and spits the same way I've seen his father do.

'C'mon, I can't be bothered hanging round these sissy girls any more. C'mon gang, I've had it.'

We sit in silence after they leave. Sonia blows a huge bubble with her gum and watches it cross-eyed before sucking it back in. She chews it and tucks it away in the corner of her mouth.

'That for real, she knocked off her dad? Howja know?'

Leadership means having no fear of the next lie. I say immediately:

'I looked in the window. He's sitting up there in this glass case.'

Pam stops sucking the end of her plait and tosses it back over her shoulder.

'He got clothes on? Or not?'

She's watching me closely.

'Course he's got clothes on. His pyjamas.'

'What colour, Sandy?'

'Blue and white stripes.'

Lies must always be switched truths. The glass case from the skeleton at the Museum. Dad's blue and white pyjamas.

Sonia blows a great flecked bubble and we all watch as it trembles, threatening to burst over her face. She deflates it masterfully and gets up.

'Time for tea.'

Leadership is never being quite sure if they believe you.

'Oooaaah Sandy you've got all moss on your shorts, your Mum'll kill you.'

Her smooth pink face expresses satisfaction at this.

Sometimes I hate girls.

122

I plan my raid carefully, and alone of course. Pam and Sonia would giggle at the wrong moment or get panicky about spiders. And although I almost believe now in the body and the glass case, I want to be alone when I make sure.

I watch from behind the oleander until Miss Spear comes out to go to the shops. She sets off without seeing me, her hair showing through the hole in the top of her hat. The cat slips through the bars of the gate and sits blinking. It yawns once and begins washing its ears.

I watch Miss Spear until she turns the corner, and wonder what she is. Women don't wear hats like that, that you can see hair through. Women don't wear sandshoes and no socks so their ankles show red and sinewy. And women don't chop the heads off dandelions with a stick as she's doing now. If Mrs Longman at school with her smooth chignon and her dainty handkerchiefs is a woman, where does that leave Miss Spear?

When she's disappeared I cross the road and pull aside a loose paling in the fence. I glance up and down the street before sliding through the hole and dragging the plank back into place behind me.

Straight away everything becomes terribly quiet. I can still hear the billycarts rattling down Bent Street, and a dog barking across the road, but all these sounds are very far away, and seem to fade as I stand listening, until I can only hear silence ringing in my ears. Miss Spear's garden has locked me into its stillness. Behind the thick bushes and the fence, the street is invisible and belongs to some other world. It may not even exist any more. A leaf gives me a fright, planing down suddenly onto my shoulder, and my gasp seems deafening. The windows of Miss Spear's house stare at me and the verandah gapes open-mouthed. The shadow of one of the tall chimneys lies over my feet and I step aside quickly. It's a few minutes before I can make myself tiptoe down the overgrown path towards the back of the house. Damp hydrangea bushes, as tall as I am, crowd over the path, holding out clammy flowers like brains. The leaves are as smooth as skin as I push through and some are heavy with the weight of snails glued to them. Sonia and Pam would be squealing by now.

123

In the back garden, the grass has not been cut for a long time, and blows in the breeze like wheat. I creep towards one of the windows on hands and knees, moving twigs out of the way so they won't snap noisily. I'm doing well, being very silent. I am feeling better about all this when a mild voice behind me says hello.

For a few mad seconds I think that if I stay quite still I won't be seen. My green sweater against the green grass, the famous chameleon girl.

'I thought you were a little dog at first.'

Since the earth does not seem about to open and swallow me, I stand up. Miss Spear is holding a carton of eggs and a bottle of milk. I see her teeth as she smiles, and her eyes under the shadow of her hat. I can see freckles across the bridge of her nose and a small dark mole beside her mouth. I've never been so close to her before.

'Exploring?'

I stand numbly, waiting for a miracle. No miracle occurs and she moves closer and says:

'You live down the street don't you? I've seen you around.'

She watches me in a friendly way while I wonder if I could pretend to be deaf and dumb. The cat comes and winds itself around her ankles, smoothing its tail along her shins.

'You want some milk, don't you. This is Augustus,' she explains to me. 'He's greedy but he's good at catching mice. Augustus, say hello to our visitor.'

She pushes her hat further back on her head so that I can see her whole face. It is a perfectly ordinary old face with wrinkles in all the usual places.

'I don't know your name,' she says, and smiles so that the wrinkles deepen.

'Sandy,' I hear myself say, and become hot in the face.

It is too late now to pretend to be deaf and dumb.

'Sandy, that's a boy's name,' she says. 'I've got a boy's name too.'

She looks at my hat.

'Your hat's a bit like mine,' she says. And we both collect feathers.

I pull the hat off my head and crush it between my hands. My hat is nothing like hers.

'I've got something you might like,' she says. 'I never use it, but someone should have it. Won't you come in for a moment?'

Even Mrs Longman would not be able to be more genteel.

'Perhaps you'd like a glass of milk.'

Anyone would think it's quite normal to be a mad spinster in sandshoes. I follow her into a kitchen more or less like most kitchens and watch as she pours some milk into a saucer and gives it to Augustus. She pours a glass for me and I sit down and drink it while she rummages in a drawer. I glance around between sips, feeling congested by this situation. But in this kitchen there's a stove and a lino floor and a broom in the corner. Just the usual things.

'Here we are.'

She hands me a penknife and I open all the blades and look at it. It's a very good one. It even has a tiny pair of scissors. When I've inspected it I become aware of her watching me. I hand it back to her, but she won't take it.

'No,' she says, 'it's for you. It used to be mine when I was a tomboy like you.'

I turn the knife over in my hands, feeling clumsy. My hands seem to be a few sizes too big and I feel that I'm breathing noisily. Here I am, sitting talking to Miss Spear the alien, drinking the milk of Miss Spear the poisoner, accepting a gift from the witch.

She takes the knife and attaches it to my belt.

'Look, you can clip it on here,' she says. 'Then it won't get lost.'

She sits across the table and with both hands carefully lifts her hat off her head. When she sees me watching, she wrinkles up her eyes at me.

'Sometimes I forget I've got it on,' she says.

Augustus jumps into her lap and whisks her cheeks with his tail. She brushes the tail away as if it's tickling her, sneezes, and says:

'He's very affectionate. As you can see.'

She strokes the cat and smiles through the swishing tail at me. I can hear a tap dripping in a sink. The sound is peaceful and I find myself relaxing. I unclip the knife and while I'm having another look at it, I try to frame some impossible question. How come you're so normal? I could ask, or: What's it like being a witch?

'It's great,' I bring out at last. 'Thanks a lot Miss Spear.'

She goes on stroking Augustus and smiling. I can't think of anything else to say. I want to go, yet I like it here. I want to find the others and tell them all about it, and yet I don't want to say anything to anyone about it. Miss Spear puts the cat down and gets up.

'Drop in any time. Next time I'll show you the tree house.'

Out on the street, the proper standards resume their places. Miss Spear is loony. I take the knife off my belt and put it in my pocket. I keep it in my hand, but out of sight. Mick has decided he wants to hear about the brains being pulled down the nostrils, after all. But now I don't want to tell him.

Stewart glows with righteous indignation.

'We oughter tell the cops about her. She oughter be locked up I reckon. Them shoes she wears and that old hat like a . . . bunch of weeds.'

Ross nods energetically, and his eyes bulge more than usual as he says:

'She's not normal my mum says. Oughter be locked up in the loony bin.'

Mick says loudly:

'My dad says what she needs is a good fuck.'

We all stare, shocked and admiring. Sonia giggles behind her hand. Mick takes courage from this and calls down into Miss Spear's backyard: What you need is a good fuck. The hydrangea bushes shift in the breeze and I feel the knife in my pocket. Sonia beside me shrills out: Silly old witch, and Pam joins in: Witchy witchy ugly old witchy. Ross takes up the idea: Witchetty grub witchetty grub. Mick·stares at me.

'What's up Sandy, you scared or summing?'

I want to push him over the cliff, ram moss into his mouth, stab him to the heart.

'She's just an old bird. Leave her alone.'

126

Sonia stares at me making her blue eyes very wide and surprised.

'Oh yeah? Since when? You gone potty or summing?'

Pam grabs my hat.

'They'd make a good pair, look at this dirty old thing just like hers.'

She stares, pretending to be frightened.

'She's turning into a witch, quick Sonia, look.'

Sonia stares at me, her mouth in an artificial smile like the one Mrs Longman uses when she explains silkily how girls don't shout like that Sandra dear. Pam is staring at me too. I see them ready to tear me limb from limb. I look at the boys and see them too, waiting to pounce, waiting for me to go further and step out of line. Their eyes are like knives, like packs of snapping dogs, like slow poison, like sharp weapons raised to kill.

Miss Spear comes into her backyard and pulls at a few tendrils creeping over a rose bush. Mick nudges me.

'Go on, say something. I dare you.'

They're all watching me and waiting. Leadership means falling into line. Miss Spear is directly underneath, her hair poking through the hole in her hat, Augustus following a few yards behind as she walks among the roses. I want to stab Mick and Sonia and Pam and rip the smiles off their faces. Or is it Miss Spear I want to stamp on and destroy? Below us, she looks small, weak, hateful. I want to crush her like an ant, to be part of the pack and hunt her down as she runs alone.

'Silly old witch, silly old witch,' I yell.

My voice is carried away on the breeze. She doesn't look up. Behind me the others are chanting:

'Ugly old witch, silly old witch.'

Sonia uses some imagination.

'Red white and blue, the boys love you.'

She laughs so hard she begins to dribble. We take up the chant, laughing at Sonia's dribble and the way Miss Spear can't hear us. Mick yells:

'Come on beautiful, give us a kiss!'

I'm laughing, or something, so hard the tears are running down my face and I can hardly breathe. I hear myself screaming:

'Nasty old witch, nasty old witch, I hate you!'

The last words carry and she looks up at last. We all stare in silence across the air. I seem to be staring straight into her flecked hazel eyes. Mick nudges me.

'I dare you, tell her she needs a good fuck.'

The tears rise in my throat and run down my cheeks and across the silent air I hear myself yell, yell straight into her eyes, see her face on a level with mine and see the freckles across her nose like mine and her smile as she says I was a tomboy like you are, I hear myself yell and see her face change across the distance as I screech, You need a good fuck, fucking witch, until my voice cracks, I see her look down and turn away and walk into the house.

It's very quiet. I look around for the others but they've already turned away. Sonia picks her way down the first part of the rocks and turns back to look up at me.

'You've got all dirt on your face,' she says. 'You look real silly.'

She turns away again and climbs down out of sight. Without looking at me, Pam follows her. Mick and his gang have already gone down the other way.

The hydrangeas, the house, the sky shudder and fracture and I stand with my hands in my pockets holding Miss Spear's knife and whispering, witch, ugly fucking old witch, until at last the tears clear and I see the garden again, and watch Augustus as he darts out from under a bush. He glances up and seems to meet my gaze for an accusing second before he slips across the grass to the verandah. The house closes smoothly behind him like water.

Sue Hancock

Sue Hancock was born and educated in New Zealand but has lived in Melbourne since 1965. She has only recently begun writing fiction and has had her first two stories accepted by *Australian Short Stories*. *Behind the Glass* is her third story. She is currently writing a sequence of short stories on a New Writers Fellowship from the Literature Board, and revising a first novel.

Behind The Glass

There seemed nothing to do but live.
— Coetzee.

There she was, we all saw her, back again; back behind the glass again. She'd been off on her own, with the child, 'wandering', no, she said, it wasn't travelling, journeying, that was closer; going through the desert places; like an unclean spirit, she said, but nobody knew what she meant. 'When an unclean spirit leaves the body of a man,' she said, 'it goes through the desert places.' 'Oh,' she said, 'the places that I have seen.' It still didn't seem quite possible to understand.

And now she was back. But this time it was harder; this time she was really doing it on her own. Sometimes in her house it was so silent; it was like a forest floor, so quiet you could not hear the sound of the distant tops; a dead-needled, brown-hued silence. Sometimes a patch of sunlight showed itself on the wall of the long corridor leading to the front door, an empty yellow patch, nothing more. Sometimes, upstairs, the child wept; being little he dreamed of flying upright through the yellow air. Once he dreamt of a forest, she found him weeping 'it was all wooden', and though she tried to comfort him, she knew what he meant.

Sometimes she opened the door and there on the wall were the shadows of the garden, nodding and dancing, in bizarre array. Outside near the front fence the saw-toothed cactus waited like a shark.

And then one day they just weren't there any more. Some people thought she'd gone up the country, but I think she went back home. She's a New Zealander, like me; we always know; not many of us ever manage to get back home.

I think about her sometimes. I wonder if they're living somewhere like Rotorua where all the cloud shadows have a yellow underside as they fall down the long heights of the light, and the air over the baking pine forests that stretch for miles is electric and dead. And I wonder about the child and if he is growing up with dreariness at his heart. Rotorua is a small town, fifty miles from the sea, and I think about that sea and how cold it is, and arid, if that's a word for the sea, moving its green waters in their unwieldy bulk.

Where the pine forests ended the grasslands began again. The smooth hills seemed to bulge with thought. They tucked into their bases narrow, surprising valleys, thick with rivergrass and in here the light was already turning into evening, a lucid, almost taffeta-patterned grey; 'air moirée' she said, thinking of the elegant, irregular stains. For the atmosphere did seem to hang in a series of watery nets. Other people were already setting up their tents in the deep grass, as she drove through she heard a radio play. She felt a moment of disquiet driving up out of that last valley onto the long road to the coast where the yellow sunlight was dry and restless, flicked with the fevers of the rustling grasslands that lay between them for thirty miles, her rusting blue car and the heaving sea.

And it was a mistake. It had got too late, for when they reached the coast it was already dark, the sky clouded over, only the sea showed a shifting light, a disk of brown-tainted mercury. On the beach the sand was grey, too, and wet, a wettish brown with the marram grass trailing in it, more like mud than sand.

'We can't stay here,' she said, 'we'll have to try to go inland and get up higher — out of the rain.'

For now here was the rain pouring down over the hills in a ragged grey fleece.

'Come on,' she said, 'we'll go camping. This is fun, isn't it?'

'No, it isn't,' he said. He stood doggedly in the sand; he was so wet already, she saw, that water was dripping straight off the edge of his canvas shorts into his gumboots, which were a few sizes too big. His small head was obdurate.

'I'm not going to get in,' he said, 'till you say we can go back home.'

The rain seemed to have a whip of sand in it, so that it stung their cheeks.

'Oh, where's "home", Matthew?' she shouted. Her voice shook him, as if she'd reached out her hands and shaken his shoulders. 'Just tell me where you think *that* is.'

'Where Dad is,' he shouted back 'idiot!'

There is no problem here, she told herself; all you need, at the centre, standing on a wet beach, in the middle of nowhere, in the pouring rain, is just one other person of equal strength. There is no reason why for him it can't be me.

'Oh you bad little Baddie,' she cried, making a mock rush at him. 'Shall I beat you now or later; or now *and* later? Come on — let's run along by the sea; let's see what we can find!'

For *thump* went the sea, thwack! on the flat beach, then ran back leaving a mirror, a surface only a centimetre thick like a clear painting of a pond that ran and dried, and left behind a green clump, a red seaweed twined about a shell; something white that scuttled off through the decaying lace; something fixed and brown. And here were the grey crests racing in again, their surface boiling with white, and the long wet pure brown beach with its swift mirrors, and the pouring rain, and this, she thought with exultation, this I have known all my life; it holds no fears for me, because this is home.

And then what a night set in. There was no light; the sea was left behind, far down at the very bottom of the pin-tucked hills through which they had been slowly climbing, along the long twist of land that ran behind the coast. Sometimes, however, though no moon showed, she saw, through the reflection of herself in the window of the car, (*had* he turned the inside light on, yet again?) a vast pale tear in the dark outside, at the same level as her, or some-times below, which made her think uncomfortably of river cliffs, of great gorge walls dropping, through which if they fell, perhaps the car would open its doors like wings and flap, like an ungainly pterodactyl, along the face of the cliff before the pointed rocks far below came rushing up to meet them. And then the road stopped against a high bank of clay over which, to a height of twenty feet, towered the gorse. The car lights pointing upwards, too high to ever light the surface of the road, showed a rattle of yellow gorse flowers shaking in the tearing rain.

But still, she thought, they'd be better sleeping out; the car leaked; they might poison the air with their own breathing. In Wellington her brother had given her a tarpaulin and two long sticks.

She turned the car round so that the lights pointed down to the left. The drop, she thought, was on the right side, down behind the clay bank. Getting out she stopped, thinking she heard the roar of waters far down at the bottom of the gorge, but she turned her imagination away from them; here there was only the squelch of mud and the gorsehiss of the rain.

The lights lit up a strange declivity, a shallow crooked dell of grey mud and a few dead trees. But strangely the ground looked dry. She tied the tarpaulin ropes in through the window to the steering wheel, then wound the window up so that there was a bit of fall; then she took the sticks and sank them into the mud. It *was* wet at the surface, but only for a few inches. The sticks, uncertainly anchored, immediately took a lean. But the weight, she thought, the weight of the whole thing once it's up, that will hold it all together.

The groundsheet her brother had given her turned out to be a black shower curtain speckled with gold.

'What's that?' the child said. 'I'm not sleeping on that.'

'Oh, yes you are,' she said, 'because if you don't you'll die. And if you die I'll have to die, and then the whole thing will have been just an enormous silly waste. So let's just not bother, o.k.? Let's just get into our sleeping bags and go to sleep and get up in the morning and go on.'

He lay down in the sleeping bag on top of the shiny plastic.

'It's all *slippy*,' he said. '*Look*, it's all falling off!'

'No it won't,' she said. 'See, I'll just tuck this blanket in underneath your feet, and now you're inside another bag, a bag inside a bag; and you're another little bag, inside the sleeping bag inside the blanket bag.'

'I'm a little brain bag,' he said. 'Mum . . . have I got any babies inside me?'

'Sort of,' she said, 'but not the way I have.'

By the time she lay down herself he was asleep.

And then the rain set in. It poured down in thick slanting lines, it changed direction and fell in what seemed like great single bucket-loads, it was full of its own ingenuities, it played endless variations on the theme of itself, it turned into a miserable creeping drivel that leaked drearily all over them, wanting to be forgiven, trying to be their friend. And through it all she slept, she lay on the mud-slope in a tangle of wet blanket and useless plastic. She seemed every now and then in her sleep to open a dream eye and see above her a passage of cloud and the rushing stars and all along she knew by some deep connection exactly where he was as they slipped down out of the cover of the tarpaulin, down the mudslope together. Until the point where she really woke and in the grey light saw that he had rolled further down and was sleeping on his back, completely uncovered, sinking into the mud. What if he'd been face down! Horrified she saw that it was like sleeping in a shell-hole in the first world war, the unnatural little hollow of the land, the dead light around the edges of their pit, the grey trees, the bodies gradually turning back into mud again. He was confused when she woke him, his skin was so chilled, yet his face was burning hot. She put him in a blanket in the back seat and turned the car back down the way they'd come.

And now they have arrived in Waihi. It is only six o'clock, but already in this early air, only sixty miles from the wet weather, there is a warm stillness. They are dazed by distance and the past night but the simple red colour of the corrugated iron fences and the fuschias hanging in great blue and scarlet drops lift them into the present, and they have been consoled.

'Shall I tell you about when you were a baby?' she says.

He smiles into the distance over his packet of chips. 'Mum . . .' he says, 'do you *think* I could get a new Transformer today? Could I get one *right now*?'

134

Soon they will go on, for this is the entrance to the Coromandel, Waihi of the massacres, whose name sounds like the grass. The road goes on to Paeroa and then all before you are the mountains of the Coromandel, peaks ringed with peaks, and all surmounted by fire from the fiery light of the sun. For the moment they dawdle in Waihi, now simple in the early redgold light. But she plans to travel on all morning down to the coast, to where far out they will see the high surf dashing against the rocks that stand off the edge of the land. They will watch the green moving hills of water, for these are the mountains of the sea.

'And always night and day' she will say, 'they were in the mountains, crying and cutting themselves with stones.' But now they are by the sea. There is a grass camping ground where a small river cuts through. There is the rain, following them from the south, but here it is a storm of magical blue; they watch it from inside her sister's tent, the canvas flapping in the strong but dewy wind. And she will explain, 'Of course we can't stay away from Australia for too long. I just had to get away for a while, that's all. But Matthew's half Australian,' she'll explain.

And she will think: But I am still here. I used to live in the large country; the day, when I woke up, was a great blue room and I was on the inside; I was centred; I was there. 'But if you live where you don't belong,' she will say, 'doesn't that mean you're imprisoned?' Even though the walls are as clear as air? As far as I can tell, she will think, there are only two conditions, if you live where you don't belong: imprisoned, or on the outside — behind the glass.

Joan London

Joan London was born in Perth, Western Australia in 1948. She was educated at the University of WA and has worked as a teacher of English as a Second Language. In 1986 she published a collection of short stories, *Sister Ships*, with the Fremantle Arts Centre Press. She lives in Fremantle with her husband and two children.

Travelling

There were four of them who had arrived in Luang Prabang that day, and now hung around the entrance of the Royal Air Lao office in light rain, waiting for a man called Ted Akhito. As far as they could make out (here Ruth for once had made the enquiries, her matric French promoted by Galen), this Ted was a Japanese English teacher who rented rooms to travellers on the second floor. Probably C.I.A. Who wasn't? An introverted, sleuthing silence fell among them, not helped by the rain.

Travellers were scarce in Laos that year, and they seemed to be sticking together, linked by a sort of professional pride. On the traveller's scale of values, Laos had an off-beat, quietly dangerous chic. Vietnam had lost its glamour even for the foolhardy, but in those days, Laos, with war flickering through its jungles so you had to townhop in a battered DC3, and sleep in the curfew to the distant sound of planes and even gunfire, still had that nice edge of controllable adventure.

In Ban-Houei-Sai, the little border town on the Laotian side of the Mekong, shopkeepers had refused to serve them, and the one cafe that would give them a meal had been full of armed soldiers and beefy American men in laundered mufti. *The place is crawling with C.I.A.*, Galen wrote to a friend back in Australia (he liked to write on-the-spot accounts in cafes), *it's probably only a matter of time before the borders are closed*. There was that Shangri-la savour of a soon-to-be-lost frontier.

But last night in Ban-Houei-Sai, while Ruth was dousing herself in a mandi bath, an unseen watcher had laughed at her from behind the window bars. There are peeping Toms everywhere, as Galen said, but there was something about the sureness and scorn of that laugh, its pause, its continuation, as she had clutched a sarong about her pink body and fled down the curfew-darkened corridors of the hotel, that she related to war. She wasn't sure that they had any right to be in this country at all.

It was nearly dark when Ted Akhito arrived, under a dripping umbrella. They followed him up a staircase that opened, loft-like, into a large rectangular room with shuttered windows at either end. It was bare except for the rows of bamboo mats along the walls.

'Five hundred kip a night,' said Ted Akhito, looking at his watch. He was young, as young as they were, dressed in Westernised tropical whites. There was no question of bargaining about the price.

'I must go now, I have a class. I'll be back later to check things out. Curfew is at ten o'clock.' He spoke excellent English without an accent, except he said 'class' like an American. What was he doing in Luang Prabang? Yes, almost certainly C.I.A.

Mats were already being claimed while he was talking.

'Here?' said Ruth to Galen. There were two mats together near the staircase. That tiny panic, like schooldays, when the gym teacher would say, 'Find yourself a spot,' and you'd jostle and circle to be at the back, near a friend. Galen shrugged. She took the mat that would be furthest from Bob, the Englishman, who as usual was hovering to see what Galen would do.

The Canadian was already striding up and down the room, looking out the windows.

'Wonder where you can get a meal in this town,' he said.

'Wouldn't mind a cup of tea,' said Bob. He was always ready to attach himself to a superior energy.

Galen was flicking through his *Student's Guide to South-East Asia*. 'Got the name of a cafe here somewhere,' he said.

There was a general movement to the stairs.

'Hold on,' Bob was muttering, arm-deep in his rucksack. 'I've lost my mac.'

Ruth hurried to join Galen, who with Canada was already at the bottom of the stairs.

Luang Prabang's wet empty streets did not seem under seige. The *Student's Guide* was pre-war, but the Melody Café still existed by the river, a dimly-lit little cave scattered with a handful of their own kind. A hang-out. Like the German Dairy in Chieng-Mai, or the Thai Song Greet in

Bangkok. Made you realise that the trail had been well and truly blazed before you. Look at the menu. Along with all the usual rice and noodles, you could get roles and jam for breakfast, bolled eggs, stek fry, bananas milkshek. They wouldn't be quite the real thing of course, they were hybrid dishes cooked up for nostalgic Western palates.

'I'm gonna have me a steak,' Canada announced soon after they had settled themselves around a table.

'Steak!' said Bob, looking at the menu. 'That's eight hundred kip. It's a rip-off.'

Canada slapped the table lightly.

'This is a rip-off, that's a rip-off, *oh* you're having *steak, I* haven't had steak since I left home.' He addressed the table in general. He was never personal. He went on, 'Why are travellers so god-damned *mean?* Like it's immoral to spend money or something. They haggle over anything to save five lousy cents. Me, if I want steak, I'll *have* steak.'

'All very well if you've got the money,' said Bob, still staring at the menu.

Ruth tried to catch Galen's eye. A taboo had been broken. They had been so conscientious about adopting the right ethos. If you let them rip you off they didn't respect you, and you were spoiling it for those who came after you. The less you spent, the more you roughed it, the better traveller you were. For some it was not just economical, it was spiritual. Working off some of that bad European karma, vaguely evening up the score. 'We lived just like the villagers.' After India, there were some travellers who never used knives and forks, or a handkerchief, or a sitdown toilet again.

Canada was untroubled by the niceties of the subculture. He didn't look like the typical traveller either. Western males in Asia seemed to become feminised. Like Galen or Bob, or the travellers at the other tables, their muscles became wasted from dysentery, their bodies were lost within their own over-sized clothes. Their hair grew, they adopted bangles or earrings or headscarves, their gestures were smaller, guarding their own space. Canada's denim shorts were tight around well-built thighs. He wore a heavy leather belt around his hips. He was square-featured and tanned like an old-time football star. The exchange of names didn't interest him. He called everyone 'Hey', they called him Canada.

The cafe-owner's wife stood before them, smiling. Young, very upright and finely attentive though a child was hovering by her thigh. A grandmother held a baby, and an older child played around the kitchen door. They smiled at her as they gave their orders. Except Bob. He was deliberating over the omelette or the fried eggs.

'Excuse me, excuse me,' he called out after her as she had turned towards the kitchen. Again she stood before them.

'Look, do you mind, I'll have the boiled eggs instead, two soft boiled eggs, two minutes each, understand? Two minutes.' He held up two fingers and tapped his watch. She nodded.

'Thank you so very much,' said Bob. He treated her to one of his weary smiles.

Ruth kept her head turned away as Bob subsided, satisfied, on the bench next to her. When they had first met Bob, in the German Dairy, a week and a country ago, she had not been sure whether in these transactions he wasn't trying to produce a comedy turn. He looked as if he was going to be funny, with all those schoolboy freckles and his hair barbered ruthlessly above his ears. He drank milkshakes for his health, he told them, by way of introduction, and his smile seemed benignly goofy under his milk-speckled moustache. Hepatitis, caught in India. Infinitely travel-worn, like all those emerging from the great sub-continent.

Like her, he couldn't seem to get the hang of foreign currency. 'This . . . can't . . . be . . . right,' he had said to the German Dairy's proprietor. 'I . . . will . . . not . . . pay . . . so . . . much.' He spoke in pained, deliberate tones, shaking his head slowly for emphasis. Galen had stepped in, and sorted it out for him. But he'd still felt aggrieved as he walked back with them to their hotel. Ruth's old hope, half forgotten in the serious business of travelling, of finding a fellow clown, died. He wasn't trying to be funny. It was a form of tantrum they were to see every time he had to part with his money.

'Nice place,' Ruth said to Galen, across the table. Galen didn't answer. He and Canada were picking their way through an abandoned Laotian newspaper, testing out their French.

'I thought you guys were supposed to be bilingual,' Galen was saying, laughing.

Their waitress brought them a pot of tea. Galen and Canada looked up, paused, motors idling over. Her swift fingers setting out the cups, her oval face . . .

'They take their time,' Bob muttered. 'I'm starving.' He reached a white freckled arm across her to pour himself a cup of tea.

Ruth's legs felt heavy as she crossed them. For a moment she thought of saying to Bob, 'Do you ever feel like you're an inferior physical species?' Like her, Bob was noticeably of Anglo-Saxon stock. Fair skin inclined to flush up in the heat. Blue eyes often sweat-stung. Beige teeth. Innocent knobbly white feet sprawling across thongs. But this was way beyond acceptable perimeters. *Too personal.* The sort of comment she used to make over wine at her own table, safe in that acknowledged femininity that she seemed to have left back in the West.

Was that what she meant? She felt she'd lost a whole persona somewhere along the trail. Become a mere trudging mate whom nobody seemed to hear. It wasn't just that mascara streaked down you face in the humidity and long hair was out of the question, you just tucked it back as best you could. She hated to catch sight of herself in shop mirrors. A large girl with a bare earnest face. Sexless as a missionary. And fat. Getting fatter. There were no shadows, no roles, no corners to hide in anywhere. Just the fact of yourself coming to meet you border after border.

'The women in these parts are supposed to be the most beautiful in the world,' Canada said to Galen. His steak had arrived. He was feeling convivial. 'Good grub heh?'

'I wish I knew,' said Bob. His eggs had not appeared.

'It pays to order what they know,' Canada said, 'if you're hungry.' His eyes glittered at Bob above his busy jaw.

Ruth finished first. Galen worked slowly through his rice, his chopsticks moving in a ruminative way like the fingers of women crouched on doorsteps, searching through their children's hair. Galen had applied himself to the art of chopsticks as he did to everything, with the natural expectation of success.

Ruth preferred to use a fork. The way you could scoop and order and round up with your aggressive Western prongs. And the fork gave her more contact with the food somehow. Sometimes she felt that the closest relationship she had these days was with the plate of food in front of her.

'Ah here we are,' Bob was saying, clearing his spot on the table. The eggs had arrived, lolling in a soup bowl. 'Not quite the usual presentation,' he had to add, but cheerfully enough, holding one down and tapping around its crown. He smoothed his moustache back, his spoon dived and was dropped clattering onto the table.

'Bloody concrete,' he said, reddening under his freckles. The eggs were both hard-boiled.

'He's infantile. It's embarrassing. It's so . . . *colonial*.' Ruth nudged Galen aside on the walk back to the hotel to share her anger with him in the dark. Bob had stood up in the cafe, waving his eggs at their waitress, calling out 'Look here'. They had left him personally supervising the timing of two more eggs in the kitchen.

'Well,' said Galen. 'So what?' He kept walking fast to catch up with Canada.

'I'm fed up with him. We've had him hanging round us since Chieng Mai.'

'Oh God,' said Galen. 'Chaos in Laos.'

'Oh very clever.'

'Honestly,' said Galen, 'when are you just going to shut up and enjoy yourself like everybody else?'

'Don't lecture me,' cried Ruth. She wheeled off and sat on the steps of a building they were passing.

'I'm going on,' said Galen. She saw him meet up with Canada at the next corner and, both hunched over with hands in pockets, disappear into the shadows of the long avenue.

Ruth didn't sit there for long. The flap of a single pair of

142

thongs was fast approaching. Like her, Bob had no sense of direction, and hated walking alone in the dark.

Back at Ted Akhito's, there was an hour left to them before curfew, but it was not inviting. A naked bulb hanging in the middle of the dormitory cast a subdued, yellowish light. Canada and Galen were making rapid male preparations for sleep. There was a flash of Galen's long hopping white legs, before he was magically prone, sheathed and flattened. It would have been indecent to watch Canada as he thrashed and muttered his way into his sleeping-bag and turned his face to the wall.

Galen re-surfaced. He lay half out of his bag, trying to read *Anna Karenin*; he maintained that he could not fall asleep without a dose of the printed word, but in this light he had to run his fingers under the lines like a ritual of prayer. Perhaps it was a gesture of waiting for Ruth. At home she always fell asleep to Galen's lamp and the soft turning of pages. She would have leaned across him, and said 'Where are you up to?' *Anna Karenin* was her book: she had read it for four whole days in the hold of an Indonesian cargo boat. She had been carried along by the book as much as by the boat, the story had unfolded to the rise and drop of the seas. Nineteenth century Russia would always be associated with the dazed hustle of their arrival in Djakarta.

Bob came panting up the stairs.

'There's not a soul to be seen out there. Do you think it's a sort of pre-battle hush?' He spoke loudly, as if he were rejoining a party.

'The light!' growled Canada from his corner. 'D'ya need that light?'

'All right, all right,' said Bob, 'it isn't curfew yet.' He lingered at the end of Galen's mat, ready to conspire. But Ruth had turned to unpack, and Galen was closing his book.

'Christ I'm tired,' said Bob. He flapped across the room to the door. They heard a hiss, 'Where's the ruddy switch?' and the light went out.

Ruth was left crouching by her pack, unresolved. Galen was still. She had intended to unpack, shake out her hair, write in her diary, all without reference to Galen, but within his range of observation: it would have been a wordless interaction that brought them to the conclusion of this day, and the battle between them that each day's travelling seemed to bring. Then one of them might have been ready to make a sign, that across these strange deprivations, their unity survived.

Darkness had pre-empted her. She was now a mere night scuffler. She moved like a thief, each sound was a betrayal. Unlayer her pack. Possessions as familiar as her hands. Book, sarong, diary, toothbrush. The layers descended in relevance. Right at the bottom, occasionally disturbed by the hands of customs officers, was a woollen sweater still smelling of home, and the photos of her family.

On the other side of Galen, Bob was crackling out his sleeping-bag. It was covered in a crisp papery plastic. For lightness. They had heard a lot about that bag. How it had been specially made for walking tours in Wales. Double thickness down, much too hot for Asia, with complicated aerations, all zip-controlled. Rolled up to the size of a giant green salami. A room-mate, French, had tried to rip it off in Calcutta.

Zip, crackle, deep sighs from Bob, more zips, more sighs. A final crackle. Enough to make the back of your skull crawl, Bob's horny feet manipulating plastic.

Galen had yawned, was turning over. Now to inch her way into her sleeping-bag, lay back her head. The big windows let in a grey translucence that had settled over the room. The night outside was silent. *You'd hardly know there was a war on*, she would write to her parents when they were safely out of Laos. She wrote them hasty airletters of cool-minded reportage, casual feats of endurance. My goodness, they would write back, you have to be young!

Beside her, Galen had started moving, in a series of subtle, strait-jacketed shrugs. Ruth listened, and understood. He was taking off his passport pouch and money belt, and kicking them to his feet. 'Trust nobody', they had been told, She shut her eyes. For yet another night, they were to lie side by side like brother and sister, burdened with old knowledge of each other. Galen, her husband for nearly half a year, had become a traveller, a different person to her. But he remained after all, like her, a well-warned child of the bourgeoisie. She turned over then, ready to sleep.

'Look after her,' Galen's father had said. Of course he hadn't had a tea-towel over one shoulder, down on the wharf, he was wearing his suit as he did whenever he left the farm, but that was how she saw him. Waving them off with a floury hand.

Every time Galen had taken her home, Norman would make scones. Rubbed butter into flour with trembling old brown hands. Cut the dough with an upturned sherry glass, up and down, swift as a process worker. 'Open the oven door for me darling,' he would say to Galen. Out the kitchen window, just beyond the chook sheds, you could see the bare brick walls of suburban houses. The poultry farm was in an outer suburb now. There had been nothing but bush and market gardens when Norman bought the place, and flatness, a convex landscape after England, Galen said. He'd been twelve. His mother died that year. He always called his home 'the farm'.

It took him an hour by bus to get to uni. He was always late for morning lectures. When she first knew him, he used to disappear mysteriously from pubs or parties. Slipping off to catch the last bus home. He got a lot of work done that way, he said.

Meeting Norman that first time, she'd been a bit breathy and overdone. She used to think she had to keep Galen entertained. She'd admired the scones, admired Norman's history book collection, pranced around the sheds and admired the chooks. Smoked like a chimney, dropping ash in her tea, but you couldn't do anything wrong in Norman's kitchen. As they were leaving (they were going to a party in Ruth's mother's Mini, Galen at the wheel), Norman had said then 'Look after her Galen'. Galen never answered.

In the humidity, Galen's face was very sallow. The acne scars across his jaw seemed to darken, reminders of an old battle. Now that he was so thin, he looked more like his father. Like this, from the side, his head bowed over the letter he was writing on his knee. She watched a tear of sweat escape his headband and linger in the hollow of his cheek. She could never imagine Galen with his mother. He seemed to spring straight from the mother and father both in Norman.

'Looks like rain,' Bob said.

They were sitting in the courtyard of a monastery, halfway up the hill overlooking the town. It didn't look like they would get much further. They were sated, even by the rich smells that hung in the humidity, of dung and damp undergrowth, and rotting overripe fruit. Even Canada, having paced the circumference of the courtyard, was sitting down now, smoking, over by the gate.

That morning, their pace had quickened with the promise and strangeness of a new place. Luang Prabang, after a night's sleep, was a beautiful country town. There were red blossoming trees along roads that still gleamed from last night's rain. High above the town, a golden dome shone from a hilltop, like a fairytale turret. Townspeople smiled at them, curiously. They shared cigarettes and sign-language with a group of soft-faced, schoolboy monks. This was how they liked to be received, as a species of scruffy pilgrim.

'Stomach's feeling strange,' said Bob. 'Think I'm in for another attack of the runs.'

Galen wrote on, rapidly. *I am sitting on the steps of a tenth century drinking-fountain*, she read at the top of his page, *in thirty-five degree humidity*. Facts she hadn't been aware of.

A bell had rung and the monks had disappeared. The sky that hung before them over the town was now a luminous grey. Palm trees in the courtyard started to rustle and wave. Nobody else seemed to be around.

Canada stubbed out his cigarette and started back down the hill.

'Coming?' said Bob to Galen.

The four of them moved towards the town like an awk-

146

ward beast whose legs wished to go different ways. Canada was off-hand, accompanying them this morning as if there were nothing better to do. He walked ahead, restlessly peering into door-ways of the ochre-coloured buildings, disappearing up alleys, looking for action. His presence made Ruth uneasy.

She was used to travelling at Galen's pace. He always had an air of elation about him, discovering new territory. He loved to plan their route, and fit together the puzzle of map and reality. His passport pouch swung out and back to its bay within his hollow ribcage. The tails of the black and white scarf he wore as a headband flew out behind him. Travelling was a feast of the eye, he said. Was there such a state as pure vision?

While she trailed, glimpsing the backdrop through a web of thoughts. Like watching ants as a child, guessing at purpose and connection in a teaming other world. Distanced by the huge eye of the self.

Sometimes she found herself silently in step with Bob. He always seemed to be holding his words in check, until he caught up with Galen. Bumping together, they didn't even bother to say sorry.

'Ouch,' said Galen suddenly. She had walked into him and trodden on one of his thongs. He held it up by one dangling tentacle.

'Sorry,' Ruth said. Galen was very attached to those thongs. His Bangkok thongs. He called them art objects. The crinkled rubber was printed with a series of red and green music notes, gay inconsequential crochets and quavers, worn away now to the hills and valleys of his feet.

'Damn,' he said. His eyes, looking at her, were as dark as the black checks in his scarf. *'Why can't you keep up with me?'*

The rain didn't matter. Running in the rain had been one of her specialities in the old days. Theatrical liberation like moonlight swims and talking for a whole evening in her 'Juliet of the Spirits' voice. Funny, you couldn't see the rain falling. Just the puddles widening, dimpling, somehow connected with the descent of the huge grey sky.

Already the aisles through the market stalls were running miniature rivers, gorges, lakes. She had to hitch up her skirt, pry up each footstep, her shoulder-bag slapping against her hip. Not such a short cut back to the hotel after all. Galen in bare feet would be nearly at the Melody by now. Untrammeled.

Most of the stalls were empty, the mats rolled up where this morning's produce had been laid out. Just a few women under one of the big umbrellas, smoking and laughing. Probably at her, the only person out in the rain. Eyes down, picking her way home as fast as she could. Focus on that emptiness three paces ahead. Do not look at me. Alone, it was always like this.

'Hey,' Canada said, appearing at the top of the stairs and turning back to the others. 'D'ya hear about the two German guys? They hired themselves a boat and went downriver. Haven't been seen since.'

'Pathet Lao got 'em I spose,' called out Bob. 'Anyone know for sure?'

'Ask Ted Akhito,' said Galen, on his way to the dormitory. The others laughed.

Ruth looked up from the mat that defined her territory. It was late afternoon, they had taken what you might call a long lunch. Whenever she was not with them they seemed to come a little closer to the action of the place.

Surprisingly they came and stood around her mat. Galen crouched down beside her. Bob started moving his hands together and apart in a little concertina movement that she had come to recognise. He was shuffling an imaginary pack of cards.

'We've decided to play bridge,' he told her.

'I don't play,' Ruth said.

The three of them were damp and breathless, seemed to be sharing a joke. Boyos returning from the pub. Galen put a hand on her shoulder. He was still barefoot.

'Bob's going to teach you. Bob's going to be your partner.'

'You know I hate playing cards,' Ruth said to him.

Bob and Canada were already settling themselves around a spare mat under the window.

148

'Come on,' Galen said. 'We'll be nice to you. Promise.'

Bob was dealing.

'You sort them into suits,' he said. 'Descending order of value. Ace, King, Queen, Jack — 4, 3, 2, 1.' He was frowning, busy, spitty-sharp. Bob came into his own when he played cards.

The faces on the cards were stern and mediaeval as they spilled out of her hand. Bob went on, about contracts, tricks, trumps.

'What?' she said to Galen.

'Just listen and play,' Galen said, not looking up from his own cards. 'You'll pick it up.' That's what he had always done.

On the other side of her, Canada lazily pulled cards in and out of the fan in his hand. He lay on his side, one heavy thigh lapping the other. His eyes had never flickered once in her direction. Why had she let herself be drawn into this? Listen. Keep up. Play.

'Nine clubs,' she offered, hopefully.

Bob flung down his cards.

'You haven't been listening, have you? You don't understand.'

Ruth couldn't help the slow smile spreading across her face.

'I can't seem to see the *point* of the game.' She heard Galen begin to laugh.

'Hey,' said Canada to Galen. 'How long have you been travelling with this chick?'

Galen couldn't stop laughing. He rolled onto his back and up again, his headband fell across his eyes.

'Oh boy.' He put a hand on Ruth's knee. 'This is for life,' he said.

'*Mais où est* Ted Akhito?' Ruth asked the clerk in the Air Lao office again.

'*Ça ne fait rien* Madame, *vous pouvez payer ici*,' came the same reply.

Ruth turned back to the others. 'It's no good. We'll just have to give him the hotel money and hope for the best.'

'Ask for a receipt,' said Galen.

'Bloody irresponsible,' said Bob, counting out his notes. 'I think we have every right not to pay.' But they had already decided that it would be too risky just to leave the town without somehow paying the mysterious Ted Akhito, whom they had never seen since that first night. He probably had friends in high places.

'Hurry up,' said Canada. Outside, the Air Lao cattle truck that ferried passengers between the airport and the town had started up its engine. As before, they were to be its only passengers.

Ruth was the first to sling her bag into the back of the truck. The others hoisted themselves up while she climbed over the boards at the side and swung in. The truck lurched off. They held on to the cabin, standing up.

'All right?' Galen asked Ruth. She nodded.

After their long walk to the Golden Dome, Ruth and Galen had told the others that they would be leaving Luang Prabang the next day. Bob said it was funny, but he'd been thinking of leaving too. Canada just seemed to be with them as they were buying their tickets. You could get used to a place very quickly, they said, it was always a relief to be moving on.

From the truck they could see behind their street now, to paddy-fields spreading under water, islanded with palm-trees and bamboo huts, dotted with bending, slow-moving figures. The truck was speeding up. Now, in their final glimpse of the town, they could grasp its strictly civic plan, its streets and squares set out under the Golden Dome, the steaming river that curved around it and disappeared into alien hills. Like the two Germans, who had never been found. A flock of camouflage-splattered helicopters rose like smoke in the distance. In those hills and jungles there would be the sort of scenes you see in newsreels at home.

'Hey!' Canada was pointing across a square. There, surely, hurrying out of a building, was the neat white figure of Ted Akhito.

'Well I like *that*,' Bob said. But they were all smiling. They had rightly been judged not to be security risks. They were too lazy. Too cautious. You'd hardly know there was a war on. If you played by the rules.

The town was behind them now, shadowed by its own hills.

Carolyn van Langenberg

Carolyn van Langenberg has published short stories and prose pieces over several years in literary journals and anthologies both in Australia and USA. Her first book of fiction, *Sibyl's Stories*, was published by Pascoe Publishing in 1986.

Hitler's Driver

I follow my course with the precision and the security of a sleepwalker.
Adolf Hitler, 1936
Hitler is not just an individual. He is a condition.
Th. Th. Heine
Simplicissimus, 1923

The dark and the sinister . . .,
strange man circling through the events of the previous evening, and I lay on a sofa recalling how he declared I was easily the most beautiful woman in the room. Then with a suddenness so complete my eyes shocked open wide, I found myself stepping from a taxi into the cavernous foyer of a hotel. Knowing but passive faces leant from pink and gold reflections and beckoned me to follow through gliding doors over soft carpets to the steel panels closing over the elevator discreetly tucked into a reddened wall. A woman whose brass hair crackled, audibly smacked purple lips, wreathed perfume around my waist, then hitched her skirt to reveal leather wrinkled thighs. I stood distinct, hat low, distaste concealed. And I paused before stepping through the doorspace, affecting lean elegance, an easy appearance, while glancing into the darkness of the night sprawling from the lobby, yellow lights thin points, traffic lights fullstopping, blue neon hazes penetrating blackness, eerie smudges, untenable. The door slid shut, inprisoning me in the elevator. I watched the numbers flit upwards, increasing. The door softly opened. I followed a corridor of dim lights and closed embossed doors and oval shaped gilt-edged mirrors. I stopped by one of these mirrors and patted my hair. Elegance transferred to nonchalance and hid indecision. Assured that even a moment's perplexity would appear as

a blankness, favoured as natural and becoming in a woman, my confidence lifted me into his room and I amazed myself volubly with the view, panoramic, a vista of a city beautifully water black and yellow lit, pushing horizons of earth and sky together, guaranteeing to startle the senses from introspection. Or jet lag. He restrained excitement. Deliberately propelled me to an easy chair. He poured champagne, held the glasses high so the light played through the effervescence and, with a slight bow, he handed one to me. The black mass of night filled the window behind him, silhouetting his red earth colour, the triangular shape of his head sloping away to firm but narrow shoulders. He asked questions about my accent, teasing me of being fraudulent, of disguising my class and origin behind an acquired manner of speaking, therefore belonging to no place, no home, whereas he, even when using a language other than his own was readily recognisable as German. I responded, playing with hands eyes mouth, creating an impression of sheer loveliness and intelligence, vulnerability and kitchen wittedness, a game I had practised so often the art was myself. He rose, stalked around the room, eyes flitting darting behind long lids, smiling, certain I would soon be a pleasant memory of his. Then, spinning on his heels, he cupped my face in his hands, announcing that if I were to stay more than two days in this city, he would get to know me very well. I let my eyes rest on his which, judging by a sudden bright gleam, he misinterpreted in his man's way to accord with his enthusiasm. A quick stride to the window meant to camouflage his apparent glee. But, at that moment, I was deciding behind my eyes if I would agree to be so well known, aware of a fine distinction between the passive action of rejecting and the passive acceptance of life's drift. My husband was elsewhere. His absence need not have placed me in the position of contacting a colleague. Indeed, the wives of colleagues do not, as a general rule, cross the threshold of a hotel foyer in the dead of night to drink champagne for the company. But, whether by adventure or misadventure, my being the wife of a colleague had established the drift. The decision to swim with the mainstream or pick along the rocky edges became a question of fastidiousness. I drank deeply, watching him move restlessly round the room, his compactness within his clothes reminding me of an equestrian, straight backed and in control. From as many angles as were presented, he surveyed the city's stretch, tossing words and phrases at me over his shoulder. I said, The disadvantage of a traveller's life is in meeting too briefly people you know you like. He, with a hint of condescension further indicating how surely he believed he had won me, smiled, and corrected my contention to, It is a disadvantage, which is also an advantage. He began to say, When I was in Bolivia . . . The unfinished sentence slipped, the drinking soothed, and the lighting in the room softened a slyness lurking round his mouth. His bearing, his presence was evil, the kind of evil I had been taught to recognise as fascist. The doors of the room flew open and a dinner of fine quails under a silver bell and strawberries chilled in silver bowls was wheeled before us. The waiter hovered at our pleasure. Charmed, I enjoyed the dexterous invasion of my senses, curious, watching myself choose whether or not to allow this man to flatter, unfold me into making love with him. We sat close together, eating strawberries by placing them gently between each other's teeth, biting them in half, then slowly pushing the remaining juicy fruit along the inner side of a willing tongue. Our conversation lapsed to gasps and grunts. I leant my head on his shoulder, a sudden aversion for his blue shirt exploding like a sharp rap in my head. The increasingly devilish mouth above my forehead grovelled, bent into my chest, twisting moist and lewd as he fumbled with the clasps of my blouse. When he had undone it, expecting to discover breasts, he shouted instead at the long scar running from my neck disappearing at the top of my trousers before descending into pubic hair. He leapt back, alarmed. A completely cloven woman! He laughed coarse ridicule, and prodded the sensitive skin stretched over the trachea, rubbed his knuckles cruelly over the breastbone, pulled at the top of my trousers to see how the scar finished. Insulted, I tugged my blouse together, adjusted my hat and composed myself as if I had never intended to be anything other than the decorous wife of a colleague. He, slumping in his chair, the back of his head black against the pink upholstery, slipped from my view where walls yawned, corridors narrowed, floors buckled and decay seered my nostrils. I could not find the carpeted corridor I had previously walked along. I fussed at a mirror hanging crooked on a roughened wall. Corrected an eyebrow. The way my blouse tucked in my trousers. But rubble scratched my boots. Dust powdered my jacket. Chips of ceiling plaster fell on my shoulders. Walls dropped away revealing caverns and smaller and smaller rooms. Dejected, I sighed and returned along one corridor where I found him again, surrounded by clowns performing slow tricks on a stage, their faces besmeared white, black around the eyes, devoid of expression. Chalk white suits clad their listless bodies. Suddenly, before I could ask his help, he cracked a whip and the clowns shook and hid their faces in the sleeves of their blouses and cowered at the back of the stage, he herding and shoving them into a huddle. Once assembled, they reached out their arms, fingers flickering the air in front of them, feeling sightlessly as they took small hesitant steps until they were able to paw his clothing, tug at his trousers, unzip his fly. One knelt and began to suck his limp penis. Others fondled, laughing noiselessly, black holes opening wide in white faces, emitting nothing. He stood stiffly at the centre of their attentions, flexed to act. One clown detached from their group, drew him away from the mechanical mouth, and partnered him to dance. Music filled the room, a scratched record of an old fox-trot turning on a gramaphone balancing on rubble, and the two danced in habitual timing. The others sat along the wall dutifully, mouths closed to form the shapes of perfect clean arseholes. I noticed then that he wore well polished black boots over grey jodhpurs. But I could scarcely believe his eyes slid under narrow lids, yellow moon rinds not seeing me alone signalling disappointment mingled with censure. My jacket sat straight. So too did my hat. He danced, controlling his sensations as well as the compliant clown whose face bobbed above his shoulder, blonde hair falling about its cheeks and she may have been his wife. His physical bearing, the tight sadistic lines of his body, attracted my stomach and I lowered my head, slightly jealous of the clown who seemed so joyless in his embrace. I tensed as if to move. Whether forwards or backwards I do not know for the clowns grappled me round the neck, dragged me by the hair and forced me to grovel the dust at his feet. My tongue and throat choked outrage. They wanted me to lick his boot. When I would not, they tore off my clothes, pulled my breasts, scratched my scar, pinched my buttocks, poked and prodded my vulva and arse. But I shook myself free of them, frowning at the way their clammy fingers sought my flesh. I looked up, one of the creatures still clawing my neck, another lapping my back with its irksome tongue, and I saw nothing but yellow unseeing slits under his eyelids, a wry smile snarling his lips. Instantly, his face stiffened. He brought down the whip, lashing me fiercely across the back, and my entrails heaved. But I had become so determined to resist and stand alone my skin did not feel the blow nor I any humiliation. Without interference, I dressed and left him. As I climbed through a hole in the wall, I realised he stared after me, his mouth agape with wonderment, his whip coiled about his feet. Clowns rolled over, curled into alcoves, their faces sliding into sleep. Before and behind me, holes continued to open and close, open and close, open and close, clowns lolling stupidly in sleep, and I stepped through and through and through basements of rubble echoing into more, larger and smaller basements as if they were one. Ordinarily, the exertion would have broken me. But a resilience overcame tears. Repetition did not reduce me, the task in itself becoming a distinctive, thrilling achievement. When I surfaced into the blue evening, he appeared in front of me, militarily elegant in a chauffeur's suit, a riding crop neat by his calf. With admiration, he clasped my hand and, pressing it, drew me to his chest saying, while staring past the clowns as if they had vaulted their spaces, You are the most beautiful presence of the evening. I received the compliment with no surprise, no fascination, expecting it, a few words whose meaning is more oblique than their banality often suggests. I looked long at his profile. He looked through his clowns. And around us the city sparked. Car engines fired. Accelerators roared. Brakes squealed. An old car chugged, coughed, fell silent. From the shadows of the foyer, a hotel doorman stretched his arm into the street for a taxi. The uniform broadened his shoulders. He flattened the palm of his hand against the small of my back and guided me to the car door which he opened. I disliked being manipulated from a curiosity in one man to the concern of another to the protection offered by a third. Accepting the doorman's palm as he ushered me forwards, I turned, pointing the toe of my boot into his instep, and kissed him full on the mouth. Satisfied no one could fault my independence, I sat down on the back seat of the taxi. The door slapped shut. The car bulletted through the city's canyons. His chauffeur's face suspended, overlapping mine in the rear vision mirror, transparent lids closing over long yellow eyes looking to the back seat, not forwards. The sky catapulted, grey black and forbidding, the car with me as its cargo leaping, never stopping, the bridge rocking buildings giddy overhead, the face in the mirror broadening diminishing distorting, thinning to a hard line resisting boredom. Gloved hands manipulated strongly the vehicle in which I sat, neither acquiescent nor protesting, detached from horror for fear of crumbling, strange, listless on a sofa, its pink upholstery too colourless beneath the black window space, the evening air cool and, if he had been Hitler's driver, did he accept the job as a good one, life's luck to him, motoring blind and in command behind the wheel of a machine through wartorn Europe?, and

Fay Zwicky

Fay Zwicky was born in Melbourne, 1933 and now lives in Perth, Western Australia. Author of *Isaac Babel's Fiddle* (verse); *Kaddish and other Poems*; *Hostages and other Stories*; *The Lyre in the Pawnshop*; *Essays on Literature and Survival 1974–1984*. She has edited two collections of poetry, *Journeys: Judith Wright, Rosemary Dobson, Gwen Harwood, Dorothy Hewett*; and *Quarry: a Selection of Western Australian Poetry*. She is currently working on another book, half prose and half poetry, based on experience in America, India, and Japan.

Hibakusha's Daughter

To keep a human voice raised against the coming of night: the cicada cries out its love but the firefly burns in silence. Hungry for speech, my lips tighten like a knife-blade on tenderness.

'A little Jap lass, eh?'
'Where you say you're from?'
'What's your name again?'
'How long you been in WA?'
'Do you like it here?'

My kind neighbours' voices are like glass splinters ...

My mother still gets fatigued in summer and goes on having blood counts done even though I was born whole and the American doctors told her she didn't have to worry any more. Her letters tell me she's still haunted by that huge desolate crater where her home disappeared before my birth. Phosphorescent blue water snakes still writhe on the dark water of her dreams. Wrinkled like an old shell, my grandmother faces the rough sea in the small fishing village where she was born.

Memory steals into a silent Australian house. I am waiting for my Australian husband to come home. My daughter, Kimika, has fallen asleep clutching her yellow bear. She looks so peaceful, one perfect had resting on her cheek, strands of shining black hair spilling down over her bear's ear.

My grandfather's hands. Always working with thick ropes. His hands are hard and thick. His fingers thick and rough. When it's really bad for him the fingernails sometimes come off. His face is dark the whole year round so I have never seen my grandfather's skin peeling off during the summer ...

The lost doll sent by my American father. How did he manage to find a Japanese doll so far away, her high glossy balloon of black hair stuck with red lacquer pins? Somewhere on a damp river beach where lamps on distant masts shone like ochre stars it must have been summer, and fireflies were casting flickering nets around the soft darkness. Grandmother's skin, grained like our thick paper and firm in the moonlight. Firm as her voice as she shooed a few straggling mosquitoes from my crouched body, pulling me roughly out of the dripping leaves of a bush.

'You little monkey! Trying to snatch the moon's face from the water again! You'll never learn, will you!'

'Learn!' I shout. 'Learn! What is there to learn? It must be here. I know it must be here!' I am crying with frustration and shock, but not so miserable that her words can't excite my curiosity.

'There's worse than lost dolls. The Lord Buddha himself would weep to see such a fuss about a little thing. Why, he told that story I heard from my own mother about the monkeys crying for the moon. You should listen too.'

'All right, all right. Tell me.' I'm no longer crying and whirling about, irritated and comforted by her ageless certainty.

'Settle down and I'll tell you about it,' and leaning awkwardly against her skinny shoulder, I give her my grudging attention.

'Don't keep pushing me like that! Just like a monkey yourself. Well, some monkeys once found a well right under a tree. They saw the moon's reflection in the water and wanted to catch it. One of them hung by his tail from a branch leaning over the well. Then another monkey hung on to him and another hung on to the second monkey and they all made a chain almost touching the water, the silly creatures!'

'Why silly?' It sounded like a clever plan to me.

'Because, Kae, they were all too heavy for the little branch. It snapped and they all drowned.'

'All of them?'

'All.'

Whenever she spoke, heaviness left my heart, but I shrugged all the same and slapped a mosquito on my arm. Clear red blood smeared my white skin and I licked it with a defiant tongue and spat on the ground.

'I'd rather be the last monkey.'

'Be the last monkey, then. Be stubborn like your mother. It's the wild ducks that make the most noise.'

Walking back on the path of wet, mouldering leaves to her house that night I was quiet for once. Her faith in the Lord Buddha was so removed from my experience that I never imagined it would touch my life. Yet here, in the shadowless foreign house of hard glass, concrete and bricks, I am remembering the Great Buddha of Kamakura...

His gentle rounded shoulders and the folds of his robe and how sunlight played on the sleeve flowing down from the shoulder and struck blinding light from his broad bronze torso. And how the light touched the bronze snails coiled like hair on his head, each standing out in sharp relief. His long earlobe seemed to hang like the pod of some dried tropical fruit. Why should I be remembering this who had a Hibakusha mother and an American father?

Gentle lulling rain on a straw roof and the mystery of shadows. Beaked dragon forms gliding by in lantern glimmers down silent shadowed avenues, mossed flights of steps and the clean shapes of bells. Murmuring of prayer from fishermen's huts by the still sea. Desolate places marked only by coiling threads of fragrant smoke.

Rain on an iron roof and the harsh white light of this new country. Jim and Kimika protect me, but something is dying. An old contract with my shadowy ancestors who were forced to live in dark rooms and found beauty in shadows. No matter what the season here, the white glare never varies and every living thing — man, bird or grass blade — is pinned cruelly for today's inspection. In such a light, memory slides furtively in at the heart's back door.

No frogs, no night clamour, no spring voices wakening in the marshes, no quickening of those soft sounds that might be the land itself speaking. I used to keep a singing frog in a little cage back home. Kajika sounded sweeter than a bird with his basin of sand and pebbles, fresh water and little garden full of tiny delicate plants under a fine gauze-wire dome.

With hands resting on the ground
reverently you repeat your poem, O frog!

My grandmother used to call me frog-in-the-well which is what you call someone innocent of the world's ways in our country.

'The frog in the well doesn't know the great sea,' she used to say. 'But,' I'd protest, 'flowers drop into my well and its waters mirror the moon,' the habit of symbolic speech coming early with such teachers. 'What about snakes? Mosquitoes?' Her knowing insistence was more than my desperate thirst for the future could stand at times.

The pumping of a remembering heart and a walk in the mountains outside Kyoto with my American father. As we followed the course of a clean swift river through a deepening ravine, my heart was pounding with excitement and exertion trying to keep pace with the long strides of the man in an American army uniform. The rock bluff on the roadside was carved with seated, tranquil Bhoddisattvas and white wisteria cascaded down in misty folds on the opposite bank. Wild azaleas that had looked faded in the valley below became more gorgeous and crimson the higher we climbed. My mind was so flooded with colour for days afterwards that I hardly noticed he was gone.

Everybody tells me
my hair is too long.
I leave it
as you last saw it
tangled by your hands

'Why do you have no hair, mother?'

'It will grow again,' said my grandmother.

They tell me it started to grow after my father died back in America. She was fourteen years old when the bomb fell and her house disappeared.

'How shall I say it? The words don't come,' said my mother, turning her head aside. 'Because I am a Hibakusha I don't want to be looked at with special eyes or treated in a special way. When I was younger, they used to call us atomic bomb maidens. Can you believe it? They have a newer word for us now.'

'What's that?' It was not an easy conversation.

'I hate the word. When people talk about young girls,

they say girls or daughters or somebody's daughter. But to call us atomic bomb maidens — dreadful! It's a way of abandoning us, this not wanting to know about death. It wasn't just bad for us — it's destroying them too if only they knew . . . I almost died. I should have died. In a way I did die, or maybe I'm not really alive now. If I'm alive now I shouldn't be. No, let me finish. My life is an insult to the dead. To be a maiden means to be pure but only the dead are really pure.'

Did she really say those things to me or have I imagined them? I do remember the day before I married Jim, the day I asked her to tell us what happened. It seemed to matter at the time that Jim should know the very worst so that he might know me better: his all-of-a-piece emancipated wife. She had started speaking slowly as if hypnotized and her face, which a moment before looked like that of a haunted child suddenly seemed terribly old.

'I wasn't feeling so well that day so I was allowed to stay home from school. I remember lying on the bed shivering with fever and hearing the air-raid warning and how good it felt to be safe at home. Mr Okada from the house across the road came to our door, and I heard him ask my mother if he could speak to my father. Listening hard, I heard him say: 'As for the eldest daughter of this family, is it agreeable that she be disposed of in marriage?'

'I held my breath while your grandfather said that no preparation for such an event had yet been made. Yes. In just those same stiff words. You might well look surprised but that's how marriages used to be arranged. It was a frightening moment for me.'

'So what happened?' I wanted to get it over with. 'What happened when the —'

'Wait!' She held up her hand and it was shaking. 'Life had already begun to look dangerous and who was I to make choices? The all-clear sounded and I thought the day was going to be all right. Why should I be bitter about someone who was a complete stranger until a certain moment in a day that has passed? Besides, Mr Okada hadn't finished his business yet. "No preparation is necessary," he went on, "so will you not honorably give her to the man for whom I am speaking? He is said to be very steady and thirty six years of age. When the war is over he will want a wife."

'"She is only fourteen," said your grandfather. "She is not ready." The words of an old poem had settled in my head while all this was going on and it wouldn't go away.

In the spring garden
in the coloured shadow
of peach blossoms
a girl stands
on a white path

His voice was courteously obstinate and I breathed more freely upstairs, sweat dripping from my forehead. "I thought your eldest daughter was at least twenty. I proposed her to him believing she was ready for marriage," said Mr Okada.

'"No, she is fourteen years old. Conditions are not favorable."

'"That being the case," said our neighbour, "I must tell the other party that the match cannot yet be made."

'"Cannot be made," said my father and your grandfather.

'I heard the stairs groan under my mother's footsteps. She came over to my bed and stroked my long lank hair without a word. I knew then that I was running for her life, my escape what hers might have been . . .

His hands are hard and thick. His fingers
thick, tangled in my hair. His face is
dark the whole year round

'And as Mr Okada started to leave our house, it happened. Suddenly, with a tremendous noise and a crackling bluish light. A flash like nothing I'd ever seen before and which I can't truly describe. It suddenly got very hot inside the house and all I can remember is that sudden flash and the heat greater than any fever that swept over me like a tidal wave. When I woke up I was underneath the collapsed timbers and roof frames of our house. At first I thought a bomb had fallen right on top of me but then I realized that I was covered in tiles and fragments of wall and everything was black and I was angry. So angry that I screamed and screamed like a wild animal whose hairy head seemed to be gradually and invisibly thrusting up inside my burning skin and I screamed for help and all around there was crying and moaning and only after I took in these sounds did I begin to think there might be any kind of danger to myself.'

The light bulb shining down circled the upstanding tufts of hair on my mother's frail grey scalp with a lunatic halo.

'The thought that I might die there, helpless and furious was becoming unbearable. There seemed to be nothing I could do. Nothing. I didn't know where I was or what I was trapped under and I couldn't hear the voices of my family. I never ever imagined the possibility of rescue. I'd simply suffocate and then die and never know exactly what had happened to any of us. And while I lay pinned and powerless in frantic darkness. I remembered quite suddenly the temple at Kobudera where my parents once took me when I was a child. I'll never know why such a memory should have come to comfort me at such a time . . . the temple gate was made of gnarled logs and there was a tiled and tilted Chinese roof that looked precarious and threatening to me at the time for I was no more than seven or eight years old. At each gable end there was a demon's head, grinning under three horns. I remember being afraid to go inside, but my father coaxed me into the green silence.

'The ground was covered with a fine thick moss, so soothing and warm that even the bright azaleas and the fragrant *mokusei* hanging above seemed sombre by contrast. And muffled by all this luminous green, the lines of stone of the ancient well and bell-tower had all but disappeared. Maples and sweet-smelling pines shielded the temple and, sniffing the air like a crazy creature, I followed behind my parents in a sort of daydream. We left the temple by a gate with big black bars and walked along the mossy paths of the cemetry that lay alongside. Incense, flowers, and water poured into bowls for the dead comforted and reassured me. So did the scriptural texts chiselled deep into granite and on the lovely smooth wood of the *sotoba*. I ran a finger over the characters as if trying to learn the secret of their beauty, as if they were mysterious words from another planet . . . but that was long ago and, blind creature that I was, I wasn't yet afraid of the dark . . . But now, trapped under our house the demon heads once again were staring down at me, their horns pinning me in a black sea of rubble and stone and once more I lay under the tiles of the fallen temple roof waiting to die.'

Jim was very quiet after she'd finished and said to me later in private that it was a wonder she hadn't become a mental case. I don't think he yet understands our long acquaintance with death or the attraction of shadows for our people . . .

Mother and I had only one more fleeting moment of communication before we left for Sydney. She wanted to tell me a last story as if to reinforce that uncanny melancholy bond of survival between us, but I was afraid to lose my resolve to leave her and Japan and I made an impatient listener.

We were sitting idly picking knotgrass in a public garden when her eyes became unnaturally bright and I was uneasy about her sudden movements.

'Don't worry about me. I felt destruction coming long before the bomb fell. I'd already seen those blue and orange flames rising in my dreams like spirits of the dead. To have made a free choice is to condemn yourself to hell, little frog. And I chose.' Still treating me like a child, still warning me as her mother had warned her. I tugged at the grass, keeping my eyes averted from her pitiful hair.

'Did you ever hear about Osame whose wonderful silk robe with the long sleeves destroyed the town of Yedo by fire?'

'My father was American, don't forget. I haven't heard your old stories,' was what I was thinking, but my heart was wrenched with pity and I said more gently than I intended, 'Go on. Tell me.'

'I don't think you want to hear the story. I was a frog in a well once too, waiting for the moon's face in my waters, but never mind. I can see that what happened to a rich merchant's daughter in the time of the Shoguns isn't going to keep you here for long.'

You would never have thought, listening to this woman, that she had once left her family and her country and gone to live in America, worn western dress and smoked cigarettes and worked as a barmaid.She made the word 'Shogun' sound like the family next door. As she was lost in thought, I let the moment pass in peace. Clusters of red flowered knotgrass bloomed and the shrilling of distant cicadas blurred into the summer mists and the smell of wood smoke.

'Snakes, flowers, the moon's bright face are all the same to the little frog,' she said, her voice ominously quiet.

From the hearth no smoke rises
in the cauldron
a spider weaves its web.
How do you cook rice
when there is no rice left?
We talk feebly as birds . . .

Under the harsh drumming rain on an iron roof I am waiting for Jim to come home

Is this the way things go?
Must it go on and on?
Yes. We are on earth.

Gillian Mears

Gillian Mears was born in 1964 and grew up with her three sisters in North Coast towns of NSW. In Sydney she abandoned an Arts/Archeology degree to work as a lab assistant and waitress. In 1985 she completed a Communications degree at the NSW Institute of Technology. She is now living with her husband Stephen Tatham in an old shingle house with an overgrown garden. Stories have been published in *Hecate*, *Fling*, *ASS* and an anthology of student writing, *13 New Beginnings*. A collection of short fiction is to be published by Pascoe Publishing.

The Midnight Shift

He hurts her with his eyes shut and his tongue poked out and the smell of hamburgers still on his fingers. Two Big Boy Special Burgers with the Lot, double cheese and sauce but not beetroot. I know exactly, because it's either me or Vorna who gets them ready. Sometimes when ordering, he'll say that just for something different I can make it hot dogs with yellow mustard. It is nothing new for him to have two cartons of chips along with a chocolate malted thickshake. No wonder he is such a shape. Like a huntsman spider with a swollen belly. And all day clinging over a power drive steering wheel with the vinyl seating getting hot in the afternoon sun.

She tries not to touch the moles that are spongy on his shoulders. Some have hairs growing out the middle. She watches them while he grunts, and the sweat that beads along his skin. Once a piece of earwax fell out. It rolled down her face like a tear.

His neck is bull red and I think that if she only dared to bite that throbbing vein he would die. The blood would spurt high in the air and pattern her skies more brilliant than any sunset.

Standing behind the front counter I can see the sunsets. Between busloads of hamburger eaters I watch them spatter, streak, light up, glow yellow, look like jam or flower colours, go smokey, go gold, go mauve, Go Shell. Go Well With Shell. Across the highway the other service station interrupts my view. It is a decrepit building that sprawls in dim oblong shapes by the side of the road, but the Shell sign is always lighted by dusk. Five minutes before Mulvy Smith who runs this place switches on our Golden Fleece ram. For a while after I started work at the Roadhouse I tried to think of original ways to see the sun through the falling clouds. The same way I used to learn a new word from the dictionary every day. Like my attempts to improve my vocabulary, all efforts have faded. My mind overloads with other people's sunset descriptions and the smell of chips in their boiling vats.

By sundown Vorna, who arranges the salads for the sit-down people is telling me about her aunt who has been in the nursing home for donkeys years.

'Those chips ready to go love?' she asks, making the rolls of Kraft-sliced stand straight in rings of tinned pineapple. 'It's a crying shame,' she is slicing the buttered bread into triangles. The crusts are only a bit stale. 'For all those years she's just a little Bean. A vegetable, you know. And now after all this they decide to operate. Diviticulitis it was. Got to wear a bag now. A colostomy.' Vorna finds the word she is looking for and spills grease from a chiko roll down her yellow zippered uniform. It coagulates in the metal teeth as the rest of the night passes.

Above the floor that gets slimy with fallen foods, above the two garbage bins filling with multi-colouring pig slops, higher than the washing-up sinks and the clock, is a strip of glass. Suns only set in the west when I'm out the front and serving at the counter. In the kitchen all I can see are the trains going past. First comes the cold chrome clanking as they slow down at the edge of the town lights. Through the high thin window I see the wooden overpass bridge bending and shaking. It seems that the bridge is right above the kitchen. I imagine disasters. Falling passengers scattering the trays of buns I butter. People splashing into the egg and milk mix the floured cutlets have to be dunked into. Sleeping babies in bunny rugs screaming awake as they crash land in the chocolate sauce bucket.

The air is lonelier after the train noises die. The night shift is the sad shift. The sound of the swings outside in the empty picnic area gives me the shivers. Vorna drops Winfield 25 ash into burgers and the other counter girl goes home. My banana thickshake dinner tastes of chemicals. I eat cold chips one by one to disguise the taste. Vorna drops a whole butt on top of a steak and egg sandwich and covers it in a pool of barbeque sauce. Maybe I know nothing at all and Vorna is out to sabotage the popularity of Mulvy and Dougie Smith's famous roadhouse Big Boy Burgers, that are even being advertised on the radio. Anything's possible

I suppose, at that time of night when the truckies begin to come in. Hearing truck gears changing in the night is a faraway feeling. The groaning of brakes as they pull in turns my insides cold. From the kitchen I can hear Vorna with the radio on listening to the dogs. She never misses a bet on Friday night. Doors slam; boots hit the tar. Gravel crunches.

Trucks heading north come to this servo. Trucks going south normally pull up at the Shell one across the road. South going trucks with drivers wanting a screw make the effort to swing across the highway and come here. There are more of these last sort of drivers than I ever would have imagined. They come through the door smelling of diesel and dust. They wear little caps and tattoos on their arms and T-shirts like I often sell, with something dirty on the front. Sometimes they go straight on upstairs while Vorna gets their meals ready. They go outside and round the back to get to the stairs. I hear them creaking up the slat and air steps and then the doors shutting.

That is not always his way of doing things. Often he'll eat chips and one burger first of all.

She knows when he arrives. She can smell the cattle in four layers moaning on the truck.

Tonight one steer with horns has got its head stuck between the rails and bellows crookedly into the night. From behind the gauze curtain that shifts with the hot air, she watches the headlights snap off. As she lies on the bed she feels her heart curl inside.

Vorna says they are King size with satin black covers and red canopies and all, but I don't know. Vorna can't but help let her imagination go when it comes to the women upstairs. Vorna says there are girls who park panel vans in the by-pass rest area and wait for truckies there. Which isn't so hard to believe.

I have a memory of the first time I saw him. It was my first week of work when I was trying to get the hang of things in a hurry. He wanted chips before he went upstairs. I scooped out two small scuttleloads. They were the remnants from the chip-display-unit; chip fragments rather than chips and some bits burnt. They barely filled the carton let alone spilled over like the photo-ads above the counter show. But I was tired and just about to clean the chip display glass. To do this you have to put your head and shoulders right inside the glass doors and angle the spray bottle into the greasy corners. I could see him through the tinted glass flipping over the box full of country and western cassettes and shovelling the chips into his mouth. He came across and pressed his face up against the glass. I could see the hairs out his nose and chips hanging onto his jagged eye teeth. And white skin the texture of bloater tripe or frozen potato. He smiled through the glass. I made him more chips because he said the others were all dried out. I had to use a detergent where his nose had been.

I am all dried out, she thinks, lying on her bed upstairs. She has tried to fill the stretch marks near her hips with vaseline and babypowder. Her ears ache with listening for the footsteps on the stairs so she unscrews her bluebird earrings and sends them flying. I hear them skitter across the floor above my head as I turn out frytol tins of frozen mince into plastic tubs and into small circles with my hands. He is still eating his chips; watching the television in the corner. The meat catches under my fingernails. It has turned green and grey at the edges of the tins. It looks poisonous under the flourescence. The colour of hail in storm clouds. The colour of the varicose veins Vorna is going to have stripped from her legs when she saves up enough holiday time. They grow like dark vines below the skin because of standing for nine hours on hard tile floors.

People should get paid more for working after twelve. The midnight shift. For every hour I get \$3.52, the same rate as daytime when all you're serving is hordes of little kids on their way home from the beach. The worst they can do is not make up their minds whether to have a lemonade icypole or a raspberry one, while the queue behind them grows longer and longer. Mothers with great welts on their shoulders from squashing their bosoms up with heavily elasticised swimmers buy suntan lotion to ease their stinging skins. They mop up split milkshakes with Kleenex and get annoyed when they realise they've been

173

sitting on a bit of a squashed pie. The pinballs are all whizzing so loud that I can't hear the silence upstairs. No-one's there. No-one's upstairs until late afternoon and never yet have I seen the women arrive. I only notice the three cars after the coach tours have gone on their way to the Gold Coast, their seats full of determined purple-waved passengers. The cars are parked out the back. I see them when I go to light the incinerator.

The Ford station wagon with the bashed headlight is hers. There are kids' toys on the back seat, spilt twisties, sweet packets, a baby restraint, an exercise book with a picture of a kitten pasted on brown paper and plastic covered. One day I will see her down the street on a Saturday morning lugging the shopping and the baby, and buying brown paper and pens at the stationer's for the kids' first day back at school. I'll know who she is. I will know and I'll give her a friendly smile. I think it's wonderful she can think still of getting proper brown paper for her kids. When I was in primary my Mum would never buy me brown paper or plastic to cover my books. I can remember having to wait until everyone had left the classroom before I handed my book up. A waste of time and money Mum would tell me, but she never knew what it felt like going with your books covered in yellow contact meant for lining drawers. A dreadful and mortifying feeling. One year I became so desperate that I used brown bags from the butchers. Only after I'd covered my composition book did I realise there were smears of drying blood all down one side. Funny the things that worry you at that age but it would have been good to have an understanding mother.

Sometimes there is a lull in people who want to eat hamburgers and I read the paperbacks from the revolving stand out the front. They have trashy covers and are full of sex. There are the truck magazines too. There is an ad for this servo in the December issue. 'Girls for Stud Rams,' it reads and the lettering is gold and black.

In between late night truckie orders, Vorna reads me the stars. It's all such bulldust but Vorna is a horoscope addict. I am a crab — a moon person linked to the water. Vorna reads that I am whimsical, wayward and a child forever. Vorna is always looking for romance. She seeks it in the to-be-continued-next-week stories, between pages of Tampax ads and Royal features. It makes her feel kind sending her magazines upstairs when she's finished with them. Minus the potato cooking supplement, or is it turkey this week?

One potato, two potato, three potato four. He throbs with the rhythm of little boys playing games. Five potato, six potato, seven potato MORE. He has eaten his chips and gone up the stairs. The door has shut and it's only him and her alone in the room.

Slut he calls her, pulling off his boots and smelling his sweaty feet. She has had everything taken out in an operation but not her ovaries. She feels them bruising, feels them hurt and squash.

Insects are self destructing over the kitchen doorway as I cut the day-after-tomorrow's onions. It is one hour into Christmas Eve. The day before Christmas and all round the house not a creature was stirring not even a mouse. It doesn't feel like Christmas this year. I suppose because this is the first time I've ever worked in my holidays. God Arrest You Merry Gentleman. Truckies buy under-the-counter magazines and stuffed kiddies toys and sandalwood perfurme and powder sets for under ten dollars. They always leave the screen door open and let the insects in. Nighttimes insects are different from the hot blundering flies of the day; more desperate to die. The purple-lighted insect ring screwed above the kitchen doorway gets them but not quickly. Sometimes their deaths seem to go on forever. Like the onion rings I must chop. Like the noises upstairs that are so loud and long. It's a wonder Vorna can stand there reading as she whacks eggs on the hotplate for his after-fuck burgers.

I slice the onions. The mattress is wheezing. He has streaked her skin with his oily fingernails, making her turn over. As a spider moves in on a stung moth, he goes for her mouth, rearranges it, sucks and spits; leaves white thumbprints on her breasts. That's against her rules but he is determined. It's Christmas time, he groans, as if that explains everything. There is a strong smell of cow shit but whether it's coming through the window or clings to his body she can't tell.

Vorna is deep in her story. Her hand flips the eggs from habit. She holds the magazine close to her face because her glasses steam up over the hotplate. I cry onion tears. It is Christmas Eve and still I can't go home until these last burgers are eaten and paid for, the hotplate cleaned, the milkshake stirrers washed. My eyes weep. Vorna yelps like a kelpie that there's a man at the front waiting to be served. It is only Winding Windows, the funeral director who lives down the road from me. He mumbles, hello, not expecting to see me here. He rubs his grey, greasy hair and makes up his mind to have a soft serve cone dipped in chocolate. It is one o'clock in the morning. As I dip the icecream into the container of chocolate sauce it falls off its cone. I put it back on. He trundles out licking chocolate off his nose. He must be on his way home from picking up an out-of-town corpse. The ads he puts in the paper make a point of emphasising that distance is no problem for a Battersly Burial. 'If you don't choose a Battersly Burial — it's *your* funeral.' I am not at all suprised that he would finish driving home a corpse with an icecream in one hand. He owns a giant refrigerator for bodies. This is also where he keeps the beer. He drinks straight from the can. He has two shining black cars each with the most up-to-date automatic features — windows that work on a button.

Winding Windows comes back in and says his icecream tastes of onions. I replace it with a chiko roll. Merry Christmas he says and drives off in his hearse.

Vorna tells me to finish with the onions and go on home. Her face is heavy with old makeup. At least it is a holiday tomorrow. It's hard not to yawn. The stairs when I go outside are as empty as the road and carpark. His truck, her car, my old ute and Mulvy's are the only vehicles left. Sometime not so long ago the other two women from upstairs have gone home. Maybe they followed Winding Windows into town. The cattle in the truck are peaceful and smell rich and sweet. They don't know the abattoirs are only four miles away.

Mulvy is doing something with the garbage, waiting for Vorna, to give her a lift home. I see his teeth smiling as he says there'll be a Christmas bonus on Boxing Day. I say goodnight. Probably it'll be a free hamburger.

'Sweet dreams dear,' Vorna puts her head out the kitchen door to say goodnight. I wave and Vorna waves back, and the wild shadows on the curtains. But it is over now. There is a stillness. The moon is bony, new, fragile, thin like a toenail shot into the sky by a blunt pair of clippers. I drive slowly round to the front to reach the road. The yellow Ram and the yellow Shell shine across the highway at each other. It will be a dull dawn, a dun coloured sky.

She lies naked on the bed while he pulls his belt underneath his belly and burps. Downstairs Vorna is putting his hamburgers into a takeaway bag for him.

Sperm sticking her thighs together feels like the thick Clag glue so good for Christmas decorations. The yellow signs look to her like the shapes her children carve out of flaky school soap for her to wash her body with. Because they know she works at the Golden Fleece servo, they have made her a yellow soap ram as a special parcel to hang amongst the tinsel and pine needles. They cannot know that she will burst into tears sitting underneath the Christmas streamers when she opens their present.

He is leaving the room now. The door opens and shuts. I see him come down the stairs a dark blob with bowing legs. A gob of spit hits the ground. He's left a packet of Drum behind and a half smoked rollie stuck to the wall above the bedhead. It glows in the grey room. She watches it burning and the bleep of the truck's red tail lights curving away.

Marianne Szymiczek

Marianne Szymiczek was born in New Guinea in
1954 and spent most of her childhood in NSW. She
spent a brief period studying Arts at Melbourne
University, then sculpture and painting at RMIT.
It was not till her late twenties that she began writing seriously. The story 'Marie and Suzie' is an ex-
cerpt from a larger series.

Marie and Suzie

We lived in an old rooming house off Fitzroy Street. Our room was small with only a bathroom leading off it. It suited us allright.

We brought clients up from the street. One of us would wait in the bathroom while the other used the bed. Sometimes, sitting on the edge of the bathtub, I'd hear them at it: the bedsprings, a brief silence the rustle of clothing.

I did them on the floor so she couldn't hear.

She was only eighteen and already she had grey hair. In the sunlight it looked a crazy blonde.

Her name was Suzie.

When she came in from the street I'd move up to her, grab her shoulders and push my tongue into her mouth, fall struggling to the floor.

She was thin. Too thin.

Afterwards, in the bath I'd enter her; my fingers angry and insistent. I'd pull it out of her — undo what they'd done. You could see it curling out in ugly clear curls of snot. I made sure she was clean.

Tattooes, bruises covered her body. She bruised easy: tiny blue patches from their hips dotting her thighs; ugly marks on her neck from when one had tried to strangle her. I soaped her back gently, gliding over the diagonal red marks we made the night before.

It was winter but I didn't feel the cold. As I crossed Fitzroy Street, the asphalt biting into my feet felt almost nice.

I don't remember how it started. I had a bad mandy habit. I slid through the days like they were slippery-dips of ice.

I remember R found me wandering down the street. I hadn't seen her for months. They'd taken my kids off me by then. I was too out of it to remember much. But R said I was uncontrollable. She took me to Danielle's. They locked me in her flat for days. It saved my life.

When there was nothing else to do we'd visit Luna Park — that insane mouth swallowing us up — we'd ride the roller coaster, go down the tunnel of horror, watch the lights flashing the people screaming. The smell of rot and salt and sea.

Sometimes we'd watch Barry down Saint Moritz rink. When he wasn't on the street he was on ice. He flew, he glided, he dropped, he spun, created another world within those circles of speed of ice. The audience a flash of blurred faces. He became winged, weightless on cold blue ice. Circles and multicircles. Flashing.

My belt was wide and thick and black, and cracked like a rattle snake above, over and across her; invisible circles scarring the air. The buckle biting and bruising. Her face all arrogance and laughter.

She asked for it. She got you feeling like you really wanted to. Now it frightens me, the way she made me feel. When I tied her up I was rough and untied the tape fast. It's stickiness sizzling in the room. She would close her eyes and sigh and I'd become wet.

Sometimes when I came home I'd find her dozing before the heater; the TV silently flashing, the radio up loud. Once the back of her jumper burned, smouldered as she lay sleeping on the floor, an awful stink in the air.

She almost went up in flames.

When she shot up her face dropped and became haggard. Her eyes two pinpoints to infinity. Then she just sat there and didn't want to do anything. When she was like this she looked dirty no matter what she did to herself. Then I really wanted to hit her.

I remember the mountains of ash falling softly from her cigarette. Our carpet was spotted with a fine grey powder.

Sometimes I thought she tried to pull me down drowning with her. There was a falling away that wasn't even a struggle. And she didn't even feel it. It was like soaking in a cold tub on a hot day. So hard to pull yourself out.

I wished I'd never met her. But deep down there was a core of pure ice. And it felt wonderful.

Janet Shaw

Janet Shaw was born in 1960, in Melbourne, trained as a teacher and has been paid for teaching, acting, labouring, and research among other things. She now lives in North Fitzroy, writing stories for children and, mostly, short stories, of which several have been published. Janet Shaw now teaches short story writing and writing for children at TAFE and CAE colleges. She has published one book, *My Hiding Place*, which won the 1983 Angus & Robertson Writers for the Young Fellowship. Janet Shaw is at present working on a collection of short stories due for completion early 1988.

Tongue

My stepfather had grey teeth and a rash on his face. Most of his hair had fallen out, but it wasn't because he was old, he said, it was in his family.

I didn't like him. He was bad enough to his own kids, our four steps, but he was worse to me and Bit and Rick and I never saw him be nice to Mum.

Someone had told him he needed a panel van for all the kids. He said he didn't — all he had to do was take the seats out of his car and he would just about have a truck, there would be so much room. So he took the seats out and left them in the yard. There wasn't any more room, of course, and we all had to pile on top of each other as usual to fit in, only now we had to sit on the rails and lumps and holes instead of seats.

One day he said we were going to visit our auntie.

He had taken out the driver's seat too, and he couldn't drive properly, and he ran over a dog that was hunching up beside the road. The dog was dead, and the poo was only half out of it. We hadn't got far from home so he sent me and my brother Rick back to get the driver's seat. We brought it back and my stepfather put it in the car, only it wasn't stuck down properly and it rocked back and forth. 'You're not going to leave that dog on the road' said Mum. 'Oh no,' said my stepfather, 'It's coming with us.' So we lifted it up and I saw the bit of poo drop off. My mother was kneeling on the floor in the front, and she didn't say anything but just looked out the window.

I don't know why we didn't put the dog in the boot but we squatted in the back and nursed it. Its head was broken and it hung over my knee, dripping on the floor. The eyes were still all right but the tongue hung so far out that I couldn't help looking at it. It touched the floor as though it wanted to taste the fluff there. I wondered where dogs keep all that long tongue when they're alive, or maybe this was a special dog with a specially long tongue that we had run over. One thing I was sure about: we'd all get into big trouble sooner or later for killing it.

Then my brother poked his finger into the dog's head. That was when my mother turned around and looked, and then made my stepfather stop the car, and she said a whole lot of stuff to him, and she got out and walked home, and I never saw her again.

After that my stepfather made us put the dog in the gutter, and then he started up the car and we went on. Bit, my little sister, said 'Where's Mummy gone?' and I said 'Ssh!'

We drove on for a while until the car made grating noises and broke down. My stepfather got out and looked under the bonnet. I said 'This car's a bomb,' and of course Trish said 'It's not a bomb. It's a good car.' And I said 'If it's such a good car then why does it always break down?' Then Katy, who is the oldest out of all of us, said 'But he can always fix it.'

That was when my stepfather slammed the bonnet down and hit the top of it with his fist. Then he walked away without even looking at us.

Nobody said anything for a moment, then Roger, who is the third youngest after Rosy and Bit, scrambled out of the car and ran after him. The rest of us stayed where we were. There was me and Rick and our sister Bit, and there was Katy, Trish and Rosy, all steps.

Katy said 'He's mad at us for fighting,' and Trish said 'We weren't fighting,' and I said 'Oh yes you were.' Katy turned to me and said 'You were too, snotty-face.' Rick, who was the only boy left, said 'Shut up Katy.' Rosy was really just a baby and she started crying, which set Bit off too.

I said 'I think he's gone to get someone to fix the car.'

'He can fix it himself,' said Trish. 'He can always fix it himself.'

'Maybe not this time,' said Rick. 'Maybe this time it's really broken down.'

Trish hit him. 'Just because he's not your Dad doesn't mean he can't fix the car. Why doesn't your Dad fix it?'

'Don't be stupid,' I said, and I opened the door I was

pressed against. 'I'm going. Do you want to come, Rick?' Rosy cried louder and Katy folded her arms in a huff and looked out the window. Trish stared at us. 'You have to stay here,' she said. 'You have to wait for Dad to come back.' I didn't answer her and Rick and I set off. We brought Bit along too since she was our real sister.

'Why do we have to go?' she asked me.

'Look,' I told her. 'What's going to happen when someone finds that dog? They're going to know it was us, and they'll follow the car and get us all into trouble. That's why *he's* gone. And if we're not there, we can't get into trouble. OK?'

Rick didn't say anything, but I knew he was thinking about it and seeing that I was right.

I didn't really know where we were but I had seen the road before through the windows of the car. There weren't many houses around. Mostly paddocks, and not much traffic, and every so often a crossroad. Bit was walking in between me and Rick and holding our hands. After a while she said 'I'm tired.' We didn't say anything, we just kept walking. Then she said 'Where are we going?' and I said 'Home.' We walked a bit more and she said 'Do sack of potatoes,' so I picked her up and put her over my shoulder and we kept walking. 'No, no!' She squealed. 'Say it. You have to say it!'

So I said who-wants-a-great-big-sack-of-potatoes in time with my steps.

We came to a crossroad with a shop and some houses and I put Bit down. She sat in the dirt and howled, so Rick said 'Be quiet Bitty.' She wouldn't, so I gave her a slap. Rick and I took her hands again and pulled her across the road to the shop. I made them wait outside while I went in to find out where we were and how to get home. The lady in there was surprised when I told her where we lived.

'How did you get all this way?' she asked me. I knew if I said anything about the car then they'd find out it was us who killed the dog, so I said 'We walked.'

'You poor little pets,' she said. 'Here, have these.' And she gave me a packet of peppermints and told me how to get home again. I didn't really understand her. I put the peppermints in my pocket and went out to Rick and Bit.

We walked on. It was about lunchtime because Bit was complaining. The houses had thinned out and there was no one anywhere and I was hot. I couldn't be bothered carrying Bit anymore so when she started grizzling I just sat down.

'What's wrong?' said Rick.

'Well,' I told him, 'we're lost.'

That made Bit scream and it made Rick sit down too. We were under a tree and just beside the road, but the road was only dirt now and nobody was driving on it.

'I'm hungry,' said Rick 'I'm really really hungry.' Of course Bit said 'I'm hungry too-oo,' and she burst into tears, which was quieter than screaming. I put my hand in my pocket and felt the packet of peppermints. 'I'm hungry too,' I said.

'What will we do?' Rick asked me and he held onto Bit's hand.

'Well,' I said, 'I'm going to the toilet.' And I got up and went behind the tree and through the fence and I squatted down in a kind of dip and I took out the peppermints. It was a roll as long as my hand when I spread my fingers out. I opened the silver paper at the end and pulled out two with my teeth and crunched them up. I closed the packet and put it back in my pocket, feeling around my teeth with my tongue for the little gritty bits of peppermint.

When I got back to Bit and Rick they were just sitting and looking at the ground and Rick was poking his foot with a stick. I sat down too, and Bit jumped on me. I had to pull my head back from her face so she wouldn't smell the peppermints from my mouth. I could see how dirty her face had got and how she needed to blow her nose, and how her eyes were scrunched up from crying.

'I want to go ho-me. I want Mummy. I don't want to play this anymore. I want Mummy and Rosy.' Rosy was our youngest step, and the only one who would play with Bit.

'OK,' I said, and I stood up and Bit fell onto the ground. 'OK. We're going home now. Come on Rick.' And Rick got up too and he held my hand and we all went along the road.

'Is this the way home?' Bit asked after a while. I told her

'Yes,' and she didn't say anything, just looked. The road was going uphill and the paddocks were empty. There weren't any houses any more and we hadn't passed a cross-road for ages.

Rick hadn't spoken for a long time, and then he said 'Are you sure?' 'You're scared' I said. I knew he'd say no, he wasn't, and he did, and that shut him up.

We walked over a little hill and there was a bridge across the road because a creek came through. It wasn't a big bridge, only twenty steps across for me. On the other side there were some huge trees along the creek. They hung right over the water and they made a big shadow all around. In the shadow was a little wooden house.

I went straight to the garden gate, but Rick and Bit, who had let go hands, stood in the middle of the road and watched me. When I went through the gate, Rick hissed out 'What are you doing?' I said 'I think you better come with me.' 'But that's not home,' Bit said, and started to cry again. 'Come on,' I said, so they followed me in and we shut the gate behind us.

The garden path was made of bricks with the corners worn off and grass growing between, and there wasn't much garden. We walked into the shadow of the big trees and it was cold. All the house was in the same shadow and it was quiet and dark. I knocked on the front door and the other two waited on the step. There was a cane chair on the verandah with a bundle of knitting in it and a pair of glasses in a glasses case. I knocked again. Bit sniffed and Rick said 'Oh.' I picked up the glasses case and took the glasses out. 'Don't' said Rick. 'Put them back.' I laughed and put them on. Everything went swirly and fuzzy and the edges of the verandah curled up to meet the guttering. I looked at the other two and their faces were flat and squished. Bit laughed and I took them off. 'Shut up,' I said. 'Do you want to get us into trouble?' and she said no.

I knocked on the door again and still no one came, so I told Rick and Bit to wait there while I went around the back.

The side of the house was all long grass and creepy bushes climbing up and the back verandah had holes in the boards. I stepped around them and knocked on the flywire door. There was no garden around the back — just a couple of sheds and the toilet. There was a chook run, but no chooks, and an apple tree with nearly ripe apples on it. I thought I saw a cat jumping.

The real back door was open, so that when I squashed my face against the flywire I could see the kitchen. It was dark and I could smell bad meat and hear a humming noise. I called out 'Hello. Are you home?' and my voice just went flat somehow in the house.

The wire door wasn't locked so I went in. The floor was only wood without any lino so I took my sandals off to feel it. The humming noise was blowflies and they were flying round and round the room and crawling all over a wire cupboard in the corner. I watched them for a while and they had a little hole in the wire they could crawl through. They would crawl all over the outside of the wire, smelling the smells coming from inside, until they found the hole and then they'd go through.

What they were smelling from outside and crawling all over on the inside of the cupboard was a lump of raw meat, and there were little squiggly maggots in it, and it stank. There were scratch marks all up the side of the cupboard on the wood part and I couldn't think what had made them. Anyway I took a peppermint out and ate it, and I stood watching the flies for a while.

It was then that I thought I heard something. Something like a little hum, or else a yawn, and it came from deeper inside the house.

The only light in the passage came from up the other end, through the red glass at the sides of the front door, and I could see Rick's face pressed up against it trying to see in.

It was in the passage that the smell of bad meat disappeared and I could smell cats. I went into the first room. It was dark but I could tell there was nothing much but dust in there, and a cat growling in the dark. There was a line of light from under the blind and I could see a cat's tail twitching in and out of it. I walked across to the window with my hands out in front of me and I pulled the cord so the blind flipped up. There was light in the room now and I turned around to look. There were a lot of cats crouching and one just running away. The cats were watching me.

'Puss, puss,' I said, and I put my hand out to pat them, but they growled and wouldn't come to me, so I jumped at them suddenly, barking like a dog and waving my arms, and they all ran out the door hissing and wowling. I kept barking after they had gone, just to hear the sound in the empty room like that. When I stopped barking it was suddenly very quiet in the house. Then I heard the sound again. It came from one of the front rooms, but I didn't go there yet. I looked back into the room. There were two plastic bowls on the floor, and a sandbox in the corner with dirty newspaper around it.

'Cats' room,' I said, just loud enough to make a little echo. I wondered what Rick and Bit thought when they heard a dog barking inside, and I thought that was funny.

The room opposite the Cats' room was dark too, but there was carpet on the floor and I could tell there was furniture in there. I felt my way, bumping into things, to the window and I opened the curtains. I looked out and saw the side of the house I had come along to get to the back door. I turned around to look at the room in the light. It was a dining room and the table still had what was left of someone's dinner on it. It must have been there for a while — there was a mess and it was mouldy. The water jug was on its side. But mostly there was cat poo under the table and in the corners and I could smell that.

I went back to the passage and shut the Cats' room door and the Poo room door. One of the rooms at the front of the house already had its door shut and I went into the other one. The window was right near the door and and I opened the curtains. It was a loungeroom with a fireplace and a bookshelf and two big chairs. I sat in one of them for a while but I got sick of it and jumped out. Then I heard a noise on the verandah and some whispering. Rick and Bit, I thought. I looked at the curtains and thought, if we could get them down they'd be our blankets and this could be our bedroom. I said 'Bedroom', but there wasn't any echo.

I opened the door of the last room and stepped in. I was

in the dark again, but what made me jump was the different smell. It wasn't bad meat or cats or poo — it was the
smell of an old lady. There was someone in the room that I
couldn't see. The window was near the door like in the
other room, and it faced onto the verandah. I held the
doorknob with one hand and leant forward with the other
for the curtain. When I drew it back, there was Rick's face,
staring in it the window, and in the next second I turned
and saw the old lady lying flat on the bed with her head up
and her eyes wide open looking at me and looking at Rick.
Then she made a noise, a moan right down in her throat
and I knew it was the sound I had heard before. I turned
back to Rick, but he had gone.

I would be Dad, I said, and Rick and Bit would be my
wives. Rick said no, he wasn't a girl and I wasn't a boy, but I
told him then he'd have to be the dog, and he let it go.

We ate some green apples from the tree and then we
fixed the house.

We left the door of the Baby's room closed because she
was having her nap, but we opened all the other windows
and doors and put the meat into the Cats' room and shut
the cat's in, but I knew they'd get out the window. We got
the curtains down in our bedroom by standing on the
bookshelf. The house didn't smell much any more with the
meat gone from the kitchen, and we closed off the Cats'
room and the Poo room, and there was a breeze blowing in
through the front door and down the passage.

It was getting darker so we sat in the kitchen and lit one
of the candles we had found. I made Rick shut the front
door and I shut the back one and we looked through the
cupboards to see what to have for tea. There were tins and
packets and some of them were no good, but we found a
tin opener and had corn flakes and peaches for tea, sitting
up at the table while it got darker and darker outside.

When we had finished I said 'Now Rick, you have to take
the baby's dinner up and Bit has to go too.' I made another
bowl of cornflakes and peaches and lit another candle and
sent Rick and Bit off with them.

I went over to the window and looked out. I couldn't see

much in the dark. I got out a peppermint and ate that while I waited for Rick and Bit to come back.

When they did, I saw the bowl was still the same and the baby hadn't eaten any. 'She didn't want it,' said Rick, 'and she couldn't talk.' Bit was clinging onto him and her eyes were staring up at me. 'The baby,' she whispered. 'The baby wouldn't eat its dinner.'

'Well she's a naughty naughty baby then,' I told them, 'and she'll have to be punished.' Bit burst into tears. 'It's a yukky horrible baby and I hate it.' Well, I smacked Bit then because she mustn't say that. 'It's our own baby,' I said. 'And you have to be nice.'

I took the bowl from Rick, and Bit sat on his knee. 'I'm going up to see her,' I said, 'and she's in big trouble if she doesn't eat this. I'm Dad, remember, and everyone has to do what I say.' Rick gave me the candle and the two of them watched me go and I knew they thought I was brave.

I stomped up the passage and went into our Bedroom, opposite the Baby's room. The big chairs were where we had moved them to make our bed, and the curtains were on the floor and the black window was bare.

'What's this about not eating your tea?' I shouted. 'You naughty bad baby, how are you going to grow big and strong if you don't eat?' Then I waited for a minute. 'That's right,' I said, 'you do what Daddy says.' And I tipped the bowl up in the corner behind one of the chairs and went back down to the kitchen.

The other two hadn't even moved. 'It's all right,' I told them. 'She changed her mind and ate it.' I put the empty bowl on the table and sat down.

Rick said 'What will we do now?'

'You two have to wash the dishes.'

They both said no, so I said 'OK live like a pig. See if I care.'

'You got that from Daddy,' said Rick.

I jumped up and hit him hard across the face. 'You shut up! I *am* Daddy. *He's* not. He's Trish's dad, and Rosy and Roger and Katy, and we never have to go back there again. So now I'm Daddy. All right? All right?'

'You're not him,' said Rick quietly, and Bit said 'No!

You're not even him.' So I grabbed her by the hair and pulled her off Rick's knee onto the floor and sat on her. 'You've never even seen him,' I said, right up close to her face. 'How would you know what he looks like? You're only the baby and you don't know anything and you've never even seen our Dad. This is what he looks like.' And I jumped up and pointed to my self. Bit scrambled to her feet and said 'But I'm not the baby now. You said I wasn't. You said the baby's in the Baby's room,' then both of them looked up towards the passage.

I had forgotten all about the baby. For a second I even thought she would be standing there in the doorway, but I looked and she wasn't.

I took a breath and then I told Bit that if she didn't want to be a baby again she'd better not be stupid, and then I sat down in the seat. 'Are you going to be the wife then?' I asked her, and she nodded and put her thumb in her mouth. 'You too?' I asked Rick. But he said no, he didn't want to be a wife anymore because that was girls' stuff, and that he'd be a policeman. 'OK then,' I said, after a minute. 'You be my son who's a policeman. And now we're a proper family — Dad, Mum, son and baby.'

'What about me?' said Bit.

'You're Mum,' I told her. 'I said that.'

She started to cry quietly. 'But you just said I was the wife.'

I put her on my knee and wiped her face. 'Silly,' I said. 'It's the same thing. Everyone knows that.' She sniffed a few times but she wasn't crying anymore. 'What do I do?'

I jiggled her on my knee. 'Oh, mostly just look after the baby.' I looked at her face and her eyes went wide.

'I don't want to.'

'It's OK,' I said, 'because Rick's a policeman and he always comes and helps you. Anyway,' I took her off my knee and stood up. 'We'd better check on the cats and go to bed.'

We took a candle and went up the passage to the Cats' room. 'You better watch out,' I said when we stopped outside the door. 'They might be ferocious and there's all bad meat in there.'

Bit, who was holding my hand, scrunched up her face, but Rick opened the door and went in.

The cats had all jumped out the window. Some of the bad meat was still there — it was the bone part and it stank — but most of the meat had been torn off it. 'Don't worry,' I said. 'They're not far away.'

Then Bit wanted to look in the Poo room. 'You've already seen it,' I said. 'Why do you want to go in?' And she said 'I have to go.' So I let her in and she crouched under the table and did a poo.

Back in our bedroom we made a bed from the cushions in the big chairs and the curtains folded up for blankets.

'Shouldn't we say goodnight to the baby?'

'No,' I said. 'The baby will be asleep now.'

'Why isn't there a television?'

'Because there's no electricity, silly.'

'Why?'

'Because nobody must've paid the bill.'

'Why?'

'Go to sleep.'

'Rick?'

'What?'

'Are you crying?'

'No.'

'Can I have more blankets?'

'No. Go to sleep.'

'I'm not tired.'

'Yes you are.'

'I'm not.'

'Sssssh.'

We lived there — Dad and Mum and the son and the baby. Sometimes the baby wouldn't eat her dinner and then I would have to go up and make her, like on the first night.

We ate up most of the tins from the cupboard and I didn't have any peppermints left. The cats never went away and there was always one or two running through the house.

Sometimes a car would drive past on the road, and if we were down at the creek I would have to get Rick and Bit back inside the house so nobody would see us, because even if they had forgotten I hadn't, and I knew if anyone found us we would be in big trouble for killing that dog.

One day we were chasing two cats through the house. Bit and Rick had one cornered in the kitchen and it was yowling and they were trying to poke it with a broom. The other one scooted up the passage and I followed it but I couldn't see where it went. I stopped near the front door for a second. I should have gone into our Bedroom, but for some reason I opened the door of the Baby's room. A cat can't go through a shut door, I know, but somehow I didn't think of that.

And there I was, standing in the Baby's room again. There was a bad smell and it was dark, but I could see her, still lying in bed just like the first time. Her head was on the pillow and she was asleep. I went up to her slowly and stood right beside the bed. Her mouth was open and I could see her tongue fallen sideways. It reminded me of the dog when it lay across our knees in the car, and its tongue hung right out, only it was wet and red and hers was hard looking and kind of grey. Her face was very very white and wrinkled all over like a peach pip.

Her hands lay down beside her. I could see that her fingernails were blue and I wondered why they were, and the nails had grown like claws curving round and I wondered why they did that. The knuckles were big and square and some of the fingers were bent sideways.

Then one of the hands moved.

I looked up at her face, and her eyes were wide and staring at me. Her mouth was opening and shutting but nothing was coming out. The hand lifted up, waving in the air, and then suddenly grabbed my arm, and at the same time she started rising up, trying to sit, her head coming up and her mouth opening and shutting and her eyes staring at me.

I swung my other arm and hit her in the neck, and I pulled my arm from her claws, and she sank back onto the bed. Her eyes were shut and her tongue waggled sideways in her mouth.

'Close your mouth,' I said, but she didn't, so I covered

her mouth with my hand. I couldn't stand to see the tongue. I could feel the hard gums through her lips, and I thought she's got no teeth. Her tongue was poking my hand from the inside. Her eyes opened again and one arm swung up and touched me and then dropped back. I looked up at the ceiling. It was dark up there and I thought there must be spiders.

Her tongue had stopped poking me. I took my hand away and wiped it on the blankets even though it wasn't wet.

'Shut your eyes,' I said, but she wouldn't. 'Shut your eyes!' So I smacked her. Still she wouldn't shut her eyes so I shut them and they stuck shut. I smacked her again. That made me shout. 'You're a bad baby and you have to do what I say.'

There was a blanket folded at the bottom of the bed so I stretched it over her. 'We don't want you to get cold,' I said, but she wouldn't speak and didn't even look at me. 'You're a bad baby,' I said, and pinched her face. I ran out of the room and slammed the door, and went straight to our Bedroom.

There was the cat, behind a chair, eating a pile of old wet cornflakes.

When the weather was hot we swam in the creek in the shade of the big trees. It was cold there, but we could play chasey or climb one of the trees, which hung right over the water. I could climb the highest, but sometimes Rick could get nearly as high and we would fight each other with sticks.

One day Bit was asleep inside the house and Rick and I were up in the tree. I was standing on the highest branch I could get to, and holding onto the one above with one hand and my stick with the other. Rick was three branches below me, poking at me with his stick. Then he poked me hard in the leg and I nearly lost my balance. I didn't yell. I just looked down at him and he stopped poking for a second, looking up at me. And then I screamed. I dropped my stick and pointed over his shoulder and yelled 'Look out! Look out! It's the dog! The dog's going to get you!'

194

With both hands he grabbed behind his back, and tried to turn, and his eyes shot wide open and his mouth went wide and he started to slip. His hands still grabbed at nothing and his feet slid each side of the branch till he went thump! sitting on it. He made a kind of sigh and then tipped sideways off the branch and his face turned towards me and his eyes went to mine and he still didn't scream. I leant forward and watched him. He hit all the branches on the way down. It was a long way. He dropped off the last branch and fell into the creek, and drifted down, and around the bend, and then I couldn't see him anymore.

When I went back inside and Bit woke up, she asked me where Rick was.

'Gone to the shops,' I said, and she only ever asked me a few times after that.

I remember what a hot day it was when the car came, and that's why Bit and I were by the creek, sitting in the shade with our feet in the water. You could just hear something coming over the hill.

'Quick,' I said. 'Inside.'

So we ran in the back door and up the passage to the Bedroom, and peeped out the window to watch the car go past.

'Why do we have to hide?' said Bit, and I said 'Ssh. I've told you. It's because of the dog.' 'But that was ages ago,' she said, and she was grizzling. 'You shut up,' I told her.

Not many cars used to come along the road. Only about one or two a week and they always kept going straight past. But this car, this car slowed down as it got to the bridge.

'It's stopping,' said Bit.

'No it's not, stupid,' I said. 'It's only going slow for the bumps.'

We didn't say anything as the car went slower and slower, and then we watched as it pulled up outside the house.

'It is stopped,' said Bit. 'It's stopped here.'

I said 'Ssh. Don't move.'

We kept watching. Two men got out. They looked pretty funny — they had black suits on. One of them had some papers and a book in his hand. He said something to the other man but we couldn't hear. They both looked at the house.

'Go away,' I whispered. 'Please go away.'

But they didn't. They came through our garden gate and up the verandah steps, and the one with the papers in his hand knocked on the door, and then they both stood back and waited.

They were so close now we could hear them talk. The one without the papers said 'I don't think so. Looks deserted.' The other man said 'Just wait.' They knocked again. They didn't say anything more but they both kept looking around. I had my hand over Bit's mouth so she wouldn't say anything, and she was grabbing me. The man with the papers said 'Let's try round the back,' and they went down the steps and around the side of the house.

I took my hand off Bit's mouth and she whispered 'They'll find us.' 'They won't come in the house,' I said. 'It's OK.' So we waited.

We heard them knock at the back door for a while, and I thought, now they'll go away.

But they didn't. They came in. When we heard them in the kitchen we crawled behind one of the big chairs. They were calling out and talking to each other and looking at things.

And then they were in the passage and we could hear what they were saying. They were talking about filth and we heard them look in the Cats' room and then the Poo room, and then they went quiet. They came up the passageway. Bit's eyes were squeezed shut and she kept twitching. I heard one of them open the door of the Baby's room just as the other one came right into our room, and then they both said 'God' at exactly the same time, which made me giggle.

Mrs Haddaway had all her friends there when the police came and I was glad about that because Mrs Haddaway and her friends didn't seem to think we had done anything wrong, and I was pretty sure the police would want to arrest us if we weren't careful.

All the ladies had cups of tea and biscuits and cake, and

Bit and I were all dressed up and clean and we could eat as much cake as we liked. They talked about us all the time and I think they thought we couldn't hear them.

One of them said 'I understand there was a woman there?' And Mrs Haddaway said 'Oh my goodness. That poor soul was dead, and really, she had been for quite some time.' Another lady said 'You mean the children were living in the house with a corpse?' and Mrs Haddaway nodded. 'The poor poor dears,' and all the ladies said 'Oh yes, poor dears, so young, what a shame,' and Mrs Haddaway said 'And only a scrap of food, and awful cats all over the house, and the most terrible, terrible —' and she stopped and put her hankie to her nose. Then they all started up again so I gave Bit some more cake and had another piece myself.

One lady said 'Do you suppose they will ever get over it? The shock . . .' and they all started talking at once and that was when the police came. I thought there would be a whole lot of them and all in uniform, but there was only one man and he just had ordinary clothes on and he didn't look like a policeman at all, he just looked worried.

Mrs Haddaway said 'This is Mr McClintock, children, and he's a policeman, but you mustn't be frightened.'

'I'm not frightened,' I said. 'I used to have a son who was a policeman.'

Everyone looked at each other except Mr McClintock who looked at his feet.

I stood up. 'I had a son who was a policeman and a baby who died and a wife,' and I pointed at Bit who said nothing, only opened her eyes wide.

We stayed with Mrs Haddaway for a week or so, and it was all right. We could eat lots of everything and do what we liked and she didn't even make us do chores.

One day Mr McClintock came back.

Mrs Haddaway was at the door saying 'Oh how marvellous. How did you find out?' I couldn't hear everything he said but I heard 'announcement' and 'shopkeeper'. Then I heard him say 'She thought there were three of them but she must have been mistaken.'

Mrs Haddaway bent down to us and said 'Do you hear that children? You're going home. Isn't that wonderful?'

Mrs Haddaway came in the police car too. I recognised the roads after a while. We came over a little hill, and yes, there was the car. I shut my eyes.

Mr McClintock said 'That bomb was there when I came past weeks ago,' and then he started to slow down.

Mrs Haddaway said 'Don't you think we should get straight on? The family will be waiting.' But Mr McClintock said 'I won't be a minute. I just want to check it. Hang on.' And he stopped the car and got out.

I kept my eyes shut and held onto Bit's hand. Then I heard Mr McClintock say 'Oh Hell' and I opened my eyes and Mrs Haddaway got out and went to Mr McClintock who was staring into my stepfather's car, and then Mrs Haddaway said 'Ohh' and covered her mouth and walked away.

I got out and went to look into the car. Mr McClintock tried to stop me but I saw in, and there was Trish and Rosy and Katy still waiting for their Dad — all huddled together, and a funny colour, and covered in flies, and flies everywhere all over the car.

When we got home only my stepfather and Roger were there. There was no one else. There were things all over the yard and my stepfather locked himself in the garage and wouldn't talk to Mr McClintock who banged on the door, and Roger just cried and cried and Mrs Haddaway said 'Poor mite' and picked him up and tried to make him stop.

Bit and I sat down on the old car seat. It was mouldy and rotten and there were things living in it.

'Where's Mum?' she said.

'Silly,' I told her. 'That's you, remember?'

Judith Lukin

Judith Lukin was born and grew up in Brisbane, but is now a Sydney-sider. For 10 years she was a bookseller, completing the Arts/Communications degree in writing and literature at NSW Institute of Technology. Presently visiting Melbourne, she works as a book reviewer, freelance writer/editor, and research officer. Her greatest pleasures are reading and travelling. Judith has had several short stories published and continues to write fiction.

Judith. 510 pieces

er gaze, after the act, is gloriously self contained. The right arm held across the belly, a hand resting intimately in his hair. Because of the frame, his unlovely head is almost hidden, resting into her side under the left breast. In the fragment of his face this much perhaps shows: wistfulness, secretiveness; peace.

Now that it's done there's no movement. She is statuesque. Luminous and fearsome. Her fine pale fingers on his severed head are bloodied. The left hand, supporting the basket which holds the head, is hidden. She bears the head as though it were a chalice.

On the morning of departure she traced her image in the dust of the mirror, her finger pursuing the arch of eyebrows, the stretch of lips, the rush of hair. Beneath the glass, oil and scent jugs waited, ashen with years of unuse, and gold ornaments gleamed faintly.

She touched her face, the skin now dry with thirst and longing for the oils, that caress of moisture after so much of the ruthless sun and a pitiless age of sackcloth. Behind her, framing her reflection whitely, her husband's deathbed yawned.

These men will strip the whole country bare: the high mountains, the valleys, and the hills will never be able to bear the burden of them . . . The Assyrian came from the mountains of the north; his armies in myriads.

For three years and four months before the coming of Holofernes and his swarming armies, on the barren rooftop of their silken bedroom, disguised even from herself by widow's garb, fasting and praying, Judith had circled this one image: the face of her husband Manasses wearing exactly the same look in death as it had in lovemaking.

An unadorned intensity of gaze as he came into her, and

200

as he died on the white bed with gold barley beads still pressed into his cheek, a mark, they said, of the sun-stroke that killed him. Throughout the afteryears of formalised wasting, the pressure, gentleness, and concentration of that look moved violent and eloquent in her belly.

She bears the head as though it were a chalice. It is a jigsaw puzzle.

On the outside of the box, the smaller reproduction shows what the picture will look like when it's put together. The package says, 'Judith. 510 pieces.'

The putting together of jigsaw puzzles helps to pass the time, now that time is here only to be passed. Rooms burgeon with slow days, each heavier with the rosary of those behind.

Outside, like the dream of a distant land, the waterless city throbs hotly day and night. Noon drifts through the grey of drawn curtains, and in sickly warm beds at night, women wake and cannot remember the names of men who lie beside them.

Anyone who's familiar with this painting will know that its name is not only 'Judith.' In gold, on the arch over her head, the inscription will read, 'JUDITH and Holofernes.'

The white bed glowed in the airy room, and Judith longed for the feeling of a man between her legs. In the mirror she saw that the unsensuous heat of mourning had worn her, that her flesh threatened to become ashes burying youth in wasted poignancies.

Always quiet at noon, the streets outside were vibrant now with the silence of fear and desire. The dry throat of the sky shimmered expectantly and Judith pulled the rough sackcloth over her head and off at last, marvelling that by virtue of her people's fear of violation, only in the light of this disaster could she be naked.

His armies in such myriads surrounded them that the citizens of Bethulia came to the end of their supplies of water. The children were lifeless, the women and young men faint with thirst. They collapsed in the streets and gateways . . . Throughout the town there was deep dejection.

From the bitter rooftop in the heat of day and the whispering cold of night, Judith had seen the people of Bethulia put on sackcloth, ashes and prostration in defence of the town against seige. They moaned, begging and blackmailing God; keeping vigil.

Still pervaded by Manasses' gaze, the rags of grief and prayer nevertheless suddenly seemed pitiful, without hope. Inappropriate. For thirty-four nights in the roof shelter Judith had listened to the feasting of Holofernes' great army, had seen the circle of joyful fires burning around the walls of Bethulia, had watched the suppliant faces within give up, excusing themselves with mourning.

For those who'd rather it was Salome, the inscription reads, 'JUDITH and Holofernes.' And in all 510 fragments the only mild touch will be the closed curve of Holofernes' one visible eye. Not for Klimt the soft and humble Judith of Boticelli, Michelangelo, Rembrandt, Caravaggio, and countless others working in peachy hues of pink and russet.

Her gaze is that of a woman in the full flight of her sensuality, abundant with the power of having destroyed an illusion. She presides at the altar of iconoclasm.

Naked in the light of this disaster, she stood before the mirror washing in water granted like gold by the elders for her cleansing. Gently her hands moved with the soft cloth, skin awash and coolly seduced by streams of water.

Her long dead and forbidden nudity revived, and the arms and thighs, shoulders, neck and breasts of a young strong woman emerged shining. In the drift of light through drawn curtains Judith washed her hair slowly, immersing face and head last. She thought of this man Holofernes, whose name came thrusting before him like a sword. She felt her hair soften, drying between her fingers, and rejoiced in his fate, singular and final, of knowing her only by her body.

The elders had sworn to surrender the town to the Assyrians after five days. They said to her, 'Throughout your life we have all

recognised your good sense and the soundness of your judgement.
But the people were desperate with thirst and compelled us to make
this promise and to pledge ourselves by an oath we may not break
. . . You are a devout woman . . . Go with our blessing, and may
God be with you to take vengeance on our enemies.' So they left the
roof shelter.

Shamed, excusing themselves their weakness with the
downcast eyes of mourning and powerlessness, the elders
had crowded and bent in the roof shelter, shrinking from
the dry blade of the sun. Modestly, ably, they avoided the
straw pallet and sordid years of widowhood, and desiring
and despising her, they were proud of their own respect
for this living memorial to Manasses. Unpossessable, she
was yet their subject and their history. Set apart, prohibited thus, she was yet possessed by their will.

They had all watched her. The rites of government in-
clude at the last resort the privilege of not knowing. Old,
ashy, crinkled, they observed jealously the pristine curve of
her throat, requiring for this deliverance by her hand only
that she be cleansed and masked by her famous expression
of devoutness. Under God's sun that had so wisely mar-
tyred her husband, their skin ran like wax. Beneath the
muttered surface of formalities they had weighed the liquid currency of virtue against the rape of Bethulia; and
found virtue wanting.

The odour of cardboard lingers among the 510 pieces. At
the altar of iconoclasm she is invincible, castrating finally
even the artist. One fragment a nipple, a piece of gold,
there a part of the smile. Seeking perhaps to make a sexual
object of luxuriant pride, Klimt has overweened himself
and in the click-click of preoccupied suburban hours he
himself becomes the severed head in her hands.

Beyond his intentions the sense of smell is evoked. She is
clouded in the bitter fragrances of blood and sex, exceed-
ing the pastels of mere picturing. Artist and voyeur are
reproduced within the embrace of her scent and touch
simply as the cypher of impotence.

In drifts of light and thirsty cities the pieces slide and

kaleidoscope into place. Printed by the thousand, smashed into jigsaws, the image shapes and reshapes into a continuity of disconnections. The whole remains. Gold, mauves, and fulsome skin. Judith. The gaze after the act.

His mortal pleasure, to know her finally by her body. Naked on the great white bed she rested, revelling in the freshness of her new body. Skin bright after washing. An image of the desert burnt hotly in her forehead. Dry, expansive, more final than the heat of this town. Origin and ending. The white sheets also fresh. Newly on the bed, the fabric brushed gently against her flesh. White being the mystic colour, translating mourning shrouds into bridal veils.

She lay in the unfamiliar haze of her whole body's breathing. Desire rippled, quietly yet, through bones and veins. In the powdery heat she slept a little, moving luxurious and slow in her dreams. The straight light hovered, herald of night in Holofernes' bed. Delighting in sensual suspension, she turned in the bed, watched through the window the undulations of sky.

The men of the town watched her until she had gone down the hill-side and crossed the valley, and then they lost sight of her. An Assyrian outpost seized Judith, then Holofernes' bodyguard and all his attendants came out and took her into the tent. He was resting on his bed under a mosquito net of purple interwoven with gold, emeralds, and precious stones. When Judith was announced he came out into the front part of the tent, with silver lamps carried before him. He and his attendants were amazed at the beauty of her face as she stood before them. Holofernes was beside himself with desire for her.

She would go down along the streets of Bethulia. Swift through the dust and resplendent as they would never have allowed her to be otherwise. Faces she hadn't seen for years watching, thirsty, from darkened doors, surprised in dusty abjection by the brilliance of their sacrificial lamb. A few wails would rise, flapping like carrion to meet her. In this way the old men waiting at the gate would mark her progress toward them.

The depiction of morality and the morality of depiction had always been their province. Now they would stand parched, attempting to appropriate, even at the gate, by authority. Within hearing of the enemy and walking distance of water, the sight of her would reduce them from rulers to chorus, jealous, dazzled blind by her consuming secret thirst.

In the light of their God and his merciless sun, they would praise her.

In the face of her appalling grandeur, the idea of jigsaws in her time is ridiculous. In godless sitting rooms we winnow the barren hours devotedly, meditating, piecing and piecing. As if it were our own life.

'Judith and Holofernes.' This painting is famous, but not popular. Ostensibly because of the severed head, the bloody subject; subtly it's her face, cruel and cunning some say, fearfully. In the splendid strength of her face the possibility of corruption and dissolution shocks. Those besieged by the domesticated hours look hopefully for the heroism of sweetness and sanity. This is what her gaze despises: the tame, the pious; passion is the only sacrament. Sweetness in this deed would be the province only of mad saints. The head of the beseiger cannot be gently cut off.

Nothing less than 500 pieces will do for the enthusiast. The smashing, fragmenting of awe-ful pictures characterises the age. The authority to create and uncreate her image assumes power over the idea of her. Towards this delusion — our corruption, dissolution, philistinism — she is stupendously indifferent. Rather than being reduced by fragmentation, she is strengthened. Each act of vandalism becomes yet another part in the total construction of her. And she grows, seeming to burn with the sensual fragrance of self-containment.

Gold choker and bracelets no longer contain her, worn now as they are like the incidental wounds of the past. Her vulnerabilities remain. Breast, navel, the secret parts of the body, soft still but strong with the refusal to be colonised. Explicit freedom.

She is faith restored. In her face and hands are regeneration, reshaping, and the purity of passion.

The severed head is the future.

The fragrance of unstoppered oils curled mustily delicious in the air. Hair and skin soaked up the rich slippery perfumes, ancient attars of ritual, scenting the arch of eyebrows, the stretch of lips, the rush of hair. Hands oiled her body, smoothly, hallowing skin. Seduction and desire moved on her lips. She longed for his body. The possession of him.

She lifted the black weight of hair away from her face and slid into the flowing silks of festivity, clasping anklets and bracelets like gilt around her bones, the great gold collar at the neck, anticipating his vulnerability. Anticipating the feeling of his rough skin and soft hair against her cheek.

She went to the bed-rail beside Holofernes' head and took down his sword, and stepping close to the bed she grasped his hair. 'Now give me strength, O Lord, God of Israel' she said; then she struck at his neck twice with all her might, and cut off his head.

Georgia Savage

Georgia Savage was born in Launceston, Tasmania and has spent most of her adult life in country Victoria where she has worked at many jobs ranging from tomato picking to the preparation of income tax returns. She now lives in Melbourne and is a full-time writer. As well as several short stories Georgia Savage has had two novels published, *The Tournament* (1983) and *Slate & Me and Blanche McBride* (1983). A new novel *The Estuary* will be released by the University of Queensland Press in October. She is currently working on a novel about street-kids living on the Gold Coast and wishes to write one more after that. Then, she plans to put herself out to permanent pasture somewhere in the country.

Irene

Soon after my mother died, I packed my things and went to live in her house at the Estuary. The sadness of leaving the Maryston Valley was softened by the fact that I'd been nuts about the house in Queensland since Irene bought it. A white stuccoed place with a flat roof, it stood in a wildly sloping garden facing the Pacific. Its windows were double-decker Queensland ones which opened outwards from the bottom. When they were all open they looked like wings and the house seemed ready to fly.

Inside, the floors were stained a soft Chinese green and scattered with rugs I'd known since childhood. In hot weather, pairs of panelled glass doors allowed the living area to be made into one vast room.

Every day about noon a breeze came in from the ocean bringing with it smells of salt and seaweed and sometimes frangipanni. The venetian blinds began to chime then and kept it up until the breeze dropped again at night.

Downstairs there was an extra bedroom, a lumber room and a laundry. In the lumber room, I found Irene's work table. I don't suppose she'd used it for years but I could remember when it was the focal point of our house in Brisbane.

Irene was a dress designer who specialised in bridal wear. Working long hours in the days when few married women had paid jobs, she more or less kept us. My father, Hal, who had a small army pension, didn't work at all.

The table I found in the lumber room used to stand bang in the middle of Irene's workroom. Scissors in hand, she'd walk around it eyeing a river of pearly satin which lay on it and fell from one end to form a lake on the floor. After several circuits she'd stand, one foot thrust forward, and concentrate on the material. Then she'd raise the scissors and move in. She always made the first cuts without the benefit of patterns or chalks or even a tape measure.

I'm certain the idea of making a mistake didn't occur to her and because of that she almost never did.

As a child I loved the workroom and longed to run my hands over the bolts of silks and satins which stood in the cupboard under the window. I also wanted to touch the spools of sewing thread, each sitting on a peg of its own in a wooden rack. I didn't dare. No one in the house but Irene touched anything in that room. Occasionally Bart was called in to help her do what she called 'finding the straight' on a length of material. I was never asked to help but I had my own workroom in a corner under the house where sunlight coming through the lattice made skinny diamond shapes on an old treadle sewing machine. The top of that machine was my cutting table and there I sliced into scraps of material while making Irene-remarks, such as 'On the bias from the hip', to my doll who sat watching.

I played there off and on until the Sunday Irene found her spools of thread thrown in a corner of the workroom with the wooden rack on top of them. I saw the mess of cream and pink and gold they made when I was hauled upstairs to be charged with doing it. To me the sight was so awful that while accusations flew around my head like lightning, I kept quiet. Some child-intuition told me that what had happened was part of the dark adult world to which things like my mother's migraines and the kidskin apron in my father's Masonic bag belonged. When sentenced to a month without mango ice-cream and trips to the cinema, I accepted it as a judgment on my inability to please Irene in any way at all. And I went outside still without defending myself.

If the person who *did* throw the spools on the floor ever owned up, I wasn't told. But touching the smooth old surface of Irene's table almost thirty years later it seemed obvious to me that a fit of unbearable frustration had caused one of my parents to do it. Whatever the case, my punishment tailed off during the first week and had ended by the second. The memory of that day stayed with me though, and I didn't ever go back downstairs to design clothes in the half-dark. Instead I played other games in the garden where the light was filtered through trees, not lattice.

The clothes Irene made were prized for their line and simplicity; the ones she wore herself were so perfect that at the age of nine I opted out of the race and started dressing as a boy. Hal was delighted at my sex-change and egged me on by taking me to his barber and having my hair cropped. Needless to say the wearing of khaki shirts and shorts was only bravado on my part. Whenever I was alone in the house I rushed to put on Irene's clothes and then posed and preened in front of the mirror.

Hal and Irene didn't sleep in the same room. My friends used to ask me about it with sly looks on their faces. I didn't understand why they were so interested and greeted the questions with a vacuity which must have astounded them. Apparently Hal was banned from the bedroom after my birth and if he visited Irene there it was in furtive dashes at night when Bart and I were asleep. One thing's certain, Hal hadn't lost his interest in women. He was mad about them. I think he was a flirt rather than a lover, but even my eyes which missed so much took in the fact that there was always some woman on the fringe of the family who was his buddy rather than Irene's.

About the time I started dressing as a boy, Hal's sister asked Irene to go into business with her. She wanted to open a shop in a swanky part of Sydney and make and sell clothes for small women. Irene, scenting a fortune, put our house on the market, but when Hal found out he flew into a temper and threatened to kill himself if she went ahead with the plan. Then he went away into the bush and hid at the place where he kept a few hives of bees. Bart and I were left at home in a state of terror while Irene searched the country roads in a taxi. At the end of the day Hal and Irene came home together. They were in unaccountably high spirits and the dress shop was never mentioned again.

In those days I was always pestering Hal to let me learn tap-dancing. As an art it wasn't socially acceptable in our circle and he held out against me for a long time. One afternoon when we were walking the dog in the park we met the local dancing teacher, Ettie Hayden. Ettie was tall and lithe with marvellous legs. A bit of her coat hem was hanging down and as I introduced her to Hal I prayed he

210

wouldn't notice. It was the kind of thing that put him off someone for life. Ettie shifted her chewing gum and gave Hal a smile. It was a stunner. Hal goggled at her, made a few feeble remarks about the weather then whistled his dog and got it to do some tricks. I was so ashamed of him I wanted to die, but I forgot it the next day when he took me to Ettie's studio and signed me up for a year's lessons. Part of the bargain, of course, was that Irene wasn't to be told.

Altogether I had tap-dancing lessons for two years. Ettie took a shine to me — I think my clothes amused her. Sometimes after the other kids had gone she let me stay and dance with her. The buzz I got from dancing with Ettie in the big bare studio with chairs stacked in the corners was something I never got over. It makes me grin even now to think of it.

Somewhere in the second year of my lessons Ettie and Hal started an affair. I doubt that it progressed much beyond whiskies in the local and a few feel-ups. Ettie had a nineteen-year-old lover in the Navy. He was a good ten years younger than she, and had long dark eyes and a squashed Greek nose. Ettie was nuts about him and I guess she egged Hal on mainly for laughs. Whatever the case she was indiscreet enough to call at our house one day wearing a new fox coat and strappy shoes. Irene answered the door and that was the end of the dancing lessons. The end of me too for that matter. At the start of the next term I was sent to boarding school and for several years I spent my holidays at my grandmother's.

Grandma had a hotel at a place called Ely in the mountains. Ely was not much more than the pub, the butter factory and a few houses. It was a wet green place with shadows that closed in on it soon after lunch. Dozens of little trails let away into the forest and every half mile or so there was a fast-running creek.

In her heyday I think Grandma was even better looking than Irene. The things I remember of her are smooth olive skin and sombre eyes which occasionally lit up and knocked the breath out of you. She had only a yardman and a kitchen-maid to help her run the hotel, so she often worked an eighteen-hour day. In the afternoons she worked in the garden; she said pottering there saved her sanity. She trained fruit trees to stand like Picasso figures against the back wall of the pub and she looked after a hive of bees Hal had given her. Every so often she put on leather gloves and a beekeeper's hat and after quietening the bees with a gadget which belched smoke, she took frames of wax-capped honey from the hive. In the kitchen she'd uncap the honey with a hot knife and let me have a mouthful of honey and wax. She was gentle, patient and kind. I should have been happy with her but I was not. I waited all the time for Irene to swoop down on us in a taxi and take me home. I imagined we'd arrive in high spirits the way she and Hal had done after his suicide threat. I thought she'd make up for my banishment by making me wonderful clothes and buying me sarsaparilla spiders. Of course none of it happened and I stayed at Grandma's.

To console myself, I used the upstairs veranda of the pub as a stage and spent a lot of time up there dancing. Nobody bothered me, least of all my grandmother. Occasionally, a drunk leaving the hotel in daylight would see me and send up some applause. Then, humiliated, I'd leap through the nearest window and hide until he'd gone.

Practically the only books Grandma had were the Scarlet Pimpernel ones. I read them over and over and when I wasn't dancing on the veranda I was rescuing French aristocrats from the guillotine. I did most of my rescuing at night when Grandma was busy in the bar. Her deaf white cat, Albert, usually played the part of the Dauphin.

One night as I stepped from the fire-escape with Albert buttoned inside my duffel coat, a hand grabbed the back of my collar. I was dragged a few steps, then spun around to face the street light. Albert leapt out of my coat and rushed back to the hotel. I wasn't frightened, merely furious that someone had taken such a liberty with me.

I glared at the man who'd grabbed me, but before I could speak, he said 'Ah, it's the androgynous child who dances on the balcony.' His voice fitted so perfectly into my Scarlet Pimpernel adventure that my anger died and I stood gaping at him. It was Max Tischler, the Austrian sculptor who lived in the next valley. I'd seen him now and then in the hotel buying bottles of wine. His European clothes and haunted white face fascinated me but when I asked Grandma about him she fobbed me off by saying, 'Don't worry about him. He's not a person for little girls to be interested in.' After that, I was even more fascinated. In time, by asking discreet questions in the kitchen, I learned a lot about him. He'd come to Ely after being involved in some sort of trouble in the city. No one knew exactly what the trouble was and at first the locals accepted him with the silent watchfulness they kept for all strangers. But Max Tischler had the kind of stunning good looks gangsters have in French movies, so it wasn't long before the Ely CWA ladies invited him to talk to them about art.

Max turned up for the talk with a pottery uterus under his arm. Inside it was a clay foetus surrounded by briny fluid. During the talk Max told the ladies that for the past eighteen months he'd sculpted nothing but uteri. Then he handed the one he'd brought with him to the nearest member of the audience and asked her to examine it and pass it along the row. Marie, Grandma's kitchen-maid, told me the uterus went along the row as if it were red hot, but when it reached the wife of the Methodist minister, she baulked and drew back her hands. The sculpture fell on the floor and smashed.

Coolly, Max stepped forward. He picked up the foetus and bowing slightly handed it to the woman. 'Congratulations,' he said 'you've just given birth.'

That night the CWA meeting was closed without supper being served and from then on Max was pretty much ostracised in Ely.

Marie told me that he went away a lot and seemed to have dozens of visitors from the city. When I insisted on details, all she could tell me was that the visitors were a weird mixture, from fat rich men in big cars to European peasants who tried to buy horse flesh at the local butcher's shop. She did tell me though that Max often worked for two or three days without stopping to sleep, and she hinted that he couldn't have done it without the help of some drug. In those days I knew very little about drug-taking and what I did know was somehow confused with thoughts of lovers exhausting each other with kisses in twilit rooms and things like the scent of Jamaican lilies. To find myself face to face with someone who'd tasted such delights was too much for me. The look on my face must've amused him because he laughed, then he said, 'What were you doing on the fire-escape? Running away? Why don't you run to my place? I'll hide you.' He was only a small man but his voice was rich and full — what Irene called a stagey voice. It broke the spell for me. 'Don't be stupid,' I said, and, like Albert shot towards the hotel.

The next morning I looked up androgynous in the dictionary. I couldn't find it and asked my grandmother what it meant. She frowned and said, 'I don't know.' She was making pastry and looked up from her floury hands to ask, 'Where did you hear it?'

But by then I was on my way outside. 'At school, I think,' I shouted over my shoulder.

From then on I began to spy on the valley where Max Tischler lived. I went there every day. I didn't go by road; instead I cut across the spicy bush behind the hotel and climbed the hill which separated our valley from his. At first I merely hung around the trees at the top of the hill but gradually I began to work my way down the slope. Halfway down I found a flat place where I could lie and watch Max's cottage. It was half hidden by a ragged cloud of almond trees but I had a clear view of the barn he used as a studio. Sometimes I saw Max moving between the buildings and sometimes I saw him washing clothes in a dish on the back veranda then throwing them over a fence to dry.

He caught me as I suppose I'd meant him to. He came up behind me as I examined some carving on a rock I'd picked up. It was of two foetuses curled around each other like Yin and Yang.

'Do you like it?' he said, and I, copying the CWA ladies, dropped the rock as if it'd burnt me.

He laughed, not a stagey laugh but one of real amusement. Then he bent down and picked up the rock and looked at it himself.

'I've been watching you,' he said, 'getting a little closer

every day. It was like watching a deer come for an apple.'
He looked up quickly and studied my face.

I went red and could think of nothing to say.

'You haven't told me if you like the carving.'

I nodded.

'Then keep it. I did it for you.'

'I wouldn't be allowed to,' I blurted the words and he put
his head back and laughed a laugh which was big and
stagey but full of amusement as well. 'Come along,' he said,
and he turned away from me and began to walk downhill.
'I'll show you some more.'

Later when Irene asked me over and over why I went
with him, I had no way of telling her, so I kept quiet and
undoubtedly that damned me forever in her eyes.

The inside of Max's cottage was a mess. I think he'd
started to rebuild and redecorate all at once then given the
lot up as a bad job. It was a shock to me to learn that
anyone could live in such a way. Our house, Irene's house,
always looked like something from the pages of *Elegant
Living*, and God help anyone human enough to leave the
newspaper on the sitting-room floor. At Max's the wall
between the two main rooms had been partly demolished.
Plaster dust and bricks lay in a pile on the floor. He'd
started to paint one of the other walls but stopped halfway.
At the back of the sink he'd begun to put old-fashioned
tiles; that job too had been abandoned. There were two
tables, one covered with plates and dishes, the other with
art materials and a dozen or so foetuses. The only orderly
thing in the room was the mantelpiece which had nothing
on it but two candlesticks and a painting of someone shot
full of arrows. It was impossible to tell if it was a man or a
woman and, in spite of the arrows, it was grinning like a
lunatic.

'Did you do that?' I asked. Max was rushing around
straightening papers and shoving foetuses into a carton.
Without looking up he asked what I meant.

'The painting. The one over the fireplace.'

'No.'

'Who did?'

Instead of answering my question, Max threw the carton

under the sink then rubbed his hands briskly. 'What do you want to do?' he said, 'stay here or go over to the studio?'

'I don't mind.'

'Then we'll stay here by the fire and I'll do some drawings of you.'

I nearly fainted with pleasure.

'Yes, that's it,' said Max. 'I'll dress you up and draw you.' He shot through the gap in the wall and was back in a moment with a soldier's tunic, 'Go into the bedroom and put this on.'

I took the tunic and looked at it. 'It's too big.'

'I know. It'll look wonderful. Wait, I'll get you some shoes,' and he dived at a carton in the corner and began to pull things out of it — a bent peacock feather, a striped jumper, a postcard so old it was yellow, then a pair of high-heeled silver sandals.

As I took the sandals, I said, 'I'll look crazy.'

'No, you won't. You'll look divine. Go into the bedroom. I promise not to peek.'

For some reason the word 'peek' worried me. It wasn't a word my family used. In fact I don't think I'd ever heard anyone use it. For a moment a doubt about what I was doing went through my mind, but it passed and I took the things and went through the gap into Max's bedroom. To my surprise it was neat and quietly furnished. The bed and wardrobe were made of solid dark wood and the material used for the curtains and bedcover was the kind of soft floral my grandmother liked. On the wall above the bed was a row of drawings of children. They were framed in gold and mounted on pale green watered taffeta. The room was so charming I forgot my dislike of the word 'peek' and forgot too about the lunatic grinning from the kitchen mantelpiece.

'Hurry up' called Max from the other room, 'put the jacket on and the shoes as well.'

I stood in front of the cheval mirror and got into the tunic. It was certainly too big. The sleeves hid my hands and the hem came halfway down my thighs, covering my own clothes.

'I look crazy' I shouted, 'I knew I would.'

Max came through the hole in the wall. 'No, you don't,' he said, 'you look the way I want you to,' and he knelt and helped me into the sandals.

I looked at myself again and repeated, 'I look crazy.'

'No' said Max, 'you look beautiful.'

'That's not true.'

'You have something more than beauty, Vinnie — something else. Later, a lot of men will see it but they won't know what it is.' I was listening to his voice rather than his words. It was soft and throaty, not his big stage voice at all. Noticing the way I was watching him, he gave a shout of laughter, sprang to his feet, grabbed my arm and said, 'Come on. Out of the bedroom. I want you to stand by the fire so the buttons on the jacket shine.' And he took me back to the fireplace and posed me there.

'While I work, I'll give you something to listen to.' Max wound up a gramophone so old it had a fancy tin trumpet on it. 'Melba singing the Butterfly aria.'

I hadn't heard Melba's voice but the one on the record was so thin and cracked I didn't believe it was hers. I was about to tell Max so when he said, 'Don't move. I'm drawing you.'

'I feel a fool.'

'It doesn't matter.'

'I don't know where to put my hands.'

'I can't see them.' Max gave another shout of laughter.

He did several drawings of me then let me look at them. I was disappointed. I'd expected to look like a fashion model, instead I saw a shadowed sexless creature wearing bomb-shelter clothes.

Max wasn't offended when I said so. He merely shook his head and said, 'You've got a lot to learn, Vinnie, but if you like I'll do a pretty one of you to take home and hide.'

He found me an old wine glass to hold. It was rose pink and had a chip in it. After he'd given it to me, he stood beside me and made a noise in his throat — a kind of European chirrup. Later I was to realise there was a sexual implication in the sound but at the time I took no notice. I was too busy staring at the frantic face of my grandmother looking through the window.

So I went home with Irene after all. We didn't go in a taxi, we went in the car with Hal. No one spoke. Once Hal tried to sing. He started 'Danny Boy', but when he came to the bit, 'From glen to glen and down the mountain-side', his song died of embarrassment. Irene sat with her feet together and eyes looking straight ahead. As for me, I watched the country go by with eyes that were hot and gritty from tears I'd been unable to cry.

Grandma had marched me barefoot back to the hotel and telephoned my mother. She arrived with Hal three hours later. She was dressed in an elegant black suit and had a little cravat of white at her throat. It looked like a judge's outfit. The first thing she did when she saw me was rush across Grandma's sitting-room and stab her foot into my shin. 'You slut,' she said. Then more slowly, 'You slut.'

I was horrified. To me a slut was someone like Patsy Garner who lived out on the road to the tip with a troop of fatherless children she couldn't be bothered feeding let alone keeping clean. I didn't answer Irene then or later. All the time she was packing my clothes and railing at me, I watched with eyes that were hot and dry, and didn't say a word.

Irene threatened to go to the police about Max but I knew she wouldn't. Hal, like me, said nothing; in fact he pretended the row wasn't happening and went outside to look at Grandma's bees. When we were leaving, Grandma tried to hug me but I pulled away from her. I thought she'd betrayed me and I felt that way for years.

After that I stayed at home with Hal and Irene. They didn't send me back to boarding school. Instead, I went to day classes like the rest of my friends. For some reason Irene started being nice to me. No, that's not quite right, she was both benevolent and condescending towards me as if she felt she'd won some major victory. But being called a slut by her had left a mark on me which didn't go away, and in four years time when I was old enough to go to dances I quickly became the wildest girl in my set as if determined to earn the title my mother had given me.

Carmell Killin

⚜

Carmell Killin was born in Brisbane in 1958 and
has a degree in Business Communications from the
Queensland Institute of Technology. She moved to
Sydney in 1979 and has worked in advertising, film
and television. Her short stories have been published in *Billy Blue*, *Australian Short Stories*, *Image*
and many other literary magazines, and included
in a couple of anthologies. Carmell Killin is currently waitressing to support her writing habit.

Vegetable Soup

Olive said it never happened. I said it did. Olive said it never happened, again, not being one for imagination, then added — prove it. Prove it, she said. The tart. The three-eyed tart. The three-eyed constipated tart. I do not have three eyes she said, convincingly, but it was beside the point. I couldn't prove it. The stupid little tart, I couldn't prove it and she knew it.

If I hadn't been the sweet child that I was I would have kicked that tart Olive in the leg until she fell over. But still I couldn't prove it.

I tried the calm approach. It's true Olive dear, why won't you believe me? Prove it, she said. I kicked her in the leg and she fell over, I had to don't you see? The tart wouldn't believe me. Sure, she believed the bit about me walking in the front door with the plate of soup but jeez why shouldn't she? Everybody in the whole damn street knew about the soup. The problem was she didn't believe the part *after* the soup, the most important part. If she wasn't my best friend I would have kicked her harder, the tart.

And something else. Not only didn't she believe the part *after* the soup she also didn't believe the part about the flavour. Couldn't have been pea soup, she said, because your mum only makes french onion. I was furious. What the hell would she know? I happen to know the difference between a french onion and a pea. For seven months of consecutive Sundays your mother has made french onion soup, she said, and you expect me to believe this once it was pea? Yes Olive. I expect you to believe that. But of course she didn't. It's outrageous, I can hardly contain myself. Anybody would think I was a liar. Age fourteen, barely out of braces, a rotten liar. But I'm not. Everything that happened on that Sunday actually did happen. Why doesn't the bitch believe me?

Is it because I'm plain and things like that don't happen to plain girls? Or is it because I'm wearing a new denim skirt and she's as jealous as all hell. I swear, I can't understand it.

I mean, the whole thing was so straightforward. I walked in the front door with the bowl of fresh pea soup, stepped over the dead man's body and barged into the vegetable's room. Now does that sound like a lie to you?

Okay, so maybe you're having trouble with the part about the dead man, but I swear it's true. It was Mr Tanhouser's house and that was Mr Tanhouser lying dead on the floor entertaining a few flies about his nostrils. I knew immediately he was dead. Some of the warm pea soup splashed onto the lino I remember and frightened the flies, but they were soon back. I called his name. Mr Tanhouser, Mr Tanhouser, I said and when he didn't answer I stepped over him, not spilling a drop mind you. What else could I have done?

Now here comes the interesting bit, the bit that Olive so boringly refuses to believe. I can't understand why. It was a perfectly normal thing to do. I just kept walking right on up that wooden staircase and into the vegetable's room. After all, the soup *was* meant for him. Mum would have bellowed at me if I'd returned home with a plate of cold, green slush.

It was still warm though when I reached his door. I kicked it open, gently, and walked straight in. The corpse downstairs made me bold.

At precisely this point in the story Olive drew in her foul breath and threw open her great staring gob as though she was the fearless one who had kicked open the door. For a moment there I had her. I really had her. Course, that's not her version. I never truly believed you for one minute, she said tartily, and then added, especially all that stuff about the gadgets.

But it was true. As true as my name is Eliza Creeber. This was no ordinary bedroom I'd barged into. I never once said it was ordinary Olive, I never once said that. No way. This was some weird bedroom, if you'd call it that even. It was more like the electrical goods department of David Jones when everybody has gone home and the machines decide to have a party. This party looked like it was just kicking off. The room was crammed alive with machines, gadgets, appliances all making quiet noises at each other. Incredible. Me and the pea soup stood in a trance in the doorway.

The first thing I noticed were the two pinball machines in the far corner. They flashed and pinged and buzzed at me. Smiling cowgirls swished their electric skirts and shifted their basketball breasts from side to side. Futuristic gladiators on the other pinging, buzzing machine were hurling nasty-looking objects. This wasn't at all like the pinball parlours on a Friday night full of mean, sweaty boys and frenzied stabbing noises. Nothing like it.

Next to the pinball machines was a giant Xerox copier flashing a green READY light and next to that an industrial clothes dryer, whirring, and next to that a gurgling expresso coffee machine like the ones in Italian cafes, and beside that a cold storage cabinet thing just like the deli's have, its shelves were bare but a light was glowing inside behind icy glass panels, and next to that, well, look I could go on forever. The whole room, I mean the *whole* room, was chocker with these machines and appliances and things I didn't even know the names of, big things with red and green lights that made chunking, clanging noises or smaller things that swished and rattled and had buttons for stopping and starting. They were all on, all of them, moving, flashing, vibrating, whirring quietly. I thought I had the wrong room. Well you would, wouldn't you? Me and the pea soup were just on the way out, had just stepped one pace backwards, when I saw him. The vegetable. Out of the corner of my eye. Propped up in a little wooden bed in the middle of it all.

Oh my god. It was him. The vegetable. Was it him? Was that really him? Had to be. Oh my god. I felt very peculiar. Finally, face to face with the vegetable. After all these months of pea soup visits and never once getting past the front door. Well, that's not quite true, once I did make it as far as the kitchen but that was only because Mr Tanhouser had been drying his underwear in the oven, terribly engrossed in it he must have been because he didn't even hear me yelling for him, so I barged in and found him there spreading a pair of Y-fronts on the top rack. He hissed when he saw me, the old fart. Bloody rude, I thought.

But now, in this weird dark room squinting at a lump in a bed, a vaguely human shape that I knew only as 'the vegetable'. Nothing of him moved. I took two giant steps closer, feeling bold all over again and slopped a fair portion of pea down the front of my t shirt and onto my brother's Addidas. I reached the edge of his bed offering him this uncontrollable grin and the rest of the green mush. Still nothing of him moved. Not a twitch even. I put the bowl on the edge of the bed next to his kneecaps. Then, I took a good proper look at him.

Well, if he wasn't the most beautiful vegetable I'd ever seen! I mean, *person* I'd ever seen. A man, actually. He must have been at least twenty. But he didn't look it, you know? You could tell he was old and that but he still sort of looked like a boy. I mean . . .

Shit. Now I'm getting all excited again, just like when I was telling this true story to my ex-best friend Olive. You're lying through your gums, she squeaked at me. I felt like twisting her scratchy, yellow hair round that great honk of hers. I am not lying, I assured her with one of my most terrifying faces, he was more beautiful than anything you'd ever see on Countdown.

And it was true. The vegetable was just a peach. I mean, gorgeous. You know. But in a scary sort of way. He just sat there with his eyes open, staring, like he was blind or mad or something. I knew he wasn't dead because his chest was moving under his blue and white striped pyjama top. Poor guy, never being allowed out of his pyjamas. I sort of felt depressed then.

Olive snorted at this point and screwed up her face, then spewed a big fat 'huh!' at me. I could have slapped her stupid. Instead I just clammed up, refused to speak to the dirty little brat and from then on I didn't tell her another word about the vegetable. I didn't tell her that he had exactly the same shiny black hair as Dan Bumper (this dreamboat who lives in Woollahra), or exactly the same colour eyes as Mick Jagger, and a gorgeous tan like the boys at Maroubra, and those little dots on his chin like my father sometimes has in the mornings.

Really, that's how close I got. I even, I actually ... touched his dots. Not in a dirty, sensual way. Not with passion in my fingertips. Hell no. I was just sitting on the edge of his bed, talking to him and stuff. It just happened, you know. It was perfectly natural.

I don't care what anybody thinks. I don't care what lies old fart face has been spreading and I know she's been spreading them because that's her nature. Tart. What would she know. She's never been in a boy's bedroom. Alone. In the dark.

Not that I was alone exactly, I mean with all those machines and stuff, but they don't count. Not really. If you don't count the machines it was just me and the vegetable, alone. It felt nice. It felt warm and safe and not the least bit strange. In the dark and that. Just me and the vegetable.

I waved my hand in front of his face the way they do in movies to test if people are blind. Nothing happened. So I leaned closer and said to him, are you in a coma? He didn't answer so I figured that's what it was. Actually I'd heard my mother use the word. I told him my name then and that I lived next door and that I was sorry he was in a coma.

I had to get close so he could hear me, I mean, maybe he was deaf. But I don't think so. I leaned right over and spoke very loudly into his ear. That's when I touched his dots. I couldn't help it. I just brushed his chin really quickly with my hand, so quickly it was all over before I realised what I had done, and it prickled. But a nice prickle, you know. He didn't seem to mind. He didn't seem to mind one bit. I'm not exaggerating, he was *gorgeous*. You just couldn't help but look at him. He stared back with his vacant Mick Jagger eyes.

We had quite a conversation then. I did the talking and he did the listening. It was really relaxed and natural, you know, like we'd known each other all our lives. He let me walk around the room and touch his machines. He let me pour myself a coffee from this appliance by his bed, not that I drink the stuff, it just seemed the thing to do. It wasn't so bad. I pretended it was wine and that I was in a midday movie, not as the glamorous heroine but the strong supporting role and this was the final scene where the vegetable miraculously becomes a human being again and declares his love for me, not the heroine, and we book ourselves airline tickets on his personal computer and fly to New Zealand for a fantastic holiday. Something like that. I told the vegetable everything I knew about him, which was nothing at all really, only that he existed. At times we even doubted that. We? Did I say we? Now why did I have to go and mention Olive, why did I have to pull her into this heaven when I could so easily have had him all to myself. Because I didn't know what a wormy bitch she was going to be about all this. I didn't know did I? So I told him about me and Olive. How we both lived next door to him. It went like this — Olive's house, vegetable's house, my house — though I didn't go calling him a vegetable, not to his face. I told him we spent lots of afternoons staring up into his window, talking about him, wondering what he looked like but never having the guts to yell out to him. I would have been slapped if my mother heard me, yelling out and stuff. We talked a long time.

At one point I was looking out the only window in his room, looking down at our cement porch where Olive and I often sat in our school uniforms, staring up. There was no-one down there now. I could see my brother's legs walking around our kitchen but apart from that no other signs of life in the Creeber house. I realised I hadn't spoken for ages, well it seemed like ages, so I turned my attention back to the vegetable. He was still staring off into the distance, same as ever. I don't know why this surprised me. As though I half expected him to have moved a little, tilted his head or something while I wasn't looking. I don't know. It's just so unnatural to sit still that long.

I was on my way back to his bedside, squeezing between a knitting machine and the warm, steel wall of a pizza oven when I noticed it. Right at the back of the room almost hidden among video equipment, film projectors and a quietly swooshing dishwasher. It's neon lights came skipping out at me in fabulous colours. I wound my way past a table of kitchen appliances, past an industrial vacuum cleaner, quickly past something that looked like an X-ray machine, further on past a whole row of electronic cash registers till finally I reached it. An old jukebox. I had to lean across the dishwasher to get a proper look at the song list, mostly stuff I'd never heard which was a downer because I felt like a bit of David Bowie or something, but there was nothing good. So I closed my eyes and pressed a couple of buttons, I didn't know if it was going to work even, without putting money in. But it did. This African bongo-type song came out. 'Spose it was alright. Felt nice just hearing music in the room, I felt all light-headed and happy or something. You know how music can do that to you. I jived on over to the photo copier and stuck my head into it. I pushed the start button. I screwed my eyes tight. The machine whirred and flashed a slow, blinding light into my face. I pulled my head away. A few seconds later the machine spewed out this foetus-looking face that was meant to be me. They're never very flattering photos. I took the copy over to the vegetable and showed it to him. I suspended the foetus face in his field of vision and told him my name again, then repeated it very slowly so that it would sink into his memory forever. The African bongo thing was still jumping around the room. I folded the foetus face and put it in his pyjama pocket. I guess I was in a bit of a trance because I said my name is Eliza, for the *fourth* time, I was mere millimetres from his face, from his huge unblinking eyes, his skin, his dots, his wet lips . . . I . . . I . . . I kissed him! There. I've said it now. I've revealed my last secret. If Olive ever gets hold of this information there'll be a story going round that I had sex with a vegetable on top of a pinball machine. That's just the sort of thing she'd say. She'd snort and giggle it out of her foul mouth. She'd find a bunch of dumb girls and whisper the filthy lie into their earholes at lunch time. She'd probably even charge money. Dollar coins. Then the really dumb girls would all be put off their food hearing the fantastic, grimy details of having sex with a vegetable and Olive would walk away with their lunches jiggling new coins in her pocket. Olive would win all round. That scumbag. That filthy rotten liar.

It was only a *kiss* Olive! A kiss. Lips on lips. A smacking sound. You know the sort of thing? Huh. What would she know. Frigid tart.

I kissed him because you've got to take opportunities when they come along. He looked like he enjoyed it.

From what I've heard Olive is still spreading the word that it never happened. A week later and it's still eating away at her, and she doesn't even know the half of it. A week later and the vegetable's house is empty. Everyone keeps saying how sad it is about the old man dying but no-one mentions the vegetable. Or the machines and stuff. They must have found the machines when they came to take them away, the two motionless bodies. It's as though the vegetable and his toys never existed. During this last week that's what I've worked out — those machines were toys for the vegetable. It's funny I keep remembering the conveyor belt. I only noticed it as I was leaving. I had to step over it to get out the door. It was a grey conveyor belt, ankle-height about 15 centimetres wide, moving in a perpetual path around the edge of the room. I nearly tripped over it, except I saw this full bottle of tomato sauce glide out from behind the clothes dryer and pass right by my ankles. There was nothing else on the belt. I watched the bottle make its journey though I lost sight of it many times because of all the stuff in the room. Pretty soon it passed my ankles again just as silently as the first time. I keep thinking about it. It's funny I only noticed it when I was leaving.

A whole week later. We're waiting for dinner in silence. My brother opposite me at the table is such a baby. He's still got a scowl on his face from last week when he caught me wearing his Addidas *without asking*. What a baby. Mum comes in with the soup. Steaming bowls of —
What's this! I blurt at her.
She says, what do you reckon it is?! It's vege —
Don't say it! I scream. She slaps me.
You eat every bit of that, she hisses.

I stare down at the little bits of carrot, the blobs of potato, curls of celery, strips of onion, peas bobbing about in the greasy liquid. And there, beached high on the side of the plate, a tiny helpless slice of zucchini.

Vicky Viidikas

Vicky Viidikas was born in 1948 to an Estonian violin maker and an Aust–Irish mother. Educated at over a dozen schools, she entered the workforce at 15, and has been writing poetry and prose ever since. Works published: *Condition Red* (1973); *Knabel* (1978); *Wrappings* (1974); and *India Ink* (1984). In addition her poetry and prose have been included in over 20 anthologies, both in Australia and overseas.

Darlinghurst Portrait

ig nose, big lips, small but definite waist, what a case. The body sustains its incongruities — like the mouth dropped open as if in a state of permanent surprise, the big lips parted all shiny with Burlesque Red. She's notorious for those lips, which can suck so damn hard it's a wonder they don't get blisters, shiny lips which gape at remote horizons, enigmatic lips to pass the body through (her speciality is 'French'). That's the lure, she's Egyptian or Eastern somewhere, and claims her name means 'Big Treat' in Arabic. That's exotic for Australia, for the streets anyway.

Shukala has tremendous staying power — she can hang onto a bleak wet morning when the other girls have left their beat, and pick up some tired man on his way home from work, and turn a trick which empties his wallet before he's even decided ... She pumps him dry with amazing vigour, before he's noticed her Islamic nose, or flat little tits all mainly nipple, or lack of height (she rarely takes her highheels off) which brings her to the level of an average man's armpit. She can tuck in under one shoulder which makes a client feel powerful and protective. With the kind of sob stories she regularly uses, that's very important. Protection. Support. Defence system. What everyone must have.

She can repeat her movements as easily as a donkey taking a familiar mountain path, without blinking, just foward, going over the contours of a man's body as if no other location ever existed. Instincts have a way of taking root in specific desires, racial memories have flavours all of their own. Her new found customer is so glad to be relieved of his ambiguity, he accepts her olive complexion and rapid-fire techniques. Her way of conversation is unique, her movements unexpected. He never quite focuses on how short she is (4' 10"), or the fuzziness of her hair which has been carefully hennaed. What amazes him is the fact he's made it with a Muslim — there's no doubt about that, her pubic hairs all shaved away, along with underarms and complete smooth legs. Australian girls mostly shave their legs up to the knee and that can feel pretty strange. There's no doubt that her big lips are wet all the time, she has licked him dry. Instinct tells him that this odd little Easterner is more hot than any local girl. Sheilas, well, they often only flash what they've got, they don't drop a bald snatch directly over your face. Cripes. He'll be back to see this one again with an 'extra heavy load.'

Shukala has it all over the other 'workers.' She's direct, all the way, with plenty of imaginative suggestions. She only discusses one thing: sex, with a thousand different ways of how to enjoy it with her. Her time means money, you don't mess around. You pay all the way, with extensions of technique which cost you extra. Each time you cum a few more redbacks are handed over. A bestial position here, a lean over the bedstead there, a putting on or off of knickers, a '69' with twenty five minutes allocated for the job. She opens that big mouth of hers like a well honed razor, and splices her way through questions to get to the immediate need — desire, the nature of it, and how quickly to take the edge off it. No unresolved actions, she'd be as kinky as her hair so long as it earned her a few thousand dollars a week. She was, as they say, in the oldest profession in the world.

'Bit Treat' meant business, all her clients said so, and were faint hearted by her tenacity, her intensity of purpose. What a challenge. No cowboy would quit the saddle until he'd ridden himself mad. She never concealed the fact she was on drugs permanently, vast quantities of them as big as her eyes, black edged with kohl, and all smokey with euphoria. Drugs kept her working, she gave herself to the nights and bags of white powder, till both of them ran out and she was forced to sleep. Her clients didn't dare argue with her habit — it was taboo, a purdah which made her more exotic. To see her contorting that muscley body of hers, with the eyelids heavy and so dark, was to feel like living a tale from the *Arabian Nights*. Spicey, wet, and weird, an original fable enacted in the 20th century.

Her lack of tits don't matter. She has a brilliant arse which fits neatly into bright coloured shorts, cut away at the sides to accentuate her strong thighs. No one else can tilt forward like that over the cars and gutters of Darlinghurst, their bum thrust out as surely as a hard boiled egg. Any man could fantasise about being squeezed by her thighs, those slightly bandy legs turned inwards . . . Australians had to suffer to get skin the colour of hers, and it was fascinating to watch beads of sweat break out across her forehead, tiny drops glinting along the creases of her body. The customers didn't realise it was the overload of drugs in her system which made her sweat that way. To see her pink tongue run over those big lips was enough to suggest delerium.

Shukala has to be fully 'on the tilt' before she'll do business at all. She can spot a mug five blocks away, and size up how much money he's carrying before he's even approached her. Those enormous brown eyes could outstare any psyched-up arrogance or challenge the meanest stance. Determined to satisfy, like a good shot in the arm, she wasted nothing, just kept stuffing her wallet with notes (she liked the grey ones best). Her future gaped in front of her like those blasé yawns which defined a man's hunger — that enigma of gratification which gave the illusion of 'forever'. She was girl/woman, demon/tonic, a pint sized female of gall and nerve . . .

Her trademark is a black glove with the fingertips cut out of it, an alluring detail which suggests intrigue or violence. With her golved hand she can squeeze a penis, a syringe, a full wallet, or a set of insecure balls, she can squeeze until exhaustion is total — this is the real meaning of staying power. Her naked fingertips beckoning from that black glove could entice an old man back to memories of his youth, some rare moment of sensation like tasting that first Turkish Delight.

When the Buddhists say — 'all sensations are temporary' — they obviously haven't experienced 'Big Treat' at her best, pouring her energy into a sexual act so intense, the memory of it can reinforce a lifetime. Each man felt like a virile lion as he roared away inside her, buried up to the hilt in a dream of horny woman. She was here, at last, tangible under his hands. She wrapped her legs around him in everything from a sailor's knot to a serpent's twist, panting in a fury while the minutes ticked away. Another knock on the brothel's door only increased his sense of power, never mind if it cost an extra $50. She demanded his seed and wouldn't let up until sperm dribbled from her mouth, or between her legs. Those lips were swollen with desire only for him. She made a man feel he'd been robbed of strength if he ejaculated too many times, just like Samson getting his hair cut off by Delilah. As if virility ever had to do with the outgoing of bodily fluids . . . What did the flowing of blood from a woman mean other than she was fertile?

Big lips, proud hips, what an arse. The mouth dropped open like a doorway to blind ecstasy. Pleasure equalled alluring repetition. Enigma of desire. Endless variation of intimate performance. Burial and resurrection. The challenge of Shukala's need. Encounter without commitment. Belief — this satisfaction of hunger. Miracle — this unexpected doing of one's most secret cravings. Love — this exchange of skin blurring into skin. Return to the deep root. Instinctive capacity for infinite pleasure. The thrill of forgetting all obligation. No remands or revenge. Special. French or Egyptian or the Muslim unveiled. 'Big Treat' — what a case, worth blowing every cent.

Mary Anne Baartz

Mary Anne Baartz lives in a semi-tropical rain forest in northern NSW. She has had stories published in a number of literary magazines. Mary Anne has just completed two plays, a novel and a collection of short stories, and is currently working on another novel.

Bella Donna

I am Bella Donna. That's who I am, though people call me Charlie. I was born Bella Donna, it was written in blood on the inside of my navel, but the doctor smudged it when he tied off the umbilicus. Because of the smudge, my parents christened me Charles William and I've had to live with that label ever since.

They say I'm old and harmless now. That I've lost my power. They tell me that when I was young I did wicked things. I laugh at them; I see what they're trying to do. They are clowns, too busy juggling balls of the very air they breathe to know anything. Old is when your teeth fall out and your hair thins and greys. And they shove you into a Nursing Home and tie you to a commode. Old is when you forget you're a beautiful woman and believe the lies they serve you with your lunch, and can't see beyond their painted faces and bright blue hair.

I have all my teeth which are solid and white and my hair is long and silky ... golden, yes, like the sun. My skin is satin smooth — true Bella Donna skin. And the breasts of the old are juiceless and droop to the waist in wrinkles, whereas my breasts are firm and rounded, pink and juicy guavas. The jokers point at me and jingle the bells on their caps, forgetting their balls of air that drop to the ground and puncture. See how they choke? Purple and swollen, their eyes are popping.

I, Bella Donna, sway through the streets of the town in my high heels, wiggling my delicious backside. It pleases me to watch the clowns' noses redden and swell as I pass by. They succumb to the power they say I've lost and sag at the knees.

At night, in the moonlight, I climb the ladder of my success and snigger over the rooftops as the fools add up their mortgages or steal kisses or hide behind their thick lips and painted eyebrows. For, Bella Donna is nourished in the moonlight. Sucks up thirstily, the juices of the enchantress, the moon goddess, Hecate. Sustained, she floats through the clowns' discontent and waves her striped tiger at their miserable snorts of ridicule.

They painted me Charles William. A horrible, dirty grey colour. They jumped up and down and giggled obscenely like it was the greatest joke ever. It was a depressing non-colour and it brought me down, just as they planned. It was so thick and sticky that I couldn't see through it. There was no way of knowing it was all a filthy trick. They forced me up the aisle, grey footsteps spreading in a murky mess behind me, and made me utter vows of love, honour and fidelity to one of their number they'd painted white. The clowns, still laughing, nailed me to this mockery in white until she gave birth to mewling, puking imps with dimpled fingers and rosebud mouths. Perhaps it was the dimples that locked me so securely in the paint, and made it less urgent to find the truth.

But, the creatures grew bigger and demanded more. The white paint cracked and yellowed and they tormented me with their sharp, gamin features and pin-prick eyes. I'd been so thoroughly painted grey that the lies were chains that they pulled ever tighter until the vows they'd forced on me jumped up and bit me on the neck. They noticed me flinch from the incisors and became worried I'd rebel. They sent their very best.

How clever of them! Smart enough to steal my own colours to paint her. She flashed her eyes and pouted her lips. I was suffocating under the grey paint and craved the green of life, the blue of love, the purple of desire, the red of passion ... Bella Donna's colours, flaunted by this imposter. It was impossible for me to know she was one of them, dressed in my stolen colours to seduce me. The irony ... They very nearly succeeded. I offered her every-thing; threw the others away — dumped them like so much garbage. Mind you, they performed well at the Tip, beating their breasts and tearing their hair, until I thought I'd go mad. But, the luminous paint was blinding.

I would have died for this viper ... braved rapids, climbed mountains, walked barefoot over burning coals and broken glass. Just as I was within reach, close enough to tell the colours were false, she spurned me. Turned her golden head away. Ridiculed me, sneered behind her hand. Tortured into shreds, I crawled to her and kissed her rosy toes. She flicked her hair and snarled, raised her foot and kicked me into a corner. I hunched there, shaking, and watched while she danced away with a fool. They'd welded match sticks under my eyelids so I was forced to watch her rub her body up against his, touch him the way she'd once touched me . . . I heard her sigh and moan and I smelled them mocking me. But, she wasn't clever enough. Before my very eyes, her creamy skin peeled away like the latex mask it was and the saggy, crinkled scales of the true clown peeked through, winking, blinking and blowing its nose. The costume fell in tatters around its ankles.

And I saw them for what they were. The dirty grey they'd painted me flaked and peeled off, revealing the green, blue, purple and red they'd stolen. The pools of their laughter dried and they were left cracked and parched — melding into a desert where nothing could grow. They hated that. They made grabs at my colours again, the green to grow their miserable pleasures, the blue to pretend that they had love, but nothing glowed and nothing grew for them. For, now I was awake. They were thieves but the treasures they'd burgled were magic and had returned to me.

The game was up. The truth unfolded like a dream. It was time to put an end to this farce once and for all. The butcher's knife glistened on the shelf behind the master deceiver and her fool. Here were two clowns who wouldn't have another chance of making it under the Big Top. I choked on my delight over the work of art I'd created. Parodies emerged out of red patterns wriggling over limp, marble sacks sprawled on the floor.

The others rushed in, costumes of blue . . . checked hatbands . . . *'anything you say may be taken down and . . .'* *'one phone call . . .'.* Metal cut into my narrow wrists . . . cold, very cold . . . hard, wooden bench . . . steel eyes. The ones I'd chucked away ran in off the Dump, their heads bowed, their eyes wet, they snuffled a lot . . . *'extenuating circum-*

*stances . . . crime of passion . . . a loyal husband . . . a kind father
. . .'* I doubled over, choked on my mirth. The last laugh
was on them.

It was then that Hecate visited Bella Donna. She rode in
on a moonbeam. She brought gifts; beauty, strength, wisdom. She showed me secrets — my name, embossed behind
my navel, caves lined with loveliness; suits with thousands
of pockets filled with words. She showed me how to mantle
the words and escape into stories. Now, whenever I need
to, I can dip into the pockets and read the stories or hide in
the caves. And I do need to when the clowns gather together and muster their forces for an attack, spilling gravy
down the bib they've fastened around my slender neck.
The joke's on them when they can't find me. They
wouldn't have a clue! I've hidden in a pocket and roared
off on my Kawasaki 1100. They can't see me for the dust
and stones from the bike's wheels.

The clowns feed me mush for they say my teeth have
fallen out and my mouth has shrunk and won't support a
plate. They nod at each other, thinking I don't know, that I
can't see through their lies. But their meagre restraints fall
away when I flash my green eyes or pout my scarlet lips.
They are pathetic, clothed in their dripping jealousy.

They've harnassed me to this narrow, iron bed and are
hammering me with old men smells; rust, pus and urine.
They've dumped me in the middle of a mess of rotting
bodies while they have busters off their monocycles and
trip over the cuffs of their baggy pants. They shout their
lies to each other so I can hear . . . *'has Charlie been fed . . .
have you washed Charlie . . . has anyone changed Charlie's sheets
. . . does Charlie need to be wheeled into the sun room . . .'* They
don't see the bed widen and turn to brass with delicate
floral patterns drawn over its porcelain wedges. They can't
see the satin cushions through the rough calico pillow slips
. . . blinded by their passion, you see. I am their passion —
it's me they want — Bella Donna. But I spit at them. I
despise their weakness, their puny dreams — they, like my
parents, can't see past the smudge behind my belly button.

I visit my lovers when the clowns are asleep. They wait
for me in doorways, my lovers, their tongues hanging out,

their eyes glazed. Often, a glance from Bella Donna is enough. A brief touch of her hand, a brush of her lips. Enough . . . Sometimes, I tease them, just as the imposter once teased me, but with a lilt and grace that the rough copy could never achieve. I tease until they would die for a word or a smile. These I give as the whim takes me. The pleasure I derive from watching them . . . shivering in corners . . . matchsticks welded under their eyelids . . .

Sometimes, the clowns change their costumes and dress in suits and ties, bryl cream plastered over their balding pates. Or they wear crimpelene and pad their bosoms. They sit on plastic chairs and brandish their false teeth . . . *'how are you, Dad . . . they treating you okay, Dad . . .'* or they dress as children with rosy cheeks and innocent eyes and blow bubbles . . . *'kiss Granpa, Bubbie . . . look, Granpa! I done dis dwawing for you . . .'* They will try anything.

Bella Donna grins at them. Poor pathetic creatures, dribbling their miserable lies. They soon tire of the game, they're not good actors. They miss their red noses and baggy pants and gasp for the balls of air they juggle for their living.

Soon, the clowns will discover their ruses have failed . . . that I'm neither old nor harmless, and am, in fact, more powerful than ever. They will bow down before me. They will strip off their costumes and prostrate themselves naked while I sit in my brilliance and glory, mildly painting my fingernails. And I will forgive them everything. For, I am Bella Donna.

Carmel Bird

∽

Carmel Bird was born in Tasmania in 1940. She has published an anthology of stories *Births, Deaths and Marriages* (1983) and a novel *Cherry Ripe* (1985). A new collection of stories *The Wood-Pecker Toy Fact* was published in June 1987. Carmel now lives in Melbourne and is currently working on a novel *The Bluebird Cafe*. She is co-editor of a new literary journal *Fine Line*.

Buttercup and Wendy

This is the legend of Wendy Trull who was the prettiest girl in Tasmania between 1955 and, say, 1959. A long time to hold any title, particularly that of beauty queen.

When you see a beginning like that, you know that Wendy must either triumph over terrible odds and end up as the wife of a diplomat, or she must be doomed. Will Wendy be found at the bottom of the cliff, broken like a wax doll, with strange juices oozing out, and her ears in a paper bag, you wonder; or will she have a wedding in the Cathedral, and an ironing lady, and a second house at the beach, perhaps even a third in the mountains and a flat in London? And for the children a nanny who is more like a second mother to them than a servant. What is going to happen to Wendy?

Wendy lived with her mother and father and brother and sisters in a reasonably nice house with wide verandahs on Windmill Hill. The needles from the pine trees collected on the verandahs, and one of Wendy's jobs was to sweep them up and put them in the incinerator. Wendy's granny lived in a grim old terrace house in a poorer part of the town. She kept the brass doorknob on the front door gleaming, and in the passage, just inside the door, she kept a cow. You opened the door, and there, standing sadly on the pink and green lino, was a brown and white cow. Cow's eyes look very big indeed when you see them up close in the narrow dimness of an entrance hall.

If there are motifs and links in the lives of people, then the presence of the cow in her granny's passage can be related to the presence of a secret lover in Wendy's attic. There were many years between the cow and the lover, but Buttercup, certainly an unusual pet, is somehow linked in Wendy's life to the man in the attic.

The attic, not yet brushed by the jacaranda which would be there by the time Wendy came, was waiting for Wendy's

241

lover at the top of a house which was waiting for Wendy. Across the water from Wendy's island, in a part of the world called Kew (thousands of miles from London, for Wendy will not roam too far), there stood a warm brick house with a fancy wooden verandah and an attic. The attic was full of attic secrets and forgotten attic dreams. The family who lived there in this long time before Wendy got there, were the Fagans: Old Missus, her son, his wife, and their fat sons who spent many wet afternoons in the attic where they read comics, did unspeakable things, and imagined that they were spying on the girls in the garden next-door. The jacarandas dropped their soft blue blossoms into the grass where the girls sat painting their toenails and rubbing each other with oil. Much of what they did was done for the entertainment of the Fagans in the attic. When Old Missus died, her son sold the house which then had a succession of rather careless owners, one of whom put an alsation in the fowl-house instead of hens. Sadder and sadder grew the house as it waited for Wendy. Would she never come? Somebody, inspired perhaps by the trees on the other side of the fence, planted the jacaranda which was going to be there when Wendy arrived and signed the contract to buy the house.

'It's very run down,' said her friends.

'Yes,' said Wendy, 'but I'm going to do it up.'

Although no cow had ever roamed the front hall of the house, there seemed to be some faint melody which sang in Wendy's heart of the memory of her granny. The lino in the front parlour was pink and green, and nearly the same as that which had been in Buttercup's domain. If Wendy changed this house, made it smell of paint and disinfectant, would she change the fact that her granny had lived with a cow? If she tidied the house, she might tidy the memory.

Before the jacaranda was planted, when Wendy was at High School, and was the prettiest girl in town, she went around with the boy who was the best tennis player, for his age, in the state. He was called Michael — a boy with ice-blue eyes and a very attractive laugh. Michael and Wendy went together to school dances to which he wore a white sports coat with a pink carnation, and she wore an orange skirt beneath which undulated a vast white petticoat edged with rope. They went together to school picnics, and to the pictures on Saturdays. In school plays, she was Portia to his Shylock, Eliza to his Higgins. The legend said that he spent every second night, just about, in her bedroom at the back of the house on Windmill Hill. However, the truth is that he went there once, and they were both so terrified of being discovered by her father that they didn't enjoy themselves at all, except for when Wendy got some licorice straps out of a drawer and they ate them. He did not go to her bedroom again. Instead, he would borrow his father's car and take Wendy to the drive-in. The car was a big black Chevrolet which had cost, said the legend, well over eleven hundred pounds. The back seat was fairly comfortable. Naturally, the legend said that they went all the way in the back of the Chev, but that isn't true either.

They left school, and the end of the chapter came when Wendy was a deb. Michael, wearing a dinner suit, was her partner, and they were the most beautiful couple on the floor. Wendy's dress was made by Mrs Winter, the ancient local maker of debs' dresses. Three times a week for four weeks, Wendy stood on Mrs Winter's dining-room table in a trance as Mrs Winter took pins from her mouth and made them go 'tuck tuck' in the white silk. Wendy wanted to look like the most fabulous fairy on the top of the most incredible Christmas tree. And she did.

Then after that, Michael went to Hobart to study the Law, and Wendy went to Kew — oh, distant, and foreign land of Australia where people ate ravioli — to train to be a kindergarten teacher. She has pastel twin-sets, and pleated skirts; smart blazers and pearls. She was a good student, and strove to look like a model from Seventeen. She put Buttercup in the attic of her mind for the time being, keeping her thoughts fixed on respectability, a certificate in kindergarten teaching, and marriage to the right man. And so Michael receded. It had not taken much, just a strip of water, to sever the bonds between Michael and Wendy. Michael continued to play tennis, seduced the professor's daughter, failed first year, and crashed his father's car, the black Chevrolet.

243

Legend suggested that if Michael had stayed with Wendy, he might have been all right. As it was, he went into his father's firm and developed an interest in racing. Before long, he was in debt to the bookmakers, stole money from his father, and ended up in prison, his ice-blue eyes staring at a window through which he could not see the sky. Prison did not improve him, however, and when he was released, he set about stealing some more money, and went back to gaol. He seemed to have set himself a pattern for life.

Wendy, in due course, became the director of a kindergarten. It was in a fashionable and wealthy suburb where the parents and children were happy with Wendy, and Wendy was happy with them. When she read to the children stories about cows called Daisy or Buttercup, she no longer thought of her granny. She would take the children to farmyards, and occasionally the huge brown eyes of a solemn cow would bring back to her a picture of the pink and green lino, and of her granny's fingers as they stroked Buttercup's ears. But this was rare. She had left it all behind her; she was a respectable career-woman. Once upon a time, in the days of the pastel twin-sets, one of her aims had been to marry. To marry the right man. Ah, but alas, she had not met the right man. The ambition faded; she had love affairs some happy, some sad.

It was a renovator's opportunity with an original fireplace, the house in Kew. Wendy hired a truck and took the fowl house and the contents of the attic, as well as some cupboards which smelt of vomit, and an ice-chest full of spiders, to the tip. Then, with the help of a builder and a plumber and a painter, she took the opportunity as a renovator. Most of the floor she covered with carpet, thick and royal blue, woolly under Wendy's bare feet. Even the little stairs which went up to the attic were blue. It was up this little winding staircase that the secret lover crept.

Wendy had not seen Michael for twenty years when he escaped from prison and found her in her back garden, sitting underneath the jacaranda with her bare feet in the grass.

Pause and picture that.

One Sunday afternoon, Miss Trull is reading the White

244

Hotel on the grass at the back of her place, when a tired man with ice-blue eyes and a dirty T-shirt comes up the path. She shuts her book, flicks a blue blossom from her skirt, and invites the man into the kitchen for a drink. He has a shower and is never seen again.

It was, in many ways, quite a good arrangement for both of them. Michael, seeking, it would seem, one kind of prison or another, had found one to his taste.

Wendy was quite used to making rules for her kindergarten, and so she easily drew up the rules of the attic. There would be no light allowed between 5 pm and 8 am. The cupboard must remain in front of the window. Michael must never come downstairs unless Wendy came to get him. The gate to the back garden was blocked off so that anybody who came to the house had to ring the front doorbell. Michael knew that when the bell rang, he must stay quiet until Wendy came to say that the visitor had gone. Wendy bought an exercise bike and another TV.

And so, in their attic dreamland, where they made love in the afternoons and early mornings, and where they ate delicious snacks and licorice straps, they lived happily ever after, the prettiest girl in Tasmania and her childhood sweetheart.

Wendy used to think about the reality of the 'ever after'. Would she die first? Would he die first? Would they have a suicide pact? When? How did people decide those things? Would the headlines in cheap newspapers say:

ATTIC PRISONER
KINDERGARTEN TEACHER SUICIDE

or

CHILDHOOD SWEETHEARTS DIE IN PACT?

As she thought about how it would be, life went on as usual. The biggest difference to Wendy's life, outside the attic that is, was the fact that she could never go away for holidays. She felt, however, no need of holidays, having as she did such an interesting home-life.

'But when are you going to Venice?' they said.

'You always told us you were going to go to Venice.'

In summer, the jacaranda bloomed. Soft blue blossoms

with no perfume, against a harsh blue sky. The branches were dark like ink, scratched in twisted twig patterns. And around the branches, in clouds like moths, hovered the jacaranda flowers, blue.

Sometimes Wendy would panic when she thought of what would happen if Michael became ill. She made it a rule of the attic that there was to be no sickness. There was none. Michael went through weeks when he was sure that she was going to be killed on the road. Whenever she took the children to the zoo, she found pleasure in the happiness of the animals, especially of the baby gorilla. These days, it did sometimes cross her mind that Buttercup in the passage had been a kind of fore-runner of Michael in the attic, although Michael was, she then reminded herself, quite different.

Beverley Farmer

Beverley Farmer lives in Point Lonsdale, most of the time, and has had three books published: *Alone* (1980); *Milk* (1983); and *Home Time* (1985). She has one son who will be 15, by the time *The Babe* appears.

As Time Goes By

By late afternoon the sky is a deep funnel of wind, damp and white. She remarks as she passes through the lamplight around his desk on her way to the bathroom: 'Doesn't it look like snow!'

'Do you think?' He squints out the window.

'That hollowness of the light.'

'It's early for snow.'

'*Casablanca's* going to be on TV tonight at eight,' she says before he can look down again. 'Why don't we go to the bar and see it and then have dinner somewhere after?'

'Mmm.'

The room is grey; only the light around him is warm and moving with shadows. The steam pipes are silent. Whenever will they start clanking and hissing and defrost the apartment? '*Isn't* it cold, though!' she says brightly.

'Mmm.'

'Maybe I should go for a walk downtown, take some photos of the lights coming on,' she says.

'It's a lot colder outside.'

'Walking would warm me up.'

'Okay.'

'Oh, maybe not,' she says. 'I might write letters home instead.' Home is Australia. It's summer there. 'Until it's time for *Casablanca*.'

He sighs and waits for silence.

She has an electric radiator on in her room — the sitting-room really, but she works in here. She has twin lamps of frilly glass at twin tall windows inside which wasps sizzle and cling and trap themselves in shreds of cobweb. The table she writes at faces the windows. Three times a day she pushes books to one side and turns papers face down, since this is also the table they eat at. The kitchen is next to it, bare and icy, smelling of gas. She pulls her radiator over by the couch and lies curled up in the red glow with her head on a velvet cushion.

Later she half-wakes: he has walked past into the kitchen. When he switches her lamps on and hands her a mug of coffee she is stiffly sitting up to make room. 'Did you get much written?' She yawns, stretching an arm warm with sleep along his shoulders.

'Fair bit.' He grins. 'Did you?'

She is glad she stayed in. 'No. What's the time?'

'Hell, yes.' He looks. 'Ten past eight.'

'Oh, we've missed it!'

'No, we haven't. Only the start.'

They gulp their coffee and help each other drag coats and boots on. 'You must have seen it, haven't you?' he says.

'Oh, yes. Hasn't everyone?'

'Then what's the —?'

She shuts his mouth with a kiss. 'I want to see it with *you*. In America.'

He smiles at that. They fling open the door and stop short. Snow is falling, must have been falling for hours, heavy and slow, whirling round the white streetlamps. 'Oh, *snow*!' She dashes back inside for her camera and takes photo after photo from the stoop, of fir branches shouldering slabs of snow, drooping in gardens, and elms still with gold leaves and fine white skin all over, and lawns and cars and rooftops thickly fleeced. Passing cars have drawn zips on the white road.

'Now we're really late,' he says. Hand in hand they tramp and slither the few blocks to the bar they like, bright as a fire with the lamps on. Outside it two young men are throwing snowballs. She gasps as one leaps on the other and they flounder giggling at her feet.

'Pussy cat!' one jeers. 'That's *all* you is!'

Her man is holding the blurred glass door open. Heads along the bar turn away from *Casablanca* to stare at them. He leads her to a stool, orders a red wine and an Irish coffee and stands at her back. Ingrid Bergman's face fills the screen.

The door opens on a white flurry and the young men stamping in, shaking the snow off. The heads turn and stare. 'Celebrate the first *snow*!' one young man announces. 'Have a *drink*, everybuddy!' A cheer goes up. The barman brings her another red wine and him another Irish coffee. The young men have flopped crosslegged on the carpet and are gazing at the screen.

'Oh, they're *so* young,' a voice murmurs in her ear; the grey-haired woman beside her is smiling. She smiles in answer and gives herself over to *Casablanca*. He is at her back with his arms round her. When it ends he goes to the men's room.

The old woman is dabbing her eyes. 'Oh dear!' She makes a face. 'Do you come here a lot? I do. We live just down the road.'

Do you come here a lot? I do. We live just down the road. You can see this bar from our stoop and I tell you it's a real temptation, glowing away down here. With that lantern at the door with snow flakes spinning round it and the way the elm leaves flap against it like yellow butterflies — it's like some place in a fairy tale. And here inside it's as bright and warm as inside a Halloween pumpkin. Those lamps everywhere, and the bottles burning in the mirror. And whenever the door opens, a breath of snow blows in and the lights all shift under and over the shadows. Even if *Casablanca* wasn't on the TV I'd have come tonight.

What'll you have, honey, another one of those? What is that, red wine? Jimmy, another one of those red wines and I'll have a Jack Daniels. Yes, rocks. And wipe that silly grin off your face, have you no soul, what kind of a man laughs at *Casablanca*? Thanks, Jimmy. Keep it.

Look through that archway, the couples at their little tables, all so solemn and proper with their vintage wine and their candles — look, their heads are hollow, like the candles burnt their eyes out. They might all have stories just as sad as *Casablanca*, but who cares? It's *Casablanca* breaks our hearts, over and over. You cried at the end, I saw you. So did that nice man of yours. Oh, a bar's the place to watch it, a bar's the perfect place. I cry every single time, I can't help myself, it's so noble and sad and innocent and — hell, you know. I couldn't watch it home, anyway. Bill, he's my husband, gets mad when I cry. He walks out. Why, am I supposed to stay and watch you slobber over this shit? he said last time it was on. Most people got all they need to slobber about in real life.

You're what *I* got, I said right back.

That's him there, over at the pool table. That your man he's talking to? I thought so. They're lighting up cigarettes and getting acquainted. Isn't that a coincidence? He looks a nice easy-going kind of a guy. But then so does Bill. I love Bill, I love him a lot. I've known that man thirteen years, I could tell you things . . . I'm not blind to anything about Bill, I love him anyway. He loves *me*, though it doesn't feel like being loved much of the time. He needs me. He has to punish me for that. There he is, an older man than he acts. His hair has a grey sheen and his skin hangs loose all over, see the crazed skin on his neck. He's affable and a bit loud with the drink, everybody's pal. Well, when we get home there won't be a word out of him. Under the skin and the smile he's a bitter, fearful man and nobody gets close to him.

He's a second comer, for one thing. He can't forget that. He's my second husband. Yours is a second comer too, is he, honey? Don't mind me sticking my nose in. It's just I can tell. You two are a mite too considerate, too careful with one another, know what I mean? It shows, that's all, if you can read the signs. So what if you are Australians. Oh no. Look, I don't mean you haven't got a nice relationship. But it's only the first time you give your whole self. After that, like it or not, you hold back. You've gotten wise — and you can't pretend *other*wise!

We've been married ten years this Thursday — Thanksgiving Day. You got to laugh. Cheers. Isn't that something, though. My first marriage never got to double figures. I had twenty years alone in between.

Do you remember the first time you saw *Casablanca*? Mine was in 1943, when it first came out, on my honeymoon with Andy. That's reason enough to cry. Bill knows. It's something he can't stand to be reminded of. He pretends it's only Rick and Ilsa making me *slobber*. Men — you tell a man the truth about your life, you end up paying for *ever*. Remember that.

1943! Andy was nineteen, I was seventeen, his ship was

sailing for Europe in a week. Our parents said no, you're too young, but we said we'd only run away, so they gave in. We had one weekend for a honeymoon in New York City. The hotel was an awful old ruin — it still is — full of cockroaches and noisy plumbing. We were so embarrassed, you could hear every drop, every trickle. Our room was on the top floor. Through the fire escape we could see the river, and the moon in the mist like a brass knob behind a curtain, and the lights of Manhattan. So it's not a bed of roses. Andy said: it's a bed of lights instead. We saw *Casablanca* and we cried. We were such babies. He was going to be a hero and I was going to wait . . . We danced round the room like Rick and Ilsa did. We sure didn't sleep much. We didn't even know how to *do* it, you know. We were scared. Oh, we soon got the hang of it. And then his ship sailed.

He came back, oh, he came back. He'd won medals in Italy, he was a hero. But he wouldn't ever talk about it. Whatever happened over there, it finished Andy. He started drinking, then he lost his job, and soon he couldn't hold down any job, he just drank and gambled and played the black market. He'd come home once, twice a week, then sleep for days . . .

One night he started hitting me. Everything was my fault, he said. Then he cried. He promised he never would again. I was fool enough to believe it. If they've hit you once and gotten away with it, honey, you're in trouble. It can only get worse.

So, one night I woke up on the kitchen floor. The table lamp was still on, the beer that he spilt looked like butter melting under it. I remember I saw the pattern of brown triangles on the linoleum every time my eyes came open, they looked wet and red, but I couldn't see sharp enough to be sure. The window was black — so it was still night time — and had silver edges like knives where he smashed it. The curtain was half torn down, sopping up the beer on the table and moving in the wind, a white curtain like a wedding veil. *Help me*! I called out. My head felt crushed. The wind must have blown my hair on my face, hair was stuck to it. A long way away something was — snuffling.

My nose was flat on my cheek, red bubbles blew out. Andy *wasn't there*. I held my head still and pulled myself up by the table leg: broken glasses, slabs of the window pane, the wet curtain but no note. No nothing. The room was going all watery and dim as if the floor was hot as fire and yet it was so icy when I lay down, I pulled the curtain down over me to keep warm.

It wasn't till morning that I saw he'd taken all his stuff. God knows there wasn't much, poor Andy. Then I got started all over again: *Don't leave me! Don't leave me alone now! I love you!* Even now I dream — I wake up and for a moment I'm on the floor again knowing I've lost Andy, he's gone for *ever*. Oh, I've never gotten over it.

I'm sorry. Don't be embarrassed. I'll be all right in a moment. Thank you, yes, another Jack Daniels would be nice. Yes, thank you.

Funny thing was, when I got up off the floor next day and my nose was smashed and my eyes looked like two squashed plums and I was shaking so hard I thought my teeth would crack — I ran out into the street in case I could see him and maybe catch him up and all the time I was whimpering. *After all you've done to me, you just get up and go?* I looked in the kitchen window. It was empty, all shadowy gold behind the edges of glass.

Another funny thing — I had a vision in the night, a ballerina came in. (I wanted to be a dancer, I was good, but first the War started, then I got married . . .) Anyway, this ballerina in white was waving her arms and bowing. It must have been the curtain that I saw. She bent down to lift me then she lay beside me, sobbing, I remember that.

Look at us there in the mirror, like two ghosts among the whisky bottles. Okay, Jimmy, laugh. He thinks I'm admiring myself. I'm not that far gone, though I'm getting there. Cheers. Is that really me, that scrawny thing with the spiky grey hair? You'd never think I was a ballet dancer. Bill hates ballet. He says that because the pain and exertion and ugliness aren't allowed to show, it's one big lie. Tinsel and sweat, he says. Dancers smell like horses, someone famous says, so Bill has to read it to me out of the newspaper. Horses aren't any less beautiful for the way they

253

smell, I say. Horses are dancers too and dancers love them. Anyway, I say, I like the way they smell. You would, he says, you're not what you'd call fussy, are you. Now wasn't that asking for it? *No, well, I married you!* I let it pass, though, and he gives me points for not saying it: just a flicker of the eyelids, but enough.

Most of our quarrels end like that. They're harmless. Nothing Bill says or does can get to the quick of me like it did with Andy whether he meant it or not. Bill can make me ache with misery when he wants, but somewhere deep down inside me now there's this little tough muscle braces itself so the barbs can't go too far in. Bill knows. He's the same. Maybe by now it would have been like that with Andy, who knows? I don't even know if he's alive or dead. My parents came and made me get a divorce. They told him I said he couldn't see me or the kids ever again.

Let me tell you the *worst* thing — let's have another drink? — the worst thing — oh, God, I've never told a living soul this. Jimmy, more of these and have one on me, okay? The worst thing is, when he had me on the floor that night — just pushed me down — and started smashing things and yelling that he wanted *out*, I rolled over and hung on to his trouser leg for dear life and begged him not to leave me. I just wouldn't let go. I — slobbered, and howled and — I kissed his muddy shoe. So he slammed his other shoe in my face. That's when my nose got broken. I mean, that's why.

I thank God the kids weren't home, they didn't see that. They saw him hit me other times, but not that. They were only little. Rick was about five, Ilsa was just a baby. Something like that, though — if they saw it happen, it'd leave a scar on them. I won't let Daddy hurt you, Ricky used to say to me. They were at my parents' place in New Jersey because I had to get a job so I couldn't look after them. We called them Rick and Ilsa — well, *you* know why! Ilsa's married, she's in Alaska now, she's a nurse. Rick's dead. He got killed in Vietnam. Got a medal doing it, too. If his Daddy ever heard about it, I suppose he must have felt proud. Or maybe not.

Don't get me wrong, I believe in sacrifice, and love and honour and loyalty, even if it turns out they were wasted — else why would I love *Casablanca*? Rick and Ilsa, they had something or someone they'd give up everything for. I only wish I still did. Real people have their moments of glory. Time goes on for them though, they can't live up to it. But the glory lives on in memory. Bill won't see that. Face facts, he says. You and your glory and your wallowing in the past. It's shit, that's all it is, shit preserved in syrup. That's better than shit preserved in vinegar, the way yours is, I say. Oh, that's good, he says. Make with the witty repartee, babe, you know I dig that. (Bill can never let go of anything. All his past is still there inside of him, pickled.) Why better, honey? Shit's still shit, he says then. Who knows the truth? I say. You refuse to, *he* says, and round and round we go.

What you never really get over, I suppose, is finding out love's not enough. Loving someone's no *use*. And you only find out the hard way. No one can tell you. You believe in love when you're young, you believe it's forever, it's the only thing that matters, it'll save you both, if you just hang in there and give more and more. I wonder if Ilsa would have gone with Rick — given up everything and gone with him — would it have ended up with her on the floor with her nose smashed? You never know.

Here they come. Look, they're wondering what we're saying. Look at those suspicious eyes and butter-wouldn't-melt smiles of theirs! Your man's been watching you all this time. Here's looking at you, kid! Easy to see you're new. It's great while it lasts, make the most. The little couples are just about all gone now. Don't you just love a black and white night like this after snow, when it echoes? And you slide and fall down on top of each other all the way and rub each other's feet dry and warm once you're inside. Okay, fellers, home time? I've lost my coat. Thanks, honey. I feel so lit up it's a wonder you can't see me shining through it! I'm sure I don't know why I've been telling you the story of my life. You cried at the end of *Casablanca*. I suppose that's why.

'Can I read that?'

'Read what?'

Her hands have instinctively spread across the pages of blue scrawl. He raises his eyebrows: 'What you've been writing half the night.'

She passes them over her shoulder. The couch creaks and the pages rustle until at last he tosses them back on the table and goes to make coffee. She stares at them, sweat prickling her. The heating is on full.

'Thank you,' she says when he brings her mug.

'Is this finished?"

'Oh, for now, anyway. I was just coming to bed — I'm sorry. Haven't you been asleep?'

'I used to respect writers rather a lot,' he murmurs. 'Now I'm not sure.'

'You're writing your thesis on one.'

'Mmm. There's writing and writing. To my mind this —' he points — 'is more like scavenging.' He waits while she swallows hot coffee. 'Perhaps if you wore a badge, a brand that meant: *Beware of the scavenger?* Then people would know they were fair game.'

'You think *that's* being *fair*?'

'She trusted you, it seems, with the story of her life.'

'I hope I can do it justice.'

'Justice.' He sighs.

She has nothing to say. He finishes his coffee sip by sip, takes his mug and rinses it, then comes back to stand behind her chair. Her mug is clenched in both hands; the light of the two lamps blurs in her coffee.

'I am not to figure in anything you write,' comes the smooth voice again. 'Never. I hope you understand that.'

Hardly breathing, she cranes her neck forward to have a sip of coffee, but he grabs the mug from her and slams it down on the table, where it breaks. Coffee spurts up and splashes brown and blue drops over her pages. This time she knows better than to move until his footsteps creak away across the boards. His chair scrapes. She hears a match strike in the room beyond, and a sigh as he breathes smoke in.

Ilona Palmer

Ilona Palmer is Hungarian by birth and was educated in Yugoslavia. A professional analytical
chemist working with CSIRO, she is married to an
Englishman and has been writing in Hungarian
and Serbo-Croatian. *Australian Short Stories* published her first story written in English. Ilona Palmer regards herself as a cosmopolitan.

In Defence of Lord Byron

Tis strange but true, for truth is always strange;
stranger than fiction: If it could be told,
how much would novels
gain by the exchange!

An old-fashioned story for this modern world of ours. And why not? For the old? Yes. They exist. For the young? Yes. There are more old-fashioned young people than one might believe.

Who is the story for?

Me.

If someone wants to say something controversial he says: '. . . there was this friend of mine who told me . . .' Well, there is no friend. It's me. I am telling the story.

The scene is a bedroom and not the matrimonial bedroom, either. I used to picture his flat over the past years, over the Sunday roast. The pictures varied but dirty dishes in the kitchen sink, a man's underwear by the bed and spiderwebs in the corner were an integral part of them. I used to be realistic in my dreams.

When my dream materialized — some dreams do actually materialize — all these components were missing.

My father, who did most of my upbringing, did not think that there was anything wrong with dreams. He used to say that dreams were as essential a component of human existence as tonsils are to the body. As long as they do a good job, they should be left alone to function. You remove them only when they become infected, harmful. He did not tell me how one can tell when tonsils become harmful.

Perhaps he didn't know.

By the pain?

What if there is no pain?

At the age of ten I used to envy other girls when the first days of European spring came. They wore socks. Their calves were blue with cold but the socks looked so good! Of course, I had to wear long stockings until the weather became warmer. When I was fifteen, my school friends went away to build a railway. The first post-war railway built by voluntary work force in the new socialist country. When the end of the school year came they went to far-away places to build socialism. My father said that all they were doing was laying down a few sleepers and getting themselves pregnant in the process. If this was building socialism, he said, it was fine with him but I, his daughter, would have no part in it.

I stayed at home in the semi-darkness of my room, read Voltaire and dreamed about railways. I also made two firm decisions: one, that I would never, never become an atheist and two, when I got my diploma I would wear short socks whenever I felt like it.

The man in the other half of the bed is someone I have known for years. I was nearing the age of thirty-five when he put his foot in my door that was about to close in on middle-age. I selected the program Elevated Thinking on my not altogether welcome but it seemed inevitable computer. The button I pressed was in accordance with our times and I am told, it does a world of good for blood pressure. 'You want to go to bed with him' the screen said but then, it sadly faded as the years went by and I still did not go to bed with him and I was no longer certain that the computer told me the truth.

He was lingering on the edge of my somewhat limited horizon, popping up occasionally, just to remind me that once, not so long ago, I was reasonably young.

There were other attractive men lingering on my horizon over the years and I wondered why I never thought of going to bed with them. But I did not.

The years went by and I cooked the Sunday roast with lots of gravy and it was good to think of him, popping up on the horizon, while my husband and I did the dishes. My husband watched 'Four Corners' and I withdrew to the study to read. After the TV was off and my reading finished, we turned off the light and it was good to snuggle up to him, to feel his arm on my hip and hear him saying 'Good night, dear . . . sleep well.' He was thinking of the famine in Ethiopia and while I felt with him, I could not help thinking, with my mind full of old, useless poetry, I could not help thinking of another pair of eyes, of the times when we, all of us, were younger.

I am here, now, in his bedroom. When he opened the door and stepped aside to let me in, it seemed that it all happened before. Some years ago, as I was making the gravy, it was just like this.

I had an uncle who was an atheist but he never said so. He used to read Oscar Wilde and did not dream. He lived alone in a cottage on a river bank and nobody knew how he made his living. Sometimes he went fishing, other times he vanished for a fortnight or so. Then he was back, sitting on the steps of his cottage, smoking a pipe, watching the sunset with a little twinkle in his eyes and said very little.

My father didn't mind my seeing my uncle but he did say that I was not to read Oscar Wilde. So, of course, I did.

My uncle lent me *The Picture of Dorian Gray* and said that it was a little early for me to read it but he knew that I could cope with it. I have read the *Picture* a few times more in my life but what stayed in my mind was what I remembered the first time: it is only suppressed, inhibited desires that turn into passion, poisoning our minds. I think he said it a little differently: the only way to get rid of a temptation is to yield to it.

My father's story about tonsils?

Possibly.

Likely.

Very likely.

He knew then what we know now.

The ancient Greeks knew what we know now.

The Greeks didn't have a computer.

Neither did my father.

In my book it reads that if the safety valve is open at all times there will be no drama in this world.

Greeks right? My uncle? My father? Oscar Wilde? I put my money on old Lord Byron. It's a purely personal choice, of course. Individual. I could say Pushkin and Petöfy, alongside with Byron and I would still be saying the same thing. (Petöfy, incidentally, was a Hungarian Byron or Pushkin.)

The Greeks have gone a long time ago and we all know how Oscar Wilde ended up; dying sad and lonely in some obscure house in France, abandoned by everyone.

Had he lived eighty years later he would be marching down Hyde Park, Champs Elysées or Bourke Street, Melbourne, carrying a placard and I am convinced, nothing ordinary, let alone vulgar, would be written on it.

Oscar Wilde loathed vulgarity.

He did not ask me when he could see me again and as I put on my clothes I was grateful to him for not asking.

Nothing to do with Oscar Wilde.

A lot to do with Byron.

This was the end of suppressed desires but it also put an end to vague, hazy dreams over the Sunday evening dishes. If I am given a choice I'll take the dreams by the kitchen sink. I may not remember much of tonight in his bedroom but I will miss my dreams over the roast.

Because they are no longer dreams. They are gone for ever.

Talk about love with a capital 'L'? I have never understood what they meant by the word.

Thea Astley

Thea Astley is three times winner of the Miles
Franklin Award, she has written eight novels. Married with one son, Thea Astley taught in the School
of English at Macquarie University (NSW). After
living for some time in the far north of Queensland, she has now returned to NSW.

Write Me, Son, Write Me

Moth tells me this. And what she doesn't tell Bo does. And what he doesn't tell I see.

She says: Dad was given to such phrases as 'a woman should fruit her loins', a rich unctuous statement of such masculine simplicity his wife had believed him. They had produced an elfin, buck-toothed girl who had entered her teen years on ballet points and had proceeded to give them all the versions of a middle-class hell. They wanted security for her, a go-ahead husband with an expense account and a house that could possibly be marked in the real estate guides with an asterisk — their version of the Trinity. She wanted success without effort (which the education system would surely have provided for her had she stayed with it), scruffy boys with bulging jeans, the pillion seats of motor-bikes, and pot.

At fifteen she was expelled from her convent school for scrawling 'Mother Philomène has it off with the bishop' on the wash-room walls. She vanished overnight with boys.

'Love,' her poor mother told her, 'isn't something you toss around like garbage. Love,' — holding her right hand somewhere on her chest — 'love hurts.'

'Not if you do it right,' her daughter said.

At eighteen she was removed from the back row of a Brisbane ballet company when, convinced by hallucinogenic drugs, she insisted she was the soloist in the only performance of the *Nutcracker* ballet that ever had two sugarplum fairies. She bought herself some cheap Indian frockery, lengths of clacking wooden beads, began to call herself Moth, and vanished into the hills.

When her parents discovered her address they wrote despairing little notes and sometimes she answered. She answered with demands for money. They sent clothes she never wore, and plastic-protected food parcels and once, after a couple of years, she came to visit them with three remarkable others and a tiny boy called Wait-a-while whose parenthood she seemed vague about.

At twenty she was still loosely connected with a large and shambling young man who, like Moth, appeared to have no regular employment though his desperate search for work had taken him to every surf-spot on the eastern seaboard. It would have been difficult to imagine such splendid physique going unwanted by those who needed to employ brawn; but apart from brief periods when a degrading love of survival forced him into well-paid terms as a strike-breaker, he took the dole. He was gentle, had a candid smile and a kind of flecked innocence.

'I can watch,' Bo explained to Moth's parents, allowing Wait-a-while to gnaw on his big harmless thumb, 'the sun come up in the morning. And I can track its progress all day across the sky.'

They were too stunned to discuss the work ethic.

'But how do you eat?'

'We manage.' His paws moved gently across Wait-a-while's fragile shoulders. 'People are kind. You wouldn't believe. And we've given up meat altogether. That's a gas saving, man. We're into fruit. We've rejected all animal products.'

'Has Wait-a-while rejected meat?'

They ignored this. 'We won't be sending him to school,' someone else said. 'We're not going to give him the hang-ups we had, man.'

'Good God!' cried Moth's father. 'Good God! Do you always travel in threes?'

They moved on and north.

There is a hypothetical quality about the aimless mists of early morning rain-forest, a demi-postulation that appealed to the very indeterminateness of their life-style. (I felt it, feel it, but then I belong to an older breed; and despite all that joy, that juice, mister poet man, I'm able to withstand those sensual assaults and stand back a bit, eh? I've always found the trappings of nature to be very soft porn, the landscape's centre-page spread.)

They found others like themselves. They skulked in lean-tos made from iron and timber off-cuts. They twanged out-of-tune guitars, sang their particular rain-forest dirges, got stoned on grass, and each fortnight, responding like children trained by the Jesuits to the vestiges of ritual, hiked in to Mango to pick up their dole cheques.

Dust. Shag-wagons. Blue Kombis.

One of them played flute, I might have told you. Its mournful embroideries would flutter in rags past my office windows and Willy Fourcorners, who now does a little odd-jobbing for me, would look up from his spading to wave, to grin. It looked like the rag-tail of Hamelin as they headed for the road-house, startling the travellers who'd paused for a bottle of soft. Some of the girls made dancing movements, doing their own eyes-down thing, absorbed by the fretwork of their feet on the smudged grass-strip. Moth, who had the edge on them, would dash off a series of *entrechats* between the beat-up tables or hold a tremulous arabesque in the bright sun long enough to catch applause. 'Hey, hey, Moth!' her buddies uttered listlessly. 'Hey! Way out!'

Some months before she had registered with the Reeftown employment office as a teacher of ballet. Reeftown, she felt, was sufficiently remote for work demands never to be made.

The official was fascinated by the small gold ring that decorated Moth's left nostril.

'Can you,' he asked, 'dance?'

'Of course.' She whipped into immediate gambades. The lethargic applicants lining the wall stirred for the first time in days.

'Certificates?' the official asked, ignoring a *grand jeté* that brought her panting slightly to the edge of the counter.

'Not with me.' Moth smiled engagingly and the little ring sparkled. 'I can send for them.'

'Do that,' the official said, checking his tea-break watch.

She returned to the rain-forest.

After a month Moth went back down to the coast and returned to the employment office. The loungers were where she had left them. They seemed to have grown a little older.

'I'm not getting any money,' she said. 'I'm starving.'

'You have to wait six weeks.'

'Six weeks?'

'Six.'

'A person could starve!'

'A person could.' He smiled at her quite nicely.

'Any jobs then?'

He hunted out her card and read it slowly. 'Could be.' He looked up at her. 'Could well be.'

'In ballet? I mean ballet? That's all I can do.'

'It so happens,' the employment clerk said deliberately, 'that we have a request for just that. For just very that. Down town here. Three afternoons a week at a private dancing school. Payment by the hour.'

He watched interestedly as she went pale.

She told him she lived out of town. She told him she had no transport.

'But you managed to get here.' He was very gentle.

'Get stuffed!' she said.

There were delays of chequeless bravado during which her friends consoled, nourished, advised.

'Longest time I've been employed was a month last year. Actually I've only had to do three months' work in the last eighteen. Not bad, eh?' one said. He was plumply in the pink and given to bib-front overalls above which his seraph smile challenged the world. 'No hassle. No sweat. Look at it this way: We're eating, aren't we? We got no problems, have we? As long as we purchase we're keeping the economy fluid. Someone pays, hey hey hey!'

But after another six weeks the rest of the commune became a little weary of her having no money to contribute. It cut right across community spirit. And at times Wait-a-while's yowling seemed excessive. Dimly, vaguely, like an afterthought, she recalled her parents.

Dear folks, went her letter home after memory had dredged up her address, *I've got it all together up here. The climate most of the time means relax relax, the family's working pretty hard at self-sufficiency (guess you city-slickers don't know what that means, huh?) and we're growing lots of our own stuff.* She chewed on her pen end and inspected the wilting banana-tree that cringed away from the door. *But it's tough going sometimes and most of us are trying for jobs in town but it's like everywhere I guess there's simply nothing going. Sometimes I feel I should have done a typing course like you suggested but who wants that sort of coop-up? Not me. Sun light trees air — we've got it all.*

Well almost all. It's like this Mum and Dad if you can see your way to sending me a little something, the clinking kind I mean to tide me over for a couple of weeks I'd be ever so. We're flat out of fertiliser and stuff and the old agro-eco system (sorry to get so tech!) needs a jolt.
Take care.

Your Moth child.

It was three weeks of shag-wagon Kombis and talcum dust before their reply came.

Darling, they wrote, *we were so happy to hear from you and know you are all right. It's a very long time since we've heard and we weren't even sure of your address. Dad and I would have answered sooner but we've been ever so busy these last weeks painting the old place up (you wouldn't know it! — bamboo beige with chocolate trim) and then the roof developed this terrible leak. I suppose you read about the floods we had last month. Anyway, everything was chaos. So we've had all this enormous expense, what with getting the mud out and the paint and the roof and everything.*

We're so glad to know you've been thinking about suitable employment. Dad says he'd be only too happy to pay for you to go to business college, but he would like you to do it down here where it would be more practical. Please think about —

Moth dropped the letter like an unclean tissue onto the floor.

'Oh, shit!' she cried. 'Those mean bastards. Those stinking shit-mean bastards!'

Wait-a-while hooked onto her dangling skirts and worked away with a banana.

'Don't worry,' Bo advised tenderly. 'Don't worry, Moth. No hassles, eh? I'll try my olds.'

He wrote them a postcard because there was less space to fill. He asked for fifty dollars.

It was a long time since he had written and even longer since he had seen them. They still had other children to worry about and wisely assumed their son's sheer largeness was his best protection. Yet now and then, moved by some memento of her eldest in the quirks of her youngest — a puckered grin, the vulnerability of large scabby knees — his mother had sent him soft concerned notes that said, 'Write me, son. Let me know if I can help.' Peering through the brightly lit picture-windows of love, she observed her own unquenchable devotion but believed it to be his.

She wrote at once, a long paragraph of tenderness. She told him about his brothers; she uttered oblique and timid pleas for his return; she worried about his health; she hoped he was able to find a job; she wondered humbly would they see him for Christmas. Also she included a large cheque — and as she gummed down the envelope her youngest child dropped from the tree where he had been terrifying some currawongs and broke his shoulder.

She forgot to post the letter.

It was a month before she remembered, for during that time as well she had discovered a lump in her breast and there had been all the bother of an operation. Her penitence expanded like some monster balloon gassed up with affection as she tore the unposted letter open, added a postscript of contrition and an even larger cheque. She didn't tell him about the lump. 'Write me,' she wrote. 'Tell us how you're getting on.' And she explained his brother's nasty accident.

Each day for that month Bo, who was worrying himself out of the boyish freshness that marked him, foot-padded the four miles into Mango, sometimes with Moth and Wait-a-while, sometimes with a very plump girl who had just joined the family after finding Jesus, sometimes on his own.

Blue Kombis, dust, shag-wagons.

In what passed for winter in this distant north, the land-scape became clear, definite, and the canopy of the rain-forest, he observed, trudging along his high ridge, looked like astrakhan across which the shadows lay in wispy layers of blue. He remained care-free; but in the third week Moth ran away to Brisbane with a passing folk-singer who was forming a skiffle band. Absent-mindedly she forgot to take Wait-a-while, who failed to miss her; but unexpectedly Bo pined as he munched on his pumpkin seeds and finally he scrounged a few sheets of paper and wrote.

Dear remembered friend,

I welcome this opportunity to dispense with bullshit say what fond memories I have of you. I can't say that the thought of you being so far away hurts, time was always the best remedy for hurt but I would really dig to hear from you, the cherished memories mean less when I realise how much you'd changed you must have. I still read the old letters you sent me a year ago when you went away P.S. with no returning address, remember those days? which stir a fondness which never seem there in old situation. I'm glad you make me realise the affinity I had for you listen kid I want to see your ass back this summer. Funny how a hick town like Mango becomes the other half just because I'm here and converse. So package yourself away from Mister Acne and other city shrinking pains and preserve thyself my child. The best package I seem to find is happy friends that's one thing I wish on you — so if you ever run short remember your own puss is magnificent. Other choice newsy items follow: — Over the last two weeks everyone has grown two weeks. Everybody is a far more interesting thing I'm starting to get a head together making more different friends is what we need most (eh? as someone once wrote me) it's easier now all is less tense pretty big 'adolescent' type problem to conquer!! Pause for a think mind is blank Wait-a-while pretty cool but pining, have been reading Nabokov man just like the old 'tin drum' beat away while I read it does me good also scrape the copper together and get along to see the first Fellini Film you come across man we miss out on so much colour speaking English (said he spelling it with ISK) *How go narcotics down there, not as good as food — I had such a* WOW *time over the last few weeks — dope mescaline music leading into a pill pop party which cooled me off for the present while Heavy*

*Heavy Scene kid it's like whiskey payout or keep dry no inbetween
Why do I tell you this What am I doing I hope Brisbane mail has
more respect than fucking Mango customs Ho hum long arm of
the Queensland law. Well kid? get the picture — saying may head
is coming together is sure sign that it aint Bliss to be insane and
irrelevant. Give us all the dope, huh, joke!*

There was further silence while Moth in the dry south
became the slightest of wing flickers around the twenty-
watt bulb.

Bo kept walking the road to town with the dust, the
shag-wagons, the blue Kombis. One of the farmers along
the river offered him a job, but he only stayed two days,
blushed, and told the bloke he had a crook back.

The weather changed. Clouds marshalled their slow
moving ranks up from the coast, nudged the hills and
burst in an apocalypse of water. After, there was calm and
penitence, a smidgin of penance during the steady wash-
away round the piles of the damp humpy where five of
them now stared miserably out through the sticky air at
Wait-a-while slushing round in the mud beneath the banana suckers. He fell and was covered in slime and came back
inside to complain.

'Cool it, man,' they told him. 'Don't make a heavy scene.'

Bo kept promising the others that the olds had to write.
The spirit of the commune was becoming impatient and
Bo felt he was a terrible burden.

When the Wet had got into rhythm, when Moth had
failed to answer, he trailed one day during a sun-burst,
lugging Wait-a-while along the highway slush into town.
The corner pub had sculptured arrangements of darkies
and despair. There was a further grouping beneath the
awning of the old picture hall. It was three days to Christmas
and Mango was sweating its expectation. An old Aboriginal woman was squatting on the steps of the hall mulling
over her shopping-list aloud with a bent old black man. 'I'll
git a poun' a' sausage mince,' she was saying. 'An' tripe.
Maybe bitta tripe.'

Bo's rush of pity changed to pain for himself. He wanted
to howl. Jesus, he thought, back home they'd be doing the

tree and all, and mum cooking herself stupid and chicken and the lot: pudding with sauce and the kids crackling round on wrappings all colours, blowing the squeakers: even the old man mellowed out after a couple of jugs. He gave Wait-a-while a hug that made the kid bellow with surprise, hollering with his mouth stretched wide and a nose that needed wiping. Write to me, mum, Bo was pleading inside. Write. And hugging away at the stringy kid.

Charlie Hanush, the postmaster, was watching through the door; he was an acid cove, filled with the wonder of near-retirement. He moved dedicated and deadly through the paper-work of his days in which each memo was planted square and each day rectangular; and he couldn't stand these bums always coming in bugging him for mail and cheques. His face didn't alter as he watched Wait-a-while yelp for a pee, saw Bo take off the kid's pants and steer the little trickle onto the grass patch.

Bo hauled the kid up the post-office steps, still holding Wait-a-while's pants, and dumped him on the office counter. Bo's candid grin was beginning to be muddled by hopelessness.

'Hi, Mr Hanush!'

'Son,' Mr Hanush said, 'get that kid of yours off the counter.'

'Any mail for me?'

'Look, I said to get that kid off, eh? You deaf or something? Don't want any bare bottoms there, see? Not where the public has to use it.'

Bo lifted Wait-a-while from another small frightened puddle.

'Oh, God!' Mr Hanush said. His wife fussed over with a rag.

'Geez,' Bo said. 'Geez, I'm sorry, man. That's a lousy scene.'

'It's a wet scene, son.'

There was a smell of Dettol. A couple of Bo's buddies lounged in the door behind him and started fidgeting near the telegram forms. Bo grinned uneasily.

'I thought this was the high-smile area.'

'What,' Mr Hanush asked, leaning his bitter bones forward in threat, 'can I do for you?'

'Any mail then? I asked. Kimball.'

'Say please.'

Bo sniggered with embarrassment. 'Please,' he said.

Elaborately avoiding the damp patch, Mr Hanush stretched over to the pigeon-holes and took down a wad of mail. Slowly, extra slowly, he began sorting it over, not looking up at Bo's strained face. 'Here,' he grunted after a bit. 'There's one for you.' And he held out a letter to one of Bo's buddies who cackled pleasantly and went down the steps. Bo shuffled his thongs about on the floor. He felt like a dog waiting for — Jesus! even a pat!

Mr Hanush went right down to the bottom of the bundle and then started again from the top. 'Might have missed it.' He gave Bo an ironic smile. 'We can't be too careful, can we?'

Finally he looked up as he extracted a bulky letter from the pile and stared hard into Bo's face.

'Here. One for you.' And he placed it carefully in the circle of wet. 'I was beginning to think you didn't have a pal in the world.'

Bo giggled, wide-eyed. 'Who, me? Me?'

He grabbed the letter.

'And listen, Bo,' Mr Hanush said, 'just get that kid out. We can do without the Wet indoors.'

'Like funny, man!' Bo said, cheeky again. He didn't care. He could recognise his mum's hand. 'Hey hey hey! They've written!'

Dumping Wait-a-while on the top step he ripped open the envelope and opened up the letter. There it was. The cheque. Jee — *sus*! Carelessly he crumpled the letter into a ball, shot it light-heartedly across the footpath into the gaping trash bin and raced down the steps flapping the cheque at his waiting buddies.

'Geez, man!' he cried. 'Geez!' And his eyes filled with tears. 'They've written!'

Margaret Barbalet

Margaret Barbalet, born 1949, has had short stories and two histories published, the latest being *Far from a Low Gutter Girl* (1983). Her first novel, *Blood in the Rain*, was released by Penguin in June 1986. Her second novel is to be published by Penguin next year. She is at present working on her third novel. She is married with three sons and lives in Canberra.

The Mincer

Joshua got out the mincer on a winter's morning at 7 a.m.

From somewhere under a tangle of sleep, blankets, a purring cat and Ken's desire, Sally heard the clatter in the dimness of their bedroom. He's six, she thought, old enough not to hurt himself. She heard in the distance the hooter for the railway workshops, imagined the fog that would hang over the town like a giant's breath, the ice that would have made every blade a whitened tooth. She snatched two more drifts into sleep before Katie rushed in, with a look of triumph at the stupid baby imprisoned by its bassinet. They lay in bed, coming-to while Katie talked.

Early morning sleep always seemed the best to her, the bed shallow, rumpled, warm. She liked to drift in, wave by wave, hated the crunch of moving bodies, the grittiness of voices. Sometimes Katie's voice, low with Ken's could put her back to sleep, so long was the accounting of Katie's dreams. She and Ken had agreed, it seemed fair, not to ask if the dreams were improvised or actual re-tellings; the child, her round stomach, protruding egg-like, between pyjama top and trousers, understood better than she and Ken what dreams might be.

'I don't dream Katie,' Ken was saying softly.

'Ask Mummy if she does.'

Katie looked.

'O she does. I know, I know,' the little girl replied not needing to use emphasis.

Sally knew she never dreamed. There wasn't time in her short bursts of sleep. Dreams were like early morning sex, impromptu meals in restaurants, sleeping-in: things that only newly-married couples sinned at.

'How do you know I dream.' She had to smile.

'You do, you do. I hear you. "N" I see the light of your dreams from my room.'

She fell on Sally's face, beginning to laugh because after one glance her parents had begun to laugh so that the bed shook. They would never convince her; she was as right and perfect in her 3-year-old shape and confidence as a newly-laid strong-shelled egg. Our best product, our best yoke, Sally thought wryly, getting into slippers and dressing-gown, turning on extra heaters.

But in the kitchen faced with the organisation of breakfast her mood wavered again. Joshua had laid out the pieces of the mincer, bit by bit, across the floor with superb organisation and precision. The box and the printed instruction booklet lay by the window, the discs and blades, the drums and the motor itself lay right across the highway between the stove and the breakfast bar.

'Right Josh, you can just pack it up again.'

He appealed, dressed, she noticed and four stages away from tears.

'We're not using it today and that's that.'

'I put it out so that you could pick the pieces, the right size,' he said angrily.

'I don't need to *see* the bits,' Sally said, pouring rice bubbles onto Katie's wheetbix.

'You forgot sugar.'

She had and went to the cupboard for the packet of brown sugar.

'I've poured your tea,' Ken said pacifically.

Sally put on Joshua's milk to heat and got out the cat's saucer. Her foot caught in the mincer cord and she saw with shame, how relieved Joshua was that she hadn't tripped. He was, like the cat jumping back now from its too hot saucer of milk, sensitive to the smallest change in her moods, so that if she was ill or irritable he would through reflected tension come within reach of making her lose her temper by becoming insistent and demanding, but like her he was open and unabashed in his affections when he was happy.

Ken fed himself slices of bread and vegemite behind the paper, not really part of the activity she noticed with a twinge of resentment. She knew if she asked him he would say 'It's between you and the kids: the mincer', but she also knew that he would back her up in whatever decision she came to. They had long ago reached this politic: provide alibis, prevent negotiations, bring in reinforcements. They went over their moves as parents in private. Spend too much time on it, she had said only last night in bed when finding some small space together they had found one such earnest conversation diluting the deliciousness of their private mutual nakedness.

She and Joshua sat down together to their muesli and hot milk in a barely maintained truce.

Outside the fog seemed thicker than ever, more oppressive every minute, simply by its blank presence, like a guest who stays without talking, a blind blocking the big window's views, breakfast's charms.

'Thank goodness we don't live on the flat,' she said to Ken as he went off to the bathroom. 'At least this'll lift by eleven.'

'I reckon actually people quite enjoy the winter. You've got to adjust, stay one step ahead.' Their one step last winter had been a rear-window demister, the year before that, an extra heater for their bedroom.

'Comfort becomes everything you mean,' she said brusquely, rejecting his smile, but feeling, with her second cup of tea and muesli behind her, at least able to attempt the hard ground of conversation. Katie wandered in to watch her father shave.

'The trouble is, I promised him,' Sally began.

Ken nodded from behind a beard of shaving foam, hesitated and gave Katie a dab of foam on her nose.

'Your treat,' he looked unsmiling at Sally, serious as always in his kindness, 'is that I'll wash up the pieces.'

His dab of generosity given, he stepped into the shower. He left at 8.40 on foot, stepping into the fog, tall and fair in gloves and overcoat and honour, not to return till five. Once long ago he had not been fair in one minor thing, and so true was he in everything that she remembered it to this day, like a single flaw in a gem.

A moment arrived when, with the baby still a-bed and Katie and Joshua watching TV, she could step into the shower. Achievement lay in getting dressed, having time to comb her hair whilst looking in the mirror not while gathering coats and bags and children on her way out. The face that looked back at her above a greasy-wool jumper was thin, young and worn; a face stilled and caught against the rich unravelled tapestry of the bedroom behind her, different she supposed to the face she never saw, the face that moved through a thousand spaces, a hundred rooms, that went from here to there, that never saw itself moving through days and lives, drawing all the whisps bobbin-like, whirring into rope. This face, a second later armed into a coat, shut the door and carried the bassinet into the hall.

'Josh, Katie, faces and teeth.'

He was supposed to remember his own but regularly slipped down to Katie's level. Between them they left dabs, little white crosses of toothpaste on the taps, on the floor, on Sally's fingers for their trying. Her hand through the face washer touched the faces they had made, scoured the ears and sent them into the hall to the coat-rack.

The thermos poured down the windows of the car and the children inside suddenly appeared through the glass, arguing, waving back through the immobility of hats, gloves and parkas. It wouldn't be long now she marvelled, before he remembered the mincer.

She drove carefully through the tiny frozen streets of the town. On days like this she always expected snow, could smell it in the air. But it never came. The fog parted around the car in whisps. The children were silent. She came in no time to the bridge that connected their outlying new housing estate with the town and slid the car apprehensively onto the iced wooden planks, driving across in third, feeling the hidden river below her, swollen with melted snow, impatient, black between its banks.

'Mummy, you *promised* the mincer today.' It burst out triumphantly as she turned towards the school.

'I know; and we'll do it today, after school.' Promises were like the law, gaols and punishments; part of a world Joshua claimed as his.

'And I'll do the pushing and you can do the chopping.'

'You can watch, Katie.' He slammed the door and darted into his other world: school. Katie craned her neck, her usual pretence of knowing what school was like, Sally noticed as she turned round to back the car, abandoned for an open-eyed stare at the children who bobbed and soared between the redbrick buildings like floats on a grey sea.

Damn, she'd forgotten the lights.

Feeling chastened she drove off, beating down waves of guilt at her carelessness, the car fumbling through the fogged streets of the town.

Ruth's house was old, verandahed, dignified until the door opened. Then an image of her own house greeted Sally. Wool lay in baskets, waiting to be spun, lego and fingermarks decked the hall, books lay awry on the hall table, a shoe stopped the door. Swatches of Ruth's hair hung out of her plaits. Behind her legs, Janet's small face was silent with barely suppressed tears. The baby Michael cried from the kitchen.

'I'm all fluey. I won't breathe my germs on you.' Ruth managed a pantomime of someone with leprosy or lassa fever from the other side of the room. Sally found herself shepherding Janet's coat and hat, while Ruth went to Michael. She shut the front door.

'When's Bob back?'

'Tomorrow.'

'We all had it last week.'

Sally thought of that chaos though this week's events which had already piled up to erase their week of illness. She looked at Ruth, saw her puffy and tangled in her reluctance to be direct.

'Look, I'll take Michael. Give you a free morning. He'll be alright with me.'

Relief flared on Ruth's face even as she began the usual disclaimers: Sally was busy, you won't have time.

'Come on, it's nothing. You need a morning in bed. I mean I know you won't—'

'But at least I can get through this in peace. I've got an Economics assignment due, too.'

Sally picked up the baby, awkwardly unhandled in his smooth bulky coat, and carried him out to the car. Ruth's morning had altered; a stroke through the ocean of parenthood became for a moment, less effort. Sally drove to the pre-school and led in Katie and Janet, a weather-clock pair, one promising sun, the other, rain, and then drove home through the husbandless streets.

As soon as she walked in she put out the meat for the mincer onto the sink to defrost. She usually liked bathing Felix alone, enjoying the warm room, the ease of his fatness in the water, their jokes. But this morning she had to put the watchful unsmiling Michael in the bouncinette, with the bathroom door ajar and despite not needing to, couldn't resist hurrying through his bath feeling the responsibility of the extra child hanging heavily on the ticking hands of the clock. Pushing down a sense of unease that Ruth might disapprove she gave Michael a Heinz rusk after she'd changed him. Felix then began to cry at not being fed immediately after his bath, presaging the pattern of the morning: a series of minor displacements, immediate demands, repeated actions, inches forward over some vast map of time that crept towards adulthood.

'They got on very well.'

Janet ran to her mother and burst into tears. Ruth was neat and recovered by 12, when Sally dropped off the children.

'You're looking very trim,' Ruth called enviously as Sally backed down the drive.

'It's the swimming. I'm going tonight.'

The day was now, as all foggy days were, brilliant with a sky of lunatic blue. Sally let Katie out of the back door and ate four vegemite sandwiches wolfishly, standing up at the sink. Then she ate a raw carrot for health's sake and put on the kettle. Setting the water running on the dishes piled in the sink she saw through the window the little girl murmuring below in the sandpit, the enchantment of the day's zenith, the willow trees along the river beginning to glow orange with August hope. Leaving the dishes in the water, against the current of her own efficiency she went out down the steps.

'Bury your hand Mummy.'

Lopsided, her arm up to the wrist in a glove of sand she gazed across the lawn. The sun surprised her back, uncramping. A space like this, had to be stolen she thought from days full of measurement and movement, of things to be done, one after another, meals, nappies, baths, grease and scraps, other people's mess, all essential, none important. She was thirty-three and had discovered her last year to be the swiftest she had known and yet it was made up of trivial minutes, no degrees worth anything, no economics courses merely grain-like tasks piled each on each, that falling through some narrow space filled a vacuum, announced something: what she wondered, half-amused; the perfectly timed egg.

On the steps at the back of the house their tabby cat folllowed the sun, lay coiled like a periwinkle shell against the sharp winds, finding in each half of the day warm patches, teaching resignation to the cold, the seasons, change.

She went in to the baby's cry.

Katie came in sandy and tired and she read her a 'quick' book. That was the second child's lot; a quick book.

When she was bringing in the washing Joshua burst in, dropped off by a friend. The stewing steak lay sullenly on the end of the sink moist in its plastic bag and he danced around it. Why did she hate dealing with the mincer so much. I'm inconsistent she thought, knowing that she didn't mind cooking mince or legs of lamb or chicken. No, it was the intimate contact with cutting and tearing that she hated, the incarnadine fingerprints, the smell of blood that lingered on the skin.

Joshua was eager, intent, untired; assembling the mincer, getting up on a chair, pushing the chunks of meat down towards the whirring blades. She tried to be at least gracious. It would soon be over. 'Makes good mince.' But her heart wasn't in it.

About half-way through the meat the machine became sullen. The six worms of mince stopped falling into the dish and twitched only crumbs down onto the plate.

'Better put some bread through.'

'It's still not working Mummy.'

Sally, coming back from planting Katie in front of 'Playschool' knew why with a sense of dread.

280

'Too much gristle. I should have cut it off.'

'What bristle?'

'Gristle. This white stuff on the meat. The blades can't chop it.'

He was fascinated.

'Why can't the blades chop it.'

Despairingly she put more squares of bread through the top, then answered. 'It gets wrapped around the screw.'

The motor whirred on louder than ever with nothing appearing.

'Bristle.' Joshua sighed with excitement, sensing a drama.

'Gristle.'

Sally turned off the mincer and put the moving parts into the sink. She tried to unscrew the end but it was stuck fast. She tried holding the parts under a running tap.

'Bristle, dreadful bristle.'

'Gristle,' she snapped at his sympathy. The motor came apart with a wrench in her hands. White shreds clotted the blades, a button of bound gristle was tied around the centre of the screw. Her heart sank and she put the pieces in the sink and let the water run on them. Outside it was nearly dark, the trees gathered in the garden into dark shapes. The phone rang. Ken.

'I'm really sorry but there's an emergency meeting over the cuts. I'll have to go.'

'But I'm going swimming . . . don't worry.'

She snapped off his sympathy to choke her own disappointment, promising him she would go another night. Walking away from the phone she saw Joshua's schoolbag had been left in the hall.

'Go and put your bag away; hurry-up. I've told you and told you.' She turned on the lights, yanked across the curtains. In the sink, small unimportant shreds of white floated; the main wad was still stuck fast. She began tearing at it, her hands the same temperature as the water, plunging deeper and deeper into revulsion, her fingernails scraping at the flesh. Joshua sidled back. When the sink was soupy with water and gristle she finally rinsed the pieces, dried them and reassembled the mincer. They finished the job in silence.

Later when the mince was steaming gently on the stove she put the two elder children in the bath and fed the baby. 'Trusting and irrelevant baby' she thought looking down at his big head. Through the doorway she could see the steamy warmth of the bathroom, the pink tiles and the heads of Joshua and Katie playing with the soap, moist hair crinkling on the lambent necks. She had been through this scene so many times; the children and their life preventing some plan or pleasure for her, that it had long since ceased to surprise her. But sitting in the warm room, the yellow curtains closed against the abyss of winter night, she still felt herself sink a little more heavily into the chair, felt the balance of the day's energies fall a little weighted to one side as she fought off self-pity. She got up and put the baby to bed.

When they were all in bed, a great silence fell. She knew it was fatal to sit down at this point, so she forced herself to wash up quickly. Near the end she gave the cupboard doors a quick wipe with Ajax and then, because it was the end and only tea and the television awaited her, and they would wait, she lent her head against the cupboard letting tiredness at last, fill up her legs and back, all the day's loneliness and trivia and work flow past her eyes, until they shut.

'Bad time to call?'

Sally jumped. A hair remained, stuck to the cupboard wrenched from her by tiredness and Ajax.

It was Marjorie; grey, energetic middle-aged. She was carrying a spinning wheel, opening the back door.

'Joys of parenthood.' Sally got out another cup.

'August is . . . the cruellest month. I never did like Elliot. Weaving was great tonight Sal.'

They sat around the table and talked and because Marjorie was old enough to be her mother, because she had had five children, Sally told and confessed, knowing she was also asking.

'No, go on, I can ring Keith.' Sally realised that Marjorie didn't want the gratitude that giving a lot, would deserve; she wanted this favour to be a little thing.

'It's nothing. They'll be OK. You go.'

Ruth-like, Sally demurred, but half an hour later found herself swimming.

The water was heated, the pool enclosed in the big new Sports Centre. She went up and down a few lengths, wet her hair, began in earnest, her mile. Ribbons of light wavered on the water. Her body fell away, felt alone, strong, perfect, at home in the water, embraced. Sidestroking her way to the end on her tenth lap she looked at the other swimmers. Serious, grey with age they ploughed on and on week after week almost submerged but always turning, persisting, labouring on to some number of lengths, some distance, some achievement that only they would remember. The end of the pool, she thought, looked so far away but if you just kept on, stroke after stroke, not fast but determined, you would get there. That was being a swimmer.

Sue Chin

Sue Chin lives in Sydney. She has had poems published in a range of literary magazines and is currently working on short stories and a novel. Besides writing, she keeps house, studies and works.

Scratch at the Dark Soil

This morning I awoke early, but too late, she was gone, already deep inside the garden which had opened up like a palm to receive her.

I crawled out of bed and over to the window of her bedroom, and then, when I saw her, I had to grab hold of the dusty pane, and wait for the dull ache that would soon start in an unspecific part of my body. (The room was sour with sleep. Once, she had said: This is what the inside of an egg smells like.) I wrapped the first thing I laid eyes on, an earth-coloured rug she brought home from India, around my shoulders, and watched her from the window. I knew she would not see me, unless I called out. As usual, I rested my weight almost completely on my left foot. My right foot was slightly weaker than my left, as a result of a sprain left unattended and only partly healed. (Luckily I was not left with a limp, but in winter it throbbed terribly, and also after long walks on the beach.) My breath made a misty circle on the glass, so I moved back a little, and settled down to watch her.

I thought, as I had so many times before: this garden is really a forest in disguise. Shrubs and bushes sprouted along the winding path which led to her front door. Huge trees crowded the sky out. They shed an endless supply of leaves all year, and she never attempted to clear the thick, crisp carpet that covered the front lawn. The sun, whenever it could, squeezed through small spaces, and fell in splinters onto the ground below, throwing dark shadows everywhere. (When I was a child, I used to paint watercolour pictures of my farm in the country. They were mostly horrible, and the ones I took to school to show my teacher were stared at, then carefully corrected. I suppose it was because I never left any room for the sky. My teacher's feathery voice would inquire gravely: but you must have *some* blue in it, mustn't you? My pictures were a claustrophobic's nightmare — house, pond, yard, animals, fence, trees, tractor and people all squashed tightly together, as if their creator was afraid they would disappear into thin air. And the sky finally appeared, if at all, as specks of diffident blue in a landscape predominantly flesh and mud.)

Later she will walk in with the first flowers of the season, I think she said red and orange roses, still pungent from being outside, where the winds blow. She will arrange them in a walnut-coloured vase, and place them on the table in the lounge. In the evening, I will start to think about dinner, and pass through the lounge on the way to the kitchen. She will be sitting cross-legged on the sofa, looking like a sleepy Buddha, head tilted at a slight angle, eyes half-closed but focused. The sun will be splashing in through the stained windows overhead, and give the whole picture an unearthly glare that will make me wince. When I pass her, bowed and blinded, she will look up, unsurprised, smile in her slow, languid way, and she will say: never ever will I tire of this. And knowing me, I will somehow manage to smile back, and stumble into the kitchen, my weak right foot knocking over bits of her handmade pottery and stepping on clean white sheets of paper, my eyes all the time looking down. (But all this happens much later. And if she is wrong about the roses and they are not yet ready, it will be daisies instead.)

I watch her, still as a ghost, at the window. She is in her garden, bent over, her fingers scratching at the damp soil. Today she is planting something new. Everything she plants grows and grows. Her neighbours learn that this is so, and come out of their homes, to knock sheepishly at her front door, cradling dead or dying plants. She takes them, telling their frightened owners to return in a week.Every day she talks to them, tends them, reveals her innermost self to them. Then her neighbours return, she has cups of tea with them, and they leave with their resurrected plants, disbelieving but insanely happy. Her fingers are forever black with the colour of soil. She is convinced that is their natural tone, that her mother had them dipped in pink dye at birth, to avoid the embarrassment. But sometimes the beauty ads prove too strong to resist, and that is why there are four kinds of handcream in the bathroom. Last night, as she applied one of them onto her hands and fingers, I sat on the floor in front of her. Why don't you stop, I said, they're beautiful like that. What, this? and she laughed and stuck her hands in front of my face. I saw the grit lodged permanently underneath the yellow nails, and the rough skin around the fingertips. They're beautiful like that, I said again. She shook her head and continued to work the cream deep into her skin. I grabbed both hands and squeezed. She jumped, then became very still. My voice sounded muffled when I spoke. Why don't you stop, I kept saying, over and over, and I must have been crying. She stayed very still. She looked at me without blinking, not even once. Please, she said at last, please don't cry. And I will not be worshipped like this. Will you let go? (But I held on. I had to hold on. I would have died, otherwise.)

From the window, in this early morning light, in this lucid morning light, she looks strong enough to bear the weight of the whole world on her shoulders. Her knees must be making two hollows in the wet earth, and her fingers still dig deep. Her hair is tied back and piled high on her head. Suddenly she straightens up. In one fluid movement she arches her back, brings her arms up above her head until they almost touch the sky. She looks up into the trees. I believe she is strong enough to face anything.

And yet, once, she whispered: I am not strong. She has a friend named Judith. They have long conversations on the phone, usually when I'm out walking or half-heartedly looking for work. Once I happened to come in early, and Judith was on the phone, so she dropped her voice to a whisper and began to watch her face in the mirror. I crouched in the doorway and heard snatches. I felt awful. Like a criminal, and I suppose I was wrong, but I needed to hear myself being spoken about, to her friends, would I recognise myself? I didn't meet many of her friends, only the ones she thought I'd be civil to, and the slightly idiotic ones, the ones she liked because they knew how to be contented, or because they were simple and undemanding, unlike me. I never met Judith, whose voice came out of the telephone like warm milk. She called the most, and they often had lunch together, from which I imagine they both left radiant and bonded even closer than they were before. (I imagined she was tall and big-boned, with eyes that people called bewitching, and that she always referred to me as 'the problem', as though I was some sort of helpless cripple.) So I crouched in the doorway like a shameful thief, and I suppose I shouldn't have, because then I heard her say, and her voice was low and desperate, and I shivered because it was strange, it was not her voice that said: I am not strong enough. How will I catch him when he falls?

Still at this window, watching. She works on, bent over, her fingers must be tired, the air must hurt to breathe in, it must be thin and pencil-sharp, but still she continues to lift and mould the earth, still she continues to breathe. Her face is full and aflame with this cold, sharp air, she is fearless to breathe so much of it. I want to do something, but she is far off. I shift my weight onto my right foot for a while, then resume leaning on my left. I watch her, I want to call out, or move, but instead I can only remember her voice, low and desperate in the hall.

A year ago, before I lost my job and took to stumbling over furniture and mumbling to myself like a ghost, she had an operation to get her appendix removed. After four restful days in hospital, the doctor said — time to go home, we need your bed. She laughed but her eyes flickered. So soon? Surely it's too soon, she said. I arrived at the hospital to drive her home. She sat up in bed, fully dressed, holding on to the sides with fists that were clenched tight. I looked around for something to do but her case was packed. A nurse stood in the corner and looked reproachful. Come on, I said. Let's go. She shook her head, closed her eyes, and held on. The nurse moved forward but I waved her back. It's alright, let's go home, I said, trying to watch my voice. Her face was squeezed shut. I'm not coming, she said. I'm not properly healed, tell the doctor I'm not ready to leave. Ask him why I can't stand up. Her face was so scared and determined I laughed. Yes you can, I said, I'll help. Finally she let go. All the way home in the car, she sat hunched-up, silent. When she got out to walk, she was doubled over. That night, I said: try to straighten up, you'll hurt your back with that bending. She growled at me, no, I'll break the stitches or something. In bed she slept with her back to me, her knees drawn up to her chin like an infant. I prodded her neck. At least change places so I can see your face, I said. But she winced when I tried to touch her, so I left her alone. For two weeks she hobbled around the house like an old woman, refusing to straighten up from her position. One day, as she sat on the edge of the bed trying to do her shoes up, I kneeled down on the floor in front of her. I traced the fine lines around her mouth and said: Why don't you stand up? You're usually so strong, you could fly if you wanted to. She looked at me, and her eyes were quiet and full. When she smiled I felt the ache begin, and for no reason I cried out. Then, with a strength I didn't know she had ever had, she lifted me bodily, off the floor and onto the bed beside her. She took my hands and held them until I calmed down. Then she got up, still bent over, crossed the room to the window, the one I'm standing at now, and looked out into the garden.

Lately I have been watching her in her sleep. Her breathing is rough, like paper when it is crumpled up. Her face is quiet. I have had to get up and leave the room, and sometimes I think I will really do it: reach over, grab her capable shoulders, and shake her with all my useless frustration, until her hair comes loose and falls over my chest like a bunch of snakes, until she cries out in pain and I am spent with shaking and hissing into her quiet face — wake up, help me, will you wake up and help me?

I have been careless. I must have called out, because she turns and waves. I wave back, and pretend that I have just strolled over to the window and seen her outside, that I must now move away, it is too cold and I must get some clothes on. She returns to work and forgets I am there. I resume my position at the window, I continue to watch her. Her arms are firm and they keep digging deep and touching new soil.

On Thursdays she goes to yoga. She tries to make me come along, but I tell her I don't want to meet people 'at peace' with themselves. The bitter edge in my voice when I say that seems lost on her. She merely shrugs and says something like: the label is yours, not theirs, or mine. They're as afraid as you are. I pretend I don't understand, it's all too deep for me, I say, my voice light as air. For three, sometimes even four hours every Thursday, the house dies, slowly. I crouch like an animal in the lounge, where it is the brightest, and stare at the walls until she comes home. (Once, she came in and found me cowering in the corner. She came at me like an avenging spirit, pulled me to my feet, and shook me until I heard my teeth rattle. Then she let go, and ran into the room, sobbing and saying over and over: Why can't you help yourself?) When she walks in through the front door, a funny thing happens. All the lights in the house, the ones that are on, suddenly become brighter, as though someone replaced all the old bulbs with new ones, or recharged them. She pounds her feet on the mat outside, saying something about the cold. As she swings the door shut, the Indian shawl around her shoulders slaps against the grill. The wind must be fierce, she rubs her hands together and the sound is red and grating. She smiles at me, and if I try hard enough I manage to pretend that the light in her eyes has something to do with me. (Perhaps she wants me to hold her.) But the fact is, and even I can't deny this: she is somewhere else, in a place I could never prove exists. I suppose it's some kind of road that we're on, and she is moving steadily along it, her step is eager and light, and I am trailing further and further behind, because of my weak right foot. So I walk into the bedroom, I get under the sheets, I curl up into a tight ball until the bed heats up. And she? She will be sitting on the sofa, in the lounge, where all the lights are on, reading another book and her hair will be falling in curls from her head.

In order to define ourselves, I said once, some of us need the help of others. She looked at me, a little surprised. I seldom spoke about anything, but this time my voice sounded brave and unwavering, and the sentence was clear and complete. But instead she shook her head, so violently I thought for a minute it would fly right off her shoulders. No, she said. We are finally alone. You must not be afraid to get up and go somewhere dangerous, perhaps even life-threatening. Because it is the danger, the fear, the dislocation that cures you. (Of course she is absolutely right. But why won't she help me?) Not all of us can afford a pilgrimage to the East, I said. No, she said, but even here, even here, there are the smells that make you look up, the books that feel like gold in your fingers, the children with wild eyes. All of that is here, too. Can you not see it? (Why won't she help me see?) I started to say something else, but she put her hand over my mouth, and her fingers started poking and stabbing at the air, as if she was trying to weave a solution I too could see and touch. Finally she said: You are helpless because you think I am not. (When she speaks in riddles, I have to smile. Secretly I wish she wouldn't. What does she mean? Why won't she help me?) Last night, my foot felt firm, as though I could walk thousands of beaches and not get tired. As I wandered through the house I could feel all the cracks in the floor, and thought: I could live here for the rest of my life. She sat at a table in the lounge, surrounded by fresh flowers, books, pens and writing paper, and several half-drunk mugs of coffee. She was writing, postcards for Amnesty, I think she said. (She was pleading for the lives of others to be spared. I knew she would be successful. Everything she touched would heal and be made whole, such was the strength and intensity of her power.) I walked into the kitchen and began to fossick for the makings of dinner. I put the garlic and the tomatoes aside, and started on the potatoes. When the mixture was ready I poured everything in, and pushed a long spoon through it. I stood over the stove and the kitchen became warm with the smell, and I concentrated on making the stew rich and thick. I could see part of her face from where I was standing. She would write for a few minutes, face pursed and firm, then she would stop and read what she had written under her breath. Sometimes she would stop for a long while, and look at the space in front of her, head slightly raised, eyes bright but unfocused. I left the stew to simmer, and set the table in the kitchen, taking care not to rattle the cutlery. (We always ate in the kitchen. She loved looking out into the backyard, where there were other flowers and plants, and clothes inevitably hung wet and clean from the line.) Suddenly, there was a loud thump, and the sound of books falling, and of breaking china, and a muffled yell. She burst into the kitchen, her face bright red. The words were caught in her throat, trying to get out. I stood still, unable to move, while the wooden spoon dripped gravy onto the floor. Finally I stammered, what's the matter? Her mouth shuddered, trying to make words. A sound started at the back of her throat. When it came, I thought something inside her was ripping open. I stood still, thinking that perhaps that would calm her. She stormed around the table, once, twice, her skirt making a swishing sound, she grunted half-words and her arm flailed like a scythe above her head. She left the kitchen, and I followed. She made for the bathroom, and threw the cabinet door wide open. I crouched in the doorway, searching for something to say. She reached for a jar of white cream. With loud slapping noises she covered her entire face with it. She swung around to glare at me, her eyes huge and alert in her pancake-face. Look, I know I've been difficult, I started to say. She hissed at me, and I moved back. She brushed past me, and I thought I heard her say: why must it always be you? In the hall she picked up her heavy coat and the front door slammed shut. I wanted to yell after her, it must be me, who would it be, then, but she was gone. Later I found the postcards she'd been working on, the ones addressed to heads-of-government. She had slashed huge crosses in red ink over her neat handwriting. The photographs of prisoners-of-conscience were shredded to bits and the pieces scattered over the table and onto the floor. She must have walked the streets for hours in her clumsy boots, invisible except for her white face and her two wounded eyes. When she stumbled in at last, it was long past midnight. The face cream had carved white lines down her cheeks, and her boots were thick with mud.

Still at this window, watching. She is deep inside her garden. For the second time this morning, she uncoils herself, straightens her back, and stretches up to touch the sky. She turns around and sees me watching her. She lifts her hand and smiles happily, forgetting that she has seen me at the window once before. It is too late for me to move away, or pretend that I am just looking out, on the way to some other part of the house. She waves again, and her mouth, although I cannot possibly hear her, is saying: come outside and help me plant this. I shake my head. She points to the sky, as though somehow that explained everything, she points to the sun that pokes through gaps in the trees and makes black patterns on the ground below. Again her mouth is saying: come outside and help me plant this. I smile, wave, and move away from the window, hoping that the dull ache will not come today. I walk into the lounge, feeling useless and heavy with sleep. My foot is hurting. It is cold. The sun is coming through the windows overhead, and fills the room with sharp white light. I can no longer see her, but I know she is still where I saw her last, digging and breathing hard, her fingers lifting and finding new soil. (I may go to her later. She will need a hot cup of tea.) She must be cold, the air is always cold and thin this time of the morning, and I am tired of tripping over the furniture.

Elizabeth Jolley

Elizabeth Jolley is the author of increasingly acclaimed short stories and novels. *The Well* recently won the 1987 Miles Franklin award. Work is currently being published in the UK, USA and Europe.

My Father's Moon

Before this journey is over I intend to speak to the woman. *Ramsden*, I shall say, *is it you?* The train has just left the first station, there is plenty of time in which to contemplate the conversation; the questions and the answers and the ultimate revelation. It is comfortable to think about the possibilities.

The woman sitting on the other side, diagonally opposite, could be someone I used to know. A long time ago. In another place. Her clothes are of the same good quality, the same materials, even the same colours. It is the tilt of the head which is so remarkably similar. She looks like someone who is passionately fond of the cello. Fond of listening to the cello. I look at her hands and feel sure she plays the piano. When I look at her hands it is as if I can hear her playing a Mozart sonata or practising something from Bach. Repeating and repeating phrases until a perfection is achieved. I am certain, as I go on looking, that she plays Cyril Scott's *Water Wagtail*.

For some time now I have travelled by suburban train to and from the places where I work. This evening I am on the earlier train. I caught the earlier train on purpose even though, because of this, I arrive too soon . . .

I sit staring out of the window at the same meeting places of unknown roads, at the backs of the same shabby houses and garden fences, at the same warehouses and the same smash repair yards and at the now well-known back of the metropolitan markets.

About once a week I catch the earlier train for a special reason. Every week it is the same. Every week I think that this time I will speak to her. This week I am on this train in order to speak to her. I will cross from my seat and sit by her and I will speak to her. I always sit where I can see her from the side and from the back and I sit close enough to hear her voice if she should speak. I long to hear the voice, her voice, to know whether it is the same voice. Voices and ways of speaking often remain unchanged.

This time I almost brought the violin case with me though I am not now accustomed to carrying it when I go out. If Ramsden saw the violin case, if the woman saw it, she would remember.

'They're both in good condition,' the man in the shop said. 'Both the same price. Choose your pick,' he said. 'Take your time.'

I could not make up my mind, and then I chose the violin case. The following week I went back for the camera case but it had gone. The violin case had once been lined with some dark red soft material, some of it was still left. I only opened it once and it was then I saw the remains of the lining. I carried the case whenever I went out.

The first time I saw Ramsden the sentry at the hospital gates had his bayonet fixed. He looked awkward and he blushed as he said; 'Who goes there!' Surprised, I told him my name and my identity card number, it was the middle of the morning and we were challenged, as a rule, only after dark. I supposed the rule must have been changed. A despatch from H.Q., I thought, seeing in my mind the nimble motor cyclist arrive.

Ramsden, on her way out, gave a small smile in the direction of the violin case and I was pleased that I had bought it. On that day I had been at the hospital for seven weeks.

Two people sitting behind me are talking in German. I begin to listen to the animated conversation and grope for meanings in what they are saying in this language which was once familiar. I begin to recognize a few words *eine Dame-keine Ahnung-langsam- Milch und Tränenbàche-mein Elend-zu grosser Schmerz-und so weiter*. But I want the words of cherishing spoken in German. I want those first words the child remembers on waking to the knowing of language. I wish now in the train to be spoken to as *du* . . .

The woman sitting on the other side is looking calmly out of the window. Naturally she sees the same things that I see. It is quite comfortable to know that I have only to lean over and touch her sleeve.

I never worked with Ramsden. I saw her sometimes in the dining room. There are several little pictures of her in my mind. The doctors called her Miss Ramsden. She did the penicillin syringes too. One nurse, usually a senior, spent the whole day cleaning and sterilizing the syringes and the needles, setting up the trolley, giving the injections and then clearing the trolley and cleaning and sterilizing and checking all over again. Whenever I passed the glass doors of the ward where she was I saw her in the sterilizing room seriously attending to the syringes and needles for the three hourly injections.

'Ramsden,' I said, 'this is the part we like isn't it. This part, this is it, we like this —'

'It's the anticipation,' she replied, 'it's what is hoped for and then realized,' she was sitting on the edge of her bed.

'This part, this —,' I said once more. I pointed with one finger as if to place the cello somewhere in the space between us. 'This going down part,' I said, 'is the part we like best.'

Ramsden nodded. She was mending a stocking. Her stockings were not the usual ones, not the grey uniform stockings which were lisle and, after repeated washing, were hard to mend. Ramsden's stockings, I noticed immediately, were smooth and soft and they glistened like honey. Dark, honey coloured stockings. Ramsden's stockings were silk stockings. She was oversewing a run at the ankle. Her sewing was done so carefully I knew the repair would be invisible. She had invited me into her room to listen to a record.

'Do you know why you like it?' she repeated an earlier question. The cello reminded me of her. How could I tell her this. I shook my head. Staff nurse Ramsden, she was senior to me. When she listened to music she sat with her legs crossed over and she moved her foot very slightly, I could see, in time to the music. How could I speak to her about the downward thrust of the cello and about the perfection in the way the other instruments came up to meet the cello. How could I say to her that I thought someone had measured the movement of the notes controlling carefully the going down and the coming up in order to produce this exquisite mixture. There were other things too

297

that I could not speak about. How could I say to her what I thought about the poet Rilke, about his face and about how I felt when I looked at his photograph in the book she had. She knew his poems, understood them. I wanted to tell her that when I looked at Rilke's face I felt clumsy as if made of wood. Even the way he stood in the photograph had something special about it and when I read a poem of his to myself I wanted to read lines aloud to her. 'Listen to this, Ramsden,' I wanted to say, 'listen to this,'

> But hand in hand now with that God she walked,
> her paces circumscribed by lengthy shroudings
> uncertain, gentle, and without impatience.
> Wrapt in herself, like one whose time is near . . .

There were other things too from *Orpheus,* but she knowing his poems might have felt I was intruding. When I read Rilke everything I was trying to write seemed commonplace and unmusical, completely without any delicacy and refinement. I never told Ramsden I was trying to write because what I wrote was about her. I wanted to write about Ramsden. How could I tell her that.

Later when she talked about the music she said the soloist was innocent and vulnerable. She said the music was eloquent and that there was something intimate about the cello. She was very dignified and all her words seemed especially chosen. I wanted her to say them all again to me. The word intimate, I had never before spoken to anyone who used this word. She said the cello, the music of the cello, was intimate. Ramsden's discipline prevented her from repeating what she had said. She continued to oversew her stocking and we listened once more to the second movement. When I listened to a particular passage in this movement I seemed to see Ramsden walking ahead of me with great beech trees on either side of her. Magnificent smooth trees with their rain soaked branches darkened and dripping. Then we were walking together, I imagined, beneath these trees, with the wet leaves deep round our ankles. Ramsden, I thought, would have small ribbed socks on over her stockings . . .

Lyrical, she said, the music was lyrical and I was not sure what she meant. She said then that, if I liked, I could borrow her records.

When I played the record at home my father, not knowing the quailities of the cello, asked if I could make the music a bit quieter. It was my day off, most of it had been wasted because I slept and no one woke me. My father asked was there a piano piece. He said he liked the piano very much. I told him that staff nurse Ramsden played the piano and my mother said perhaps Miss Ramsden would come some time and play the piano for us. She said she would make a fire in the front room and we could all sit and listen . . .

Because I caught the earlier train I have an hour to spare before it is time for the clinic to open. The people who attend this clinic will be setting off from their houses in order to keep their appointments.

I walk to a bus stop where there is a bench and, though I am in a familiar place, I feel as if I have come to a strange land. In one sense there is a strangeness because all the old houses and their once cared for gardens have gone. In their place are tall concrete buildings, floor upon floor of offices, all faced with gleaming windows. Some lit up and some dark. The buildings rise from parking lots all quite similar but unrecognizable as though I have never seen them before. Small trees and bushes planted as ornaments offer a few twigs and leaves. The new buildings are not at peace with their surroundings. They do not match each other and they have taken away any tranquillity, any special quality of human life the streets may have had once.

The Easter lilies, uncherished, appear as they do every year with surprising suddenness, their pink and white long lasting freshness bursting out of the brown, bald patches of earth at the edges of those places which have been left out from the spreading bitumen.

If I had spoken in the train I could have said, 'Ramsden,' I could have said, 'I feel sad. Lately I seem unable to prevent a feeling of melancholy which comes over me as soon as I wake up. I feel nervous and muddled and everything

299

is accompanied by a sense of sorrow and futility.' Should I join a sect? I could have asked her. A cult? On TV these people, with a chosen way, all look light hearted. They jive and twist and break-dance from kitchens to dining rooms carrying wooden platters of something fresh and green neatly chopped up. Perhaps it is uncooked spinach. Perhaps it is their flying hair and their happy eyes which attract, but then the memory of the uneasiness of communal living and the sharing of possessions and money seems too difficult, too frightening to contemplate. In real life it won't, I could have told her, it won't be the same as it is on TV. Probably only the more sparkling members of the sect are filmed, I could have said this too, and something is sure to be painted on the spinach to make it look more attractive. Food in advertisements, I could have been knowledgeable, food in advertisements is treated before being photographed. I left the train at my station without another glance in her direction.

Perhaps the lilies are a reminder and a comfort. Without fail they flower at Easter. Forgotten till they flower, an unsought simultaneous caution and blessing.

It seems to me now, when I think of it, that my father was always seeing me off either at a bus stop or at the station. He would suggest that he come to the bus or the train just as I was about to leave. Sometimes he came part of the way in the train getting out at the first stop and then, waiting alone, he would travel on the first train back. Because of the decision being made at the last minute, as the train was moving, he would have only a platform ticket, so, as well as all the waiting and the extra travelling, he would be detained at the other end to make explanations and to pay his fare for both directions. All this must have taken a lot of time. And sometimes in the middle of winter it was bitterly cold.

The strong feeling of love which goes from the parent to the child does not seem a part of the child which can be given back to the parent. I realize now with regret that I never thought then of his repeated return journeys. I never thought of the windswept platforms, of the small smouldering waiting-room fires and the long, often wet, walks from the bus to the house. I simply always looked ahead, being already on my journey even before I set out, to the place to which I was going.

The minutes which turned out to be the last I was to have with my father were at a railway station. When it was time for my train to leave even when the whistle was being blown my father went on with what he was saying. He said that if we never saw each other again I must not mind. He was getting older he said then, he was surprised at how quickly he was getting older and though he planned to live a long time it might be that we should not be able to make the next journeys in time. It is incredible that I could have paid so little attention then and the longing to hear his voice once more at this moment is something I never thought of till now.

He had his umbrella with him and when the train began to move he walked beside the moving train for as long as he could waving the umbrella. I did not think about the umbrella then either. But now I remember that during the years he often left it in trains and it travelled the length and breadth of England coming back at intervals labelled from Liverpool, Norfolk, St Ives and Glasgow to the lost property office where he was, with a kind of apologetic triumph, able to claim it.

The huge Easter moon, as if within arm's length, as if it can be reached simply by stretching out both hands to take it and hold it, is low down in the sky, serene and full, lighting the night so that it looks as if everything is snow covered, and deep shadows lie across pale, moon whitened lawns. This moon is the same moon that my father will have seen. He always told me when I had to leave for school, every term when I wept because I did not want to leave, he told me that if I looked at the moon, wherever I was, I was seeing the same moon that he was looking at. 'And because of this,' he said, 'you must know that I am not very far away. You must never feel lonely,' he said. He said the moon would never be extinguished. Sometimes, he said, it was not possible to see the moon, but it was always there. He said he liked to think of it as his.

I waited once for several hours at a bus stop, a temporary bus stop on a street corner in London. There was a traffic diversion and the portable sign was the final stop for the Green Line from Hertford. It was the long summer evening moving slowly into the night of soft dusty warmth. A few people walked on the pavement. All of them had places they were going to. A policeman asked me if everything was all right.

'I'm waiting for someone,' I told him. I waited with Helena for Ramsden.

In the end, in my desperation, I did write my letter to Ramsden asking her to help me to leave Fairfields, the school where I had gone to live and work taking Helena with me. It was a progressive boarding school. There was not enough food and I was never paid. In my letter I told Ramsden everything that had happened, about my child, about my leaving home, about my loneliness, about my disappointment with the school. I had not expected, I told her, such fraudulent ways. My poverty, I thought, would be evident without any description. After writing the letter I was not able to wait for a reply from Ramsden because, when I went to give notice that I wanted to leave in a fortnight, Patch (the headmistress) replied in her singing voice, the dangerous contralto in which she encouraged people to condemn and entangle themselves; 'By all means but please do go today. There's a bus at the end of the field path at three o'clock.' Neither she nor Miss Myles, after exchanging slightly raised eyebrows with one another, said anything else to me.

I sent my letter to the last address I had from Ramsden almost five years earlier. She was, she said then, still nursing and had a little flat where I would be welcome. Five years is a long time.

I told her in my letter that I would wait for her at the terminus of the Green Line. As I wrote I could not help wondering if she was by now playing the piano in concerts. Perhaps on tour somewhere in the north of England; in the places where concert pianists play. I tried to think of likely towns and villages. As I wrote I wept remembering Ramsden's kind eyes and her shy manner. Staff nurse

Ramsden with her older more experienced face — as someone once described her, and her musician's nose — someone else had said once. She had never known what there was to know about the violin case I carried with me in those days. It had been my intention always to tell her but circumstances changed intentions.

I begged her in the letter and in my heart to be there. Five years is a long time to ignore a kind invitation from someone. A long time to let pass without any kind of reply. With failing hope I walked slowly up and down the pavement which still held the dust and the warmth of the day. I walked and waited with Helena who was white faced and hungry and tired. Sometimes she sat on our heavy case on my roughly folded school winter coat. I tried to comfort myself with little visions of Ramsden playing the piano and nodding and smiling to Helena who would dance, thump-thump, on the carpet in the little living room. I seemed to remember that Ramsden said in the letter, sent all those years ago, that the flat was tiny.

'You'd best be coming along with me.' It was the policeman again. He had passed us several times. Helena was asleep on the folded coat and I was leaning against the railings at the front of an empty house.

The woman in charge of the night shelter gave me a small huckaback towel and a square of green soap. She said she had enough hot water if Helena and I could share the bath.

'She's very like you,' the woman said not trying very hard to hide her curiosity behind a certain sort of kindness. She gave us two slices of bread and butter and a thick cup of tea each. She handed me two grey blankets and said Helena would be able to sleep across the foot of the bed she was able to let me have for one night. The girl who had the bed, she explained, was due to come out of hospital where she had been operated on to have a propelling pencil removed from her bladder.

'The things they'll try,' the woman said, 'I or anyone, for that matter, could have told her she was too far gone for anything like that. All on her own too poor thing. Made herself properly poorly and lost her baby too.' She looked at Helena who was eating her bread and butter, crusts and all, neatly in what seemed to me to be an excessive show of virtue.

'There's some as keeps their kiddies,' the woman said.

'Yes,' I said avoiding her meaning looks. The night shelter for women carried an implication. There was more than the need of a bed. At St Cuthberts the nurses had not been too sympathetic. I remembered all too clearly herding A.T.S. girls into one of the bathrooms every evening where they sat naked from the waist down in chipped enamel basins of hot water and bicarbonate of soda. In her lectures the Sister Tutor reminded often for the need to let patients be as dignified as possible. The hot basins defied this. Many of the girls were pregnant. Some women, the Sister Tutor said, mistook the orifices in their own bodies. All this, at that time, belonged to other people.

Later my own child was to be the embodiment of all that was poetical and beautiful and wished for. Before she was born I called her Beatrice. I forgot about the A.T.S.

Grateful for the hot bath and the tea and the promised bed I addressed the woman in charge as Sister.

Did the Sister, I asked her, ever know a staff nurse called Ramsden. The woman, narrowing her eyes, thought for a moment and said yes she thought she had — now she recalled it. There was a Ramsden she thought, yes she was sure, who joined the Queens Nurses and went to Mombassa. I tried to take comfort from the doubtful recollection. Yes, went to Mombassa with the Queens Nurses. Very fine women the Queens Nurses. And one night, so she'd heard, the cook in the nurses' quarters was stabbed by an intruder. Horribly stabbed, a dozen or more times in the chest, the neck and the stomach. Apparently the murder was justified, brought on by the cook's own behaviour — him having gone raving mad earlier that same day. But of Ramsden herself she had no actual news.

I understood as I lay under the thin blanket that she had been trying to offer some sort of reply to my stupid and hopeless question. Perhaps the cook in Mombassa was often murdered horribly in these attempts to provide answers.

I tried to sleep but Helena, accustomed to a bed to herself, kicked unbearably all night.

Being at a bus stop, not waiting for a bus, and with the dusk turning quickly to darkness, I think of my father's moon. This moon, once his moon and now mine is climbing the warm night sky. It hangs in the branches of a single tree left between the new buildings.

The journey to school is always, it seems, at dusk. My father comes to the first stop. This first journey is in the autumn when the afternoons are dark before four o'clock. The melancholy railway crawls through water logged meadows where mourning willow trees follow the winding streams. Cattle, knee deep in damp grass, raise their heads as if in an understanding of sorrow as the slow train passes. The roads at the level crossings are deserted. No one waits to wave and curtains of drab colours are pulled across the dimly lit cottage windows.

At the first stop there is a kind of forced gaiety in the meetings on the platform. Some girls have already been to school and others, like me, are going for the first time. My father watches and when the carriage doors are slammed, one after the other, he melts away from the side of the train as it moves slowly along the platform gradually gathering speed, resuming its journey.

I sink back at once into that incredible pool of loneliness which is, I know now but did not understand then, a part of being one of a crowd. I try to think of the moon. Though it is not Easter, my father said before the doors had all been slammed, there will be if the clouds disperse, a moon. Because he pointed with his umbrella I felt embarrassed and, instead of looking up, I stared at my shoes. I try to think about his moon being behind the clouds even if I cannot see it. I wish, I am wishing I had smiled and waved to him.

In the noisy compartment everyone is talking and laughing. We are all reflected in the windows and the dark shadowed fields slip by on both sides.

The school bus, emblazoned with an uplifting motto, rattles through an unfamiliar land. The others sing songs which I have never heard before. There is no moon. The front door of the school opens directly on to the village street. Everyone rushes from the bus and the headmaster and his wife stand side by side in a square of light to receive us.

'Wrong hand Veronica. It is Veronica isn't it?' he ticks my name on a list he has. 'Other hand Veronica. We always shake hands with the right hand.'

When I unpack my overnight bag I am comforted by the new things, the new nightdress, the handkerchiefs and the stockings folded carefully by my mother. Especially my new fountain pen pleases me.

Almost at once I begin my game of comparisons, placing myself above someone if more favourable and below others if less favourable in appearance. This game of appearance is a game of chance. Chance can be swayed by effort, that is one of the rules, but effort has to be more persistent than is humanly possible. It is a game of measuring the unfamiliar against the familiar. I prefer the familiar. I like to know my way, my place with other people, perhaps because of other uncertainties.

I am still on the bench at the bus stop. My father's moon is huge and is now above the tree in a dark blue space between two buildings. A few cars have come. I have seen their headlights dip and turn off and I have seen the dark shapes of people making their way into the place where my clinic is. They will sit in the comfortable chairs in the waiting room till they are called in to see me. Unavoidably I am late sometimes but they wait.

At the other place where I work there is a scent of hot pines. The sun, beating down on a near-by plantation all day brings into the warm still air a heart lifting fragrance. There is a narrow path pressed into the dry grass and the fallen pine needles. This is the path I take to and from the railway station. Sometimes I suggest to other people that they walk on this path. The crows circling and calling suggest great distance. Endless paddocks with waving crops could be quite close on the other side of the new tall buildings. The corridors indoors smell of toast, of coffee and of hot curries. It is as if there are people cooking at turning points on the paths and in corners between the buildings.

It is as if they have casually thrown their saris over the cooking pots to protect them from the prevailing winds.

From where I sit it seems as if the moon is shining with some secret wisdom. I read somewhere that it was said of Chekhov that he *shows us life's depths at the very moment when he seems to reflect its shimmering surface.*

My father's moon is like this.

But the game. The game of comparisons. Before meals at school we have to stand in line beginning with the smallest and ending with the tallest. The room is not very big and the tallest stand over the smallest. We are not allowed to speak and our shoes and table napkins are examined by the prefects. It is during this time of silence and inspection that I make my comparisons. Carefully I am comparing my defects with those of my immediate neighbours. I glance sideways at the pleats of their tunics and notice that the girl next to me bulges. In my mind I call her Bulge, her pleats do not lie flat, they bulge. She is tall and awkward, taller than I am and more round shouldered. I try to straighten my back and to smooth my tunic pleats. I can be better than Bulge. She has cracked lips and she bites her nails. I try not to chew my nails but my hands are not well kept as are the hands of the girl on the other side of me. She has pretty nails and her hair is soft and fluffy. My hair is straight but not as greasy and uneven as Bulge's. Fluffy Hair's feet turn out when she walks. My feet are straight but my stockings are hopelessly wrinkled and hers are not. We all have spots. Bulge's spots are the worst, Fluffy Hair's complexion is the best. She is marred by a slight squint. We all wear spectacles. These are all the same except that Bulge has cracked one of her lenses. My lenses need cleaning.

It is the sound of someone closing a case very quietly in the dormitory after the lights have been turned off which makes me cry. It is the kind of sound which belongs to my mother. This quiet little closing of a case. My night dress, which she made, is very comfortable. It wraps round me. She knitted it on a circular needle, a kind of stockinette she said it was, very soft, she said. When she had finished it she was very pleased because it had no seams. She was telling our neighbour, showing her the night dress and the new clothes for school, all marked with my name embroidered on linen tape. The cabin trunk bought specially and labelled clearly 'Luggage in Advance' in readiness for the journey by goods train produced an uneasy excitement. My mother, handling the night dress again, spoke to me;

ein weiches reines Kleid für dich zu weben,
darin nicht einmal die geringste Spur
Von Naht dich drückt —

'Shut up,' I said, not liking her to speak in German in front of the woman from next door. 'Shut up,' I said again knowing from the way she spoke it was part of a poem. 'Shut up,' I crushed the night dress back into the overnight bag, 'it's only a nightgown!'

When I stop crying I pretend that the nightdress is my mother holding me.

On our second Sunday afternoon I am invited with Bulge and Fluffy Hair and Helen Ferguson and another girl called Amy to explore a place called Harpers Hill. Bulge is particularly shapeless in her Sunday dress. My dress, we have to wear navy blue serge dresses, is already too tight for me and it is only the second Sunday. Fluffy Hair's dress belongs to her Auntie and has a red lace collar instead of the compulsory white linen one. The collars are supposed to be detachable so that they can be washed.

I wish I could be small and neat and pretty like Amy, or even quick like Helen Ferguson who always knows what's for breakfast the night before. Very quickly she understands the system and knows in advance the times of things, the difference between Morning Meeting and Evening Meeting and where we are supposed to be at certain times, whose turn it is to mop the dormitory and which nights are bath nights. I do not have this quality of knowing and when I look at Helen Ferguson I wonder why I am made as I am. In class Helen Ferguson has a special way of sitting with one foot slightly in front of the other and she sucks her pen while she is thinking. I try to sit as she does and try to look as if I am thinking while I suck the rounded end of my new pen.

During Morning Meeting I am worrying about the invitation which seems sinister in some way. It is more like a command from the senior girls. I try to listen to the prayer at the beginning of Meeting. We all have to ask God to be in our hearts. All the time I am thinking of the cross roads where we are supposed to meet for the walk. Bulge does not stop chewing her nails and her fingers all through Meeting. I examine my nails, chew them and, remembering, sit on my hands.

Between Autumn-berried hedges in unscratched shoes and new stockings we wait at the crossroads. The brown ploughed fields slope to a near horizon of heavy cloud. There are some farm buildings quite close but no sign of any people. The distant throbbing of an invisible tractor and the melancholy cawing of the rooks bring back the sadness and the extraordinary fear of the first Sunday afternoon walk too vividly. I try not to scream as I screamed that day and I try not to think about the longed for streets crowded with people and endlessly noisy with trams. It is empty in the country and our rain-coats are too long.

The girl, the straw coloured one they call Etty, comes along the road towards us. She says it's to be a picnic and the others are waiting with the food not far away. She says to follow her. A pleasant surprise, the picnic. She leads us along a little path across some fields to a thicket. We have to bend down to follow the path as it winds between blackberry and under prickly bushes. Our excited talk is soon silenced as we struggle through a hopeless tangle of thorns and bramble. Amy says she thinks we should turn back. Bulge has the most awful scratches on her forehead. Amy says, 'look, her head's bleeding.' But Etty says no we shall soon get through to the place.

Suddenly we emerge high up on the edge of a sandy cliff. 'It's a landslide!' I say and, frightened, I try to move away from the edge. Before we have time to turn back the girls, who have been hiding, rush out and grab us by the arms and legs. They tie us up with our own scarves and rain-coat belts and push us over the edge and down the steep rough walls of the quarry. I am too frightened to cry out or to resist. Bulge fights and screams in a strange voice quite unlike any voice I have ever heard. Four big girls have her by the arms and legs. They pull her knickers off as she rolls over kicking. Her lumpy white thighs show above the tops of her brown woollen stockings.

'Not this man but Barrabas! Not this man but Barrabas!' They shout. 'She's got pockets in her knickers! Pockets in her knickers!' the horrible chant is all round Bulge as she lies howling.

As quickly as the big girls appeared they are gone. We, none of us, try to do anything to help Bulge as we struggle free from the knotted belts and scarves. Helen Ferguson and Amy lead the way back as we try to find the road. Though we examine, exclaiming, our torn clothes and show each other our scratches and bruises the real hurt is something we cannot speak about. Fluffy Hair cries. Bulge, who has stopped crying, lumbers along with her head down. Amy, who does not cry, is very red. She declares she will report the incident. 'That's a bit too daring,' I say, hoping that she will do as she says. I am wondering if Bulge is still without her knickers.

'There's Etty and some of them,' Helen Ferguson says as we approach the cross roads. It has started to rain. Huddled against the rain we walk slowly on towards them.

'Hurry up you lot!' Etty calls in ringing tones, 'we're getting wet.' She indicates the girls sheltering under the red-berried hawthorn.

'I suppose you know,' Etty says. 'Harpers Hill is absolutely out of bounds. So you'd better not tell. If you get the whole school gated it'll be the worse for you!' She rejoins the others who stand watching us as we walk by.

'That was only a rag. We were only ragging you,' Etty calls, 'so mind you don't get the whole school gated!' Glistening water drops fly from the wet hedge as the girls leap out, one after the other, across the soaked grass of the ditch. They race ahead screaming with laughter. Their laughter continues long after they are out of sight.

In Evening Meeting Bulge cannot stop crying and she has no handkerchief. Helen Ferguson, sitting next to me on the other side, nudges me and grins, making grimaces of disgust, nodding in the direction of Bulge and we both shake with simulated mirth, making, at the same time, a pretence of trying to suppress it. Without any sound Bulge draws breath and weeps, her eyes and nose running into her thick fingers. I lean away from her heaving body. I can see her grazed knees because both her stockings have huge holes in them.

Before Meeting, while we were in line, while two seniors were practising Bach, a duet on the common room piano, Bulge turned up the hem of her Sunday dress to show me a large three cornered tear. It is a hedge tear she told me while the hammered Bach fell about our ears. And it will be impossible, when it is mended, she said, for her mother to lengthen the dress.

I give another hardly visible but exaggerated shiver of mirth and pretend, as Helen Ferguson is doing, to look serious and attentive as if being thoughtful and as if listening with understanding to the reading. The seniors read in turn, a different one every Sunday. It is Etty's turn to read. She reads in a clear voice. She has been practising her reading for some days.

'Romans chapter nine verse twenty one,' her Sunday dress is well pressed and the white collar sparkles round her pretty neck.

'Hath not the potter power
over the clay, of the same lump
to make one vessel unto honour
and another unto dishonour?

'And from verse twenty,' Etty looks up smiling and lisping just a little,

'Shall the thing formed say to
him that formed it, Why hast
thou made me thus?'

Etty minces from the platform where the staff sit in a semi-circle. She walks demurely back to her seat.

'These two verses,' Miss Vanburgh gets up and puts both hands on the lectern, it is her turn to give the Address;

'These two verses,' she says, 'are sometimes run together.'

'Shall the clay say to the potter why has thou made me thus . . .'

Bulge is still weeping.

Miss Besser, on tiptoe across the creaking boards of the platform, creeps down, bending double between the rows of chairs and, leaning over, whispers to me to take Muriel;

'Take your friend out of meeting, take her to . . .'

'I don't know her. She isn't my friend,' I begin to say in a whisper, trying to explain, 'she's not my friend . . .'

'To matron,' Miss Besser says in a low voice, 'take Muriel.' I get up and go out with Bulge who falls over her own feet and kicking the chair legs, makes a noise which draws attention to our attempted silent movement.

I know it is the custom for the one who leads the other to put an arm of care and protection round the shoulders of distress. I know this already after two weeks. It is not because I do not know . . .

I wait with Bulge in the little porch outside Matron's cottage. Bulge does not look at me with her face, only with her round and shaking shoulders.

Matron, when she comes, gives Bulge a handkerchief and reaches for the iodine. 'A hot bath,' she says to Bulge, 'and early bed. I'll have some hot milk sent up. Be quick,' Matron adds, 'and don't use up too much hot water. Hot milk,' she says, 'in half an hour.'

I do not go back into Meeting. Instead I stand for a time in a place where nobody comes, between the cloakroom and the bootroom. It is a sort of passage which does not lead anywhere. I think of Bulge lying back if only for a few minutes in the lovely hot water. I feel cold. Half an hour, that is the time Matron has allowed Bulge. Perhaps, if I am quick . . .

The lights are out in our dormitory. I am nice and warm. In spite of the quick and secret bath (it is not my night), and the glass of hot milk — because of my bed being nearer the door the maid brings it to me by mistake — (it has been sweetened generously with honey) in spite of all this I keep longing for the cherishing words familiar in childhood. Because of the terrible hedge tear in the navy blue hem and, because of the lumpy shoulders, I crouch under my bedclothes unable to stop seeing the shoulders without an arm round them. I am not able to weep as Bulge weeps. My tears will not come to wash away, for me, her shoulders.

At night we always hear the seniors, Etty in particular, singing in the bathroom. Two of them, tonight, may have to miss their baths. Etty's voice is especially noticeable this night.

little man you're crying, she sings.

little man you're blue

I know why you're crying

I know why you're blue

Some-one stole your Kiddi-Kar away from you

The moon, my father's moon, is too far away.

The Easter moon is racing up the sky. The stunted ornamental bushes look as if torn white tablecloths have been thrown over them and the buildings are like cakes which, having taken three days to ice, are now finished.

Tomorrow is Good Friday.

Next week I shall take the earlier train again and, before the journey is over, I shall speak to the woman.

Ramsden, I shall say, *is it you? Much water has gone under the bridge* — this is not my way — but I shall say it carelessly like this — *much water has gone under the bridge and I never answered your letter but is it you Ramsden, after all these years, is it?*

OTHER VIRAGO BOOKS OF INTEREST

THE MIDDLEMAN AND OTHER STORIES

Bharati Mukherjee

'A romance with America itself . . . handled with the same rapturous affection and acuteness of ear that Nabokov . . . brought to *Lolita*' – *Jonathan Raban*

In this stunning collection of stories, Bharati Mukherjee confronts the American Dream head on, as immigrants and exiles transform and are transformed by the experience and the idea of America. Larger than life and greedy for it, they have travelled to live and find fortune, love or adventure in a culture still uneasy in their presence yet partly remaking itself in their image. A Trinidadian girl housekeeps for a 'radical' family in Ann Arbor; an aristocratic Philippine woman negotiates a new life with an Atlanta banker; an Indian student tours New York with her husband and wonders if, 'freed from the dignities of old world culture, he too could get drunk and squirt Cheez Whiz on a guest'; a veteran finds himself in a Florida more foreign than Vietnam. Through them, we experience the allure and the ugliness of America, the urgency and danger of the search for a place within it.

Passionate, comic and razor sharp, these wonderful stories confirm Bharati Mukherjee's gifts as a writer of eloquent prose and astounding imagination.

ON THE GOLDEN PORCH

Tatyana Tolstaya

'The most original, tactile, luminous voice in Russian prose today' – *Joseph Brodsky*

Poetic, magical and piercingly funny, this is a stunning debut from a remarkable new Russian writer. With lyricism and zest, Tatyana Tolstaya evokes the longings, fears and romance in all human encounters, from childhood to old age. A small boy at his summer dacha dreams of marriage to the *louche*, mysterious Tamila as she smokes and drinks on her veranda . . . Balding Simeonov falls in love with the festooned orchid of Vera Vasilevna's voice on his old, cracked records as he eats processed cheese . . . While his wife nurses their sick child, Depression makes room for Ignatiev in the marital bed, enfolding him in her embrace . . . Shura, an old woman with pre-revolutionary legs, recalls her three husbands and the lover she left waiting at a railway station until the stars came out . . . Men and women fall in love, but rarely want the same things. Souls escape from tea-cosies and table-cloths, slithering snake-like out through napkin rings. These are the characters of Tolstaya's extraordinary imagination: people who refuse to grow wise or relinquish the poetry of their souls, into whose hearts we are allowed a captivating glance.

BROKEN WORDS

Helen Hodgman

'The pond on the Common froze in the night. Thirteen ducks were caught by their feet. The big dog came along and bit each bird off at the knee. Later the sight of a stubble of duck's stumps poking through the ice like a five o'clock shadow was to fracture Hazel's morning . . .'

So begins this extraordinary story of life in South London. Here we meet the out-of-work designer Moss, her young son Elvis and her lover Hazel from Goodiwindi, Australia, scraping their living from the DHSS and a spot of moonlighting on the side. Then Moss's ex-husband, Harold, tips up, pursued by the orange-robed cult he has abandoned, while Hazel's ex-husband Le Professeur de Judo, begins to think of her murderously back in Vancouver. We meet Walter, too, walking his dog Angst on Clapham Common; his novelist wife, Daphne, and their motley collection of children. And there are Buster and Beulah from the Women's Design Collective, their offspring a result of the milkman's sperm donation in a yoghurt carton (swapped for a rare Beatles' bootleg). Finally, there is the Bogeyman with his chipped junkie eyes who Elvis watches and shadows, dizzy with love.

A bizarre black comedy of contemporary urban life, *Broken Words* is written with sparse elegance and a fierce wit. This, Helen Hodgman's third novel, is a *tour de force*.

BLUE SKIES & JACK AND JILL

Helen Hodgman

Blue Skies – The Tasmanian sun flashes upon weather-boarded houses and a holiday-brochure beach. Early-morning hoovering gives way to empty afternoons when the clock always says three, and women and children huddle together in steaming heaps by the sea. But this stagnation will be shattered – by incest, suicide and murder.

'A born writer with a style and an elan which are all her own' – *Auberon Waugh*

Jack and Jill – While Douggie is away, his wife dies; his grief-slimed and hungry young daughter Jill gives a kookaburra laugh on his return four days later. Thereafter they live hand-to-mouth amidst the dogs, dust and flies of the New South Wales outback. Then Jack arrives on their doorstep. Like the nursery rhyme, it is the start of no ordinary romance.

'It's ferociously funny to the end. Immensely stimulating, like a small dose of strychnine' – *The Times*

MY PLACE

Sally Morgan

'The sort of Australian history which hasn't been written before, and which we desperately need' – *Weekend Australian*

'A moving and quite remarkable account of personal discovery' – *Sydney Morning Herald*

In 1982 Sally Morgan travelled to her grandmother's birthplace, Corunna Downs Station in Western Australia. What started as a tentative search for information about her forebears turned into an extraordinary emotional and spiritual pilgrimage. Sally and her family were confronted with their own suppressed history, and with fundamental questions about their identity. Through memories and images of growing up in Perth in the fifties and sixties, hints and echoes emerge, hidden knowledge is uncovered, and a fascinating story unfolds – the mystery of her Aboriginal identity. The momentum of her narrative in turn sparks responses in her great-uncle, her mother and, finally, her grandmother, allowing them to tell their own stories. *My Place* is a powerful autobiography of three generations, a poignant yet often humorous account of a search for truth into which a whole family is drawn.